The Ship to Look for God

D. Krauss

Second Edition April 2022
by Indies United Publishing House, LLC

Cover design by *Damonza*
Book design by *Caryatid Design*

ISBN 978-1-64456-400-4 [paperback]
ISBN 978-1-64456-401-1 [Mobi]
ISBN 978-1-64456-402-8 [ePub]

Library of Congress Control Number: 2021949738

INDIES UNITED PUBLISHING HOUSE, LLC
P.O. BOX 3071
QUINCY, IL 62305-3071
www.indiesunited.net

To Colonel Bob and Captain Bob
You guys made it all clear.

"This joy in God is not like any pleasure found in physical or intellectual satisfaction. Nor is it such as a friend experiences in the presence of a friend. But, if we are to use any such analogy, it is more like the eye rejoicing in light."

- St. Augustine, The City of God

Chapter I

Otto Passes, or He Doesn't, but He Is Certainly Somewhere Else

Otto died in his driveway. He should have died a half-mile down the road, but the indignity of crashing into a parked car and drooling all over himself while people gaped and called him an idiot had kept him going. He somehow negotiated the uphill street and reached his carport without mishap, even though a trip-hammer slammed his chest, his ears roared like a tidal wave, and his eyesight tunneled. But his legs no longer worked and the car cruised up the incline and nudged to a halt against his son's truck, supposed to be on the street but, hey, this kid.

Son, washing the truck (which explained why it wasn't on the street and maybe a good thing because, otherwise, Otto would have kept going right through the carport and into the backyard pool), jumped out of the way, carrying hose and bucket with him (lacrosse player, great reflexes), then ran up mouthing, "Are you nuts?"

Otto didn't hear a word, further evidence he was dying. He wanted to say, "Sorry about the truck and, no, I'm perfectly rational. It appears my heart's exploding. Mind calling an ambulance?" but couldn't quite muster it. He did manage a slight smile. Then, gone.

Otto had, over the years, developed certain expectations about death: it starts with severe pain, of course, because the transition from life to death must be a bit traumatic, otherwise, everyone would go right to it, but then the pain fades and a beacon appears that he is impelled to follow, while a darkly magnificent voice coaxes him along. He'd float around for a while until finally reaching Heaven, an unbelievable golden city spread along light-years of stars and clouds and nebulae, with the Light of God Himself shining out as Otto descended, in awe and rapture, to the center. He wasn't exactly up for sainthood, but Otto had lived a good enough life to earn a spot on Heaven's portico, at least. Probably.

We'll see.

If he landed in a Buddhist or Islamic Afterlife instead, or a nihilistic vortex of chaos, or in simply nothing, well, better a letdown than a burning. Although, if the Islamic picture held, he'd burn anyway.

But nothing of the sort happened. (Except for the pain. Naturally.) Blackness enveloped him as his heart disintegrated and organs shut down, processes marked by a terrible sense of drowning while someone shoved a red-hot poker into his sternum and pried it open. Took way too long running its course and for a bit, Otto feared death was nothing more than eternal pain. What joy.

But eventually, it stopped, after what felt like twenty hours, and Otto gasped and said, "Damn."

Probably not the best first word to utter in death but nothing was following the expected program, which meant maybe he *wasn't* dead; more likely, he'd suffered through one helluva heart attack and revived, which called for appropriate commentary. But he wasn't lying in a hospital bed or an ambulance or a recovery room; he was face down on a hard surface. Best not to say any more until he figured out what in the blue blazes was going on.

So what in the blue blazes was going on?

Had he fallen out of the car? No. This surface was cool, whereas his asphalt driveway should be at summertime temps, hot enough to fry eggs. He lifted his head for a better view.

"Cobblestones." Otto rendered his second word with appropriate surprise because, yes, he lay on cobblestones, Quite well-made ones, perfectly even and free from all detritus. Well swept, too. Otto blinked a couple of times but everything remained and, so taken was he with the workmanship, he stayed there, admiring it.

He finally batted the praise out of his eyes and looked to the side. Feet. Well, shoes, lots of them, stepping quietly over and around him, sandals and boots and flats and sneakers (they don't call them sneakers anymore, do they?) of all types and colors and styles. Shoes attached to legs clothed in pants and skirts and slacks and dresses and what – a kilt? No way.

The cobblestones, cluttered with so many active feet, ran for quite a distance to a sunlit intersection bustling with brightly painted wagons rolling to and fro. Horses, beautiful dapples and greys and whites, pulled the wagons, and Otto heard the music of their hooves. Guys with very straight postures, elegantly dressed in top hats and tails and carrying long-handled whips, guided the horses with a gentle tap on the shoulder … withers … whatever. Otto didn't know anything about horses. Some of the wagons were empty; some had persons riding in the back while others carried nothing but flowers. One passed with someone sitting at a large piano playing it. Otto didn't recognize the tune.

Interspersed among the wagons were other vehicles, including a 1961 Volkswagen Bug, exactly like his first car, down to the same crap baby-blue paint job. Otto smiled. Good ole Buggy. What a great car. It had no working instruments. For heat, he screwed open a floor valve to let in engine fumes, and only one wiper functioned. (Passenger side, of course). Otto ran Buggy like a madman over south Jersey roads with frequent stops at Seaside, Groveton and the Spectrum, or merely tooled around the Barrens, pulling in WMMR with an FM converter lying on the passenger floor. (Which made changing over to that upstart WYSP a hazardous proposition.) After about a week of said tooling around, he'd figure he needed gas, the useless gauge offering no clue, so he'd pull into the Getty station and yell, "Fill it up!" Eighty cents, dollar twenty, that was it.

Buggy met its demise at the hands of Otto's sister's idiot boyfriend, speed-shifting it in the parking lot and thereby destroying the transmission. Otto's last sight of Buggy was heading down Route 38 toward Mt. Holly, dangling from a tow truck. Be something if that was her, lovingly restored, a member of the distant parade.

The other cars ranged from vintage to ones so sleek and modern, they had to be experimental. Bicycles zipped among them, half the riders layered up in safety equipment like plastic knights, the other half in barely-there shorts and Tees, the barely-wearers such beautiful specimens of humanity that Otto was grateful they'd chosen so little clothing.

"I'm in Central Park," Otto concluded.

Had to be: strange parade of ill-suited vehicles flanked by unconcerned crowds meandering across tasteful sidewalks … yep, fitted the description. Not that Otto knew; he'd never been to Central Park, although he'd gotten close, when Sherry and he drove to New York City a very long time ago in her 1969 Dodge Coronet, looking for a party that his crazy friend, Tree, was throwing somewhere near Battery Park. (Or was it *in* the Park?) Hopelessly lost, they ended up in Harlem. Gulp. But a festival of some kind was in full swing and crowds danced up and down the streets in full rainbow colors and everyone was in a good mood. A delivery guy cheerfully gave them directions. Never did find Tree, but Otto's impression of NYC ever afterward was of a town overrun with street festivals peopled with nice guys.

This looked like that.

Which prompted a few questions, such as how in the heck did he end up in Central Park? And where was Sherry? God, she was going to *kill* him. This wasn't an unfortunate over-drinking episode where he ended up passed out in the back of his car somewhere near Bethesda. (Never do that again.) He was hundreds of miles away without a single clue about how he got here. The first order of business, then, develop said clue. That way, when he called her, he'd have a story. Maybe not a plausible one, but one nonetheless.

Otto turned over, staring straight up, and froze. Wow. The sky.

All the colors of cold-stirred winter air spread above him, shades of the wine-dark sea that he and Homer had the privilege of sailing on, thousands of years apart, of course, he with Sherry on that Greek Island cruise. Not the pale-blue-almost-white of the current summer diffused by haze and particles, but an endless dark blue. Otto could almost see through it, sense and touch its texture, four- and five-dimensional soaring to heights well beyond the point it should dissolve into the blackness of space. It glowed with beauty, with health, if that were possible.

"Good God in Heaven," he whispered, awestruck. He had an overpowering urge, like coming across a clean pool on a hot day, to swim in that live, caressing, rich blue; to jump up and find the stairs of a tall building and burst through the roof and launch himself over the side because a sky like that would reach down with gentle, loving fingers and catch him and he would soar in blue streams of air forever, riding its currents across a world of many colors.

He looked at the surrounding buildings for a set of convenient stairs and gasped. Not your run-of-the-mill office or apartment towers bordering the Park, these. Temples, enamel and pearl and crystal against the living sky, diamonds running up and down edge inlays which might be copper or gold or ruby, Otto couldn't tell. Thousands of windows caught the blue and cast it back in celebration, like sheer panes of pale opal under fluorescent light.

Marvelous and stunning and nothing like he had ever seen, Otto wanted to know what genius, what overwhelmingly brilliant architect, designed them, but they weren't the point. The buildings inclined in his direction as if to urge him to spend a moment admiring the workmanship: such lines, such craft, the obviously precious materials woven into perfect form asked to be ignored, gently nudging the eye to something even they, in their glory, thought more glorious. Yes, Otto, don't forget the sky.

The sky.

"What is this?" Otto whispered. The buildings caught his question and offered it to the deep, deep blue and Otto, for a moment, believed he would actually get an answer. The expectation was delicious. But nothing spoke, nothing explained. He was not disappointed. Somehow, keeping the mystery of the sky was more important.

But he really, really needed an explanation because this was all too weird. Fortunately, lots of people walked about so, ask. Otto sat up. An Asian man dressed in jeans and a pullover, about to step over him, smiled politely and stepped around instead. Otto watched him stroll nonchalantly away. Several other people passed around Otto just as politely: this was a very busy street and he served as a speed bump. Oddly, no one seemed to mind. That wasn't in keeping with even a cheerful vision of New York, where he should have gotten, by now, "Gedouddadaway" from at least one or two of the not-so-cheerful. These people were excessively tolerant; if Otto wanted to lie down in the middle of a busy cobblestoned thoroughfare, well, fine, they'd simply go around him.

"Definitely not New York," he concluded, as if the sky and the buildings had not so convinced him before.

All right then, one scenario considered and discarded, leaving him with … what? He peered at the street and the buildings and the people, avoiding the poetry of the sky because he'd get lost in it and he needed answers right now, not rapture. No street signs, no billboards, no marquees and no flyers pasted to telephone poles.

Hmm … no telephone poles For that matter, no power poles either.

No wires crossing the streets and interlacing the sky, black-line weavings cutting his view of it, sectioning the azure diamond of the forever sky while the buildings bent in worship and pointed him once again to that lovely, wonderful, soul-filling blue …

He shook his head hard. Concentrate, dammit!

He took a deep breath and, while focused on the wagons and cars in the distance, rapidly shuffled through all possible scenarios and reached the only possible conclusion.

He was in a coma. Had to be.

There was no location on Earth even remotely like this, not even Paris, Otto's idea of the Most Beautiful City Possible. Their first night there, Sherry and he stood on the steps of the National Museum across the Seine and watched the full moon rise behind the Eiffel Tower, a tableau that had taken his breath away. It remained for him the perfect image of what a city should be, and he'd always meant to go back on the full moon and see if it had been the moment, or illusion, or was standard fare. Because, if that was normal, then Parisians were the luckiest people in the world.

But this place beat that all to hell with magnitudes of beauty well beyond what he idealized in Paris, and well beyond human capability; either this was the most intense heart-attack-coma-induced hallucination ever, tapping areas of his brain he had never accessed before, or he was no longer on Earth. With no experience of either coma or extraterrestrial travel, he could not say which was which. The latter was ridiculous, the former more likely.

Let's find out.

"Excuse me," he said, raising a finger at a woman walking by.

She stopped and smiled, middle-aged and sun-freckled with bronze hair and perfect teeth. "Yes?"

Otto swallowed because, wow, she was quite beautiful. "Uh, sorry to bother you and I hope this doesn't sound like a stupid question, but can you tell me where I am?"

She laughed aloud, ice cubes tinkling on crystal, and Otto's heart melted. Good God! How was such beauty possible?

"You're new here, aren't you?" she said.

He nodded dumbly, struck through, Sherry forgotten.

She reached down and patted him gently on the shoulder, "You'll be all right," and walked away.

He sat dumbfounded, whether from her sheer beauty or sheer cheek unsure. Probably both. He watched her retreating form appreciatively but c'mon, what's this? His hallucinations should be a little more cooperative.

"Excuse me," he said again, more insistently, to a black man with the most luxurious set of dreds he'd ever seen flowing and shaping around the guy's head like they were separately alive.

"Yes?" The voice of a tenor sax, smile of pearls.

My God, is everyone in my head beautiful? "Uh ..." Otto was in danger of getting lost in the man's eternal black eyes. "Can you tell me where I am?"

"Ah!" The man roared out a laugh of pure delight. "You are new here!" He reached down and vigorously shook Otto's reluctant hand. "You will be all right!" And he walked away.

"What the hell?" Otto spoke to the man's back. No response except a cheerily waved hand as the man kept going. Well, good to know everyone thought he'd be all right. Too bad no one offered much more info than that. Didn't need to get hit with a board to deduce that if he wanted to know what was going on, he'd have to figure it out himself.

Otto stood up and brushed at his clothes, the same ones he was wearing in the driveway during the heart attack, he noted. Botany blue suit, white shirt, blue tie: day uniform of the mid-level DC government worker. He checked himself thoroughly but there wasn't a speck of dirt on him, nor an abrasion, heck, not even a wrinkle.

Odd. Should be some sign of wear or trauma, like a ripped-open shirt as EMTs applied CPR and defibrillator paddles, gunk all over him, tubes shoved down his throat, that sort of thing. But no. Strong evidence this was, indeed, happening in his mind while he sprawled in an ICU, airways and cords poked into him, grim-faced doctors walking in and out while Sherry stood outside the glass wringing her hands. Anoxia-induced daydream. Sit back and enjoy it then, man. Otto hoped he remembered it all when he came around because, man, what a story!

Someone cleared a throat and Otto looked up. A brown-skinned young man stood in front of him; Asian-looking, Filipino or Indonesian, maybe Vietnamese, had that look. In his twenties, wearing a colorful short-sleeve shirt and white Dockers, brown sandals. Reminded Otto of a business owner he once knew who owned a building outside the Mabalacat gate of Clark Air Base, further evidence this was a coma.

"Hi," the young man said.

"Hi," Otto replied.

"You all right?" The young man showed genuine concern.

"That seems to be the general opinion."

The young man chuckled. "Yeah, you get a lot of that around here." He reached out a hand. "My name's Frank."

"Otto." They shook. Firm and friendly, two good guys meeting each other for the first time. Okay, relax.

"You're probably a little disoriented," Frank said.

"That's a good call, Frank." Otto looked around. "Where exactly am I, and, yes, I am new here, and please don't tell me I'm going to be all right."

Frank laughed, "Okay, okay. You *will* be all right, by the way, but everyone quickly forgets how confused they were when they arrived and, well …" he made an amused gesture at the passing crowd.

"So where am I?"

"The City."

"The city ... where?"

Frank smiled. "The City. That's all, just the City."

"Oh, you say it with a capital 'C', huh? Cities have to be somewhere, Frank."

"In one way of thinking. Not in every way."

Otto shook his head. "Metaphysics. Oh, no. What's the sound of one hand clapping, then?"

Frank regarded him warmly. "I think that's one of those unanswerable questions. Are you hungry?"

"Frank, why won't you tell me where I am?"

"Because that's a hard question to answer, Otto. Best I can do right now is to ask you where you think you are."

"Strapped in a bed in ICU."

Frank approved. "That's good for now. Question stands, are you hungry?"

Otto considered. "I could use a cheese Danish."

"Okay. I know a good place. C'mon." Frank turned, waving a "come along" hand, and headed toward the intersection of piano-playing wagons and cars.

"Great," Otto muttered.

This was all so stupid. But, the thing about dreams, you play along, trying to figure out the ham-handed metaphors one's overly theatrical brain presents. So be it. He lurched behind Frank's receding back.

Chapter II

In Which Otto, Unfortunately, Remembers Frank

"These are really good." Otto licked the crumbs of his third Danish from his fingers.

Frank grinned. "Best in the City."

Otto glanced around. The place was a Starbucks' wet dream, all crystal and mahogany, with soaring windows of lead glass inlaid with what looked like pearl, reaching up to tin ceilings supported by slender wooden columns that couldn't possibly hold the weight. Murals of fractal patterns swirling into themselves – quite hypnotic –plastered the walls and Otto caught himself drifting into their lines. *Hmm*. Like the sky. Recurring theme?

The baristas wore gold brocade tunics with elaborate green embroidery suspiciously Celtic in design, but not quite. They smiled cheerily and took in everyone with happy server eyes, making contact with Otto quite often and, subsequently, bringing him more stuff to eat and drink.

"I mean *really* good." Never had a more perfect Danish, ever, and Otto had made strenuous lifelong efforts to find them. Could go for a fourth, maybe even a fifth.

"Should be. The guy who runs this place invented the doughnut."

"Don't say? What's his name, Dunk'in'?"

Frank laughed. "Dunkin' doughnuts, that's funny. Should be

the name of a store. No, his name's Hansen. Says he got the idea while sailing on a ship."

"Sure he did. And you're putting me on about the store name, right?"

Frank furrowed a brow in excellent deadpan. Deadpan. Hilarious, given the circumstances.

Otto wiped his mouth with a cloth napkin – cloth. Wow – and contemplated that fourth. Or fourteenth.

Man, toasty cheese with a mere hint of sweetness, exactly the subtleness of flavors that's eluded me in fifty-plus years of Danish munching. Funny, that.

And he wasn't full, either, even though two earthbound Danishes, even ones approaching this level of deliciousness, usually did him. Bet he could eat hundreds of these and never suffer a moment of biliousness, or stop right now and be completely satisfied. And no weight issues, either, since, somehow, in the past four or five hours, he'd lost four or five inches from his belly. Back down to the ole fightin' weight, it seemed.

Funny, that.

Lots of funny things here: a sky that held him captive, junk foods he could eat with no discernible health consequences, beautiful people all over the friggin' place ...

Trap. A rich, colorful, mind-ensnaring trap.

While he slowly ossified into a fetal position in some VA Hospice hellhole, an aging Sherry stopping by once a month or so to see if there'd been any change, here he'd be, enjoying his 12,000th Danish lying in the street staring at the sky or tooling Buggy around. A loop of infinite pleasure as he rotted, Sherry despaired, and his son disappeared.

So what?

If he were vastly entertained while dissolving into pudding, felt no pain, indeed, quite the contrary, indulged every possible pleasure his rather creative mind conjured, why not give in to it? Seemed a just reward for a hard-lived life.

Because, dude, that ain't you.

Otto delicately wiped the tips of his fingers. That's right – it ain't me, babe. Wasn't built that way.

He didn't seek his pleasures through the suffering of others.

And Sherry would suffer if he sat here stuffing his face for the next twenty years. Obviously, he wasn't dead. Death, real death, was God the Father on His Great Golden Throne wiping away Otto's tears, not some doughnut feast, even with cloth napkins. And if he wasn't dead, then he still had things to do, like wake up, give Sherry an assuring pat on the hand, and get started on rehab.

Time to go.

"So, how much?" Otto slapped around for his wallet which, naturally, wasn't there. Great. You'd think a fertile imagination would leave me some cash. Or did one of the beautiful people lift it?

He had an instantaneous vision of that freckled babe emptying his accounts. He'd have to stay here washing an infinite number of Delft dishes engraved with fascinating domestic scenes. It'd make for pleasurable labor but he'd still be trapped.

"I already paid for it," Frank said

"Oh? Well, thanks for that, because I seem to have lost my wallet. But I'm good for it. Catch you later." Otto slipped the chair back.

Frank made no move. "You don't need a wallet here. It's a credit system."

"System?" Otto eyed him. "Rather odd way of putting it, Frank. How does it work?"

"Like any credit system."

"What, a card? Because I didn't see you give one. You pay on the way out?"

"Uh-uh. They know me here."

"Ah." Otto got it. "You have a tab. Tell me how much it was and I'll get you next time." Like there'd be a next time, Frank. Tomorrow, Otto starts physical therapy and laughing about all this.

"It's not actually a tab, either, but you don't owe me anything."

Okay, great, freebie, thanks for that, gotta go, should go, but Otto's curiosity piqued. "No tab? So how does it work?"

"Like I said, they know me here."

"But that's a tab."

Frank smiled. "Not in the way you're thinking of it. I don't owe anything. It doesn't accumulate. Everything is properly compensated."

"So they have your account number? They just go straight and charge your checking account?" Quite foolish that, no matter how nice the baristas appeared.

Frank laughed out loud. "You're funny. It's really not like that, not at all. There are certain values. I have certain ones and they have certain ones, so it balances."

"That makes absolutely no sense."

"It will."

Otto closed his eyes and let out a long exasperated breath. "Okay, I'm getting very, very tired of this."

"I know and I wish I could make it easier with some simple explanation, but it's not that way."

"What's 'not that way,' Frank? What? And please don't say 'this,' because I don't like riddles. I'm very bad at them, in fact."

"How angry will you be if I say it's a gradual realization?"

"Very."

"Then I won't." Frank looked down. "I'm not doing this right."

Otto had half a mind to reach across and throttle him until he got a straight answer, which would be unfair because Frank was obviously sincere. But damn, man, just say it! Dream? Coma? Dead? "Just say it, Frank."

Frank looked up slowly, then turned his head, the light from the front door profiling him perfectly.

Perfectly.

Something dormant stirred in Otto's memory. That face … Otto studied it intently and a sense of familiarity, a disturbing one, washed over him. "Frank?"

Frank turned back, still looking sad. "Give me a few moments to figure out the best way to explain it to you."

"No, no." Otto waved a hand. "Frank, this may sound a little out of left field but, do we know each other?"

Frank cocked his head. "No, don't think so. First time I ever saw you was back there on the street."

"You sure?" Otto intensified his gaze. "'Cause, I swear, I've seen you someplace before."

Frank now scrutinized Otto's face. There a flicker of

recognition. "I'm … not sure ..." Frank turned his head to get the various angles right. Each movement stirred Otto's memory even more.

"Yes, yes," Otto said, "Now I'm sure I know you from somewhere, but ... can't place it." Otto paused, angling and maneuvering as much as Frank, trying to get the puzzle pieces to fall in place. Not working. More info, please. "Frank, where you from?"

Genuine surprise. "Well ... here!"

"Here? What's 'here'?"

"My home."

"But, what's its name?"

"I told you, the City."

Here we go. "Look." Otto waved a hand, exasperated. "Please stop. This place has a name and a location and much of what I need to know is in those two, so." And he made a "go on" gesture.

"The. Ci. Ty." Frank said it as if Otto were an idiot. "And. It's. Here."

Otto was no idiot, had a fairly reasonable level of intelligence, and could grasp most things if given proper explanation, but condescension triggered his usually-in-control temper.

"That's crap," he growled, temper emerging. "There's no way this place is just 'the City' and 'here' is not a reference point."

"But they are! It is!" Frank looked at Otto like he was crazy, which Otto had not ruled out but, *hmm*, wait a minute ...

Now he had it, the string that unravels. Time for this silliness to end. "Frank, no way you're from here. This place is ... it's, well, it's either where you go after you die or where your mind goes, or in this case, my mind goes, when you're in a complete and severe coma. So you've either come here from some other place after you died, or you are a startlingly clear figment of my imagination. And I'm going to vote for 'imagination' because I know you from someplace." And Otto sat back, satisfied.

Frank gaped at him. "You're wrong," he announced, "completely wrong. I've always been here."

"I really don't think that's possible, Frank."

"How can you say that? What do you know? You just got

here!" Agitation roiled Frank's face, alarming Otto. "Let me make sure you understand. I've *always* been here!" He stabbed a finger into the richly wooded tabletop.

A little too loud, that, and the baristas looked over, concern dropping their smiles to frowns. Otto briefly wondered what kind of police patrolled here, nice guys who put their hands on your shoulders and said, "There, there," before kneeing you in the groin? "Listen." He decided to match Frank's tone. "If you've always been here, then, you're something else. You're an angel, right? Is that what you are?"

"An angel?" Frank yelped, which startled the baristas and four or five other customers into open-mouthed astonishment. "I'm not an angel! How could you even think such a thing? *Wheoouf!*" – pure exasperation – "Boy, they really gave me a live one this time!"

Otto narrowed an eye. "'They'? What do you mean 'they'?"

"The bosses, of course." As if that was sufficient. Frank waved the baristas away. "New guy," he called and they all went, "Oh, okay," and turned their server smiles back at Otto, maybe with a touch of sympathy.

Which was irritating, but one irritation at a time. "Who's your boss?"

"Mr. Latchemondy," Frank replied, offhand.

Otto concluded this line of questioning was going to dead-end very quickly. Shift direction. "What's your job, Frank?"

"I'm a greeter."

"What do you greet, Frank?"

Good humor spilled across Frank's face again. "Why, you, of course!"

"Right." Play along, Otto, don't get mad. "And how did you get this job?"

Frank glared at him. "It's my job!"

"Right." Patience, patience. "But how did you *get* it?"

"That's a silly question. It's my job."

"Were you appointed, did you go to school, did you pick this line of work out of a book? How actually did it come about?"

Frank leaned forward. "It's the job they gave me ..." and his voice trailed off. He looked confused, "... when I got here. Wait."

Frank's face transformed into a mask of doubt and Otto half-regretted doing this to him. But, hey, going to get some answers, even if it made Frank's skull explode.

"I've ..." Frank gazed inward, struggling to capture something, which was quite painful to watch. "I've been here ... a while. Quite a while, I think. Since I was about ten." He wasn't talking to Otto; he was muttering to himself. "After Lawton."

A chill ran down Otto's spine. "What did you say?" he breathed.

Frank, eyes clouded, face pinched. "Lawton. I remember a town called Lawton."

"Lawton, Oklahoma?"

Frank's brows furrowed. "Yes," he said finally, snapping his eyes open. "Yes, that's the place. Lawton, Oklahoma. That's it." He regarded Otto. "How'd you know that?"

Otto was barely breathing. "Frank, what's your last name?"

"I don't use it."

"Frank."

"I don't use it ... I don't want to."

"Frank, tell me."

Distant, Frank went somewhere he hadn't gone in a long time and there was a storm in there, something he didn't want to see. If right, Otto knew what Frank was seeing and he knew why Frank didn't want to see it. If Otto was right, then—

"My God," Otto whispered, "you're Frank Vaughn."

Frank paled and his mouth opened. "Yes," he said softly, "that's my name." He paled. "How do you know my name?"

"I was there, Frank."

"There?"

"Lawton. I was there. When it happened."

"When it happened ..." Frank's voice died and Otto watched him go away again.

The last day of school. Bell rings. Ten-year-old Otto skips along the sidewalk and sings the "School's Out" song along with dozens of others of his just-freed peers. Peanut butter sandwich at home, flops on the couch and watches TV all the rest of the afternoon because he could and the Six O'clock News came on and there it was.

"Oh," or some noise like that came out of Frank's mouth and he was far away, so far away, seeing it again. Probably for the first time in what, fifty years or so?

The chill detonated, a glacial wave that froze Otto's spine into a gigantic shiver of pure fear. Heart pounding, he backed as far into his chair as possible, seeking escape. Oh, no, no, this is impossible. This is a nightmare. This is a *Twilight Zone* episode, conjured by my coma-frozen mind. It's not real, not real at all.

It's only a movie; it's only a movie.

"She just kept beating me. With my own bat. You know? My own bat! It hurt!"

The news showed Frank's blood-streaked bedroom and blood-soaked sheets, his head covered but his arms out, still and boneless. The aftermath. But Frank was there while it happened.

"I told her I'd go back but she kept screaming, 'Stupid boy! Stupid boy!'" Frank's voice rose to a loud falsetto.

The baristas and other customers faced him, their surprise turning to fear, all of them going back to their special moments, that car accident or slip-and-fall or the simple giving out of a heart, which had moved them from there to here. And right at that moment, Otto knew exactly what he, and everyone here, was.

Ghosts. They were ghosts.

"Stop, Mommy, I'll go back, school's still open, it's still open, I can go back. I CAN GO BACK!" Frank screamed and leaped to his feet, chair flying across the room and knocking over a table, elbows covering his face.

Everyone else screamed, too, Otto right along with them, a red-hot coal exploding in his chest and bursting out like the creature in *Alien*, drenching him in red-hot pain and red-hot despair and he was lost, lost forever.

Frank, still screaming, still with his arms up, ran out of the shop, aimless, turning one way or the other and running, just running, bouncing into corners and walls and doubling back to the shop door and ricocheting and then, finally, rushing out of view.

Otto followed his progress by the Doppler effect of screams from everyone Frank swept by as he made them relive what had brought them here. It was a city of screams moving off, fainter, gone.

Otto lay his head on the table, weeping. So did everyone else. He'd got this wrong. Otto wasn't tubed and intubated in ICU, oh no, not at all. He was dead. He was gone; his life was gone; everything he had ever done and wanted to do, gone, the agony of it woken by Frank's screams.

No. Please, no. I cannot bear this.

There were steps, quiet and hesitant, near him. Someone hovered near Otto's shoulder; he turned his head, keeping it in contact with the wood surface, and saw a gold brocade tunic. He followed it up.

The barista's tears still flowed down his beautiful black face, his teeth all gold, a couple of them inlaid with diamonds winking at Otto. "His mother?" he whispered in an accent that sounded vaguely West African.

"What?" Otto croaked.

The barista hesitated, looking fearfully out of the window for a moment. "His mother did this?"

Otto stopped crying, sat up. "Yes," he answered flatly, "Because he left his report card at school."

The barista put a shocked face to the window. "How ... trivial," he whispered.

Chapter III

Heaven and Hell and Angels, Maybe

"Mr. Boteman?"

Otto sat on the curb, head in hands, staring down at the cobblestones that ran so perfectly under his feet and into a storm drain cut into the gutter.

So, it must rain here, or maybe they hose the streets. Were there sewers? Were there toilets?

Otto checked himself. No particular urge, but instinctively knew he could take a very pleasant dump for as long as he desired in what would probably be the Taj Mahal of bathrooms. A superior crap in Hell.

And it *was* Hell, but not as advertised: lovely buildings and people instead of fire and demons. Which, Otto had to admit, was a relief. Getting singed and skewered wasn't a pleasant way to spend eternity. 'Course, spending it wrapped in despair and hopelessness was no picnic, either. Almost better to get the tines and coals because at least he'd know where he stood. This ... uncertainty, this limbo, was worse. It hinted at eventual redemption, else why make things so pleasant? Which meant this was Purgatory, right? Except Otto didn't believe in Purgatory. Seemed like cheating. Either you made Heaven or you didn't. And he hadn't. So, this was, what? A staging area for reincarnation, get to do it all over again?

Great.

"Mr. Boteman?" The same voice again.

"Go away," Otto replied, not moving. Oh, man, Frank, sorry, sorry. Didn't mean to do that to you. Got to find you, wherever in this City of Dis you are, and apologize.

"The apology is not necessary, Mr. Boteman. Frank is all right."

Startled, Otto looked up. A tweedy man stood there, big wire-rimmed seventies-style glasses, checkered suit and pants always popular with the over-sixty set, greying hair cut military short and big brown eyes, magnified by the thick lenses. "You can read my mind?" Otto asked.

"No, no created being can do that, but I am trained in physiognomic responses that indicate what's on the mind. And I'll say it again. You have no need to apologize. In truth, I should apologize to you."

"Who are you?"

"I'm Mr. Latchemondy, supervisor of this section." The man smiled without showing any teeth and offered a gentle hand.

Otto ignored it. "No offense, but I'm not feeling warm and friendly right now."

Latchemondy withdrew. "Perfectly understandable, Mr. Boteman, and I take no offense. You've had a rough experience."

"What gave it away?"

Latchemondy smiled broader, this time showing evenly capped white teeth, "Ah, Humor. One of the Gifts. You'll be fine."

"*Phuuh.*" Otto fixed on the perfect street lined with marvelous crystal-and-lead storefronts stretching back to another wagon parade. Or maybe it was the same one. Frank hadn't taken him all that far. Stay on the wagons, bud, don't look up or you'll get lost in the sky again, and, right now, you need to focus.

"Yes, it is a wonderful sky, deliberately so." Latchemondy leaned back, pressing his face up to the blue, rapture washing over his features.

Otto quick-glanced him and, just as quickly, back down because one level too high and he'd get caught. "Stop doing that."

Latchemondy came back to him, eyebrows raised. "Looking at the sky?"

"That and reading my mind."

"I can't actually read your mind—"

"Yeah-yeah." Otto waved a dismissive hand and then pushed

himself up. "Listen, supervisor of this section, things are pretty effed up right now and I am really, really tired of riddles. Just tell me, straight up, no dancing, no mystery, what is going on?"

Latchemondy frowned at the "effed up" but looked sympathetic. "All right. You're dead."

Otto flipped his hands out. "Finally! A straight answer! Thanks for that. Although I gotta tell ya, Mr. L, I'm not completely convinced this isn't all some stroke-induced dream."

"'Mr. L.' *Hmm*, I like that. And I thoroughly and completely sympathize and empathize with your confusion, but you are definitely not in a coma, you are definitely passed on, and all of this will come clear in time."

"I'm going to be all right, right?"

Latchemondy laughed out loud, like a bell ringing, very pleasant, "Yes, Mr. Boteman, yes, you will be all right."

"Call me Otto."

"All right. Otto. I can take you to your place right now so you can get started."

"My place?"

"Yes. We've got a condo selected for you, just a little north of center, rather pleasant, but don't feel you're obligated to it. Try it out and if it's unsuitable, we can see what else there is." Latchemondy made a gesture to follow.

"Wait a minute. What?"

"I'm sorry. Was I unclear?"

"Well, no, you were very clear, but ... condo?"

"That's the closest term I can use for it. Most *arrivées* are quite satisfied with them, but some want to go to other places, even Out, and that's fine. I suspect you're one of those."

"Ahreevays?"

"It's the term we use."

Otto glowered. "Well, how ... French. And euphemistic. Try something a little more spot on, like 'deadheads.'"

Latchemondy grimaced. "That sounds a bit rude."

"Not to fans. And, 'Out'? What's 'Out'?"

Latchemondy brightened. Happy to help. "'Out' encompasses the areas beyond the City. Whatever terrain you find appealing, mountains, desert, jungle, can be found there. Although, it is quite a journey."

"So, that means the City has boundaries."

"In a sense."

"In a sense of having boundaries and a location and an outside, all of which strongly indicate a physical location. So. Ipso facto." Otto lowered on him. "Where is this place?"

Latchemondy smiled, a pleasant, knowing look crossing his face. "Ah, Curiosity, another Gift. You are blessed, Mister ... Otto. The City is, well, how do I explain? I don't mean to impugn your intelligence, but this 'location,' as you will, is a hard concept for mortals to grasp—"

"Would you just tell me?"

"Sorry. The City is beside everything."

"Beside? You mean, like in another dimension?"

"Well, no, not really."

Otto's temper flared. "Look, I'm not a complete science idiot, you know, and if something unseen exists beside something else, then it's in another dimension, behind a closed door. But not a real door, which is in the same dimension. Another kind of door. You know?"

Latchemondy's puzzled look conveyed otherwise, so Otto went straight to it. "Is that what this is, a closed door?"

"No. It's not a door. Nor a parallel dimension. That implies a corporeal ability to reach here, and you cannot, it cannot be done. All connections to material planes have to be severed to reach here."

"In other words, you have to be dead."

Latchemondy raised a triumphant hand. "Exactly."

"Woowee," Otto blew out a breath. "Okay, I'll buy it, but, there's something wrong with that because I can still remember everything about who I was, which means there is some kind of material connection—"

"But memory is not material."

"A lot of people on Earth would disagree with that."

"No doubt, but it's true."

"So what is memory, then?"

Latchemondy tapped a finger, impatient. "We have some rather extraordinary libraries here, Mister ... Otto. All your questions can be answered there, although it will take some rather involved research."

Otto let out a slow breath. "You won't tell me, will you?"

"It would do me little good to tell you. There are certain preparations necessary, certain concepts you must grasp. With your

Curiosity—"

"Yeah-yeah," Otto palmed him quiet, "A gift. Which bespeaks a Giver, don't it? So, then—"

"Where's God?" Latchemondy finished for him.

"Stop doing that. Yes, where is God?"

Latchemondy pushed his face to that forever sky, "You see this, Mister … Otto, you are transported by the sheer ecstasy of it, and you ask?"

Otto stepped back. Latchemondy's face turned serene and light. Whatever men had long decided was tranquility or nirvana or fulfillment – pick your term – glowed on and through him. Otto almost went to his knees because the light from Latchemondy's face caressed, like Mom easing the pain of a scraped knee, a girlfriend soothing the lost game, Sherry the missed promotion. So comforting, so peaceful. He swayed with the power of it. With the alien, the otherworldly, the infinity ...

"What are you?" Otto breathed.

Latchemondy's beatified face turned toward him and bathed and soaked and succored Otto in the same light as the sky – and Otto was gone, transported, forever soaring. "I am like you," Latchemondy's voice, so far away, a stirring on the breeze.

Otto held up his hand to block that light and return to this planet, whatever that was. "No, you're not."

The light stopped and Otto took in a deep breath because he was whirling around a center he could not identify and he could easily, easily, let go. Just let go ... No! His mind screamed, No, not yet! I must know!

"Yes," Latchemondy's voice was normal again. "You must know. You are Humorous and Curious and you Seek. Good, very good. There is a ship."

"Huh? Ship? What ship?" Otto did a Bugs Bunny headshake. "You speaking metaphorically?"

"Perhaps."

Otto squeezed his temples. "One profoundly baffling topic at a time, okay? I asked what you are. And don't tell me again you're like me because you're not. You said something about us mortals and about being created so, no more crap, what are you?"

Latchemondy gave him a graceful smile. "Attention to detail, too. Also good. No need for hostility, Mister ... Otto. I am like you because I am a created being but of a different creation from you."

"An—"

"Angel? And yes, I know, stop doing that." Latchemondy paused, considering. "An angel," he muttered, "I suppose that's as good a label as any. Yes, let's use that."

"What?" Otto frowned. "Are you an angel or not? That's a pretty straightforward question."

"And I have given you a straightforward answer."

Otto laughed, "Oh, no you haven't, but I'm guessing that's about the closest you'll come." He stopped, his eyes narrowing. "Wait, if you're created, then—"

"There is a God? Of course, I thought we were past that."

"But—"

"No," Latchemondy shook his head, "you're quite right, Mister ... Otto. This is not the Heaven the churches taught you, clouds and harps and giant throne rooms. It is so much more."

"But—"

"Then this is Heaven? Sorry." Latchemondy waved an apology. "I can't help the mind-reading, although it's not really mind-reading. Certain physiognomic responses ..." Latchemondy trailed off at Otto's murderous expression. "It is my training, after all." Latchemondy pursed his lips and Otto almost exploded waiting for him to say something, which the big geek took his sweet time doing. "I can't really answer your question. This is the Afterlife, the place where Seekers end up, but calling it Heaven is somewhat inadequate because your concept of Heaven doesn't quite fit."

"Seekers? Is that another euphemism? You mean believers, right? Christians?"

"Among others. 'Seekers' is the better term."

Otto's frustration peaked. Latchemondy looked unbothered, serene, an almost post-coital peace about him – the effect of the sky, Otto knew. He also knew his chances of getting a straight answer were about nil. Try the opposite tack. "All right," said with some antagonism, "let's table that for now. So, answer this, Angel. Where's Hell?"

"Wherever you want it to be."

"Now what does that mean?"

"You asked me 'where' and I told you." Latchemondy's face remained serene but Otto detected annoyance in his voice. So, angels can get mad, huh? "The better question would be 'what?'"

"Okay. What?"

Latchemondy regarded him mildly and swept an encompassing hand across the landscape. "Hell is like your Heaven, not what you expected, so much more than you thought. It is exactly the opposite of all of this. But it is not actually a place, and everyone here, everyone, including me, is not safe from it."

"Huh?"

Latchemondy's eyes took on a strange light. "We are not safe from it." And his look hardened, froze, glaciers of pain and terror, lost, so lost, buffeted by dark winds, no up or down, no one else in sight, no answers.

No answers.

Otto was on a flat plain of nothing that stretched to nothing, the last person in the Universe. Alone. Completely. Running over a featureless void toward the black horizon and never reaching the end of it, never finding his way, the emptiness a mockery, laughing at him, sneering at him. Forever.

He screamed.

On his knees, gasping, the cobblestones stark and hard, it took him a few seconds to realize the Void was gone. He moved drunkenly, large turnings, and the blessed sky reeled in and out of his vision, centering him, a sympathetic Latchemondy standing there watching.

"My God," Otto said.

"Yes," Latchemondy clucked, then paused. "I think you're ready to go now?"

Otto nodded and wobbled to his feet. Latchemondy turned and headed toward the parade. Otto followed.

Chapter IV

Perturbed by the Wonderful

Otto sipped a martini, gazing at the traffic and pedestrians fifty stories below, which all looked like ants. He smiled. Some analogies fit anywhere.

Otto's condo, apartment, whatever, topped a red-brick skyscraper, its walls pearled and inlaid and bejeweled like every other building here, gems cascading down merging lines, like one of those fun distance illusions in a Psych 101 textbook; cream-colored balconies – same as his – jutted from the brick in perfect step all the way to the street, no doubt accessed by cream-colored French doors identical to his. 'Course, the other doors might be painted circus colors for all he knew – the geometry of this place prevented him from seeing much beyond the edges of the descending balconies – but probably not. Symmetry prevailed. Take his patio furniture, for example; wrought iron chaise and rockers, all red-and-cream cushions, with a glass-topped table supporting a red-and-cream umbrella rising from the middle. It all matched, the varying shades of chair and umbrella and balcony and building masterfully blended into an eye-pleasing palette. Sherry'd love this place. He presumed she'd be along one of these days to take its measure. That would be good.

At least he'd know someone.

He looked at the building opposite, a dark-brown, granite slab version of this one. Deng Xiaopeng, on a charcoal-and-tan balcony across the gap, raised a glass to Otto. Well, it wasn't actually Deng Xiaopeng; it was a Chinese guy, or close enough to one that further distinction wasn't necessary; rather stout, grey-haired and wearing pince-nez. Otto didn't know his name, so Deng will do. Otto raised his glass in response and they toasted each other. They'd been doing this every day at about sunset for the last two weeks (or what seemed like two weeks, anyway). They simultaneously lowered their glasses and then Deng did what he always did next: smiled at Otto. No attempt to communicate, no shouts or waves or exaggerated mouthings; not even a paper airplane across the way. Just stood there, smiling. And then Otto did what he always did after about ten minutes of Smiling Deng: decided enough was enough and walked back inside.

Deng was the only person Otto saw. If it weren't for random lights switching off and on after dark in the windows opposite, he'd swear they were the solitary inhabitants of their respective buildings. Testament to the engineering, sound did not travel. Occasionally, shadows moved around the lower balconies, but Otto had no idea if humans were causing them. Could be squirrels.

Otto returned to the balcony after dark. The night sky wasn't hypnotic so he could look at it and remain in control. That is, if he didn't let the weird stars get to him. And, boy, were they weird. Not as weird as the moons, but close enough.

He saw things he'd never seen from Earth – nebulae and novae and comet groupings and, of course, stars – doubled and tripled and formed into wondrous patterns, celestial fireworks – but it was all flying by like a gigantic, left-to-right version of that Windows 95 screensaver. Otto couldn't tell if the Afterlife was whipping through the Universe at breakneck speed or if this was some kind of show. Not a popular one; he appeared to be the only one staring at it. Even Deng stayed away. Maybe it was too disconcerting.

He'd never seen the same constellations twice, at least, so far. Otto had turned it into a game, coming up with more and more outlandish labels for the singular patterns: the Dervish, the Mongoose, the Inside Out Man, but they were gone as soon as he named them and he was, frankly, running out of titles. He could double-name them, but what if the first constellations came back? After all, he'd been observing for only a couple of weeks (or what seemed like a couple of weeks), so there was a good chance this was a function of orbit and, sometime down the road, the Inside Out Man would reappear. But, by then, he wouldn't remember it, so not an issue.

He suspected that the same stars came by two or three times a night so he'd stayed up to see if that was so, but, nope, all different. He'd walked back inside as the sun rose, not sleepy at all, and wondered about that; he should at least be punchy or wired but felt fine. He stretched out on the couch and half-jokingly said, "Go to sleep, bud," and, lo, he did. For about eight hours, he figured, waking up very much refreshed, feeling very much at peace and very much wondering why. No dreams, which didn't seem right: if there was one place he should have the best dreams ever, it was here. But, since the whole thing was a dream, maybe that was overkill.

Further testing needed, he willed more sleep and did a subsequent eight hours, equally dreamless, which took him into the early morning; he stayed awake for two straight days, sitting in the condo after sunrise to avoid the hypnosky, and on the balcony at night, watching stars. And suffered no deleterious effects.

He discovered he could sleep or stay awake, whichever he wanted, didn't matter, he was good either way. Insomniacs must love that but Otto included a sleep cycle. It was more natural. He usually hit it at what he called midnight, when a moon, exactly like Earth's – except it was movie-screen sized, accompanied by a featureless, golden, dwarf companion to its right – stood directly overhead, after first appearing on the horizon right above the setting sun (let's call that "west") and reversing the sun's track. Apogee, both globes went right back where they came from, straight down the middle of the sky until dipping below the western horizon as the sun peeped opposite.

Talk about weird. At least they weren't speeding by.

He struggled to remember all the science classes he took, especially a freshman astronomy course that quickly became uninteresting when it moved away from meridians and orbits to the chemical compositions of various stars. A grasp of orbital dynamics might help him understand what was happening. Like, how do the sun and moons follow the same paths every day and night while the stars were different? And how was it that the double moonlight did absolutely nothing to obscure the stars, which shone as brightly as if it were dead dark? Can that even happen?

It's happening, isn't it? Do you seriously believe Earth's physics apply here, bub?

His observations left him with more questions than answers. Need at least an entire year to establish baseline data before making any sense of this mess, but what constituted a year? If the sun traveled exactly the same arc every day, how would he know? Simply count off 365 days and, on day 366, blow a horn and yell, "Happy New Year!"? That's Earth physics, bub. He didn't want to sit out here for however long it took to mark the seasons, even if he had all of eternity to do so. That may be fine for Zoroastrians, but he'd go bonkers.

Besides, he had more than local celestial rules to figure out. Take his condo. What a great place. Lots of highly luxuriantly cushioned, tastefully designed loungers and couches and ottomans and settees, all properly placed and properly complementing each other. White carpet in the living room with glass tables and marble highlights; black carpet in the oaken guest room (guest room, that's rich), Persian rugs in the master bedroom underneath his king-sized Queen Anne bed, squared by a marvelously carved headboard ... the place was unreal. Sherry would love it as much as the balcony setup, be astounded in fact, and have absolutely no inclination to adjust anything. Which may, or may not, be good, because then what else would she do, sit and admire it all day? Or, would *her* condo require constant rearranging so she was happily occupied until her chosen bedtime? Would she even have her own condo? Did husbands and wives get back together, or was that "death do us part" stuff inviolate?

Questions, questions.

Like how 'bout these floor-to-ceiling bookshelves, stuffed floor to ceiling with books, lining every single room, even the bathroom. Yes, a bathroom, marble and gold with a toilet and a huge Whirlpool tub/shower/sauna and his choice of piped-in music, falling a little short of the Taj Mahal facilities he'd imagined earlier, but nice, all the same. And even though he had no particular urge to download, he decided to give it a go, so to speak, and the resulting session – crampless, odorless, messless – had been so completely satisfying, he figured toilet use could become quite the pastime.

How unseemly, yet it didn't feel that way. Felt wonderful.

He used the Whirlpool a lot, sitting neck deep in decadent bubbles and swirling water that massaged him almost to the point of sexual excitement, puffing a cigar and sipping brandy. Nothing ever got wet except him, unless he wanted it to, like the time he had deliberately dropped a cigar in the water to see what would happen. Nothing. Wasn't a big deal, he simply got another one and reached up and grabbed a book, a John Banville he'd always intended to read but never did.

All the books were ones he'd intended to read but never did. Like Dostoevsky. He had everything the mad Russian ever wrote, shelved alphabetically in lovely gold script and leather binding, and Otto went through it all as fast or as slow as he desired, savoring the long passages of brilliance with a reading pace outstripped by a first-grader, then zipping through the long boring descriptions with a speed that would astonish Stephen Hawking. (Say, shouldn't Hawking be around here somewhere? Wonder what he makes of the skies.) And he remembered whole passages; heck, whole chapters! And he had the urge to read all that Dostoevsky again, which he did. When he no longer had the urge, Dostoevsky was gone, replaced by others he had forgotten about and others he suspected had never been written, at least not on Earth. Mark Twain, *Sojourners Among the Galaxy*? Nevah hoid of it.

Questions, questions, questions. Like, how did someone know he was a big reader? How did they find all the books he had forgotten? And how were they replaced?

Similar questions applied to television. Oh yeah. A big plasma TV dropped down from the ceiling with a touch of a button as the lights dimmed and the leather lounger warmed and purred and adjusted to give him a perfect view. (And that was another thing: he didn't need his bifocals anymore. He still had them, still wore them, but didn't need them, unless he wanted. The toilet principle.) All the channels broadcast all the shows he had enjoyed before his somewhat rude departure. And they appeared to be current. Right now, he was watching football, his Eagles, and knew it was real-time because they sucked as much as ever.

Switch a channel and there was an entire library of movies, from D. W. Griffith to stuff released a few months before Otto died, like that Spiderman in Europe thing. Even porno. Not nasty lowlife stuff either, quite exquisite. He watched it and was exquisitely stirred and had no desire to pleasure himself because the stirring was sufficient.

Playstation, too, or a reasonable facsimile, with some of the most stunning, realistic games he'd ever seen. He invaded Normandy and raced in Monte Carlo and even played a stand-up comic on an improv game requiring snappy patter to advance. But the games were all earthbound; he hadn't found a game based on this Afterlife yet. And none of the games were multiplayer. Indeed, he'd found no Internet connections of any kind, not even a computer. No Google. Now, why was that? Someone afraid we'd all turn into *Warcraft* geeks or something?

Or find out what's going on?

Don't forget the refrigerator and pantry all stocked with stuff he loved – pork loin, Cocoa Puffs, artichokes and every salad mixing possible. Plates of the most luscious foods, all fresh, and never running out. He had, much to Deng's astonishment, barbecued wondrous meals on the wondrous charcoal grill (not gas, sacrilege) cleverly placed on one side of the balcony. Not that he needed lip-smacking meals, or any meals, for that matter. Eating was like crapping, only when he chose, and the two functions weren't even related. He could go days without food or water and feel no effects or pangs and could toilet on command, with no need for a requisite meal as a pump primer.

Very, very weird, and all prompting additional questions, ad infinitum, and all of those questions pointed to one, Eternal and Omnipotent Answer.

God.

Only God could be doing this. No creature, no other thing, had the ability. And that raised the biggest, most profound question of all, the Keystone of Questions:

Where was God?

Obviously, around here somewhere, else, how could all this be happening? But, the Big Guy was not apparent; at least, Otto did not glimpse a throne room or some golden staircase winging by in the night, and God hadn't dropped by to say welcome, good to see ya, how 'bout a spot o'tea?

Why so coy?

Maybe God was actually some small-fry nerdy-looking dweeb and He didn't want his rep diminished. 'Course a God Who could do all this could easily make Himself Schwarzenegger, or at least come up with pretty nifty *Hulkbuster* armor. But no.

No God. Anywhere.

If God wanted to stay behind the curtain, fine. Otto could easily shrug his shoulders and dive right into all the toys and joys and pleasures of this Afterlife, which God was certainly taking great pains to provide. Otto had plenty of things to distract, get lost in, and forget the Source of, the grace of, but, ya know, no.

Not his style.

First of all, Otto was grateful. He had, despite numerous and severe shortcomings, done well in his life, keenly aware of God's hand in that. Otto needed to say thanks. Secondly, it was God. The Unmoved Mover, the Father of Us All, the Source. The Man with the Plan and All the Answers to all the questions. Like, f'rinstance, purpose of all this?

The purpose of all this.

Otto had to know why. Why life? Why the Universe? What is man, that Thou visiteth him? We're maggotry, yet you, God the Father, have certainly spent an inordinate amount of Your Time and Effort looking after us. Yeah-yeah, the Fall of Satan and the angels and using the lesser creature to condemn the greater but, geez, Dude, complicated. You're God: You can just fingerflick Satan across the Universe. And yeah-yeah, the essence of God and the compromises: Otto understood the theology, but it had all been filtered through centuries of interpretation and translation and it'd be nice to get a straight story from the Source Himself.

And so far, nothing. No hints, no clues, no answers, not even from the books; they were all pre-death. Even the Twain galaxy sojourner book used Earth and Life as its base. The TV was equally worthless because there were no local channels, no *Ten O'clock News*, no *DIY for the Died*. If God was holding a half-hour chat session on some channel, Otto hadn't found it yet.

Frustrating.

And that's why he was going out.

Otto sipped a little more of the martini and then, whatthehell, gulped down a mouthful, which was a mistake, because the same characteristics of a good Earth martini applied here and he choked and spluttered and got all teary-eyed. Deng leaned on his balcony edge, concerned. Otto waved and gulped and choked some more and then burst out laughing. Even in Heaven, you can't glug gin and vermouth. Still laughing and choking, he went inside, feeling Deng's surprised eyes following.

He cleaned up and went to the closet and poked around and selected a white Bagutta shirt (which sounded expensive) and a midnight blue suit labeled "Welsh and Jeffries." Nevah hoid of 'em, but the richness of the wool and the perfection of the fit strongly indicated quality. So who knew his measurements well enough to ...

Oh, never mind.

He grabbed a bright yellow tie, a Hakashi, which he supposed was another tasteful label, and tied it big, leaving the top button of the shirt open. He stepped back and looked at himself. Okay, an ensemble that would have cost him half his earthly paycheck and he looked damned good in it. Not preppy, not overbearing, but classy, as if the down-to-earth (yuk yuk) guy in the mirror had developed a sense of style and understanding over the years. Exactly the impression he wanted to convey.

How does that happen?

That's why you're heading out, dude, to get those answers. And if you stand here admiring your Rico Suave self all night, you'll not get any answers. To anything.

Otto left the bedroom and went down the hall and opened the door for the first time since Latchemondy had ushered him inside with a, "You'll be all right," and boldly stepped out.

Yeah! This is me doing this!

The door closed gently behind him. Right at the moment Otto realized he didn't have a key.

Great.

He grabbed the handle, jiggling it to see if, by magic, it would open and – by magic – it did. He felt a bit foolish and then walked in and peered at the inside doorknob. Yep, a lock. He pushed the button and tested it.

Yep, locked.

He then went back out and deliberately pulled the door closed. Okay. He turned the knob again and it opened.

Obviously, key not necessary.

Did that mean anyone happening by could breezily enter and rummage around his place? He checked up and down the hall to see if his neighbors were pouring out to burgle him. So what if they did?

It's not like anything in there was actually his. The idea was bothersome, though; it felt like vulnerability.

He watched, suspicious, and when no black-clad-masked-bag-over-shoulders thieves appeared, walked about six apartments down and grasped the handle of the first door on the right. He twisted it, but nothing happened. He twisted it again. Nothing. That didn't mean anything, though. What if his was the only door that unlocked at the touch?

The door yanked open. Otto gaped at the small, swarthy man dressed in a red brocade smoking jacket standing there. "Yes?" the man asked.

"Uh." Otto was at a loss. What did you say in this situation, I was merely seeing if I could break into your apartment? "Sorry," was all he could come up with.

The man's exquisitely shaped eyebrows went up. "For what?"

"Uh," Again, loss of words. "For ... disturbing you."

The man nodded, waiting, and Otto realized he must sound like a salesman and Eyebrows was ready for the pitch. Did that mean salesmen operated here? *Hmm.*

Seconds ticked by. If Otto didn't do something, they might tick for a year or two. He held up a hand. "That's all. I'm not selling anything. I didn't mean to disturb you."

The brows furrowed and the man looked at Otto suspiciously, then shook his head and turned to go back inside.

"Wait," Otto said.

The man's brows came back. "I thought you were not selling anything."

"I'm not, I'm ..." Otto cocked his head. Guy had an accent. "Are you Spanish?"

"Spanish?" The man regarded Otto. "No, Castilian."

"Isn't that Spanish?"

"No, it is not. Spain is the peninsula, but I am Castilian. I was lately of the Plata."

"Plata? The River Plata? You're from Argentina?"

"Argentina?" The man looked puzzled. "Oh, yes, yes, that is what it was called later. Much later," and he smiled.

"Later? When were you there?"

"In 1780 by the Church calendar. I was born there. I left there in 1799." He leaned forward conspiratorially. "Diphtheria."

Interesting. "You mean you've been here since 1799?"

"Not right here. I lived a few other places before this but, yes."

"Here in the ..." and Otto paused momentarily before saying it, "... City?"

"Yes." The man's suspicion reappeared. "But so are we all. Why?"

"Uh, well, nothing, I'm just a bit surprised, I guess."

"Surprised? Why would you be surprised?"

"Uh ..."

Eyebrows got stormy and, no doubt, he was wondering what kind of a crazy person had shown up on his landing and Otto wondered, again, what kind of police handled such situations when the man brightened. "Oh, of course! You are new here!"

"Well, yes."

"You will be all right."

Otto couldn't help it, he laughed out loud. The man goggled and stepped back warily.

"No, no." Otto waved a hand. "It's okay. It's just that every single person I've met here has told me that."

The man smiled broadly, suspicion relieved. "I am sure they did. We who have been here for a while tend to forget what it was like on first arrival." He peered at Otto. "And when did you get here?"

"I'm not really sure."

"What year was it when you left?"

"Left?"

"Earth."

"Oh." Otto now understood. "Twenty-nineteen"

The man's eyes rounded. "Truly? It is that year on Earth?"

"It was. I'm guessing it still is. I'm not sure how time works here."

"Yes, yes," the man said absently, self-absorbed for a moment, then snapped awake. "But I am being most rude." He held out a hand. "Ferdinand Silva de Astorga."

Otto took it, "Otto. Otto Boteman."

"You are Prussian?"

"No. American."

"American." Ferdinand smiled pleasantly. "We all were very impressed by your victory over the British."

"Which one?"

Ferdinand cocked his head. "You fought them more than once? Well, that is understandable. They must have been quite displeased with the Revolution."

Otto stared at him. "You remember the Revolutionary War?"

"The American War for Independence. Not exactly. I was too young to follow your battles but my father regaled me with the stories and I did know of your subsequent struggles to establish a country. Quite intriguing, an inspiration to us all. A catalyst for the French, yes?"

"Well, yeah, but that didn't go as good."

"No? I am afraid I have not kept up with Earth history since my arrival here and would be very interested in hearing about it." He stepped aside and swept an arm back to the door. "Would you like to come in? I have a very fine Madeira that begs company."

Otto hesitated. "I was about to go out."

Ferdinand looked him over. "Yes, I can see that. Something pressing, an engagement, perhaps?"

Otto shook his head. "Not really."

"Ah." Ferdinand nodded. "An exploration of the City. Your first, I am sure. If I promise not to detain you long, would you spare me the time to share a glass?"

Otto looked at him. Ferdinand's smile was genuine and his eyes sparkled with intelligence and interest and, you know, a little insider info might not be a bad idea.

"Sure," Otto said.

Chapter V

Value and Vice-royalties and a City so Immense

"Do you smoke?" Ferdinand asked.

"Cigars," Otto said absently, luxuriating in the overstuffed alpaca lounger. Man, this is nice.

"I am sorry, I do not have any of those, but I keep a collection of exquisite pipes, one of which I would be pleased to offer you." Ferdinand looked at him expectantly from an identical lounger placed opposite, the two of them sitting like bookends at the hearth of an immense, blazing fireplace.

"I've never tried one," Otto admitted. Pipes seemed so – grandfatherly. His grandfather smoked one. Case closed.

"Then, it is a pleasure you have too long deprived yourself, and if you will allow me the honor of introducing you to its decadence, you will forever be indebted." Ferdinand rose smoothly and walked across the room to a waist-high mahogany chest, opened the top and fooled with the contents. Otto watched idly, feeling quite content. This has been a pleasing detour.

He swirled the last of the Madeira, catching the glow of fire and candles and lamps in the bottom of the glass. What a place. Elegant, like its owner. Thick red parchment with green fleur-de-lis papered the walls, trimmed with ironwood wainscoting. Copper and brass wall-fittings contained the lamps and candles, crystals and small mirrors mounted behind them, magnifying and cross-hatching the light in such a way that it gently brightened the room. Great paintings in heavy gilt frames of dark and brooding countrysides, broken up by a distant windmill or two, hung from every wall. Otto could not name the artists; heck, if it wasn't Norman Rockwell, he was lost, but they were probably Rembrandts or Van Goghs or some other Dutch guy. Windmills, see. Then again, could be Spanish. Didn't Don Quixote attack windmills?

Iron and wool furniture, a wonderful combination of hard and soft, ran like a broken line of comfort around the room. A long sofa faced the two chairs, flanked by ironwood tables holding elaborate candelabrums, also backed by golden mirrors. But the linchpin was the marvelous fireplace: black-veined marble mantle dressed with golden fixtures that gleamed in the light, the hearth great blocks of brown granite cut to expose the grain and laid without mortar. How they did that, Otto couldn't fathom. The fire, cheery and airy, gave off pine and cedar smells, throwing an occasional waft of smoke for atmosphere. Stylish gold pokers and tongs lay alongside a golden wood carrier holding three perfectly cut logs.

A real fire. Otto had confirmed that by advancing a hand until he singed a finger. Yet the room was comfortable, not hot, and the smoke was chokeless, no coughing, no burning eyes. Otto wanted a fireplace exactly like it, a mental wish he fired toward The Great Condo Furnisher in the Sky. Put it alongside the TV, will ya, Chief?

"Here you are." Ferdinand handed him an ivory meerschaum carved in the face of a smiling old man with a long beard, so realistic Otto expected it to laugh aloud. Otto put the stem to his mouth and pulled as Ferdinand applied a brand. Sweet, humid smoke curled about his mouth. "*Mmm*," Otto approved.

Ferdinand smiled and drew from his pipe, a dark wooded monstrosity that looked as though it had been banged together with a rock. Darker smoke, richer, and far more pungent clouded about his head.

"This is great," Otto said, puffing again and then admiring the pipe's carving.

"I am so pleased you like it. That is a mild mix, an aromatic

Scottish with a rum casing."

"I'll take your word for it. What's yours?"

"A Burley."

"Okay," Otto savored another pull and regarded his host with growing amusement. What a throwback. All courtly and mannered and Edwardian. The guy was straight out of *Downton Abbey*. And the way he talked, so old school, so correct. "And I must say, your English is impeccable."

"As is your Castilian."

Otto raised an eyebrow. "But I don't speak Spanish."

"Nor I English. We hear each other in our most familiar language."

"Seriously?" That's a bit startling. And handy. "*Hmm*. A universal translator."

"Indeed."

"How does that work?"

Ferdinand tipped the pipe. "I do not know."

"Aren't you curious?"

"Very. But it is not where my explorations have taken me."

"So you've been out and about."

"I have not been Out."

"Oh." This universal language thing didn't translate expressions. Or Ferdinand was a literalist. "I meant, you've looked around. By the way, have you heard about some ship?"

"Not per se." Ferdinand recharged his pipe. "There are ships on the oceans."

"Oceans, huh?" Otto considered. That may be worth checking out. "So where have you explored?"

Ferdinand waggled an indulgent finger. "I do not mean explore in the physical sense. You will soon understand what that is. I meant my penchants, my urges."

Here we go. Otto made an impatient gesture. "I'll be all right, right?"

Ferdinand raised his pipe in apology. "Forgive me. I imagine the answers you have received to this point have not satisfied your questions. I do not wish to be another source of frustration, either, but it is a difficult concept to explain."

"Would you, at least, give it a try?"

"I will, but please, be prepared to come away with as much

ignorance as when I start."

"Okay, deal."

Ferdinand cocked his head. "Deal? Ah. I understand. An agreement, not a card action. All right." He took a breath. "I have found, since I have arrived here, that I am drawn to certain things. I have an interest in flavors, textures, the elegant. Not in the prurient sense, but in the elevated. In the superior. The sublime."

Otto got that. "It shows. The Madeira. The tobacco."

"Exactly." Ferdinand looked pleased.

"That's not so difficult to explain." Otto pointed out.

"In the concept, but its function is more obscure. In my case, I found that I was, subtly, in ways I did not realize, led to explore a part of myself I never knew about. It was not something I recognized while on Earth, there actually being little time for it. Although I did partake of the excellent Spanish wines and the occasional Guyanese tobacco that came in, and there are, of course, local delights in the Plata, like yerba and mandioca, but I did not know I had such interests."

"What do you mean, 'led'?"

"That is the part I cannot explain. On my first explorations," he pipe-gestured toward the door, "I found myself on streets talking with persons who had certain insights or wandering about in shops that nudged my interest ... a small bistro that specialized in honeyed wines I had never before tasted, or a fifteenth-century friar who mentioned an interesting wool."

Otto regarded him balefully. Random friars dispensing cloth wisdom? Watery tarts flinging swords ... are we, by chance, having the new guy on, Ferd? All right, dude. "Friar Tuck?"

"I ... do not believe that was his name."

"Never mind." Otto puffed. "Let me see if I get it. You arrive, start running around, see a white rabbit, go down a hole, drink from a bottle and, next thing you know ..." Otto's gesture took in the room.

Ferdinand looked at him like he was crazy. "What are you talking about? I have never seen a rabbit here."

All right, all right, stop it. Otto grimaced an apology. "Sorry. I think I'm being too much of a smartass. So, after all these ... encounters, let's say ... what's been the upshot?"

Ferdinand regarded him suspiciously for a moment and then took another puff. "I am now a successful purveyor of rare wines and exquisite tobacco blends. I, also, speculate on wool futures and have an interest in a blanket factory."

Intriguing. And weird. "Purveyor. You own a store?"

"Several. I believe the current term is 'chain?'" and he raised an eyebrow for confirmation.

"What's the name of it?"

"Pardon?"

"Your store, your chain."

Ferdinand shook his head. "It does not have a name. It is a place where my customers go for certain things of high-quality taste and texture, at least as it pleases them."

"So, capitalism reigns." Otto tipped his pipe in toast, which Ferdinand hesitantly copied, looking a bit puzzled. "I take it you make a lot of money, then." Otto waved a hand around the apartment. "Which is how you afford all this."

"We do not use money here."

"Oh, that's right," Otto corrected himself, remembering what Frank said. "Credits."

"For lack of a better term."

"What's a better term?"

Ferdinand thought. "Value," he said, after a moment, "Your value determines your credits, er, money."

"And you have greater value because you own the chain?"

"Oh, no, not at all." Ferdinand set the pipe in a holder and offered more of the Madeira to Otto, who refused, then poured himself a half glass. He swirled the liquid and held it to the fireplace, examining the color, and then sniffed the glass, closing his eyes. Otto waited. Ferdinand's eyes popped open. "Delightful," he murmured, sipping the wine. A man of such exquisite taste apparently needed to indulge it. Frequently.

"You were saying?"

"Oh, yes, forgive me. The chain is an interest, something I was guided to and developed, which many others now enjoy. But it is not the source of value. Who you are is that source."

"Like Steve Jobs." Who also should be around here, somewhere. Otto made a mental note to look him up.

"Pardon? I do not know what steve jobs are." Said with the

Spanish 'y' instead of the 'j.'

Otto laughed appreciatively. "'Steve Jobs' is a person, after your time. He had such a great tech reputation that everyone bought from him, no matter how silly the product." Apple Watch. Get real.

Ferdinand's brow clouded. "That is not what is meant by value."

Otto gave a dismissive shrug. "Seems dead-on, if you'll pardon the pun. That guy could sell ice cubes to Eskimos."

Darker clouds descended. "It is not selling. It is not reputation."

"Then I don't get it."

Ferdinand appraised him, and not benignly. "No, you do not, and that is understandable. It's something so un-Earthlike that many who have been here for centuries still do not grasp it. But, to summarize, your intrinsic value determines your credit. It often leads you to interesting pursuits, such as mine, but the value, itself, remains your cash source." Pause. "If I may be so crude."

Huh? "I don't think we really have an intrinsic value, unless you mean reducing us to our component parts. I think we've got about four dollars' worth of gold in us."

Ferdinand sighed, clearly irritated, then settled and swirled Madeira. "No, that is not it." A further swirl. "Let me try to illustrate," his air patronizing, and Otto felt his dander rising. "I do not wish to bore you with personal stories, mind you, especially of my history, but I have found that anecdotes do more to explain a concept than any poor rendering of definition or explanation of theory."

He swirled a moment longer. "I was born in the Vice Royalty of Buenos Aires, the third son of a Castilian noble who had come to the Plata seeking his fortune. My father was a robust, shining man who held his life cheap and the experiences of the world dear, qualities I inherited from him, as they somehow managed to evade my two older brothers, my two younger ones, and all but two of my sisters. My mother was a court beauty, a passionate, bracing woman who loved my father with a purity and excitement that was dazzling. To be in their presence, as they sang or read or danced, was to enjoy a rare moment of souls who have bound their hearts and thoughts together, forever, and because of that, my childhood memories are golden and sunny and wondrous." Here Ferdinand raised the glass in salute.

What the heck is this, *Storytime*? Guess we're going to break out the whist decks and invite the ladies in from the parlor.

Ferdinand continued, "Being the third son was, in those days, an assurance of mediocrity, with the Army or the priesthood the only respectable options, depending upon which profession the second son chose. The elder inherited, of course, and the youngest sons were in his employ, so my immediate brother, Juan, could decide my future. But I was the mirror of my parents' light, my father's favorite, so, in a manner completely at odds with the social norms, I became his advisor, his champion, the one he sent into the Plata for this or that exploration—"

Otto cut him off with a swing of the pipe stem. "Is there a Cliff Notes version of this?"

Ferdinand, who had been in full-blown declaiming stance, came up blinking. "Pardon?"

"Can you summarize?"

"I am!" he responded with true bewilderment and Otto realized he'd careened headlong into a generation gap. Several generations' worth of gap. Back Before TV, hours-long stories were all the rage, whether via radio or via a pipe-smoking, wine-swishing Argentine.

Otto blew out his cheeks. Might as well enjoy the ride. He sat back.

Ferdinand, a bit perplexed, eyed Otto then resumed: "Naturally, such behavior engendered talk, and we were looked upon with great suspicion. *Peninsulares* distrusted *criollos*, such as I. We were considered the source of all discontent, the seat of disruptive ideas, like those arising from your Revolution. That my father, politically aligned with the peninsulares, would place so much of his wealth and power in the hands of an unvested younger son caused great concern. It was necessary, not only for my continued survival but the survival of my parents, that I prove my value." Ferdinand paused for a sip.

Ah. So we are finally approaching something like a point, are we? Otto puffed good-naturedly. "You know what's odd?" he said, "I heard those terms, peninsulare and criollo, just like that. No translation."

"As you should," Ferdinand sniffed. "Some concepts retain original language. 'Mainlander' and 'colony-born' do not really convey the meaning of those words."

"Yeah, they do. They're like Redcoat and Yankee Doodle."

"No," Ferdinand put down the glass. "I just heard you speak those two terms in English, because I do not know the subtleties of the relationship."

Otto raised an eyebrow. "Now, that's interesting. You'd have to be pretty read-up on the respective histories to know those subtleties, right?"

"Correct."

"So they stay in original form. Nice. But yet, we get the gist."

"Yes," Ferdinand said. "So do you get the gist of value?"

"Not at all."

Ferdinand rolled his eyes. "All right, then I shall continue."

Otto's turn to roll eyes as Ferdinand did as threatened.

"As I was taking over more and more of my father's concerns, our beloved Aires was eclipsed by the more successful Montevideo, and there was much talk that our Royal warrants would be transferred if we could not catch up. At the same time, both of our cities, indeed, the entire colony, were suffering unwarranted incursions from the Portuguese, who attacked from the upper Plata. These troubles allowed my value to emerge, tipping the balance to our side.

"You see, I had a natural gift for the land. It was etched in my soul. There was no part of the *llano* I had not explored, no Indian language of which I did not have a rudimentary understanding, no tributary of the Plata that resisted my navigation. I had demonstrated this ability before I was fifteen and it was this that caused my father to place so much faith in me, using my abilities to advance our fortunes. For example, when I discovered the manner of a Portuguese approach, I devised methods, from my natural understanding of how the Plata worked, to interdict them. I guided at least four expeditions, some of them deep within the estuary in places we had not yet traversed, and we inflicted severe defeats on the Portuguese, sending them fleeing for their lives. I was at the height of my worth when I contracted the diphtheria." He shook his head. "I often wonder how much more I would have done." He sat the glass down and took up the pipe, lost in thought.

It took a moment for Otto to realize the narrative was over. Time to wake up. So, what's the proper old-timey parlor protocol here? Comment on the delivery, he supposed. "Excellent story," he said. "Very ... detailed."

"Thank you," Ferdinand looked satisfied.

Otto mentally patted himself on the back. Good call. Let's extend the compliment, then. "I think I see it now." He didn't but, please, no more stories. "You had proved your worth and that advanced your stock. You, being you, have this value. Everyone can depend on it."

Ferdinand nodded. "That is correct."

"Okay. Good." Otto puffed. Keep it going. "So, tell me, what's your value here?"

Ferdinand's brow furrowed. "Pardon?"

"Is it the shops? Are texture and flavor so important here, your value is enhanced? Or is it that you employ a lot of people?"

Ferdinand rubbed the side of his temple. "No, that is not it. Value is not something you earn here. It is what you bring with you."

Great. Guess another story's coming. Need to short circuit that. "Just tell me what you mean, Ferdinand."

"It is the value I amassed in life which determines my credit here."

"Really."

"Truly."

Otto mulled. "Okay. So you walked in here at a certain value level."

"Yes."

"And that's based on what you did in life."

Ferdinand beamed. "You have it."

"Let's see if I do." Otto narrowed on him. "Your natural ability to ambush Portuguese soldiers there earned you a lot of wampum here."

Ferdinand was pained. "You put it in rather gross terms."

"Don't mean to, but that's the way it looks. You were really good at ambushes and, as a result, got a lot of credits, enough to start up a chain." Otto took a long slow pipe inhalation, without any urge to cough. Excellent. "The Almighty puts a lot of premium on that?"

Ferdinand's lips snapped about the stem, his eyes cold. "The value is not in the action," he said stiffly, "but in its effect. Many people benefited from my abilities."

"And many suffered from it." Otto streamed smoke.

"That is not the point."

"What is, then?"

"That my value enhanced, protected, indeed, improved, the life of my family and my country."

"At the expense of such things for the Portuguese. And, I'm betting, the Indians. And the slaves, let's not forget them."

Ferdinand matched him puff for puff, his furious, Otto's snarky. The silence stretched. "Are you endeavoring to provoke me?" Ferdinand asked quietly. Deadly. Like the preliminaries to a shoot-out.

"No. Yes. Maybe. I don't know." Otto shook his head. "Can people be provoked here?"

"Yes, they can."

Ferdinand's threatening tone gave Otto pause. This was terra incognita. Do they fight duels here? Who knows? But here he was, making smart-alecky remarks in a social context he did not understand. Talk about fools rushing in. That no angels showed up to rescue him indicated how much he'd stepped in it. So what do you do when you've stepped in it? Apologize, of course.

Otto held up a placating hand. "I have offended you."

Ferdinand visibly relaxed and Otto congratulated himself on getting another parlor rule right. "I am out of my depth here. Chalk it up to my ignorance."

"It is not ignorance." Ferdinand tapped his stem. "It is your misunderstanding of value. I said earlier that I would not be able to explain and I have proved myself true. It is unfortunate." Ferdinand attended to the pipe, ignoring Otto.

Otto realized something had gone out of the room. The bonhomie gave way to a distinct chill. Winning friends and influencing enemies, as usual. Perhaps a change of subject was in order.

"Do you see them regularly?" Otto asked.

Ferdinand looked up. "Who?"

Yep, distinct chill. "Your family."

"My mother, my father, my siblings?" Ferdinand shook his head. "No." He paused. "I have not seen them since I came here."

That seemed a bit odd. Little bit of family tension, mayhap? Well, yeah, younger son displacing the elder in dad's affections. "Really?"

"I have not seen them." Said with emphasis as if Otto had called him a liar. Confirmation that the translator did not convey meaning. "I do not know where they are."

Otto leaned forward, all thoughts of correcting the translator's error gone because, what? "How's that possible? This is the Afterlife. You're supposed to see all your family and friends and neighbors and old dogs and parakeets and everything. I mean, that's the big selling point."

Ferdinand laid the pipe down. "It does not work that way. The City is immense."

"So?"

"Finding a particular person is difficult. The City is the size of a world. Everything you see around you is replicated for thousands and thousands of square miles, even more. Many mansions." Ferdinand stated flatly.

"Yeah, okay," Otto said, "but that shouldn't be an issue. I was planning on looking up some people myself." Dad, for instance, although, there was a better-than-even chance the Old Man was, right now, screaming at a black horizon. "That is, after I got a better handle on this place. It's the Afterlife. You should be able to find anyone."

Ferdinand pursed his lips. "Yet I have not."

Otto felt helplessness rising in his chest. That can't be true. Just can't. "Have you looked? Have you looked for your dad?"

Ferdinand sat back and tented his hands. "I saw him briefly. He was on a trolley bus that passed me in one of the business thoroughfares. He recognized me and called out and we waved at each other." He shrugged. "That is all."

"That's all."

"Yes."

Otto examined Ferdinand. What kind of a cold-blooded sonofabitch is this guy? His dad sounded like a good egg, so what's the deal? The everlasting reunion of family, the eternal picnic in the grove of golden apples while the Smiling Countenance of God beamed over the extended generations reunited in death, the cares of the world gone, love and happiness forever ... that's what's supposed to happen, Ferdinand. Especially for a man like you who comes from such a tradition. You should be immersed in all of your passed-on relatives, down to obscure fourth cousins.

You shouldn't be indifferent.

"That's not right. That's just not right," Otto concluded. "I mean, what about your mom? Have you even tried? Isn't there a Celestial Yellow Pages? Eternity's Facebook or something?"

"I do not know what those are."

Otto made a helpless gesture. "A registry. A way to find someone else. You at least had something like that in Argentina."

"Argen ... oh, yes, the Vice Royalty. Yes, we all knew where each other was. There. But not here."

"Not here."

"No. Because there are other ..." Ferdinand paused, thinking of the word. "... considerations."

"*Pfhht.* I'm not buying it. I know for a fact people meet up here. I ran into someone I knew when I was ten, about ten minutes after I arrived, in fact."

"Yes," Ferdinand agreed. "As I have met, and still see, such persons of some peripheral contact during my life, like a Guarani guide I once used, a horse trainer on our estate."

"But not your family."

"No. The City ..." and he made a gesture indicating size.

"Bull." From Ferdinand's reaction to that, the universal translator had conveyed the proper sense of the word. "People move all through this City. Some go out of it."

"Some do," Ferdinand conceded. "But not that many. Only

the dissatisfied ones."

Momentary silence as Otto absorbed this. "Ferdinand, is this Hell?"

Ferdinand cocked his head. "No. You would know if it was."

Otto wasn't convinced. Heaven was a carefree place, no conflict, no fear, but now here he was, filled with care, worried ... fearful. He had not bargained on this. Meeting Ferdinand had seemed one of those fortuitous little events nudging him along some necessary path, the first step on a delightful road of self-discovery replete with magic and wonderful insight. It wasn't turning out that way. Unless he was meant to discover that this Heaven, this Afterlife, was a baffling, cold and lonely place.

And God was not here.

At all.

That thought staggered him. God was not here. Instead, there were billions of His subjects, pampered, coddled, indulging textures and tastes since about, oh, the year 3000 BC or so, living at His expense. But He, Himself, was not to be found. He had abandoned his children to their eternal pleasures, eternal pursuits, and gone away.

Ferdinand stood and carefully retrieved Otto's pipe from his numb fingers. "I think it is time for you to go."

"Yes," Otto said numbly and got up numbly and was shown the door and stood outside as Ferdinand gently closed and latched it, not inviting him back, he noted in his numbness, and he was in the hallway.

Alone. Forever.

Chapter VI

Carriages and Moonlight

Otto wished he had a cigarette. For atmosphere. He was alone on an unknown street of an unknown city and bathed in moonlight. Er, double moonlight. Noir.

Well, not really; no menacing shadows and not alone, either. People bustled by, as did cars and horse-drawn carriages, the fake Central Park scene from his first moments here. He stood on the corner of the street closest to the building foyer, eyeing the passing traffic and wondering which way to go. The sidewalks led in every direction and it didn't really matter which one he chose, except he needed to keep a map in his head. There were no street signs or building numbers, no references of any kind. No Google maps, no 911, so who you gonna call? Otto hummed the *Ghostbusters* theme and chuckled quietly. Maybe no one got lost here. Odd things guided, a gum wrapper blowing in the wind, a strange flash in the sky, a magical unicorn surrounded by rainbows and nickering in the right direction.

Beautiful evening. Of course. Nary and never a cloud in the sky. The big moon and its little buddy hung at forty-five degrees. Nine o'clock, Otto's designated time for that angle. The streets, as a result, glowed in silver and gold. Is that what the verse meant? Yes, we said streets lined with gold, but we didn't mean actual gold. Don't be so literal. Much of it is allegorical. Take that "eternal happiness and fellowship and basking in the glory of God" trope; the happiness is relative, fellowship is with strangers and God is not here.

Not too different from Earth.

The passersby smiled and said, "Pardon me," an expectation on their faces of a return greeting but he ignored them. Sorry, not in the mood. Which was odd for Heaven; should always be in the mood. But he was feeling a mite surly.

Not too different from life.

Which meant, like life, he could count on more surprises, and not all of them pleasant. And, if he wanted any answers, he'd have to figure them out for himself.

Okay.

Otto threw away his imaginary cigarette and stepped off the curb. Immediately, one of the horse-drawn carriages pulled up. "Ride, sir?" the top-hatted-and-tailed driver asked cheerily. Mid-sixties, white hair, pince-nez (must be popular around here), merry look, weird English accent, so, what, a nineteenth-century Dickens character? Must be, guy's driving a carriage, after all. "How much?"

"Much? Oh ho!" The man laughed. "You must be new! Hop in."

Otto did so, muttering under his breath what he would do to Carriage Boy if the guy said anything about him being "all right."

"Do my credits cover this?" Otto asked.

"You have more than enough."

"I do? How do you know?"

Carriage Boy smiled. "I simply do. Now, where to, sir?"

"Not sure. Where are we now?"

"Here, sir."

"Right. Okay. Where's here?"

The driver raised waggish eyebrows and Otto raised a stopping palm. "This is about to turn into a frustrating metaphysical discussion about place, isn't it? Well, then, let me ask you this, if I'm on the other side of the City and wanted to get here, how would I tell you?"

"You'd just tell me, sir."

"What would I tell you?"

"That you wanted to come here."

Otto resisted a sudden urge to strangle the driver and then wondered what would happen if he did. Probably fry in Heaven's version of the electric chair and then wake up in Hell. He flashed back to Latchemondy's little demonstration and shuddered. No thanks.

Besides, look at the guy, patient and cheerful. Let him live.

"All right, I'll play." He paused. So, how to do this? A light bulb went off in his head. "I want to go where it all started."

"Very good, sir." The man cracked his whip at the horse, which strained joyously against the harness. They bounded off, doing an impressive U-turn back into traffic.

Otto absorbed the scenery. Lots of brightly lit shops here: an art house, a jewelry store, a wine cellar, a theater ... man, each one of those places cried out for a visit. Which one was Ferdinand's? He almost yelled, "Stop!" but he had to test this out.

"So, tell me," Otto asked Carriage Boy's back, "Where are we going?"

"Where you said, sir."

"But what does that mean?"

"As you asked, sir."

Here we go. "No, what does that mean to you?"

"It isn't important what it means to me, sir, it's important what it means to you."

Drat. Triggered a logic bomb. Unless you want to get stuck in this maze, Otto old boy, change tack. "Let me guess," he said, "A chimney sweep, a porter?"

"Excuse me, sir?"

"You. Back on Earth."

Carriage Boy turned, looking a bit surprised and not losing any control of the horse. "Oh, no, sir. I was an engineer in Glasgow." (Said it "Glassgie.") "Worked for West of Scotland Water Authority. Came here in ought three."

"Nineteen o-three?"

"Two thousand and three."

"So we're sort of contemporaries. I just got here, myself." Which Carriage Boy already knows, idiot.

"And how are you finding it, sir?" Good customer service, not letting the passenger know he was an idiot.

"Confusing."

Carriage Boy let out a big laugh. "It can be that, sir, it can be that. But, it all clears up."

"When?"

Carriage Boy shrugged. "I'm not sure. It depends on your definition of 'all.'"

The Metaphysics Alarm went off in Otto's head, but he decided to press it. "So, I take it you haven't got it 'all' cleared up, either."

"Oh, no, sir, not in a long course. I have some very detailed questions regarding evolutionary theory versus the Bible that I am having one devil of a time with." Carriage Boy smirked a little self-consciously at his unintended pun.

Otto's interest piqued. "Really? What have you discovered so far?"

"Well, in a nutshell, that there's very little separation of the two, if you examine the original Biblical languages. There's enough of a time gap between the first two or three verses of Genesis to allow for several millions of years of development."

"Huh?"

"Yes. The verb tenses between 'null and void' and the Spirit moving over the face of the waters strongly indicate an indistinct period of time, an archeological age, possibly. It also strongly indicates the Earth was packed in ice."

"Sorry to repeat myself, but 'huh'?"

Carriage Boy chuckled. "Yes, well, it is a bit mind-blowing. We all grew up thinking the Lord created the Earth in seven days, but it's more likely He was restoring it."

"Restoring? So, what, the Earth existed before Genesis?"

"That's how I'm reading it."

"*Hmh.*" Intriguing. "Where are you reading that?"

"The library."

Mental note, get to a library soon. "Is that then, 'all' for you?"

"Heavens, no." Carriage Boy deftly dodged a very nice Mercedes tricked out like an LA pimp's with a scrawny, beaming white kid driving it. "It is one of my many things, all just as involved and time-consuming."

"Time," Otto snorted, "There's a concept."

Carriage cocked his head. "Yes, it is, one I haven't had the time to look into, excuse the self-reference. Are you planning on doing so?"

"No. Yes. Maybe. Who knows?" Otto sat back.

Carriage Boy, a slight look of pity on his face, stuck out his hand, whip and all. "Name's Ian."

Otto took it, avoiding the whip. "Otto."

"So where do you hail from, Otto?"

"DC."

"Truly? And what did you do there?"

"I was a government analyst."

"Ah. Which governments did you analyze?"

Otto wasn't sure how to respond but then saw the twinkle in Ian's eye. "Your other job is comedian, I see. I analyzed trends. Actually, counter-trends."

"Pardon?"

"Things that don't go according to plan."

Ian attended the traffic. "That should serve you well here."

"You think?" He watched more of the shops go by, making mental notes to visit each one. "So, Ian, how'd you get this job?"

Ian waved at a passing carriage driver, who cheerfully saluted. "I can't say for sure, sir. Sometime after I got here, I started driving the carriage."

"How'd that happen?"

"I don't really know."

"I mean, did you get up one morning and this seemed like a good idea?"

"Yes, actually."

"You're kidding."

"No, truly I'm not. It came to me after a particularly satisfying sleep session. I went outside and there stood the carriage. And George. I've driven ever since."

"And you're not bored with it?"

"I like George far too much to be bored," and the horse, on cue, tossed its head and let out a pleased whinny.

"But, driving a carriage ..."

Ian looked down at him. "Somewhat demeaning, especially after being an engineer?"

"I didn't mean it that way."

"No, no, don't apologize," Ian brushed that away. "If I were home, that'd be the same reaction. But I can safely, easily, say I am far more satisfied tooling about town in this carriage than I ever was tweaking chlorine levels and adjusting flow rates."

"And why is that?"

Shrug. "Hard to say. When I saw George, it felt like the right thing, the perfect thing, what I always should have done even back in Scotland. I, apparently, have this secret love of horses."

Like Ferdinand's penchant for textures and tastes. The essence of

Heaven was finding your essence, the hidden one, that is. So there was a very good chance Otto would end up crocheting straw into fine gold and loving every minute of it. Discover what charms you and then spend eternity doing it. Family, friends, and God becomes secondary. The old concerns dissolve into a pleasant lassitude.

Which is diametrically opposed to the long-proclaimed Divine purpose of reconciliation and joy, rendering all this a bit less charming. Otto frowned, a stir of unease making him fidget.

"Here we are," Ian said.

Otto looked. Yes, by God, this was where he had awakened face down on the cobblestones. Okay. Good place to get started. Otto stepped off the carriage then turned back to Ian. "Can you tell me where this is?"

"Where you asked to go."

"Uh, I meant the add ... oh, never mind." Otto waved at the street. "How do I get back?"

"Would you like me to wait, sir?"

"No, no. I have no idea how long I'm going to be."

"Very well then, sir. When you are ready, step to the curb and a cab will collect you. Who knows?" Ian smiled, "It may very well be me. Good evening, Otto." Ian cracked the whip and George whinnied and they drove off.

"See ya, Ian." He paused. "You, too, George." Otto swore the horse looked back at him and grinned, but it may have been a trick of the light.

Otto jammed his hands in his pockets. Okay, now what? Stand here at the intersection and watch the parade for a while, try to guess what the more exotic cars are? The traffic hadn't let up since he first saw it, might even be a little stronger. That indicated a rather intensive nightlife, probably quite diverting, lots of fun and downright weird, like skeet shooting at stars or bouncing your head off the moons. What to do, what to do.

Get a cheese Danish? Yeah, why not? From that place Frank took him. He looked up the street but wasn't sure of which direction. He'd been reeling a bit when they went there and hadn't paid attention. He didn't even know the name of the place.

Do you think that matters?

Otto mentally flipped a coin and turned to his right and strolled. In some mysterious manner, he'd find himself at the pastry shop. And there'd be a hot cheese Danish waiting for him. He grinned. The City had some definite advantages.

About halfway up the block, Otto heard undertones of music coming from somewhere across the street. *Hmm*, familiar. He strained to catch the tune but passing cars and carriages blew too many holes in it. He narrowed the source to an obscure doorway wedged between a shop filled with glass sculptures and a restaurant modestly advertising the best pre-Colombian cuisine. No signs, but light and movement flashed out from underneath.

Otto crossed, stopping to admire a futuristic gull-winged car that amiably jousted with him until he gave it a thumbs-up and continued. Nice ride, man. He stood in front of the door and cocked his head. Yes, definitely music, with singing.

"...and it's no, nay, never, (clap clap clap clap)
No nay never no moooore, will I plaaaaay the wild rover
No nay neveeeer no more."

Man! No wonder it sounded familiar! Sherry and he had enthusiastically rounded it alongside a dozen or so local musicians in a small pub outside Londonderry. What a wild, fun, crazy night that'd been. Drank way too much, sang way too loud and off-key, and got appreciative calls from the musicians when Sherry had, finally, dragged him off to bed. Good times.

Well, what are you waiting for?

He pushed through and ... wow.

Chapter VII

In Which Otto Meets Another
Who Is Humorous and Curious

A monstrous oil-burning iron chandelier hung from the ceiling, supplemented by torches and candles on every wall. A stone fireplace, even more impressive than Ferdinand's, stretched completely across the far side. Long wooden tables lay parallel to each other with crude wooden benches slammed up to them, wall-to-wall bearskin rugs supporting the whole mess, shields and axes and spears, oh my, covering dark Scandinavian paneling.

A Viking mead hall.

Packed. And roaring. People two and three deep at the tables swayed and bellowed and flourished gigantic steins, slopping beer all over each other and the platoon of male and female attendants, dressed in kilts and leathers, hauling huge platters of even more steins back and forth among them. Musicians wielding guitars and bodhrans and pipes and fiddles on a raised platform off the fireplace thrashed the next round of the chorus, heartily supported by practically everyone in the room. It was a weird mix of Irish songs, Oktoberfest, and Norse mythology, plied by an even weirder mix of ethnicities, ranging from Chinese through North African.

Too cool.

A hand rose from behind a low-slung mile-long bar at the right of the door and waved him over. Otto wormed his way through, enduring a gauntlet of spilled beer and hands slapping him good-naturedly on the back. He struggled to the edge of the bar, fending off a barrage of even more insistent backslaps and peered over it.

Hamana, hamana.

A short woman, a gorgeous woman, gorgeously short with everything in proportion, stood fast behind the bar and grinned up at him. Blonde, as expected given the milieu, Swedish blonde, with iceberg blue eyes and small, even teeth. Cute, very cute, way too cute, and the merriment in her shone through. Otto's heart skipped a beat. Skipped several more beats. My goodness gracious. The last time Otto's heart had so skipped was that moment way back in 1968 when he'd strolled into a Gino's on Route 38 in Cherry Hill and spotted Sherry across the room. Love at first sight. Then. And now. In Heaven. Who'da thunk it?

"Welcome to Grendel's!" the gorgeously short blonde blue-eyed Viking princess yelled over the music, "Your first time, right?"

Quick, think of something clever and witty to say ... "Right."

Good job, Romeo.

"Then the first one's on me." She studied him as Otto studied her right back. "Dark, something full-bodied?"

"Yes, I am."

"Ho, Ho, a funny one, you." She fixed him with a half-teasing look.

Good job, Romeo.

"Yeah, sorry, born smart-aleck. A dark sounds good."

She ducked out of sight for a moment, emerging with a barrel-sized stein frothing with amber foam. "Tell me what you think."

Well, I think you are the most beautiful woman I have seen in this weird maybe-the-Afterlife City filled with beautiful women but that's not what you're referring to, is it, gorgeous Viking princess? Otto balanced the stein and sipped. Peaty, washing over his tongue and leaving a lot of itself behind. "Whoa!" he said, drawing back a little. "That's definitely full-bodied."

"You like it?"

Among other things, gorgeous Viking princess. "Absolutely," he said and drank, the beer falling like cool, smooth sludge down his throat. Exquisite. Just like the gorgeous Viking princess.

She beamed. "I just laid that ale. Had a feeling someone was going to show up who appreciated the craft. No one else here," her hand swept the bar, "would want it."

"I pity them." He smacked his lips.

"Oh, don't. They're very happy with my browns and some of the pilsners have a honey undertone that's quite catching."

"Maybe so, but you're not a real hophead until you love a bock."

She laughed. "Well, then, you will have to convert them." She paused, the sun lighting her eyes. "My name's Claudia."

"Otto," and he reflexively held out his hand.

She reacted with some surprise, then took it. "You're a Briton, are you?" she asked.

"Well, no. American. Why?"

"American, American ..." puzzled for a moment, then her brow cleared. "Oh, yes! The New World!"

"New?" He cocked his head. "Exactly how long have you been here?"

Her face dimpled pleasingly when she smiled. "Well, that is a question, isn't it? Let's see ..." She tapped the bottom of her chin. "What's the last year you remember?"

Kind of an odd question, but let's play along. "Well, it was twenty-nineteen when I left. What it is now, I can't say."

"You are a recent arrivee, then?"

Arrivee? Latchemondy's word, un-Frenchified. Still too euphemistic but save the snark. "I ... think so. I mean, it only feels like a couple of weeks."

"It feels the same to me."

"So how do you know I'm recently arrived, then?"

Her smile was slight, tinged with sadness. "Because you still remember the year."

That was a bit off-putting and Otto regarded her with some concern. "You don't remember your ... arrival year?"

Slow shake of the head. "I don't remember it so much as know it, like a date in history."

Otto considered. "That makes sense."

The sad-tinged smile remained. "As you will discover. So tell me, this twenty-nineteen is that the Christian era?"

"Well, yeah." Odd way to put it, but keep playing. "I suppose. We call it AD. Although now, the atheists call it CE."

"What does that stand for?"

"Common Era."

A dismissive flip of the head. "And the AD?"

"Anno domini."

"'The year of our Lord.' Ah, yes!" She clapped her hands. Otto found that delightful. "I've heard that used. Many of the guests," a nod at the mob, "measure their years that way. I must confess, though, I have a hard time converting it." She arched coquettish eyebrows. "I'll tell you, Otto the American, what my years were but you will have to figure out how long it's been." She paused. "When I died, Diocletian was Caesar."

"Diocle—" Floored, he was. "Caesar? You lived during the Roman Empire?"

"Yes. And died then, too, thanks to that very same Diocletian."

"Wow!" Otto was almost speechless. Almost. "That's, well, that's just ... something! So let me see, subtract a thousand, carry the one ..." Otto made exaggerated counting motions with his fingers, "... that means you've been here for two thousand years."

"Two thousand?" Thoughtful look. "Has it truly been that long?"

Otto waggled a hand. "That's ballpark. I'm not sure when Diocletian was running things, but figure around there."

"So you know what Hastati are."

"Excuse me?"

"I heard you say '*Hastati hurling pilum.*' You know close to or generally at the target."

Otto goggled at her then tapped his head. "Ah, I get it. 'Ballpark.' So the universal translator DOES convey expressions. Back and forth, apparently, but it still falls short. I have no idea what Hastati are."

"And I have no idea what 'ballpark' is."

Otto grinned. "You have, indeed, missed much. So how do you know about America?"

She pointed at a grizzly bear of a man far down the room belting out the next song – "Alive, Alive O!" – while enthusiastically pounding his stein on the table. "That one there, Ralph Hamor, has told me many tales of Jamestown."

Otto added another entry to his long list of mental notes: have a conversation with that guy. One of Sherry's distant ancestors came from Jamestown. Wouldn't it be a hoot if Ralph knew him? "So, why did you ask me if I was a Briton?"

"Because you offered your hand. That is a Britannic custom."

"So it is. And we Americans were mostly British, so it follows. But I thought the Romans did the same thing, grasped forearms, at least."

"They did. But not women. And usually only soldiers. It would have been somewhat forward for you to have done that to me."

"Oh. Sorry." Otto ducked his head in apology. "I didn't know."

She waved that away. "Quite all right. If there is one thing I have learned in two thousand years, it's not to worry about differing customs."

"Good, I don't want to offend." At least, not anyone else. Right, Ferd?

The sad smile turned genuine, warm, and then she curtsied and there was something so anachronistic and wonderfully pleasant about the gesture that Otto thrilled and felt his heart skip. Again.

Definitely love.

She turned and dealt with some of the kilted platoon laughing and joking and backslapping their way to giant casks lining the wall behind Claudia, where they refilled the steins and plunged back into the crowd. Otto cleared his throat, afraid he'd lose her to business. She looked at him, one eyebrow raised. "Are you ready for another, Otto the American?"

"Just Otto, please. And no, I'm still enjoying this one. But, I gotta say, it looks like you're well steeped in all things Britannic."

Her smile went lopsided, a personable look, and Otto was lost. Again. "And why, sir, do you say that?"

Otto took in the bar with a flourish of the stein. "This. The name, Grendel's. The music. The kilts. Although the décor looks early Norse."

"How observant. Yes, I am rather fascinated by the Isles, which were part of the Empire, as I am sure you know. So barbaric. Grendel's is part tribute, but you are a little off about the Norse part."

"How so?"

"This is actually patterned after an Irish king's hall built in Dublin after the Norse settlement. So yes, keen-eyed American that you are, it is Norse, but Celtic Norse."

"Celtic Norse. There's a concept. It works, though." He raised his drink. "You've done an excellent job with it."

She smiled and curtsied again and made to move off but Otto didn't want her to leave. "So," he shot from the hip, "how did you find out about Britain's history?"

She pursed her lips. "Here and there. Conversations. Library. The usual."

"Let me guess. The first conversations sparked something in you, a hidden interest you were unaware of, which has now flowered into a full-blown passion. Right?"

She inclined her head. "So, you have been here long enough to know that."

"At least to have seen it, although I'm not feeling any particular urge myself. Yet. So, tell me," and he set the stein down. "Do you think it odd that a citizen of the Roman Empire would develop a love for all things Celtic?"

Her eyes frosted and Otto had a sudden terror that he had, unknowingly, violated another protocol. Idiot! Can't you keep your mouth shut?

"Well, not really, considering that I am Tectosage," she said after a moment, as Otto realized, with relief, that the eye-frosting was introspection, not hostility, "and that I had no great love for the Empire."

"What's Tectosage?"

"Why, Otto, do you not know your recent history?" She dimpled again. "The Tectosage are Celts who invaded the Galatian plain."

"'Recent history'? You're the funny one. But why dislike the Empire?" Otto asked as he raised the stein for another quaff.

"Because the good Emperor Diocletian drowned my sisters and me."

"Good God!" Otto spluttered through his beer, "That's terrible! Why did he do that?"

"Because we were Christians."

Some of Otto's college history came back to him. "Of course. Diocletian. The persecutions of the Church." He gazed at her, fascinated. "What happened?"

She leaned her elbows onto the bar. "We were Galatians of Ancyra. My father was a wealthy metals dealer, specializing in iron for weapons and armour. We were a Christian family, tracing our faith back to Paul's time, and my father was an intimate of Clement, the Bishop. When Galerius seized Clement and took him to Rome, my father became deacon and helped administer the charities until Galerius returned and threw us all in prison, my parents, my six sisters and me. We were raped repeatedly, scourged, burned, broken, but we refused to renounce Christ, so they weighted us all with chains and threw us into a lake." She tilted her head.

Otto, open-mouthed. "I don't even know what to say."

She smiled a bit. "There is nothing really to say. I have been here ever since. It was a good trade."

"Y-e-e-e-s, I can see that. I can also see why Britain would hold more interest ..." His voice trailed off. "Who's this Galerius?"

She shrugged. "One of Diocletian's generals. He hated Christians. He convinced Diocletian to purge us. Someone," vague wave of the hand, "told me he later became emperor." She shook her head, exasperated. "Why God allowed that, I do not know."

Sharp intake of breath. She names God. Has she seen Him? Because, if there was anyone the Big Kahuna should have granted an audience, it was to one of His martyrs. This woman, for instance. This beauty. Who may know where He is. "Have you ... asked Him?"

"In what sense?"

Bit of a puzzling response and Otto flailed a bit. "Well, I mean, in person."

She regarded him, the light glowing in her eyes and the small smile still there. "You seek God, don't you?" she asked softly.

Clear and simply put. "Well, yes, yes I do."

She leaned in closer and Otto smelled the perfume of her, the stirring musk of a young, beautiful woman. "Then you must seek the ship."

He was so intoxicated with her, he almost did not ask, "What ship?"

"The rocket ship. The one they're building in the desert. To look for God."

Chapter VIII

Love. And Trains.

Otto stepped out of Grendel's and into full daylight – my, how time flies – wrapped in a warmth generated by a night's worth of bocks and pilsners and the stir of Celtic music. And Claudia. And what she'd told him.

He tilted his head back and deliberately stared into the Mesmer sky. In moments, he was lost, jaw slack and eyes vacant. More than a few passersby joined him. Time ceased ... only a convention here, anyway ... and, after a few years or a few moments, Otto shook out of it. "I am going to find You," he told God, hiding up there somewhere, and stepped to the curb.

"Ride, sir?"

Ian.

"Don't you ever go home?" Otto asked as he scrambled up.

"Oh, yes, sir," Ian laughed as he cracked the whip over George who whinnied with pleasure and stepped into traffic. "In fact, I have just come from there. You're my first customer."

"You know, Ian, if this were any other place, I'd call that odd."

Ian smiled. "In any other place, it is," and attended to the traffic.

They bounced along quite pleasantly for a while and Otto contemplated the streets and shops, even falling into the sky from time to time, until it occurred to him that he had not called out a destination. "Ian, where are you taking me?"

"Home, sir."

"I'm not going home, Ian."

"Oh. Sorry, sir. I assumed that, after a night at Grendel's, you'd seek a quieter venue."

"You know Grendel's?"

"Oh, yes, sir, it's very popular."

"That it is. Do you know Claudia, then?"

"I've had the pleasure. She makes some of the more extraordinary ales in the City."

"True that. Have you talked with her?"

"On occasion. She has an astounding command of British history. I once engaged her on the Scottish kings, only to be schooled."

Otto chuckled. "I'll bet. Have you noticed her blue eyes?"

Ian turned. "Why, Otto, one would think you're in love."

"I think you're right." He paused. "How does love work here, Ian?"

"Very much like it works everywhere, sir."

"*Hmm.*" Otto considered. "Good to know. But, I'm guessing, after two thousand years, she's managed to find herself a boyfriend." Otto hoped he wasn't too obvious.

Hope dispelled as Ian smirked. "No doubt, sir, a woman that attractive has a boyfriend or two, but it isn't the way you think."

"So, how is it?"

"Well," Ian flicked the whip playfully at George, who flipped his mane. "You know, of course, the object of romance on Earth was family, children, stability, right?"

"Maybe in theory. Hardly in practice."

"Yes, reality does bung things up, doesn't it? But, overall, that was the purpose, any prurience subsumed to the object. Here, not so. Romance, the attraction between men and women, is for the attraction alone."

"That sounds hippie, Ian."

"To be sure, but I am betting you still think of it in the physical sense."

"Physical. You mean, like sex?"

"Indeed, sir."

Otto frowned. "Does that mean there's no sex here? Because, I gotta tell ya, Ian, I have stirrings."

"As do we all." Deeper smirk. "Tell me, sir, do you remember the first time you saw your wife?"

"You betcha. And funny, the moment I saw Claudia, I relived that moment."

"Oh, so very romantic, sir, but please tell me what jumped to mind during that first glance of your wife?"

"Well, Ian, obviously, being seventeen, I wanted to jump her bones."

"Ha!" Ian's laugh caused George to whinny. "I have not heard that phrase in years! No doubt you have those same stirrings even now. But what is your *thought* of Claudia?"

"Well, Ian, obviously, being a lecherous seventy-year-old in a seventeen-year-old body – at least, that's how it feels – I want—" He stopped.

"Sir?"

Otto considered. He had stirrings of the jump-bones variety, true, but they were mere background to a better stimulus, that of Claudia herself, with all the attendant interest and flush of new love.

"I'll be damned," he said in wonder, "Or not."

Ian beamed. "See? It's not lust. It's from the heart."

"You're right, old bean. And I'm a bit astonished. I mean, I want to bed her, but it's not the primary drive. I want to sit in her presence and smell her perfume and listen to her laugh and look deep in her eyes and buy her presents and maybe shag every once in a while and that's a mere part of the whole package, a smaller part, at that."

"And that, if I may be so bold, is real love." He pulled George over and waited patiently for some car traffic to pass.

Otto mused for a bit. "Say, Ian."

"Sir?"

"You got a girlfriend?"

"Several."

"You dog!" Otto chortled and slapped him on the back. "How do you manage that?"

"Carefully, sir."

Otto and George fell into a gut laugh while Ian grinned and

attended to the traffic. Otto wiped his eyes. "Too much. But, hey, doesn't your wife object?"

"My wife?" Ian's brows furrowed. "I believe she's still living."

"Oh. Right. Sorry." He sat back as a thought struck. "So how will you know when she's here?"

"I guess after an appropriate amount of time, I'll presume she is. But, to answer your question, I won't actually know."

"Why not?"

"Because."

Casually tossed-off answer and Otto stirred uneasily, remembering Ferdinand's lack of family contact. "Why is that? I mean wouldn't you want to see her?"

Ian shook his head. "No," he said, "not really. And that's not out of callousness. On Earth, your family is limited to blood. Here," he swept a hand over the City, "everyone is your family."

"In the sense that we're all in the same boat, you mean."

"No, it's not circumstance. Think of it as a higher connection, more than blood."

"What's more than blood?"

"Favor," Ian said, simply.

Favor. Otto considered. By the grace of God placed in this fabulous City, magically provided with every need and then some; interesting people like Frank Vaughn and Ferdinand and Claudia, beautiful Claudia, to engage and really, why limit yourself to relatives, most of whom you don't even like?

But that isn't the way it's supposed to be. Not at all.

"C'mon, Ian," Otto said, "You know that's not right. I mean, don't you miss them? Have you looked for anybody, say like your father?"

Ian shrugged. "Not really. My father wasn't such a good 'un I'd want to reacquaint. But, even then, I have no real urge. Tell me, how many times have you thought of your wife since you arrived?"

"Uh." Otto reviewed. Three times? Four? Six?

Not very much.

Ian clucked at George who whinnied them back into traffic and Otto was not very happy with himself. He loved Sherry. They'd had bad moments but, overall, they worked. He enjoyed her company, always looked forward to meeting up at the end of the day for the mutual passing of stories, even if they were nothing more than dreaded office tales. She made him laugh. After all the years, she remained his favorite person.

But he'd barely considered her since waking up face down on a City street. Worse, barely considered his son. And now he was head-over with Claudia, practically a stranger, which somehow wasn't right. Which he repeated to Ian.

"Right?" Ian dodged a Corvette. "Not sure that applies. On Earth, yes, paternity and property being so important."

"But, it's a betrayal."

"Certainly, if Earth considerations were in play but, they're not. There's a higher concept."

"What?"

"As I said, love."

Confusing and circular. "I don't get it."

"Love, itself, that attraction we've been talking about. Here, it's freed from other considerations which means there's no jealousy because love, real love, is not exclusive."

Otto let out a long, disbelieving sigh. "There's also something not right about *that*, Ian."

"What? Isn't that the ideal?"

"No, I don't think so, because love IS exclusive. One woman moves your heart. Everything else is hound-doggery."

"So God loves only one believer?"

"Huh?" That certainly came out of left field. "What are you talking about?"

"You're familiar with the Bride of Christ?"

Even more out of left field. "I vaguely recall a couple of obscure Sunday school references, yeah."

Ian rolled a concluding hand. "There you go."

"There does what go?"

"A bride made of millions. Not just one. Billions of people sharing the same love."

Otto sat back. No, it didn't mean that ... or did it? Is that another busted metaphor, then, like golden streets and many mansions? He eyed Ian suspiciously. "So, you're telling me that if I was smooching with Claudia on a park bench and Sherry walked by, she wouldn't cut my throat?"

"Well, first of all, you're unlikely to conduct such brazen public displays because that's lust, not love. And, no, she wouldn't. She'd probably sit right next to you, give you a kiss just as passionate, and ask Claudia where she got her dress."

Otto laughed derisively. "Ya know, Ian, I doubt that. I really do. Sounds way too hippie-ish."

Ian smiled. "Doesn't it? Nonetheless ..." and Ian rolled an "oh well" hand.

"So I've got celestial permission to carry on an affair with Claudia, even though I'm a married man?"

"The phrase was, 'till death do us part.'"

Otto snorted. "Yeah, but it's looking like death is a business trip and the old lady will be showing up. And I certainly don't want her barging into the hotel room and finding me wrapped around another woman."

Ian snickered. "You have my assurance it's not that way. There won't be any lamp throwing or calling of lawyers."

"Are there lawyers here?"

"Two or three."

"What do they do?"

"Someone has to sweep up."

Otto chuckled appreciatively. "So, Ian, I guess I should tell you where I'm going."

"Yes, sir, you should, although I've been so enjoying the conversation that I was merely driving about aimlessly to prolong it." He cocked a jovial eye. "I shall ask you formally, then, what is your destination?"

"Out."

"Out?"

"Yep."

"You mean Out Out?"

"Yeah. That's what I was told. So, how far is that, and how long will it take?"

"I ... don't know."

Unexpected answer, and he watched with growing concern as a somewhat perplexed Ian consulted an equally perplexed George. "I thought you knew where everything is."

"I do, but not Out. I've never taken anyone there. No one has ever asked to go."

"Never?"

"Never."

Hmm. Not the impression that Mr. Latchemondy and now Claudia had given him. Lots of people had gone Out. Including those Otto now sought. "Okay, so do what you do if you get a call for a place you haven't been to yet?"

"I've been everyplace."

"Wait." Otto held up a hand. "How's that possible? I thought the City was huge, like planet-sized huge."

"It is."

"So ..." and Otto spun his fingers to get Ian to continue.

"There's an innate sense of everything's location."

"*Uhm*, what?"

Ian made an impatient gesture. "If you do this" – a pass of the hand over the carriage – "or that" – pass of the hand at the surrounding cars – "or even take a long stroll, then you know where you are going."

"Okay. So you should know how to get to Out, then."

"Out is not where everything is."

"At the risk of being repetitive, uhm, what?"

A pitying look from Ian. "Out is called Out because it is out. Completely out. Do you recall what medieval cartographers scrawled across unknown territories?"

"Terra incognita."

Ian raised "there you go" palms.

Otto leaned slowly toward him. "That doesn't make any sense. The place exists. People go there."

"Yes," Ian agreed, "A small percentage do. The wanderers, the unsettled, the ... dissatisfied."

Otto was taken aback. "Is that what I am, then? Dissatisfied?" He stilled. Was he?

Well, yes.

"I do not mean to insult," Ian said hastily, in an apologetic voice, "but, why go there, when you have here?" And he stretched out both arms to encompass the boulevard and the jeweled buildings and the crystal and music and the Mesmer sky and Otto had to admit, Ian made an excellent point.

As did Otto. "Because, Ian, my innate sense tells me that's where I need to go."

Ian and George regarded Otto sorrowfully. "All right, sir, you are the customer," Ian deferred and he and George exchanged sorrowful looks and then he pulled a sheet from his jacket and studied it. "It depends," he said, after a moment, "on which Out you mean."

"Huh?"

"Out surrounds the City, so the part of Out you intend to visit will determine our course."

"Oh." *Hmm.* "Problem is, Ian, I only know it's Out. Didn't occur to me, deep in my cups, to ask *where* in Out. And that's another thing, Ian, eight beers and I'm not drunk. Just happy. And very relaxed."

"Yes," Ian smiled. "You get the benefits of alcohol here, not the detriments. Unless you *want* to be drunk, and then you'll be amazed how little alcohol that takes. Although, no one here gets drunk because sobriety is so interesting. As to your exact destination, perhaps if you tell me what you are seeking?"

"A ship."

"What kind? Cruise, sailing?"

"A rocket ship."

Ian gaped at him. "A rocket? Here? What for?"

"To look for God, Ian."

Ian's mouth dropped open, which tickled Otto to no end. So, the new guy could surprise the old guy, huh?

Otto kept a straight face as Ian shook himself and gave Otto an odd look before scrutinizing his sheet again, frowning, then looked surprised. "Well, crivvens, there is such a ship." Ian tapped his chin. "Yes ... yes, I'd heard rumors of this. A fool's errand, so no one took it seriously. Yet," he slapped the paper, "there it is." He stared hard at Otto. "Are you sure you want to go?"

"Dunno." Otto, immediately irritated. "Convince me it's the fool's errand you just said and I might change my mind."

Ian made a pleading face. "It's simply ... unnecessary!"

For a moment, Otto wavered. Yes, given all this, a wondrous City of eternal delights filled with delightful people, what he sought was obviously right in front of him.

Then he remembered Claudia's eyes and the blue fire deep within them And the answering fire deep in his soul. A different fire. "Maybe for you, Ian. Not for me."

Everything stopped. Time, traffic, thought ... and Otto felt a distinct shift. A ship waited in a far desert. And beyond that ...

"... let's see ... ah!" Ian consulted the sheet and traffic resumed as did time and Otto slipped off one track and slid down another long, very dark, and somewhat frightening one. Ian peered at Otto over the edge of the sheet, as if he noted a change of some kind, turned and clucked, and pulled George toward a side way. George broke into a brisk trot, downright grinning with the joy of it.

Enjoying it as much as George, Otto said, "So, what, at this pace we'll be there in about a day?"

"Oh, no, sir, it's much too far to reach by carriage. I'm taking you to the train."

Hello. "Train?"

"Indeed." Ian flipped the reins to urge George on. "The train that circles the world."

Chapter IX

Out Being More Out Than Otto Considered

Circles the world, indeed.

Otto glared at the scenery whipping by and swore they'd passed this way a hundred times already. It had been two, counted 'em, two sunrises since Ian had shuffled him off the carriage and into this very slick bullet train. The conductor, a sumo-sized jovial Hawaiian who converted to Christianity in the 1860s and once sailed on a clipper ship, blabbed Otto to the best set of windows in the observation car and periodically returned for more blab. Otto hadn't seen him today; must have gotten off at one of the million or so stops they'd made. And if it turned out they were doing nothing but a giant loop around the City, Otto'd follow him.

Do the math. Bullet train 160 mph, but figure optimal conditions here, so more like 200. Forty-eight hours times that, minus a fudge-factor for the stops every flippin' twenty minutes ... 9,000 miles so far, give or take a hundred. And the scenery had not changed. Not one bit. Buildings and shops and stations, ad infinitum, ad nauseam.

Either a giant loop or this place was huge. Jupiter huge.

Think about it. All this way and still no Out, which had to surround the City otherwise, why call it Out? If it were some little park or forest, it wouldn't be called Out, it'd be, well, City Park or City Forest or City Green Space, something. But it was "Out," which contrasted with "In," like "in the City," so, for the sake of geographical argument, halve the City into, say, an Upper and a Lower, then that meant Out was twice as big as both halves ... no, that's not right; have to take surround into account the compass points, which means *four* times as big but, c'mon, be reasonable. Make it simpler and use quadrants: Right, Left, Up, Down. Multiply by miles traveled so far (give or take a hundred) and that meant Out was at least 27,000 miles wide, with the City (9,000 miles of it, that is) smack in the middle. But wait, have to cube that, right? To get area?

Boggles the mind.

What was the circumference of the Earth, 15,000 miles? No, no way. Had to be bigger than that – 30,000? Maybe that was too big. Otto racked his brains to recall fifth grade science but failed to connect. So, for the sake of argument, split the difference and call it twenty-two five. Out, by itself, was already bigger than Earth. Which meant this was a very big planet, indeed.

Made sense. Storing practically every person who died since Abraham required major real estate. All those condos needed anchoring to something, and all those residents needed a local Grendel's and theaters and libraries and ... Out. If you're the Almighty, conjuring up an accommodating planet wasn't that hard. Especially one that defied physics.

Because a very big planet should exert a very big gravitational pull. *That* much of his fifth-grade science he recalled, but he didn't feel heavier and things weren't sluggish or massive to compensate. So what's the deal here? Otto snorted. Asking that of a place with Mesmer skies and baffling stars? You can't even remember the circumference of the Earth, bub.

Which fueled his impatience to reach the ship. Claudia said very smart people attended it – "masters," she called them – which Otto interpreted as Class A scientists. They had to have worked out some theories about this place by now. Had to.

But jeez, how much longer? Otto blew an exasperated breath. Ten more minutes, ten more centuries. Maybe this was a test of faith and endurance, along the lines of forty years in the Wilderness. In this case, forty years to *reach* the Wilderness. Otto chuckled. Get there when we get there. If it's actually there.

In the meantime, let us seek further diversion. Otto pushed

away the tea and croissants some tuxedo-clad and always-laughing waiter, an Australian transportee, guv'ner, brought him every half-hour or so, stood, stretched, and commenced his one-millionth exploration of the other cars. He'd made earlier contact with a pair of Nestorians who were off to see a mutual friend of theirs some ten stops away. All three of them had lived in a Dark Ages Chinese city that no longer existed. While their description of China's evangelization in the 600s was fascinating, Otto was more intrigued by how they'd found each other in the City.

"Oh, yes!" Cyril the Greek had said, "Well, funny that. I was having a chocolate in some shop when Theodore walked in," here, Theodore nodded enthusiastically, "and I was completely blown out of my socks. Completely. It'd been a thousand years or so."

"Yeah!" Theodore laughed. "My last view of Cy was a mob near Xi'an chasing him down as I was beheaded. So, imagine, you walk into a place to get a bun and there's your fellow traveler, just sitting there, looking all refreshed and happy." They beamed at each other. Otto had been tickled, but when they got on the subject of *qnome* and *parsopa*, he was kind of glad their station showed up. He never did find out how they'd run into their other pal. But stumbling across people stumbled across on Earth seemed a feature here.

Otto doubted that was random or accidental. There was a method here, some purpose, and Otto had a pretty good idea Who was orchestrating it. But why didn't God do stuff openly, like put people who wanted to see each other (even if they didn't know they did) in contact? Otto, this is Claudia. She's a fourth-century Galatian martyr with forever eyes and a sassy attitude you'll enjoy. Now you two kids run along and I'll see about locating your parents for a big get-together.

Why so coy, God? You'd think a Guy Who waved the Universe into existence wouldn't have self-esteem issues; au contraire, He should be Large and In Charge and Overjoyed to see His children. Then again, Otto, there were a few kids in your family you hoped got lost on the way to the reunion.

Yeah, but this wasn't Earth and this wasn't family: sinful, mean-spirited, backstabbing family. This was Family and the Pater was Grace, and He should be right here, right smack dab in the middle of the City (or in the middle of Out, if He was That Big), astride a giant glowy throne that could be seen from everywhere, beckoning everyone to come on over and attending to all the children who came on over, even the ones He Wanted to Strangle: "Hey, God what about them dinosaurs?" "Oh, those? Some pets. Kinda fun actually, but bad-tempered."

But, no, not here. Or there. Or anywhere.

Which was strong indication that something else was going on, something not advertised in the various holy texts, whether Bible or Torah or Koran. Otto had a growing suspicion that the Afterlife was not the end of all things; it looked more and more like the beginning. Of what, Otto had no clue.

"Like a game, friend?" a voice called softly.

Otto zeroed in on a man sitting behind a table set against the bulkhead of the car he'd just entered. Reedy build, straight blond hair, blue eyes like lasers, and a thin, consumptive face. Shuffling a pack of cards from one hand to the other, expert and skillful, he had "Mississippi gambler" written all over him.

Otto grinned. "Sure," he said, and sat down.

Gambler eyed him and then, wordlessly, low shuffled one-handed and laid the cards for a cut. Otto tapped and Gambler scooped them cleanly.

"You've done this before," Otto said.

"A few times." Gambler's expression did not change.

"What's the game?" Otto asked.

Gambler dealt five cards each. "Draw," he said.

"Stakes?"

Gambler shrugged. "You want some chips?"

"What's the currency?"

"What do you want it to be?"

"American."

Gambler nodded and reached below the table, coming up with a thousand dollars' worth of wooden chips, white and blue and red. "Five-dollar ante, no limits," he said and pushed the chips at Otto.

"Uh, I didn't give you any money," Otto pointed out.

Gambler arched an eyebrow. "You new here?"

"Yes," Otto said and braced for the "you'll be all right."

Gambler shrugged. "Your credit's good. For now," and gave Otto a lip twitch as he stacked his chips.

Otto watched Gambler's deft movements. "Yeah, for about an

hour, I'm guessing." He held out a hand. "Name's Otto."

"Henry." Gambler shook then attended to his cards.

"Just us?" Otto asked as he picked up his own.

Henry shrugged again. "We play, usually a couple of others will step in," he paused. "What's your pleasure?"

"*Hmm*? Oh," Otto looked at his cards, a seven and nine of hearts, a three of clubs, a jack of spades, a king of hearts. "Two," he said, throwing away the non-hearts.

"You need to ante and bet first," Henry said.

"Right." Otto threw in ten. Henry matched and they discarded and drew and Otto lost that hand. He lost most of them over the next few hours.

"Yep, you've definitely done this before," Otto said as he mused over his significantly dwindled chip stack. A New York Dutchman named Augustus, from Stuyvesant's time, threw down his cards and left, grumbling. He'd been the third of some passersby who joined in, the other two being a woman from twelfth-century Malta and a soldier killed in the Battle of the Bulge. The soldier, Frank from Brooklyn, enjoyed the game but enjoyed the Maltese, named Frida, more, so left with her.

Henry peered at Otto from behind his mountain range of chips, "May I comment on your game, friend?"

"By all means," Otto waved his hand expansively.

"You don't cheat."

"Well, thank you. I don't win, either."

"That's because you don't cheat."

Otto chuckled, "Does that imply you do?"

"Of course."

"What?" Otto was surprised. "You're telling me you cheat? That you're cheating?"

Henry nodded.

Otto was speechless. "How," he finally spluttered, "how can you say that? How can you just come out and, and tell me that?"

"'Cause it's true." Laconic.

Surprise, incredulity, now anger. "You know, I'm sure that would get you shot in most games."

"It certainly would, and there were many occasions when I was shot at and shooting. But that's only if you got caught. Or accused."

"But cheating is okay, you're saying."

"Expected." Henry shuffled the deck one-handed again. "And since I know you're not cheating, I don't have to spend my energy trying to catch you. And since you haven't caught me yet, I can continue."

"How are you doing it?"

Henry gave him a small smile. "You have to catch me."

Otto frowned. "I don't think I can. I'm not that skilled. And cheating as a premise is never how I played the game. And, furthermore, it's a bit out of place here."

"You mean the City?"

Otto nodded, perturbed.

Henry canted an eyebrow. "Not if it's expected."

"So you're telling me you play with an expectation of cheating on your and everyone's part, therefore, it's not a dishonest game. Part of the game is catching the other person and accusing them, right?" Otto shook his head in disgust. "Sheesh, where in the world did you learn those rules?"

"Here and there."

"Like where?"

Henry raised a soft, but warning, hand. "No need to get edgy, friend. We learned in different places, that's all. I started out in Dallas, then on to Cheyenne, Denver, Deadwood, Dodge City. Others."

Otto blinked. "Deadwood? Dodge City? Did you know Wyatt Earp?"

"Well, yes, friend, knew him rather well. Went with him to Tombstone, in fact, he and his brothers."

"Tombstone? Wait a minute," Otto's eyes narrowed. "What's your full name?"

"John Henry Holliday."

Blown out of his chair, he was. "Holliday. Doc Holliday?" Otto blurted. "You're ... you're Doc Holliday?"

"Been called that. I was a dentist, after all."

"But ... you're Doc Holliday! I mean, you're a legend!"

Doc frowned. "Well, some dreadfuls said that, but that ain't me. Now, Wyatt, he was a legend."

Otto went back to spluttering. "But ... but ... you are! I mean, you're a giant! They've done movies about you!"

"I heard about those. The one with, what's his name, Quaid? That one seemed true to form."

"Did you see it?"

He shook his head. "No, friend, not my venue. I prefer plays."

Otto's grin almost split his jaw. "I can't believe it. I've been playing cards with Doc Holliday! Doc freakin' Holliday! Who's been cheating the whole time."

Doc's face froze. "You callin' me a cheat, friend?" Soft. Deadly.

Otto reacted. "Huh? What? You said so yourself!"

"It's one thing for me to say it. It's another if you do."

The cold in Doc's eyes chilled Otto like an avalanche and unexpected sparks of fear cascaded up and down his spine. Fear in Heaven? No way. But look at this guy, rigid and filled with murder. The last face many unlucky gamblers had seen on Earth, Otto figured. But this wasn't Earth. If it were, he'd know what to do: reach for his shootin' iron with the forlorn hope of outdrawing and outshooting the master gunfighter sitting across from him. But here?

"What are the rules, Doc?" he asked, making his voice sound a calm and deadliness he did not feel.

"Rules?"

"About this situation." Otto wanted to sweep his hand but was afraid any movement would lead to the Afterlife's equivalent of a weapons grab.

So here Otto was, in a staring contest with one of the most fabled gunmen in the West. Great. This wasn't going to end well, Otto was sure, but, what else could he do? He wasn't going to back down; he was just as tough as Doc Holliday ... well, he could pretend he was, anyway. So Otto stayed on Doc, and time, however it was measured, stopped.

After a moment or so of stopped time, Doc shrugged and said, "Ain't no rules." He picked up the cards and shuffled them. "Wanna play?"

We are, most definitely, over the rainbow, Otto thought and shrugged back. "Sure. Deal." Because, really, how often did you get to play cards with a legend?

Otto looked at his new hand while reviewing the last few minutes. Fear and anger, he'd just experienced fear and anger.

They were sins, according to the Methodists, the Baptists, and the Lutherans (during his brief flirtation with them). And, according to them, real trust in God meant no fear, even if Satan and Dracula and a thousand gibbering zombies suddenly leaped out of a closet; a test Otto was pretty sure he'd have failed. Not supposed to be angry, either, all that "turn the other cheek" stuff, another one Otto failed. Repeatedly. But on Earth, such failure was a given. Shouldn't be here. Shouldn't be a hint of sin anywhere of any kind here. And have we addressed those frequently rapacious thoughts about Claudia?

Otto played his pairs and won the hand and looked at Doc suspiciously but couldn't read him. Centuries of poker-face practice. So, back to it. Otto picked up the next hand and considered what Ian said, that his interest in Claudia was normal, expected, so how could it be sinful? Which must mean Heaven-based anger and fear were, also, not sinful.

How can that be?

"Doc, do you ever get scared here?"

"Scared? Not that I can recall."

Idiot. This is freakin' Doc Holliday. He doesn't fear; he inspires fear.

"How 'bout angry?" Better question.

Doc paused. "'Spect I do, from time to time."

"Over what?"

"Bad play. Insults. Nobody willin' to sit for a few hands. That kind of stuff."

"Doesn't that seem out of place here? Getting angry, I mean?"

Doc considered. "I don't think so. You read a lot about anger in the Bible. It was justified."

"Yeah, but that was mainly an anthropopathism to illustrate God's viewpoint. His anger wasn't sinful because it always meant something else. When *people* get angry, though, it's supposed to be wrong."

Doc looked at him flatly. "You some kind of preacher?"

Otto shook his head, "No, just reasonably well informed when it comes to the Bible. Don't ask why, I just am."

"Then you got preacher in ya." Doc examined his cards and threw one down. "Why you askin'?"

"I'm trying to figure out what's going on around here."

"Nothin'. It's the Great Beyond. That's all."

"Yeah, but," and Otto's sense of frustration returned; in itself, a perplexing thing. Heaven wasn't supposed to be frustrating. "It's not making any sense." Otto gestured at Doc. "You, for instance."

"I don't follow."

"Don't get me wrong, I'm not insulting you. Please don't shoot me or whatever passes for an equivalent here but, given your well-documented history, I'm surprised to see you here."

"Not half as surprised as I was to end up here, friend," Doc chuckled. "I figured I'd end up in the Other Place."

"Exactly!" Otto waved a hand in emphasis. "I mean, again, no insult intended, but you're not exactly Heaven's poster boy."

Doc's eyes narrowed again. "I'm not sure what that means, friend, but now I gotta question your so-called knowledge of the Bible. Since when did behavior decide your entry or exclusion from Heaven?"

Otto thought for a moment. "You know, you make a very good point."

Doc nodded. "I seen Kate a few times since I been here. She likes to ride the train, too. Going with what you just said, I should never have run into her. At least, we both shudda run into each other in a lot nastier place. But what you seem to forget is that most of the people of my time believed in Christ. It was a given."

Otto considered. "Yeah, I guess that's true."

"Believin' was a part of us, no matter how we turned out." Doc won the hand and scooped the chips. "From what I'm hearin', it's mostly you modern folk who've turned your back on God."

"That's also true."

"So if there's someone who should be mightily surprised to be here, should be you."

"Even more true. And accurate."

Doc took in a long breath. "Grace is grace. No matter what your century." He dealt another hand.

Wow. Schooled in the ways of God by a murderous, bad-tempered, whore–mongering gambler. "Thanks, Doc, I needed that." Otto chuckled at the unshared reference. "But, can I ask one more question?"

"Sure."

"Where's God?"

The Hawaiian conductor suddenly burst into the car, lurching with the train's motion and shouting, "Coming in to Out, in to Out!"

Otto stared at him in surprise.

The conductor hovered over Otto. "I believe this is your stop. So, Doc, how much did you take him for?"

Again the lip twitch. "Enough."

The conductor roared a giant laugh and slapped immense thighs. "I bet! I bet!" He turned amused eyes on Otto. "Well, come along, then, and be grateful you've arrived in the nick of time."

Otto got up, gaining his balance. "So we're really here?"

"Yep!" the conductor bobbed his head enthusiastically. "As far as the train goes, anyway."

"Huh? What does that mean?"

"If you're going farther. you'll have to find some other way."

"How?"

The conductor shrugged. "Don't know. Never got off the train to find out. But!" And here he beamed, "You'll be all right!" With a slap on the back, he drove Otto toward the end of the car.

Reeling from the good-natured pummeling, Otto looked back at Doc shuffling the cards again. "Doc, where?"

Doc Holliday, legend, icon, historical giant, raised his eyes and regarded Otto with a veiled, unreadable expression. "Wherever you want Him to be, friend."

Otto got off the train.

Chapter X

And Once Again, Doubt

God must love the Western motif. Trains, Doc Holliday, and now this.

Otto stood on the huge plank deck of a station right out of a Glenn Ford movie: low-slung brick structure, wide, open portal leading inside, long benches like church pews scattered here and there, and another portal opposite framing a dirt road and an open plain. Cheyenne, Wyoming.

Otto shook his head then turned and watched as the train picked up rather astonishing speed on the looped return track. More cars than he'd realized, forty or fifty, were attached, but it only took about three minutes to get the whole thing around. Benefits of better physics. The train appeared empty – at least, no one was at the windows. Where'd everybody go?

Certainly not here, because Otto was alone.

The train disappeared ... man, fast ... and Otto walked to the end of the deck to get a last look, promptly blown out of his socks. Wow! This view! Just ... wow! Mountains, glorious monstrous blue leviathans stretched to the sky and beyond, peak after peak crowding the horizon until they were lost in the distance. Clouds hovered over them, their shadows dancing across rock face and fissures and waterfalls, tiny details he could see clearly, even on the most distant peak.

"*Bwa*," was all he could say.

The plain, all short grass and tumbleweed, ran from the station to the mountains, the dirt road passing through some little town about a mile away and then going on quite the meander until it leisurely reached the Himalayas. Otto took in where the road diverged; one fork careened around the mountains' base and another followed the natural shelving straight up. He walked down some wooden steps and went around the front. The mountain panorama continued but there was a distinct bowing, as if the range curved back on each end and ran the other way.

Bwa, indeed.

Admiration washed over him, as did satisfaction. This was certainly postcard appropriate; the view alone worth the trip and he stood for what felt like a half-hour and then did a Bugs Bunny shake of the head, wondering if the Mesmer sky had snuck one in on him.

Stop it. Things to do, places to go, God to see. He gazed at the distant town. Now, why didn't they build that next to the station? He sighed and figured a half-hour slog. Maybe should check schedules first.

He walked up the front steps and into the station, the view now out of the back portal toward the track. It was wide open in that direction, flat and featureless. Nebraska.

There was a vending machine jammed against the inside wall to his right. Otto chuckled.

Looks like the prop man screwed up.

The machine had a coin slot without a price and didn't show any products so he punched some buttons to see what would happen. A bottle popped out from the side, a Coke, a real Coke with a sealed cap, and he pried off the cap with the machine's bottle opener and took a drink.

Ah, the pause that refreshes, or was that Pepsi?

Didn't matter, this one was cold and brisk. A bulletin board to the side of the machine had some papers thumbtacked to it and Otto scrutinized them. Train schedule, yes! It looked as if the Bullet came back every day at noon, which couldn't be right. If it took three days to get here, how was it able to leave so frequently? Must be more than one train involved, which was a bit puzzling. Not exactly a rush of people back and forth.

Other notices on the board offered various services in keeping with a frontier. Someone named Nellie Cashman boarded visitors; a Charley Utter provided cartage.

Charley Utter? Wait a minute—

Otto frowned. Utter was Hickok's friend and business partner on the TV show *Deadwood*. Otto'd been a fan of the series, watched every episode. In fact, Charley Utter had been his favorite character.

Didn't that seem the slightest bit odd?

People whom Otto found interesting on Earth kept showing up here: Old West legends, early Christians, explorers like Ferdinand. Frank Vaughn. And they did so in locales he found equally interesting – Viking mead halls, moving card games, the frontier.

Yes. Very odd.

"Can I help you?"

Otto located a ticket cage, paneled with wood halfway up to an iron grate, a cash box behind the grate with an old-fashioned adding machine next to it, and over the top of it all, a big, classical clock hanging from the ceiling. A Chinese man, dressed in the striped shirt, vest, watch chain, and hat of an 1850s conductor, stood inside.

Otto's suspicion mounted. "I don't know. Can you?"

"Well, depends on what you want," the Chinese man replied. "I can get you tickets for the next train, if that's your pleasure."

"I just got here," Otto said.

The Chinese man shrugged. "Some people like to ride the train."

"Yes, well, not me." Otto stepped closer and peered at the man, who returned his stare carelessly. "Are you for real?"

The Chinese man pinched himself on the arm, "Yep," he replied.

"I mean," Otto cocked an eye, "real, real. Like a real person standing there. Like this is a real station, and those are real mountains and a real Western town off there somewhere."

"What makes you think it's not?"

"Well, for one, everything about this place seems to be coming out of my imagination."

"The station?"

"Yeah." Otto waved an irritable hand. "But not just the station. Everything else. The City. The sky. The stars. Charley Utter."

"Oh. You know Charley?"

"No, I don't know Charley. I know *of* Charley. That's the point."

"What's the point?"

Otto breathed, regaining patience. "That all of this, including Claudia, are people right out of my own set of interests. Like my mind is making all these weird connections while under heavy sedation in a hospital bed. Ya know?"

"Claudia, Claudia ..." The Chinese man pursed his lips. "You mean, the girl who runs Grendel's?"

"Well, yeah! You know her?"

"Sure." The Chinese man picked at some lint on his sleeve. "She comes out here a lot."

"She does? Wait." Otto repeated the Bugs Bunny head shake. "We're off subject. How is it that all the things I favor are showing up?"

"Please." The Chinese man waved a dismissive hand. "Haven't you ever heard that like calls to like?"

"Well, yeah."

"Well, yeah," the Chinese man mocked him. "So, don't you gravitate to what you like?"

"Well, yeah."

"Okay. So, why isn't what you like gravitating to you?"

Hmm, God, being God, would have no trouble working out a Heaven of personal interests.

Yes, as would your comatose brain.

The Chinese man finished his grooming. "I see that you are not convinced. Well, let me ask you, in your wildest imagination, would you have a Chinese station master?"

"I-i-i-i ... guess not. Seems out of character."

"Right. Out of *your* character. Not mine. Since I worked on railroads, it's my pleasure to actually run one."

"You worked on the railroads?"

"Yes, I did. In fact, I built an all-Chinese railroad in California."

"Really? I didn't know there was such a thing."

"You see?" The Chinese man opened his hands. "How's that coming out of your imagination?"

"I guess it couldn't," Otto admitted, "unless ..."

"What?"

"The idea tickles me and I'm just creating it."

"Ach," the Chinese man clucked. "Well, I can safely state I'm not from anyone's imagination." He stuck a hand out through the bars. "Name's Moy Jin Mung."

"Otto Boteman," he said and shook. "So, is it Mr. Mung?"

"Moy Jin."

"Okay. Moy Jin, tell me, then, how it is this whole area looks like Promontory Point?"

Moy Jin laughed. "Doesn't it? Which is why I'm here. Why a lot of us Old West types are here. It's what we remember. You go that way," and he pointed east, "and you'll find steppes filled with the Khan's hordes and a bunch of Cossacks, all whooping it up because that's what they remember. You go that way," he pointed west, in the direction of the mountains, "and it's the Chiricahua and some Kentucky hillbillies." He swung south. "There, great rivers and lakes and Eskimos and Portuguese fishermen. And there," he swung around, "hills and valleys and farmers and cattlemen, Picts and Zulus." He paused. "If this is all your imagination, it's a fertile one indeed."

"Wait," Otto pointed out the back toward the tracks. "The City's there."

"And?"

"Well, how can the City and great rivers and lakes and Portuguese Eskimos, like you say, all be there at the same time?"

"It isn't. The City is where the City is."

Spidey-sense tingled and Otto raised his hands. "Metaphysics. I surrender."

Moy Jin smiled. "Accepted. So, you need a ticket back?"

"Eventually. Maybe. I don't really know."

"So this is a well-planned excursion. Maybe you'd do better with an open ticket and a long lead time, say thirty days?"

"*Hmm*. Okay, but it may be longer."

"No problem." Moy Jin pulled a handle on the adding machine and papers rolled out. He stamped some things and yanked some carbons and handed Otto a long envelope. "There you go. Don't lose it."

Otto stuffed it into his jacket pocket. "Right. Well. Ah, can you give me directions?"

"Sure you really need them?"

Otto considered. Maybe, maybe not, but let's play it safe. "I'm not sure how to get there."

"And where would that be?"

"The ship."

"Ship?"

"The rocket ship."

"Oh." Moy Jin drew out the word and examined Otto closely. "You're one of those."

"'Those'? I don't know who 'those' are. This is my first time here."

Moy Jin shrugged. "First time, hundredth, doesn't matter. You're one." He pointed at the mountain portal. "You saw the little town, right? Okay, go there, ask for Pashtun. He'll take care of you."

"Pashtun. Right." Otto paused. "Thanks."

"*De nada.*" Moy Jin turned and bustled around the back, slipping papers into a giant pigeonholed desk. Otto watched him for a moment and then walked onto the mountain porch. The breeze had picked up, a coolness to it, an underlying touch of snow from far-off peaks. He threw his head back, savoring, but kept his eyes closed to avoid sky hypnosis.

So, a Chinese stationmaster working out of a Warner Brothers' back lot who throws out Spanish phrases directed him to a guy from New Delhi.

"Wacky," he muttered and headed toward town.

Chapter XI

Dreamers In A Land Of Dreams, And The Limits To Credit

"Are you Pashtun?"

The obviously Indian man dressed in Dockers, a Nike ball cap with a Washington Nationals logo, and a plaid shirt, sat comfortably in a wooden chair tipped back against the wall of a clapboard building, "Feed and Grain" crudely painted in white above him. Soooo Wild West. Except for this guy.

"I am," the man replied, not moving, "and how may I help you?"

Yep, Indian. Otto loved that accent. It made talking sound like opera.

"Moy Jin sent me."

"Ah, my friend Moy Jin." Pashtun smiled wide and dropped the chair's front legs and placed his hands in a flagrantly satisfied manner on his knees. "He is a good man, that one. We are most fortunate he runs the station. I am not so sure anyone else would bring the efficiencies to bear that he does, because it is all so complicated and he has the gifts for it, thank God."

God? Otto eyed him suspiciously. "Which God?"

"'Which God?'" Pashtun looked at him with astonishment. "Why, are you crazy? There is only One." And he pointed skyward.

Otto wasn't going to fall into a staring-at-the-sky trap; he kept on at Pashtun. "But I thought you believed in a pantheon."

"Who?"

"Well, you," Otto gestured at him. "You're Indian, right?"

"Yes, from the kingdom of Maratha, but why does that not mean I do not believe in one God?"

"Uh ..."

"Consider this." Pashtun made a sweeping gesture. "The whole Vedic tradition speaks of Brahma and his Oneness. How is that wrong?"

"I guess it isn't."

"All right then," Pashtun said with satisfaction and leaned his chair back.

Otto blinked. "So, uh, Moy Jin said you could help me."

Pashtun blinked back. "With what?"

"To find something."

"That is very possible." Pashtun looked serious. "I am probably the most versed in Out of all the dwellers herein because I make the most travels. It is what led to my calling here, the helping of persons in Out to see a direction, find a place, even a person. It is a very remarkably versatile employment, one that I find very rewarding. And fun."

"Fun?"

"Oh, yes, very fun." Pashtun was satisfied again.

"So, then, you could help me."

"Undoubtedly."

Pause. And pause. Otto shuffled and glanced down the road and wondered if he should talk to someone else when it occurred to him that establishing Pashtun's credentials were part of the business here. "Okay. I'm looking for the ship."

"Which ship? There are many."

"Really?" Puzzled, Otto then figured they weren't talking about the same thing. "I mean the rocket ship."

"Oh. In that case, there is only one."

Pashtun paused, again, the silence stretching into moments. Again. Otto concluded exasperation was also an element of Out business and said, "Well, okay. Good. Makes my search easier. Can you tell me how to get there?"

"No."

"Excuse me?"

"No."

Otto was bewildered. "I thought you knew where everything in Out was."

"Is. And yes, I do."

"Okay." Downright baffled, now. "So where's the ship? The rocket ship," he added, hastily.

Pashtun pointed back toward the mountains to their left. "That way."

Otto followed his pointing finger, fixing the direction. "So, what, do I start walking?"

"It is too far."

"Then what do I do?"

"I can take you."

"You can take me?"

"Yes."

Otto let out the peeved breath he'd been nurturing. "I think that's what I asked you in the first place."

"You did not," Pashtun crossed his arms. "You asked me about God and if I could help you and where the ship is, but you did not ask me to take you."

"That was implied."

"Many things are implied, few are known. You must speak to what is known."

Otto eyed him. "Is that out of something?"

"It is out of me," Pashtun dropped the chair back down.

Was it this easy? Otto's shields went up because nothing was this easy. Nothing. Come Heaven or Earth. "How do we get there?"

"In my taxi."

W-a-a-ait a minute ... "You drive a taxi."

"As stated."

"An Indian guy drives a taxi. Here. In the Old West." Otto snorted. "That is just too much."

"Too much of what?"

"Too ... much a stereotype. I mean, come on!" Otto threw hands skyward. "This is like every comedy routine I've heard in the past fifty years. What, you drive like a crazy person one-handed through traffic while eating curry and telling me stories about your grandparents?"

Pashtun stared at Otto as if he were the crazy person. "Now why would I do that? You did not know them."

"I ... no, I did not. That's not the point—"

"Then what is your point?"

Yes, Otto what is your point? How to explain to this now bristling Marathan Man, or wherever the heck Pashtun was from, that he was a stock character in a whole cast of one-dimensional throwaways populating Otto's subconscious? And in so doing, would Otto throw away a golden, apparently God-given, opportunity to reach the ship, no matter how odd the means? Discretion, dude, that better part of valor. "I don't have a point."

Pashtun waggled his head. "It did not appear that you did, so one must be careful about engaging in a discussion that is ultimately fruitless." Satisfied last wag of emphasis. "So do you still wish to go to the ship?"

"Yes."

Satisfied nod. "Then we shall go." Pause as Pashtun scrutinized the area where Otto stood. "Where are your bags?"

"I didn't bring any."

Pashtun, suitably astonished, raised eyebrows. "And how can you spend a week at the ship without a change of clothes?"

"A week? I kinda thought I would be staying longer." I kinda think I'm going to board the ship and blast off into the Mesmer sky on a quest for God. At least, that's what Claudia led me to believe.

Or he had led himself to believe that based on Claudia's story?

"Even more of a reason."

"Uh, well ... as has already been pointed out to me, this isn't a well-planned expedition."

Pashtun clucked and threw a thumb behind him. "Go into the store and buy some clothes. Supplies."

"What kind of supplies?"

Pashtun shrugged. "Whatever you need. I am not one to tell a man what to think he needs."

You aren't one to tell a man much of anything, Otto thought of saying, but wondered how that would also affect his chances of getting to the ship; instead, he gave Pashtun the stink eye and clunked up the wooden steps, pausing before pushing through the swinging doors. "Why did you say a week?"

Pashtun was tipped back against the wall again, the top of the ball cap facing Otto. "I go out there only when someone arrives to go out there. But I do not come back for a week," the ball cap said.

"So, does that mean the people you take out there come back after a week?"

"Most do."

That doesn't bode well.

Otto considered the possible reasons, from loss of enthusiasm to discovering the rocket was shot out of a pop bottle.

But, Pashtun said 'most,' not all, so hang hat on that. Speaking of hat ... "You a fan?"

"Fan? That is an odd word. I am hearing it as 'admirer.' It is slang?"

"Wait," Otto interrupted. "You hear my words in English?"

"I do."

Otto leaned forward. "But I thought everyone heard their own language."

"Yes, but if you know enough of the other language, as I know English because I heard it quite frequently, then you hear it while it is translated in your head."

How 'bout that? "Well, good to know, and, to your question, yes, it's American slang. Worldwide, now. It comes from the word 'fanatic.' I don't know when it got started but it's used for people who obsess over sports teams, rock bands, that sort of thing."

The silence yawned and Otto knew by now to fill it. "So, are you a fan or not?"

Pashtun dropped down and turned a puzzled face to Otto. "Of?"

"Baseball."

Now it was Pashtun who looked baffled and Otto enjoyed the momentary payback.

"Ah." Pashtun tapped the brim. "This. I do not know of the squadron or of the game. A passenger named Gene Mauck gave it to me. He had something to do with their early history. It is a comfortable covering." Another tap of the brim and tilt back.

Gene Mauck, Gene Mauck ... nope, not familiar.

'Course Otto was hardly Mr. Baseball, so no surprise. And Pashtun wasn't, either.

Baseball squadron? Chuckling Otto went through the doors into...

Woolworths.

An old-time Woolworths, 50s, 60s. Just like every single Woolworths he'd run through when he was a kid.

Toooo cool.

Otto savored the linoleum floors, banks of overhead neons and the waist-high metal shelves stretching to the back, some set parallel, some perpendicular. Round wire baskets lay strewn across the front, one holding beach balls – beach balls? – another with notebooks, and – too funny – flip-flops.

Man, look at that card rack, at the too-skinny roof support columns fading in the distance, and, what's that in the back, a lunch counter?

How can I resist?

Grinning, Otto almost skipped his way down the aisle and selected a middle stool and surveyed the countertop's long sweep. An aircraft carrier, that's what he'd always thought when Mom plunked him and Art and Cindy down and they all, clamoring and fussing and throwing napkins around, spun stools and hit each other and cried while Mom, always at the end of her rope, ordered cheese sandwiches.

"Wadillibe?"

The perfect short-order cook with a big belly, three-day-old stubble, white paper hat greasy and askew, stained apron and T-shirt and, of course, an unlit cigar stub, was draped over the counter opposite, lip-pointing the stub at him.

Delighted, Otto didn't miss a beat. "Cheese sandwich."

"Cuminup." Cook walked away and Otto watched him through the order window: intent, gruff, unable to hide the glee. A man who'd found what moved him.

"Seems a little slow today," Otto called.

Cook shrugged. "Nodaladacussumers."

"Ever?"

"Spurts. Nataday."

"When?"

Shrug. "Crew shift."

Crew? "The rocket ship crew?"

"Dem, udders. Earyewgo."

The perfect toasted cheese, the perfect pickle and pile of Lays potato chips already staining the napkin. Otto smeared mustard on the sandwich as Cook watched in horror. "How do you stay in business?"

"Dunno." Cook stepped back from the desecration of his masterpiece. "Askdaboss," and fled behind the window.

"There's always enough to keep us going," someone said next to him. Otto looked up from crunching the perfect crust.

An old black man stood there, smiling. Bald, except for white side hair, Alfred E. Neumann ears, big kindly brown eyes. Everyone's grampa.

Otto savored the swallow. "Really?"

"Yes. Sometimes, I even get bought out."

"What causes that?"

"Tourist season. May I?" He gestured at a stool and Otto waved permission. "Although it's not by the calendar. It's episodic, based on movement. Say a whole troop of steppe dwellers arrive and stock up for a few years. Miners, too."

"Miners?"

"Yep."

Now that was interesting. "What are they mining?"

"Whatever they want," Grampa stuck out a hand. "Name's Henry, Henry Brown. You can call me Box."

"Box?"

"Long story." Henry grinned. "And you are?"

"Otto. Otto Boteman."

"Well, Mr. Boteman, what brings you to Out?"

Otto took the last, excellent, bite. "The rocket ship."

A pause. "Oh," Box said, softly, "one of those."

Otto wiped crumbs off his lips. "That's the second time I've gotten that reaction."

"You should probably get used to it." Box waved at Cook, who brought them cups of great smelling coffee then backed away, still looking mustard-hurt. "Rocket people are a peculiar lot."

"How so?"

Box raised a kindly brow. "You serious?"

"Well, yeah. I'm sort of new at this."

"*Hmm.*" Sympathetic. "Okay, ask yourself, what's the rocket for?"

Otto shrugged. "Well, I'm guessing – and, mind you, I haven't actually seen it yet – but to go into space."

"For what purpose?"

Otto laughed. "You might as well ask why Sir Edmund climbed Everest."

"Because, as he told me, 'it's there.'"

Well, how 'bout that? "You know Edmund Hilary."

"Comes in here every once in a while. Stocks up between trips. He's guiding some writer named Haggard. They're mapping the highlands, which is an obvious, and understandable, goal." Box looked meaningfully at Otto.

Haggard, Haggard, familiar but Otto couldn't place it. "Okay. You're right, there's a goal. And it's quite understandable." Dramatic pause. "The rocket is going out to look for God. I'm going with them."

"And why do you want to find God?"

Otto was somewhat perplexed by that. "Doesn't everybody?"

Box shook his head. "No. No, they don't. Out of all the billions and billions of souls here, only about forty or fifty want to find God."

Otto narrowed an eye. "That can't be true."

"Have you seen the sky?" Which Otto knew was rhetorical. "Have you seen the City?" Box pointed back out the front of the store. "Those mountains? You have tasted the best of foods, breathed the purest of air, met the most wonderful and interesting people." Box sipped his coffee and looked straight at Otto. "How much more evidence do you need?"

Otto didn't reply.

"This is a land of dreams and you rocketeers are shooting yourselves right out of it. Have you heard of people who spent their whole lives looking for something that was right in front of them?"

There was a response to this, Otto was sure, a cogent, pithy, irrefutable explanation of the urge within him to look God dead –

so to speak – in the Face but, for the life of him, Otto couldn't articulate it. "I know what you're saying," he said, lamely. "Others have more or less told me the same thing." Ian, for one. Latchemondy, for another. "But ... I have to go see."

Was that cogent, pithy, and irrefutable enough?

Apparently.

Box scrutinized Otto's face for a long moment, searching for ... what, Otto didn't know. Signs of insanity? Then he raised an "oh well" palm. "Okay. Man's gotta do what a man's gotta do."

"So you think I'm crazy."

"Yep." Vigorous nod of the head. "I think all you rocket people are crazy. But, sometimes, you gotta box yourself up and go. Follow me," and he waved Otto behind him.

Obviously, the odd reference had something to do with Box's nickname; Otto was about to ask for details but they moved so quickly up three aisles that within moments they fronted a long shelf packed with tough stuff: Dickies, jeans, chambray shirts, wool socks and boots, and the chance was lost. Box gestured, "Get what you need."

"The work is that hard?"

"From what I hear. You don't want to be getting that nice suit all greasy now, do you?"

"Bet it would come off with just a light brushing."

Box laughed. "It would. More proof of God, rocket man, but you want to look the part. Have at it. Dressing room's over there, if you're modest."

No need to be; no one else but Box and him in the aisle and Otto spent the next fifteen minutes putting together a workman's ensemble. Oshkosh and Carhartt and whatnot, no sizes, but every shirt or pair of pants he randomly selected fitted. Perfectly. "Wadja expect?" he muttered, slipping on a pair of perfect fitting Timberlands.

Box, marking up some clothes at the end of the aisle, muttered back, "More proof." Then looked at him critically. "That should do. Now, you need to get some camping equipment."

"Really? Why?"

"They don't have a lot of accommodation out there. Aisle 7. Keep it simple." And he walked away.

Tucking his suit under his arms, Otto located the aisle and picked out a sleeping bag, a one-man tent, and some toiletries. "Camping tonight on the ole camp ground," he sang under his breath and wondered how that would be. Probably as sublime, as mesmerizing, as every other experience here, with coyotes singing a chorus of Verdi operas on some bluff while Comanches rode by silhouetted against the moon. Er, moons. He dumped everything into a cart at the end of the aisle. Probably done.

No.

"You'll need a couple of bags," Box called from the front and, of course, right in front of him was a variety of duffles. Otto selected two, dropped them on top of everything else, and wended the cart forward.

"Over here." Box gestured from a cash register. Otto loaded the belt and watched it convey to the end. Box, hitting random keys as items slid by, frowned. "*Tsk*," he *tsk*ed.

"Something wrong?"

"Yes." Box pursed his lips. "You're broke."

"Huh?"

"Yep. Used up all your credits." Box fiddled with some keys and pulled out a clipboard, seemingly from nowhere. "You've enough for another cheese sandwich or two. Definitely not enough," Box swept his hands over the equipment, "for this."

"What does that even mean?" Otto strained his neck to look at the clipboard.

"Like I said, you're broke. Says so right here." Box flipped the clipboard around, but all Otto could see were columns of meaningless numbers. "Rent, utilities, food ... how many times did you go to Grendel's anyway?"

"Just once."

"Expensive place, you know."

"But ..." Otto was thoroughly baffled. "How's that possible? I mean, rent?"

Box looked at him in amazement. "Did you think all this is free? You get a lifestyle commensurate with your credit, but you don't get to fling it around like a trust fund or something. Gotta stay within your limits."

Well, great. Been nice if someone – Latchemondy, f'rinstance – had explained that. "So, okay, how do I get more credits?"

"More credits?" Box laughed. "You think you can earn more credits here?" Box chortled as the clipboard magically disappeared then turned away, still highly amused, and sorted through the equipage, folding it for re-shelving.

"What put me over?"

"This," Box flipped a hand at the clothes. "It's the same with all you rocket people. Except for the boss, of course."

"All the rocket people overdraw? And who's the boss?"

"Yep to the first question. And some Russian named Chilkovsky, Tsiolkovsky, something like that, for the second."

Otto looked around. "So, what do I do?"

Box stacked the clothes. "You'll need to change back to your suit."

"No, I mean about credit."

"Have to recharge."

"Thought you said I couldn't earn more."

"It's not earning more. It's replenishing what you had. Like waiting until payday. You know?"

Yes, Otto knew, having at various points in his life, lived from payday to payday.

Maybe at more points than he should have. "So what it's like every two weeks or so? Or is it monthly?"

Man, what would he do around here for a month? Stock shelves?

Box was puzzled. "Is what monthly?"

"Our payday."

Box was even more puzzled and then his brow cleared. "Oh," he smiled, "no, it's not an actual payday. You have to recharge."

"How do I do that?"

"Just go back. And wait." Box pushed the refolds behind him. "You wanna change here or in the dressing room?"

"Go back where? The station?" Walk down the road, recharge, then walk back again and resume purchasing? That seemed silly.

"The City."

"But," spluttering again. Otto hated to splutter, "I just got here!"

Box threw out "oh well" arms.

"But ... but ..." Stop it! Otto did, took in a breath. "How will I know when I'm recharged?"

"You'll know," Box held out Otto's suit.

Otto walked back to a dressing room, changed, and wordlessly handed the ensemble back to Box and walked outside and stood on the porch, bewildered. All the way here just to have that proverbial rug yanked from under, and rather rudely and weirdly at that. Hey, God, is this some kind of joke? A very elaborate one, and not in the least bit funny, Dude. He eyed the road to its vanishing point and wondered how long it would take to reach the rocket hoofing it.

"Are you going?" Pashtun, sitting on the lowest step, whittled a piece of wood.

"Apparently not," Otto replied bitterly. Another emotion he didn't think possible in Heaven. Was very possible in a coma, though.

"Why?"

"No credits."

"Ah." Pashtun concentrated on the wood. "I'll take you."

"Huh? What? Really?"

"Yes. It is no problem. I have to go there anyway and it is a long and lonely trip."

"But I don't have the equipment."

"You'll be all right," Pashtun stood, brushing off the shavings. He gestured at a black London cab parked at the corner. "Coming?"

Chapter XII

British Wars And Indian Converts And A Heaven Strangely Empty

Otto absently rubbed the upholstery on the back of Pashtun's seat while still puzzling over this whole credit fiasco. Maybe God was toying with him. Didn't want to be found, and having a little fun with idiots who insisted on so doing.

"This is a great car." Said absently

"Thank you," Pashtun called back. "I take good care of it."

"I'll say. I always wanted one of these."

"Indeed. I have heard much similar commentary from many other passengers. When I first saw this vehicle, I immediately felt the same way. And I do not come from a car culture. There is apparently something about this particular model that we find joyful."

"Think you're right," Otto agreed. "When I was in London I took one just for the experience. The driver was a hoot, dressed in tails and a top hat and sure knew his way around. Ended up at a tavern named The Grenadier, used to be Wellington's mess, and the driver and I raised a glass to his ghost."

Pashtun looked back at him. "Did you now? I would not have joined you."

"Not a fan?"

Pashtun shook his head. "No. I am not a ... fan."

"I thought you Indians admired the British."

"After my time. And not so much admire as tolerate. We very much considered them a barbarous people."

Otto chuckled, "So do we. As they, us."

"Indeed. I am thinking that every race has the same conception of every other race. It is a sad thing, because ultimately, are we not the souls inside?"

"You'd think. But, Pashtun, we look here like we did there."

"That is not so odd." Pashtun moved gracefully into a long curve. "There is a sense of identity with your body, no? You look in the mirror and you see yourself. Could you recognize your soul?"

"Dunno. But this body is the showroom version. Makes me think I'm dreaming."

Pashtun nodded. "We all do."

That was actually comforting and Otto settled back, looking at Out. It was a mix of Arizona and Colorado, or Afghanistan and Saudi Arabia, your druthers. Everyone's concept of hinterlands. God accommodating the trope, or his mind doing so? Otto frowned. How do you tell the difference?

By gathering data, of course.

Otto stared at the back of Pashtun's wonderfully coiffed hair, a lovely mixture of smoothness and curls in a pattern he could not identify. Here was an opportunity to gather said data. Let's see how creative his brain could get. "So why do you dislike the British?" he asked.

"Because I spent most of my adult life fighting them. Because my last days were spent in a rude hut by a rude river, mourning my losses."

"That sounds pretty harsh."

"Indeed, it was a harsh time. Are you familiar with the wars of the continent?"

Other than what he'd gleaned from old movies and Rudyard Kipling, Otto didn't know a blasted thing about them. Which was perfect for present conditions. "Can't say I am."

"*Hmph.*" A tad contemptuous. A tad. "I am not surprised. From what I have gathered from the visitors I have taken to and fro over this wilderness, the histories are known by only a few specialists. I am thinking the British have done a very clever job of glossing over their rather brutal subjugation of a people they had no business subjugating in the first place. It does not make them look very good."

"No doubt."

"But I am thinking there are such histories somewhere in the early-ons of every people. I am believing you have such histories yourself?" Pashtun looked back at Otto with expectation.

"You betcha. Just ask the Indians."

Genuine bewilderment. "You mean me?"

"No, no," Otto said, hastily, "not you. Native Indians. Native Americans, I mean."

"Why did you first call them Indians? Is that not the name others have designated for my peoples?"

"Geographical mistake. Columbus thought he had sailed to India, so he called the natives 'Indians.' The name stuck."

"*Hmm*, most amusing. Although I do not understand how he could have made such a mistake. Even if Columbus had landed at the meanest and lowest place of my continent, it would have been obvious by the silks and good manners of even our lowest caste that they were not savages." Pashtun chuckled. "I must ask him about that."

"Wait ... what?" Otto was startled. "You know Columbus?"

Quick nod. "Oh, indeed. He is always with his fleet up and down the Inner Ocean and the Sidelong Seas. He is enjoying himself immensely."

"There are oceans?"

"Oh yes, many, and Columbus told me he has barely scratched the surface of them with all of this time and with all of his captains sailing so much here and there, up and down. He is a very happy man," and Pashtun slapped the wheel in emphasis.

Waddyaknow. Otto made another entry in his mental notebook: find Columbus. Ironic phrasing.

"I was," Pashtun launched as if no intervening conversation had occurred, "a noble, not Peshwa, to be sure and I would never rise to command an army, but blessings on Shahu for bringing us all as one, because I was a captain in the lancers and I must say I was most fortunate to have that position, the grandson of a clerk and all. Those were not the best of times for Maratha, even if I felt the glory of it. We had already fought the British twice, the East India Company spiriting away our kinsmen and our lands so they could advantage themselves for trade." He spat out of the window as Otto wondered if he was in for another Ferdinand-style narrative.

Yep.

"I did well in those two wars, leading my company when Shinde trapped the British in the ghats until we surrounded them at Wadgaon and they had to surrender. Can you imagine, the vaunted British Army forced to surrender to the wogs?" He laughed, pure delight in his voice and Otto grinned, even though he had no idea what Pashtun was talking about. No idea at all.

So where was his brain getting this?

"But of course, of course." Pashtun waved a hand, "they came back and they bested us at Sipri and Shinde had to give up those lands. I was wounded there," Pashtun rubbed his shoulder, "a bullet, and I could no longer lance with this arm so I had my saddle remade and a sling constructed to show my major I still had the power to run through, so he said I could stay as captain." Pashtun gave a satisfied smile to himself in the rearview and Otto figured this was one of those triumphant moments cut out of circumstances not so.

"So, and do you think, do you not think this was enough for the East India Company? No, no, of course not. They are rapacious, those British, and it was so very important to them to own everything and everyone." He shook his head. "Warriors testing warriors, that I can see. Match man to man and see who has the heart of a tiger, but not for trade." He spat out of the window again.

"Twenty years, it was twenty years we stood quietly. I was in my prime, strong and regarded, my company now the Peshwa's favorite and we led the parades. My wife, so beautiful and adoring, and my sons, my sons ..." His voice trailed off and even Otto recognized this was a bad moment and he thought furiously of something consoling to say but Pashtun went on.

"All that life was supposed to be. Rao, that fool, that traitor!" He spat again. "A snake, a pig. I lost my eldest at Laswari, my youngest at Assaye, my leg to Wellesley." He was silent for a moment. "The last I saw of my wife she was being carried away by a gang of British soldiers." The silence grew.

"Pashtun," was all the consoling Otto could muster.

"No," he raised a hand. "I was not done. No, I was not. We were not done. With a useless arm and a missing leg, I took my saddle again and waved my lance to the old men and we charged, hard and fast with the songs of war on our lips and we died, they died. I woke, trapped under my horse, and saw the remains of my company, the remains of all Maratha, broken and bloody and lost. I crawled away to the river. I stayed there until my death, holding my broken lance."

He turned and looked at Otto squarely. "So I am not a fan of the British."

Otto, for a second, didn't know what to say. Only for a second. But," he blurted, "this is Heaven."

"Yes?"

"You're not supposed to harbor ill will toward your enemies."

"Who has said that?"

"Well, jeez!" Otto struggled to find a specific verse, but realized it was extrapolation. "Everybody!"

"I have not read or heard everybody yet."

"You know what I mean."

"Yes," Pashtun agreed, "I know what you mean, but that is a Christian tradition, not Vedic. Our wars go with us."

"But I thought you were a Christian."

"I never said I was. I may be. I heard the Christian gospel many times, in the prayers shouted by the British I ran through. It is ridiculously easy to become Christian, a mere thought, withdrawn a moment later. I think that is what happened to me."

"So you don't consider yourself a Christian?"

"I consider myself a warrior of Maratha, sworn to the Peshwa, the thrill of war in my blood, the love of one woman, just one, in my heart, the pride of tall sons in my eyes. And my gaze turns in rage toward the British." He seethed. "I am still seeking the justice sworn to me by gods and God."

"So then," Otto wasn't sure how to phrase it. "You don't think this is Heaven?"

"Of course I think it is. But I think there are many others. Why is it that you seek the rocket ship, if you do not think the same thing?"

"Many others," Otto considered. "Maybe that's it."

"Of course it is it. Look around you." Pashtun swept an arm at the desert to their left: endless, burning, and exquisitely harsh. "If you consider the billions of people who have lived and died on Earth since its inception, then I must ask you, why do these lands remain so empty?"

"Because not all of them went to Heaven."

"At least not this Heaven," Pashtun concluded.

"No. A lot of them don't go to any Heaven at all."

"Of what are you speaking? Do you mean Hell?"

"Well, yeah."

"And what is the criterion for that?"

"To reject Jesus Christ as your Savior."

"*Pffht.*" Pashtun made a derisive sound. "I already told you how ridiculously easy it is to become Christian. As criteria, it is very, very broad. There are possibly only approximately maybe about forty-five people who never actually heard and considered the Christian gospel for the split-second required to gain its advantages."

"Yeah? So then it's a Christian Heaven, is it? And those forty-five, which, I think is a gross underestimate. By the way, where'd they go?"

"I do not know. I have not met them."

"*Phwwft!*" It was Otto's turn to be derisive. "And how would you know if you did? And if they're in Hell, all forty-five of them, how would you ever know that?"

"I am not sure that can be known," Pashtun conceded.

"All right then," Otto sat back, arms crossed. He felt like he had just won an argument, but he wasn't sure what it was. Then something occurred to him. "Pashtun."

"Yes?" A hint of pique in his voice.

"Have you ever met anyone here before the Christian era?"

"I was not here before the Christian era."

"No, no," Otto waved a hand, "I mean, people before the Christian era. Greeks, Babylonians, Hottentots, whatnot."

"What are you talking about? All of that was the Christian era."

"No it wasn't. The Egyptians? That was well before Christ's birth."

"You are mistaken. I have read some of your Bible. All of those peoples are mentioned quite prominently."

"Yeah, but that's in the Old Testament. That's before Christ was born."

"Yes, and that is all in the Bible, too, is it not? So that means they are all part of the Christian era, does it not?"

"Augh!" From derisive to exasperated. "It's not the same thing! That was the time of the Jews. The Israelites. King David, you know?"

"Oh, I have met Jews here. There was one young man who said he helped build Solomon's Temple and another who said he fought with that King David you mentioned against some other king. I do not know the name."

"Saul?"

"Perhaps that is it. I do not recall."

"I'll be," Otto sat back, pleased. And puzzled.

"What is the significance of these Jews?" Pashtun asked.

Otto chewed his lower lip, "Tell you the truth, Pashtun. I don't quite know the answer to that. But, this Heaven, it's not fitting the template."

"We all think that," he said. "And, by the way," he pointed through the windshield, "There is your rocket."

Otto leaned forward and sighted along Pashtun's directing finger. The brightness of the sun and dun colors of the desert washed away contrast but there, in the distance, a thin, shiny needle of reflected sunlight.

"Your ship," Pashtun emphasized, "to the other heavens." He fell silent, then added, "God help you."

Chapter XIII

Old Russian Rocketmen
And The Continuity Of Dreams

"Star City?"

Otto frowned at the hand-painted sign leaning on the gate. Wasn't much of a gate – just a hole in a flimsy chain link fence.

"You do not like the name?" Pashtun asked as they drove through the opening.

"Not at all. That's what they called the Russian launch complex in Siberia."

"Is it not a launch complex and is this not Siberia?"

"Not cold enough, but, yeah, I see your point."

They drove on, Pashtun's cab pulling up a vortex of dust behind them. The rocket loomed in the windshield. It wasn't, as Otto first concluded from the distant reflection, an elegant silver needle, the stuff of fifties pulp magazines. It was anything but. The gantry holding it was a crosshatch of stairs and ladders and smoking hoses just as in every photo of every launch complex he'd seen since 1st grade. The ship itself, well ... Otto didn't know what to make of it. It was a hodgepodge of bulging metal plates and forms, a collision between the Space Shuttle and Mir. The boosters attached to it looked weird; those Russian ones – Balalaika, Ballyhoo, something like that – married to ancient V2s.

Overall, quite crappy.

Otto wondered what he had gotten himself into as they spun through government-drab buildings and hangars fronted by white-painted rocks arranged in clever titles: *Metal Men, Liars and Fabricators, Wires Guys,* et cetera. So, a sense of humor pervaded the place, no doubt inspired by that joke of a rocket.

Titles ...

"Say, Pashtun, can you read that?" Otto pointed at a *Trawlers and Haulers* logo as they passed.

Pashtun was suddenly hostile. "Do you think I am illiterate?"

"Well, no!" Man, touchy guy. "I'm just wondering if you read English."

"It is not English. It is in lovely Devanagari and says, 'Trawlers and Haulers.' But you are reading it in English, no?"

"Yes."

"Barbaric language," Pashtun muttered as Otto marveled. Wow. The universal translator was, indeed, universal. Good work, God.

But wait, wait a minute here ... Otto frowned at Pashtun. "I thought you said you understood English. So why don't you see the words in English?"

"I never said I understand English." Pashtun cut suddenly up a street.

Otto raised a finger, "Oh, yes, you did! When we were talking about the word 'fan.'" Aha! A flaw in the logic of this world! Otto leaned forward. Was this, finally, the crack in the prison wall?

Pashtun gave him the fisheye. "I said that I had HEARD English enough. Many of the British troops yelled long and intense phrases when I ran them through. So, I know the words. Especially the bad ones," and he chuckled.

"Oh." Drat.

People walked back and forth, most of them carrying something from a bag to large pieces of metal or coils of wire. Almost all of them waved at Pashtun and he waved back. "You're popular," Otto observed.

"I am their only outside contact."

"Yeah?" Otto looked back toward the fence. "Then what's that for?"

"Ambience."

They drove through a row of hangers, open bay doors revealing giant engines slung inside as well as swept-wing jets suspiciously like Foxbats, tool stands and tool chests and activity. Welding sparks flew. Vehicles towed giant masses of metal while people with clipboards stood around consulting each other. Smokestacks in the distance belched vapor and dirty clouds.

Otto was amazed. "Regular little complex they've got here."

"Now you see why it is called Star City." Pashtun stopped in a turnaround that curved back in front of a one-storied, glass-doored building – a headquarters if Otto ever saw one. "Come with me," Pashtun said and got out.

"Pashtun!" a woman squealed as they entered. She was a fortyish looking, print- dress wearing, pointy light-blue eyeglasses-with-holder-straps secretary right out of a 1950s movie, sitting behind a too-high wooden counter with "In" and "Out" baskets arranged properly on one side. Otto suppressed a smile.

"Angela," Pashtun responded, gravely.

"Wha'd you bring me?" Angela squeezed her shoulders up to her ears and smiled wide. Cute and flirty. *My Little Margie.*

Pashtun dug into a pocket and took out some red licorice. Angela squealed again and took it from him. "Is he in?" Pashtun asked.

She pointed the licorice down the hall and Pashtun moved. Otto fell in behind. "Friend of yours?" he asked.

"Shut up," Pashtun said and Otto grinned.

At the end of the hallway, a door stood partially open. Pashtun led through it without ceremony. It was a small office, rather bare, organizational-beige walls with graphs and formulas tacked to them, a battered metal desk set before a large picture window framing the rocket.

"Konstantin," Pashtun said.

A thin balding man with a lovely beard and moustache, sitting behind the battered desk in an equally battered chair, looked up from a laptop and smiled. "Pashtun! So good to see you again."

"And it is always a good day for me when I can say hello to you, sir." Pashtun half bowed and then pointed back at Otto. "I have brought you another recruit."

"Indeed?" Konstantin raised an eyebrow and looked Otto up and down. "Well, good, good, we certainly need the help. Your name, sir?"

Otto stepped up to the desk. "Otto, sir. Otto Boteman."

Konstantin stood, extended a hand and shook warmly. "American?" he asked.

"How could you tell?"

Konstantin laughed. "We have many Americans here. I have come to recognize their accents."

"And yours," Otto said, "is ... Russian?" He raised an eyebrow and Konstantin beamed back an affirmative.

"Well, then," Pashtun said, "I must check the depot and deliver some packages and then I must be going."

Otto looked at him. "Really, you gotta go?"

"Yes, I must. I will be back in a week. I always stop here first so if you wish to speak with me or need a ride back, please be here. Goodbye," and he headed out.

"Pashtun!" Otto called as he stepped through the door. Pashtun turned. "Thank you so much. You didn't have to give me a ride. It was very decent of you."

"I was coming this way anyway. And it is a real pleasure to see everyone here. They are all interesting," and he walked away. Otto heard Angela squealing and chuckled as he turned back to Konstantin.

"That Pashtun," the Russian said admiringly. "What would we do without him?"

"He's a real good guy. Doesn't like the British, though."

"Who does?" Konstantin sat down and gestured at a folding chair leaning behind the door. Otto unfolded it and pulled up to the desk, peering through the window behind the Russian. Vapor drifted from various connections on the rocket, almost hiding it, and there were lots of people running up and down the gantry. "Wow," Otto said.

Konstantin shifted the chair, which squeaked properly, acknowledged Otto's gaze. "It is beautiful, is it not?"

"It's ... unusual," Otto said. "Quite a mix of different styles."

"Oh, indeed. We took the best from available systems. The Russian rockets are strong, the Americans powerful, and the Germans efficient. Put them together ..." and he flourished a hand.

"I'da thought you'd build it like the ones you built in Russia."

"I never built a rocket in Russia," Konstantin said absently, watching a tractor pull some large containers up to the gantry.

"Really? I thought you were a rocket scientist."

"Not me. I was a math teacher in Kaluga, well before there was a Russian space program. This is my first real rocket," and he smiled in pure delight, almost enraptured. A man who had found his place.

"So how did you get into rockets?"

"Oh, I've always been 'into' them." Konstantin made an expansive gesture but his eyes never left the window. "I like that American phrase, 'into.' So descriptive. I designed a lot of rocket features, air locks, bio systems, things like that. I wrote a lot. I even wrote some science fiction." He turned an inquisitive eye on Otto. "Did you read science fiction?"

"Avidly."

"Good!" Konstantin smiled. "Any of mine? *On the Moon?*"

Otto realized it was a title and shook his head. "*From the Earth to the Moon*, I know that. *The Moon is a Harsh Mistress*, one of my favorites. But yours? Sorry."

"It's all right." Konstantin was unfazed. "It was out of print rather quickly. I know the Jules Verne one, but the *Mistress* one, I don't know. Who wrote it?"

"Robert Heinlein."

"Oh, him!" Konstantin clapped delighted hands. "He comes here from time to time. Engaging man. I will have to ask him to bring me a copy."

"Robert Heinlein comes here?"

"Yes. He's a consultant on our space suit design. It's his first real space suit."

"*Have Space Suit Will Travel.*" Otto made the connection. "Amazing."

"Yes it is. Not that we're sure we'll actually need one, but it's always good to have backups. So," by the change of tone, Otto knew the interview had started. "What did you do, Otto, and what is it you want to do?"

Do? On Earth, in life, before coming here, obviously. That was the easy part of the question. "I was an analyst."

Konstantin raised approving eyebrows. "Excellent. What kind, electrical, hydraulic?"

"Uh, no, nothing mechanical. Intelligence."

"Pardon?"

"I looked for spies and terrorists."

"Spies and terrorists?" Konstantin was instantly worried. "Are you from the American McCarthy period?"

"No, after that. Twenty-first century, just ..." What, a few weeks ago, a few years, a few decades? He didn't know. "... recently. And how do you know about McCarthy?"

"One of the propulsion engineers lived during that time frame. We had a very interesting discussion, comparing McCarthy and the Cheka. Are spies and terrorists that much of an issue a whole discipline must be devoted to them?"

"Mostly terrorists now. Not so much spies anymore. But, when they were," Otto smiled, "they were Russian."

"Ah, yes!" Konstantin laughed. "We were very good at that, weren't we? So, you do not bring us any new technologies?"

Otto pointed at the laptop. "You seem to be doing well."

"Wonderful, isn't it?" Konstantin stroked the screen affectionately. "It makes things so much easier. Are you a programmer?"

"No. I can work in code, but only the old stuff, COBOL, like that. 'Fraid I don't really offer that much."

"You would be surprised. You have concepts that you, no doubt, take for granted but which would be a revelation to us. See, we progress as persons like you find your way here, drawn by whatever draws you." Konstantin's eyes narrowed. "So, what *does* draw you? Optics? Equations? Metallurgy?"

And now the hard part of the question. "No." Otto hesitated and then took a breath. Time for the hard answer. "I want to look for God."

"Ah." Konstantin drew it out, appreciatively. He looked at Otto, then stood. "A crewman," he said, and saluted. "Welcome aboard."

Wordlessly, Otto returned it. And knew something had, irrevocably, changed.

Chapter XIV

A Crew Ill-Suited To A Purpose

"Come with me," Konstantin said as he zipped around the desk, beckoning furiously, and led Otto quickly down the hall. "Oh!" Angela squealed as they reached her, "Doctor, where you going? You have that meeting ..." But he waved her off and they were out the door and down the street, careening through switchbacks and side alleys until Otto was hopelessly lost. They finally entered a barracks some old boot must have designed – open bay, cots, and lockers. About twenty men and women sat around cleaning equipment.

Konstantin screeched to a halt just inside the double doors. "Can I have your attention?"

Everyone looked up. Konstantin threw a hand at Otto and said, "Another crewman!"

Suddenly Otto was the center of a cheering, smiling blob of handshaking, backslapping people yelling, "Welcome aboard! Good to have ya! What's your specialty?" in a mix so jumbled, Otto looked at Konstantin helplessly.

Konstantin smiled, "You'll be all right," and walked out.

"One more! One more!" a huge guy sporting swathes of layered blond hair shouted, holding up a finger to emphasize his point. Several others enthusiastically joined him.

"All right! Okay! Let the man breathe, please!" A female

voice cut through the chatter and the blob parted. A tall woman stood opposite, hands on hips and exasperation on face. Obviously, the one in charge. She was plain but big-eyed, hair arranged in a pleasing flapper style.

"Hello," she said, sticking out a hand, "and welcome aboard. I'm the captain."

"Hello." Otto took it. "I'm the buck private."

She laughed. "A sense of humor. Good. We don't need any more Gloomy Gus's on this trip," and she looked pointedly at a young man dark-haired and dark-browed, who shook his head and sighed, "Don't get one joke." They all laughed.

Otto smiled at her. "Yeah, I've got that. Too much of one, my wife used to say."

"Is she here with you?" the captain said, expectation reflected in the sudden leaning forward and collectively held breath of the group. Otto, taken aback, replied, "No, no she's not." He measured the distance to the door, should escape be necessary.

"Oh," the captain looked momentarily disappointed. She turned to the big blond guy, who looked even more so. "One more, Karl, just one," she consoled, putting a reassuring hand on his gigantic arm.

"What does that mean?" Otto asked.

"Karl will explain," the captain said. Karl handed her a clipboard and she flipped through some pages, scrutinized them, and then looked at Otto sharply. "Well, what can you do?"

"What do you want me to do?"

"Engineer? Machinist? Mathematician?"

Otto shook his head. "No none of those. Nothing technical, I'm afraid."

"*Hmm*," the captain tapped a finger to her chin, studying him. "You're a big guy," she observed. "Look pretty strong, too."

"That's an illusion," Otto said. "I have no upper body strength. Legs, though," and Otto slapped his thigh, "are like rocks."

"Well, if I need something kicked, I'll let you know," the captain observed dryly, which got a big laugh and some mock kicks thrown at the periphery.

Otto chuckled and looked at Gus. "I see what you mean."

"I'm thinking," the finger-tapping continued as the captain looked at Karl, "outside repair?"

Karl examined Otto critically. "Let me have some time with him and we'll see."

"What's outside repair?" Otto asked.

"We don't know what we're going to run into out there," the captain said, "Maybe meteorites, asteroids, little green men," she grinned, "so we're training a segment of the crew for spacewalk and frame repair. That might be you."

Coulda knocked him over with a feather. "You want me to spacewalk?"

"If Karl agrees, absolutely. Is that a problem?"

"Uh ... no! Not at all! That'd be great!"

The captain beamed appreciation. "Well, good. You belong to Karl now. He'll make the decision." Karl beamed his appreciation, a huge smile almost an acre long splitting his face in half.

"Okay!" Otto said. Wow, spacewalking!

The crew, including Karl, looked satisfied and turned away. The captain flipped through the clipboard.

"So, what do I do now?" Otto asked.

"*Hmm?*" she looked up. "Oh." She pointed after Karl. "Go with him."

Karl had moved to a bunk and was sitting on the end, absently folding a long shirt. A few of the others, including Gus, gathered around him, watching and talking.

Otto took a step that way when someone called, "Hey, Amelia!"

The captain waved a hand. "In a minute."

Amelia?

Otto pirouetted and stared at her. Flapper hairstyle from the 1920s. A captain of an aircraft involved with cutting-edge aeronautics ... could it be? "Not, by chance, Amelia Earhart?"

Genuinely surprised, she arched eyebrows. "You know me?"

Smacked across the forehead, he was. "You're Amelia Earhart?"

She cocked her head. "How do you know me?"

"Why!" Otto laughed, pleased and excited. "Everyone knows you!"

She waved at the crew. "They don't. Except for Marc over there." She gestured at a brown-haired man standing at the back. "And he was unimpressed. You're from a recent era, right?"

"Yes, how did you know?"

"You said 'buck private.' How recent?"

"Two thousand nineteen."

"Really?" she mused. "It's that year? Do we have flying cars yet?"

"No," he smiled. "Nor jet packs, nor are we living on the moon. So, you're really her?"

She flourished hands. "In the flesh. So to speak."

"My God." Otto suddenly loved this place even more. "You know you're a big hero, right?"

"Still?" She looked a little puzzled. "I mean, they hyped it all up back then. The idea was to promote flying, you know. All I did was ride along that first time and they made such a big deal." Rueful shake of the head. "It wasn't actually a big deal until I flew it alone. Now *that* was something. I got lost, you know," and she elbowed him in a joking manner.

"You're an icon" Otto said "There's statues of you. All the kids study you in school. You're an example of what women can do. Sky's the limit, no joke intended."

"Really?" She looked pleased and hugged the clipboard to herself, smiling. "Who'da thought that? I figured everyone forgot about me."

"No." Otto waved that away. "Quite the contrary. There's a big mystery about your last flight. So?" Otto's tone made the question.

She clucked, annoyed, "Don't ask."

"I mean," Otto couldn't leave it alone, "really, what happened? Is Fred Noonan with you?" and he looked around.

"I said 'don't ask.'" She was definitely annoyed. "And no, I haven't seen Fred since I got here."

"Is that right? You mean, he's not interested in ..." and Otto gestured in the direction he thought the rocket stood.

"Probably not. Not a lot of people are. Even fewer actually want to be on the crew. And if you do, you need to convince Karl. He decides who goes, so do what he says if you want to come along." She slapped the clipboard and walked away.

Otto watched her leave. Man. Amazing. What a fertile imagination I have. He walked over to Karl, standing next to a bunk with a line of folded shirts on top of it. Karl and Gus and he were examining a long, denim-looking coverall and arguing about stress points.

"Pretty wild, huh?" a voice said in his ear.

Otto turned. Marc stood there, arms folded, idly watching Karl.

"I'll say," Otto replied, "Amelia Earhart, of all people."

"Yeah," Marc said, "although, you shouldn't be too surprised. I mean, heading into the unknown, that was her."

"True. Did she ever say what happened?"

"Nope. Very closed-mouthed about it. I think they screwed up."

"*Hmm*," Otto mused. "Guess I'd want to keep that quiet too."

"Yeah!" Marc laughed, "Not like me. I'm very proud of the stupid way I died."

"How was that?"

"I was killed by a hatch."

"A hatch?"

"Yeah," Marc grinned mischievously, "a hatch. I was going out on the observatory platform. There was a design flaw no one knew about and the dome was still moving, even though I had shut it off. A ladder attached to the dome smacked into the hatch. *Thwack!*" he made a smacking sound with his hand.

Otto grimaced. "Oh, man."

"Wasn't pretty."

"'Observatory.' So, you were an astronomer?"

"Still am." He held out a hand. "Marc Aaronson. Lately of Kitt Peak."

"Otto Boteman." He shook it. "Lately of DC. I always wanted to be an astronomer."

"What stopped you?"

"I suck at math."

Marc chuckled. "That'll do it. So what did you do?"

"Chase terrorists."

"Really?" Marc raised an eyebrow, "You a cop?"

"Never had the privilege. An agent."

"FBI?"

"No, something better. DoD IG."

"Never heard of them."

"Not surprising. We were small. Kept to ourselves."

"*Mmp*." Marc made a small sound of appreciation. "Bet you have some stories."

"Eh." Otto waggled a hand. "I'd rather hear yours. Like, what do you make of the moons?"

"I don't think they're natural."

"What?"

"I mean, the big one is, but the little one is artificial."

"What makes you say that?"

"Their motion." Marc moved his hands to demonstrate. "It's all wrong. The big one's about a third farther out than good ole Earth's moon, but this planet has about a third more mass, hence the motions should be similar. The smaller moon is not behaving under gravity as I know it. It's wacky."

"How do you know all this, mass and distance?"

Marc smiled. "I don't suck at math. Besides, we have lasers. Scales. Mirrors. Real good ones – eighteen, twenty-four inches, perfect polish. They make 'em over there." He made a vague gesture toward the outside. "Dutch and Venetian lens grinders from the Middle Ages, can you believe it? They just go nuts over the modern equipment."

"Where'd it come from?"

"The moons?"

"No, the equipment."

"There's a big industrial base here."

"Where'd that come from?"

Marc shrugged. "Search me. Was here when I arrived. So, you want to know about the moons?"

"Yeah. And what's with the sky? And the stars?"

"Ah." Marc smiled. "From the sublime to the ridiculous. The big moon looks real enough, craters and oceans and rills, but I think it, and the little one, which I'm pretty sure is fabricated, are artificially powered. The orbits are too tight. Lots of comings and goings between them."

"What?"

"Lots of movement. I don't have enough resolution to figure out what it is, but there're shadows and reflections. Stirred up dust, too."

Otto considered that. "What do you think it is?"

"Couldn't tell you. That's why I want to go up in that thing." He gestured again, out toward the rocket. "To see."

"And the stars?"

Marc *whewed* his bafflement. "Another reason to go out there. None of my physics work. Oh, I mean, they work, but there seems to be another set functioning."

"Are we moving?"

"I don't know."

"Is the Universe moving?"

"I don't know. But we intend to find out," and he folded his arms, determined.

"So." Karl stood then, his discussion with Gus over, and regarded Otto. "Let's do this right. I'm Karl Voorsen." He extended a hand. "In charge of structural repair, both inside and out."

"Otto Boteman." They shook.

"Gustavo Guerricaechevarria," Gloomy Gus said and they exchanged handshakes, too.

"That's a mouthful," Otto commented, "Sounds Spanish." He suddenly flashed on Ferdinand. "You wouldn't, by chance, be from Argentina?"

"No," Gus said, "Pamplona. Where's Argentina?"

"South America."

"South America?"

"One of those lands in the New World I told you about," Marc said to Gus, who replied, "Got it."

"He's a Basque from the tenth century," Marc explained to Otto.

"Have you worked with metal?" Karl, with some impatience, interrupted, looking straight at Otto.

Otto shook his head. "Not really. I can bend gutters into the right place but if you mean welding, shaping, things like that, then no."

"*Hmm*," Karl was obviously disappointed. "How 'bout framing?"

"Like I said, nothing technical. I'm very unhandy. I helped my Dad build small sheds and things, did wall framings, stuff like that."

"Carpentry." More disappointment. "I'm afraid we're using very little wood. Wiring?"

"Outlets, receptacles, things like that."

Karl raised eyebrows at Marc. "House wiring," Marc explained.

"Wait a minute." Otto held up a hand. "You don't know what house wiring is? Karl, where you from?"

"Falkenberg. I was a blacksmith." Karl paused. "I know metals."

"But not house wiring. Okay. *When* are you from?"

"Eighteen sixties, eighteen seventies."

Otto regarded him quietly, then turned to Gus. "And you're a tenth-century Basque, a weaver of some kind, I take it?"

Gus gave him a thumbs-up, speaking to the antiquity of the gesture.

Otto turned to Marc, "You've got to be kidding."

"*Ha!*" Marc was thoroughly amused. "Then I guess you don't want to hear about our fourteenth-century Chinese court scribe, our nineteenth-century Maori warrior, twelfth-century geisha, although she's really hot, and the Wehrmacht supply sergeant, *hmm*?"

Otto was a bit put-out. "That's the crew?"

"Some of it."

"But," Otto spluttered, "I mean, where's the real astronauts? The Space Shuttle Columbia guys, for instance."

"They haven't shown up."

"Well, what about more modern people? People who get this?"

"You and me." Marc pointed between them. "We're it. At least, so far. Amelia and the sergeant, if you want to count outliers."

Otto was speechless. Karl and Gus stood quietly, arms folded, regarding him. "Do you wish to change your mind?" Karl asked gently.

Did he? Otto considered. A rocket under construction by a Russian science-fiction theorist who never actually went up in one, captained by a woman who splashed her airplane somewhere in the Pacific, and relying on a Swedish blacksmith and a *Song of*

Roland cotton weaver for its maintenance.

Absolutely, completely, insane.

"No. Sounds like fun. Count me in." Otto said.

Karl smiled. "All right. But we still have to find a use for you. Everyone has to contribute something, or they can't go. So, what can you do?"

"Wait. I thought you wanted me to do outside repair, which involves spacewalking, which I am definitely up for."

Karl waved that down. "I don't mean ship tasks. We've already assigned you to that one. What do you bring to the mission?"

Not sure what Karl meant, but let's take a stab at it. "An overwhelming desire to find God." He said it simply.

They were all silent for a long moment. "That's what brought you here," Marc said, breaking it. "That's why we're all here." He gestured at Karl. "He's a Swedenborgian intent on proving the Trinity. Gus there," Marc waved at the Basque "wants to resolve issues raised by the Andalusians. Me?" The astronomer shook his head. "I'm just mostly stunned."

"A skill set." Karl explained, "Something you bring, an important capability. Like, for instance, pathfinding. Can you fix our place in the stars? Can you find the way back?" They looked at him expectantly.

Otto eyed Marc. "I thought that was your job."

"Not completely," he said, "I deal with motion. The Hubble constant was my thing. Fittingly, I'm going to work out drift and tidal movement. We need a navigator to apply it. I can't do both."

"Why not?"

Marc glanced askance. "That you have to ask, in this weird Universe with its weird physics, tells me you're definitely not a navigator."

"So, what can you do?" Karl repeated.

They looked at him again, waiting. Otto thought hard. Good question. He knew nothing of star fields or Hubble constants or forging a track through endless space, fuels or hydraulics or quantum mechanics or any other kind of discipline that made a rocket launch successful. If the ship were to leak, best he could do is slap on duct tape, which meant they'd all get sucked into space. Would they then drift, cold and hungry, for eternity? And wouldn't that be his fault, because he bumped some MacGyver who could fashion a patch out of chewing gum and a paper clip?

The silence grew, long and uncomfortable. Otto reviewed his internal résumé several thousand times more but couldn't find anything. Anything at all.

Which meant he brought nothing to the mission. Nothing.

Which meant he couldn't go.

Otto swayed, something within him falling hard. He wanted to collapse straight to the floor, weeping, but that would be undignified. "I'm afraid," he said softly, "that I'm wasting your time."

He saw deep disappointment in their eyes. The thing that fell earlier hit bottom and detonated. Waves of despair washed through him ... despair in Heaven, how's that possible?

Easy. When your dream of seeing God is crushed.

He turned, a thousand pounds heavier, and took a cumbersome step toward the door.

"Wait a minute," Marc said, pulling Otto around so they were all facing each other again. "This man," Marc patted Otto's shoulder, "brings a unique talent we desperately need."

Karl and Gus raised eyebrows, as did Otto. He did? Really? "What are you taking about?" he asked.

"Bear with me," the astronomer said, "You were a detective, right?"

"A bit more glorified than that."

"Okay, fine, you still analyzed bits of disparate information and came up with a conclusion, right?"

"Well, yeah."

"Okay!" Marc turned to Karl and Gus. "We're going in blind. Despite the telescopes and measurements, we have no idea what's waiting for us. Could be nothing, could be one of the most boring trips in history. But I'll bet not. I'll bet we'll encounter stuff and events that no human has ever encountered before, a lot of it dangerous and baffling and downright scary. We won't even know how dangerous until it's too late. Unless we've got someone who spent his life looking for dangerous and baffling and scary things." Marc dramatically flapped hands at Otto. "*Ta da!*"

Karl and Gus exchanged looks and then turned on Otto,

expectant. "But," Otto said to Marc, "you're the scientist."

"Right."

"So unbaffling things, isn't that your bailiwick?"

Marc nodded. "Sure. With hard data, I'm the master. But with intuitive stuff, flotsam and jetsam and offhand remarks, I'm clueless."

"Do you expect to run into a lot of offhand remarks out there?"

"Best to be prepared for any eventuality."

Otto gave him the fisheye, but Karl stroked a thoughtful chin. "Marc's right. Future people think differently, and you might see something we don't. Okay, then, you're back on." He extended a hand toward Otto. "Welcome aboard. Again."

The thing that fell came roaring back, lifting Otto's heart and he smiled, downright glowed, actually. "Thank you!" he grasped Karl's, then Gus's, then Marc's outstretched hands. They all started laughing.

"All right, all right!" Amelia's voice cut from behind, "Enough dilly-dallying."

They turned. She stood frowning and slapping the clipboard impatiently on her hip. "Time's wasting." She pointed the clipboard at Otto.

Man, that clipboard was like a weapon.

"We need you trained up as soon as possible, in case the last one shows up."

Otto looked at Marc. "Last one?"

Karl fielded it. "The last crewman. We are taking thirty. You're number twenty-nine. When the last one shows up, we go."

Uh, what? "You mean, the ship is ready?"

"Has been for years," Amelia answered.

"And we're only waiting for the last crewman?"

"Like we've been waiting for you," Gus said.

Otto reeled with the implications. In the next five minutes, some hotshot test pilot comes diddlybopping through the door shouting "Let's go!" and they do. He spun toward the door, expectant. "So who is it?"

"Who's who?" Amelia asked.

"The last crewman," Otto said impatiently, straining at the

entrance. Doesn't have to be a hotshot test pilot. Could be a Paleolithic sheepherder, for all he cared. Just be someone. Now.

They all shrugged at each other. "We don't know," Karl said. "When he, or she, gets here, then we'll know."

"How long'll that be?"

"Who knows?" Marc said, "You sure took your sweet time getting here."

"And even more time getting ready." Amelia slapped the weaponized clipboard impatiently again. "So, buck private, grab your gear and let's get going."

Uh-oh. "About that ..."

Amelia regarded him. "You do have gear, don't you?"

"Well, no."

Amelia made an exasperated sound and the others exchanged concerned looks. "Didn't Box tell you what you needed?"

"He did, but ..." Otto felt suddenly embarrassed. "Well, it looks like I ran out of credits."

You could have heard a pin drop. They all stared at him, aghast. "Not again," Gus said.

The sudden mood change was alarming. Otto took a wary step back and aimed at Gus. "What does that mean?"

Amelia glared at him. Yep, definite mood change. "A couple of others showed up with the same story and had to leave."

"But I can earn it."

"Not here you can't." Marc, grieved, threw a helpless palm. "You can only bring it."

"Why's that?"

"We don't know."

Amelia's expression ran from disgust to sorrow to anger. She turned on her heel and stormed out the other side, leaving Otto somewhat astonished. A hand fell on his elbow. "You'll have to go," Karl said.

"What?"

"You have to go." He said it more firmly and the pressure on his elbow brooked no argument and Otto was down the aisle as some returning crewmen, including a petite Japanese girl, stepped out of the way. Marc was right, she was hot.

Karl, with Marc trailing, guided Otto down the front stairs and then released him in the yard. Without a word and without looking back, he walked back inside.

Marc remained on the landing. "I'm sorry," he said.

"But ..." Otto was perplexed, "what do I do?"

"You have to go back," Marc said.

"But Pashtun doesn't return for another week."

"That's true, but you still have to go back," Marc said. He turned, hesitated, then looked at Otto. "If the last two show up while you're fixing this ..." and he waggled a hand, then went inside and closed the door.

Otto waited by the door as the shadows lengthened and the first volatile stars pitched over the horizon, the self-propelled moons revving behind them. No one came out. No one came by.

Sighing, he turned and scrutinized the area, picking out the main road, white and gold in the moonlights, between the other buildings. He walked over to it, looking in both directions, but nothing moved. In the distance was the fence. He headed that way.

Chapter XV

Sebastian Cabot Was The Valet

"Screw this."

Otto sat down on a big, flat rock conveniently placed by the side of the road. He'd walked about five or six miles or five or six hours – who knew – the roaming stars outpacing him. Everything was silver and gold, the self-propelled moons high and shining. He glared at them.

"This is CRAP!" he roared, the last word flinging back at him from an escarpment maybe a mile on the opposite side. "CRAP!" he roared again, with more agreement from the rocks. "Bullcrap," he whispered to the road. No reply this time, but he sensed commiseration.

What in the blue blazing hell IS this? Otto suddenly flashed on a classic *Twilight Zone* episode where a petty crook was shot to death and woke up in a gangster's paradise of casinos and tracks and nightclubs. The crook's horse always came in first, every slot pull was a jackpot, and beautiful women hung on his neck. After a while, the crook was bored stiff and moaned he was better off in "the Other Place" – euphemistic early 60s TV, when censors ruled. "This IS the Other Place!" was the payoff, his valet's evil laugh closing the show. Otto heard it now, in Latchemondy's voice.

The Other Place.

No flames and dancing devils, not even Latchemondy's pit of endless despair, but a hell, tailor-made; in Otto's case, everything just out of reach, never quite able to pull things off. Tantalus. He'd missed a scholarship to Dartmouth by a few points on the SAT, missed a promotion because a rival had gone to Dartmouth, his pay raises were lower than expected, and the cases he cracked went on the boss's résumé, not his.

"I could have given up, you know," he told the escarpment. Could have. Accept he was second best, an also-ran, adjust expectations accordingly. But then, how do you quell the constant urge for better, the conviction you *were* better than the yahoos who climbed ladders solely on a wondrous ability to suck up? So he never quit and, well, never made it. What was that old Despair Inc. poster? "Failure – When Your Best Just Isn't Good Enough."

And now, this.

Otto fumbled with his thumbs. He could see it now: God a tad out of reach, forever. He'd catch a glimpse of Him off in some distance and head that way, barking his shins on various outcroppings, until the Brooding Old Man he swore was a couple of miles off turned out to be rock face. But then, swish of Divine Beard on a cloudy horizon and off again, an eternal search to nowhere, like that Ray Bradbury story where the guy went from world to world looking for Jesus, always missing Him by a few seconds.

An eternity of 'day late, dollar short'.

He looked back toward the rocket, a little bright spot on the plain. He wondered why they illuminated it. Not like there was anyone out here but us rejects to admire the view, fellas. Round-the-clock maintenance, he figured, while waiting for the last crewman. The last *real* crewman, Otto, ole boy, not you. We had a big Divine Belly Laugh leading you out here and kicked your legs out from under you and, boy, did you tumble! Ha ha! Shoulda seen your face! If you want, sit a while, wait for the rocket to go. When it does, you'll know that you have, once again, been bested.

The thumb thing got boring so he simply watched the rocket. Any second, any second … Stars whipped past his line of sight from time to time, but he ignored them. Marc was going to have a blast out there. What *was* a Hubble constant, anyway? Maybe if he'd actually become an astronomer, he'd know.

"You remember that dream, God?" Otto asked the escarpment. He supposed every halfway intelligent kid dreamed it at some point but realized, in enough time, that they're only halfway intelligent and couldn't grasp enough physics to figure out Earth's orbit, much less something like the Hubble constant. So, give up and move on to running the family store or fixing cars or putting up drywall, normal stuff. Not him. Kept that stupid 60x telescope he got for his thirteenth birthday well into his twenties, outside at night, straining through bad optics at moon craters.

"And what was I looking for?" he asked again, loud enough that the words came back. He didn't wait for an answer because he wouldn't get one. "You," he whispered. He'd always been looking for God, always sure the next time he placed his eye against that crappy eyepiece, he'd see another Eye looking back.

Quest denied.

All right.

Otto levered off the rock and sat down on the sand. He peered at the two moons and wondered about the dust stirrings Marc described. Add that, now, to the long list of things he'd never know, like the origin of it all, the purpose of life, the purpose of *his* life. Did you meet people randomly, or was it all ordained? Was there more than a glib churchman's response to the question of suffering? Did Otto leave a mark other than some fraction of a population stat, idly studied by some demographer twenty years from now?

Not for you to know, bud.

Otto fixed a spot next to the golden moon and anchored his gaze. Maybe if he held this reference point long enough, he'd pick up a pattern among the stars, a la one of those 3D photos in a mall window, random bits suddenly falling into place and *lo*! A dinosaur, a flying saucer, so, stay on it, stay focused …

Something prodded his arm.

"*Hmph*?" It was a coming-awake sound and Otto realized *he* was coming awake, which meant he fell asleep, which was rather disconcerting. He'd grown used to sleep as a recreational activity, something done by choice, so actually drifting off didn't seem right. Prodded awake also didn't seem right. As he gained consciousness, a lot more didn't seem right.

For instance, the spear point against his shoulder.

Otto looked at it. Thin, swept-back head, very sharp tip, ditto for the edges, bound to a long staff by multicolored leather straps and feathers. Nice. And painful. Easing back to relieve the pressure, he followed the long shaft back to its owner, silhouetted by the exceedingly bright sun almost directly overhead.

"Hi," the owner said.

Otto blinked hard for more detail. Beard and moustache, furry hat with a hard shell on top that came to a shellacked point, ear flaps, big hairy overcoat with lots of feathers, astride a leather-encased horse with more feathers tufted in its mane. Three or four other similarly dressed guys on similarly dressed horses flanked him.

"Hi," Otto said. "Can you stop poking me?"

Spear Boy leaned forward conspiratorially. "Play along," he stage-whispered.

"Huh?"

"Just play along." He winked encouragement and leaned back in his saddle. "Brothers of the wind!" he suddenly proclaimed to the other horsemen, "The spirits of the plains have been kind to us! They have delivered a spy into our hands!" and he jabbed Otto a bit too hard.

"*Hey*!" Otto knocked the spear point away. "Are you nuts or something?"

The horseman grimaced at Otto and gestured with his head at the other horsemen twice, so obviously trying to get him involved that Otto almost laughed aloud. What the heck was this?

Another spear abruptly pushed, with a lot more enthusiasm than Spear Boy's, into Otto's chest, just above the heart. Not cool.

"My liege," growled the other spearman as Otto's eyes widened, "Shall I run him through?"

"No, no!" the first guy said as he desperately tried to signal Otto. "We shall not kill him here. We shall ..." and he looked around wildly, "... *uh*, take him back to camp! Yes! We shall take him back and torture him for our amusement!"

Whoops of joy greeted this and spears pinned Otto to the

ground as two or three of the horsemen jumped down and trussed him with long leather cords. Otto struggled but the spears held him. The kidnappers yanked him to his feet, the first guy's horse pulling back on the cords, and Otto fell forward, against the saddle.

"You trying to get killed?" Spear Boy whispered fiercely as he bent down and made a pretense of cuffing Otto about the head.

"Can you actually get killed here?" Otto whispered back, just as fiercely.

"I dunno," Spear Boy said, "Wanna find out? Then play along!" and he spurred the horse, yanking Otto off his feet and dragging him behind.

Not cool. Not cool at all.

Chapter XVI

Denizens Of The Plains

In short shrift, Otto discovered that some Earth physics still applied here, such as the rules governing what happens to a body pulled through rock, scrub, and sand by an overeager horse. Very much akin to a 300-pound Russian masseuse going over him with a Brillo pad. Hurt. Man, it hurt. As did the earlier spear point. Pain in Heaven?

More evidence of the Other Place.

Or, maybe, when you blasphemed, doubted, called God out, certain protections were removed, like, say, a Pain Barrier that shielded against razor cuts or stubbed toes or being dragged through the desert by a nutcase on a horse.

Hmm. What an interesting idea. Needed ruminatin' at Grendel's, stoked with twelfth-century mead while Claudia flashed a bit too much cleavage. Certainly not here.

Otto grabbed the cord and hauled back on it, acquiring his feet and settling into a shambling run. The other nutcases took that as invitation to ride up and trip him with spears, hooting and whooping as he fell into a cactus patch. He fought his way back up, only to suffer through several repeats; he was figuring out how to loop the cord in such a way it would catch one of these idiot's horses and send *them* flying into a cactus patch – see how you like it – when his host suddenly accelerated and pulled Otto off his feet and over a ridge top. Naturally, he landed dead on his stomach, dead on top of the ridge.

Whoof!

All the air drove out of his body. Then, it was a matter of grimly hanging on as Spear Boy, yelling insanely, whipped the horse to a frenzy, whipping Otto from side to side in the process, as they descended to a huge encampment of round tents and horse corrals. A mob surged out to meet them, also yelling insanely.

Uh-oh.

The horse stood on its heels, bouncing him off a rock, and about three thousand screaming little kids, dressed in miniature fashion of the horse idiots, surrounded Otto, every single one of them carrying large sticks. They were joined by about four thousand similarly armed women, wearing costumes ranging from hijabs to Xena the Warrior Princess. All of them surged forward to enthusiastically pound Otto deep into the sand. Quite annoying.

A hand reached down through the crowd and yanked him to his feet. "All right! All right!" Spear Boy waved viciously at the crowd while dangling Otto by his collar. "We'll do this again later! Get out of my way!" and he pushed through the crowd, using Otto as a battering ram. The crowd fell back, but not without some well-aimed hits at Otto's shins.

By this time, Otto was in a rather bad mood. "I am going to kick your ass," he hissed, spitting blood at Spear Boy.

"That's the least of my worries," Spear hissed back, avoiding the spray. "I gotta figure out how to get you out of this."

"Get me out of this?" Otto whirled, aiming a fist at Spear's face, "You got me into this!"

"I know, I know." Spear looked contrite as he dodged, "But this won't help. Let's get past it and seek a solution."

"I'll solution you!" and Otto whacked him with a good haymaker.

"Dammit." Spear Boy backhanded Otto, who fell down, his legs still shaky from the wooden stick tattooing he'd just received. "Would you listen to me?" Spear stood over Otto, rubbing his jaw. "They want to torture you!"

"And what do you call that?" Otto jerked a hand viciously at the crowd, which had followed at a distance, throwing rocks at him.

"That's nothing." Spear blocked a badly thrown rock. "These people are creative. You don't want to find out. Would you just come along? Please?" and he held out a hand.

"I'm still going to kick your ass," Otto said as he took the hand and pretended Spear had gotten him rudely under control.

"Yeah-yeah. Just come along," and he pushed Otto, somewhat gently, toward one of the round tents.

There, three black guys dressed in turbans and harem pants and little else trussed Otto to a center pole and roundly kicked him to a sitting position. The three stepped back, grinned at him, and then high-fived each other. Hilarious in other circumstances. Otto wasn't laughing. He eyed the big scimitars hanging on their backs and giant gold earrings pegged through their earlobes. "What are you, refugees from a Bob Hope Road movie?"

The three burst into cheerful laughter as Spear Boy went, "All right, all right," and waved them outside. "I will now interrogate the prisoner!" he announced through the tent flap to loud cheers as he closed and tied it down. He took off his pointy helmet and sat on the ground opposite Otto. "Name's Kenny," he said, offering a handshake.

"Kenny, is it?" Otto glared at him. "Well, Kenny, I'm still going to kick your ass. And, if you'll note, my hands are tied."

"Oh, right, sorry," and he withdrew. "And sorry about all this. But you were trespassing."

"I didn't see any signs."

"There are no signs in the desert."

"I was on the road. You know, right of way?"

"Technically, you weren't. You were off the road."

"We make such fine distinctions here, do we, Kenny?"

"Yep." The barbarian fished around inside a horsehair bag until he pulled out a pipe. "There are rights and traditions, you know. No one leaves the road without our consent." He lit the pipe with a coal from the fire, offering it to Otto, who glowered his response. "You sure? It's a mild mix, an aromatic, Scottish with a rum casing."

"Wait. What?" Where had he heard that before? His eyes narrowed. "You know Ferdinand?"

"Everyone knows Ferdinand." Kenny sat back, puffed luxuriously then regarded Otto. "So, the question becomes, what to do with you?"

Leave the question of how everyone knows Ferdinand for later. "You're going to let me go."

"Eventually, eventually," Kenny agreed, puffing large clouds of smoke. "But, first, there are forms to be observed."

"Those traditions you referred to earlier?"

"Yes!" Kenny brightened, "Yes, indeed! You catch on quick."

"Kenny, untie me. Now."

"Can't do that." He gestured outside with the pipe. "They're expecting a show."

"What kind of show, Kenny?"

Well, first of all, they're expecting you to be screaming in pain about now. So, would you?"

"Excuse me?"

"Scream. In pain."

Otto blew a raspberry. "I am not going to scream. In pain, in high hilarity, in anything."

Kenny frowned. "Well, that's a problem. They're either going to think I'm not doing a good enough job, or you're one tough customer. Either way, they'll want to see for themselves and they'll come get you. It'll get ugly, then."

"Like it's not now?"

"I watched them skin a guy, salt him, spit him, and roast him over a fire for a few days."

Otto arched eyebrows. "You're kidding."

Kenny's hands went out, a gesture of not kidding. Otto considered. "All right." He let out a sigh of exasperation and then took in a breath, "*Ahhhhh!*"

"Oh, please," Kenny said, "Am I a doctor checking your throat? You're being tortured, okay?"

"How's this? *Aaaahhhhhhhhh!*"

"Pathetic," Kenny shook his head. "You need some incentive," and, with no warning, he flipped a coal from the fire onto Otto's lap.

"What the— *AAAAAAHYUUUUUUUGH!*" Otto screamed as the coal burned through his pants and settled onto his thigh.

Kenny's head bobbed enthusiastically "Now that's a scream!" Apparently, the others thought so, too, because enthusiastic cheering burst out around the tent.

"Get this DAMN thing off my leg, you cretin!" Otto roared.

"Oh, yeah, right!" Kenny hastily smothered the coal with a cloth and shook it back into the fire. "Sorry."

"When I get free, I am going to skin you, salt you, and spit you over a fire, Kenny!" Otto snarled, looking down at his charred leg. "I am going to ... hey, look at that." Otto's tone morphed into wonder as he observed the first degree burn pale, knit together, and heal completely.

Kenny leaned over, "*Hmm.* Pretty quick. You must have special healing powers. Are you Wolverine?" and he giggled.

The pain vanished. Otto was amazed. "Does this always happen?"

"Yep, which made the guy on the spit doubly unfortunate because he kept healing and burning, healing and burning. Torture takes on a rather exquisite character under these circumstances." Kenny looked at Otto curiously. "Didn't you know about the healing?"

"No. I haven't been hurt. Until now, jerkface."

"Oh, well," Kenny picked at his toes. "Consider it a lesson, free of charge. And, now that you know what it feels like, can you go ahead and give out a few more screams while I figure out what to do?"

"Kiss my butt."

Kenny shrugged. "Have it your way," and he reached for another coal.

Otto hastily discharged a series of very loud and, apparently, convincing screams, each met by resounding cheers. Kenny spun one hand encouraging him to go on while digging in the dirt with the other. Suddenly, Kenny's head popped up and he smiled. "Eureka!"

Otto was in mid-breath for another scream. "What?"

"I've got it!" Kenny stood and undid the flap. "Follow my lead," he said and stepped outside.

"I can't follow you while tied up," Otto protested.

"The prisoner has confessed his sins!" Kenny called out and there was an answering roar of approval. "I find him an honorable and brave man! Let us adopt him! What say you?" and there was another, even louder, roar of approval.

"Now wait a minute!" Otto struggled against his bonds.

The three harem guys came in high-fiving each other and Kenny. They grinned at Otto as they untied him and pulled him to his feet. "Wait a damn minute!" Otto said and Kenny gave him a warning look.

The harem guys dragged him through the flap where the joyful five thousand or so screaming women stripped him down to nothing, most of whom were rather too caressing. He watched his nice suit, containing the return ticket, get spirited off.

"I might need that," he protested but no one was listening.

Draped and folded into various odd cloths, the three harem guys hoisted Otto to their shoulders and danced him around the camp with the five thousand women and all the children, and about twenty thousand warriors, in attendance, everyone calling and ululating and singing and waving spears and swords around.

Otto had to conclude it was an exceedingly strange day.

Chapter XVII

True Diversity

"Man, this is pretty good." Otto smacked his lips and threw a well-gnawed rib onto the growing pile in front of the fire.

"Told ya." Kenny belched contentedly and contributed his bone. The three harem guys – Moses, Jakto, and Sam – nodded agreement.

"Camel. Who'da thunk it?" Otto searched around the big platter suspended over the fire for a choice bit.

"Yeah," Moses laughed, "you'd think it'd be greasy." He leaned back into the lap of a particularly lovely barbarian girl, her hair trussed in leathers, gold-capped teeth glinting.

Sam held a thigh piece critically to the firelight. "We should try another sauce."

"Here we go." Jakto rolled his eyes, which made the others laugh.

"No, seriously." Sam waved the thigh, "Something more North Carolina."

"Well." Kenny licked his fingers. "You can always go over to the cooking tents and see what you can come up with. The ladies won't mind." He winked at the barbarian girl, who laughed in agreement.

"No time," Sam said.

"*Hmm?*" Kenny peered over his decimated ear of corn.

"Yeah, been meaning to tell ya." Moses casually stroked the girl's cheek. "We're heading out at the end of the week."

"What?" Kenny's yelp drove the ear onto the fire.

How popcorn got invented, Otto figured.

"Uh-huh." Sam took a long swig from a goatskin and wiped his mouth on his arm. "We're joining up with a pirate crew on the Inland Sea. Some of the girls," he chinned at the barbarian, "are going with us."

Kenny was almost in tears. "But, why?"

"Some of the girls want to be pirates."

"Okay, yeah, but, I mean, why are *you* guys leaving?"

"We want to be pirates, too."

"Pirates?" Otto interrupted.

"Yeah!" Moses was enthusiastic. "Want to come with us?"

Kenny looked so stricken that Otto said, "Well, no, I mean, I just got here." Kenny visibly relaxed and Otto continued, "But, pirates?"

"*Um-hmm.*" Sam dug around the platter.

Otto couldn't grasp it. "What do they do?"

"Oh, the usual. Capture ships, make people walk the plank, bury treasure on islands, you know." Sam pulled out what looked like a drumstick.

"But, who do they attack?"

"Merchants."

"Merchants? Ocean-going, hogshead totin' merchants?"

"*Um-hmm.*" Sam set about an enthusiastic chawing of the drumstick. "There's even a British Navy. Pretty good one, too."

Otto was intrigued. "Who runs that?"

"Some guy named Forester."

"C. S. Forester?"

Moses raised an affirmative finger. "That's him. Know 'im?"

Otto shook his head in admiration. "How 'bout that?"

"So, did I do something wrong?" Kenny asked.

"No, no," Moses assured him, "it's not you. We've been having a great time. But, you know, so much else out there. Besides," Moses indicated his costume, "this is getting a little silly."

Otto grinned at him. "I've been meaning to ask."

Moses and Jakto pointed at Sam. "His idea," they both said.

Sam held up a hand of innocence. "I asked if you guys wanted to try it. That's all." He turned to Otto. "Got the idea from a movie."

"Which one?" Otto asked.

"One of the Bowery Boys. Saw it in St. Louis."

"That where you from?"

"Yep," Sam said, "I was a porter on the railroad in the thirties. A crate fell on me. I came here."

"*Hmm.*" Otto looked at Moses.

"Field slave in Louisiana in the thirties. Different thirties." He winked. "Got sick."

"So you've been here a while."

"Not as long as him." Moses flipped a thumb at Jakto.

"I was a soldier in Axum," Jakto responded. "You probably know it as Ethiopia. Got ambushed by some Egyptians."

Suspicious, Otto dropped an eyelid. "How's that possible?"

"The Egyptians were pretty good."

"No. I mean wasn't that way before Christianity?" Otto's earlier conversation with Pashtun came roaring back. Now, an opportunity to test theories.

"Yeah, by about 800 years." Jakto stretched luxuriously and lay back on his elbows. "Right after Queen Saba's time, in fact. You probably heard of her. She and Solomon were good friends, if you know what I mean," and he nudged Sam suggestively.

"Wait. Solomon? King Solomon of Israel?"

"Same guy."

"Was this Saba the Queen of Sheba?"

"I've heard her called that before, but only here. I think 'Saba' got a little garbled in translation." Jakto settled comfortably.

"How 'bout that." Otto was impressed. "So, you were a Christian."

"Don't think so." Jakto contemplated the rushing stars. "More likely Jewish."

"Well that's ... unusual."

Jakto smiled. "Isn't it?"

Otto stared at him, trying to work out the timelines and theologies and simply couldn't. Need more information. "So, then, how is it you three are running around together?"

"We're pals," Moses said, simply.

"Right. But *how* are you pals? I mean, seems there's gigantic gaps between your individual arrivals and backgrounds. So ...?"

The harem guys exchanged nonchalant looks and all pointed at Kenny. "Ran into him," Moses said.

Puzzled, Otto followed their point. "You mean, Ken brought you guys together?" Ken? Captain White Guy?

Kenny, still aggrieved, busted right through the conversation. "Well, this is all very nice. You're all getting to know each other right before bugging out. That's just perfect."

"Ken," Moses said, "We've had a really good time, but we want to do other things, ya know? I mean, weren't you a Goth or something before you started the Tartars?"

Otto cocked his head. "That's what we are, Tartars?"

Kenny shrugged. "Sort of. More like Mongols, since we have a lot more of them than any real Tartars. Same principle, though."

Otto contemplated that as he licked the last smidgeon of camel sauce from his fingers. "Okay. We're a horde of some kind. I still don't get how y'all found each other. If you don't mind my asking, Ken, how'd you end up here?"

Kenny belched. "I was an accountant in West Kankakee, Illinois, back in the 1970s. Slipped and fell, came here." He looked quite satisfied.

"Can you elaborate?"

"You mean, how'd I end up running the Tartars?" Kenny waved a hand. "You ever been to West Kankakee, IL?"

"Can't say I have."

"Well, then," and he settled back into the rugs, as if that answered everything.

Which it didn't. "Okay," Otto pursued, "I get that. The unexamined life and all. But how did you three ..." and he waved a hand at the Harems.

Sam dismissed the question with an airy, "Just how things worked out," and focused on Ken. "It's not a big deal, Ken. We'll send you some pirate recruits to make up the difference."

"Sixty. Send sixty."

"Sixty?" Jakto eyed him suspiciously. "Why, what are you planning?"

"Well." Kenny played coy for a moment then leaned forward

conspiratorially. "I was thinking about going after the train."

"The train?" Jakto was incredulous. "You can't do that!"

"Why not?"

"Since when did Tartars ever go after trains?"

Kenny considered then frowned. "Okay, the rocket, then."

"What?" Otto sat up. "The rocket they're building over there?" and he pointed over the desert.

"More over there," Kenny corrected his direction. "And, yeah."

Otto shook his head vigorously. "No. No way."

"Why not?"

"Same reason as the train. Besides." Otto raised a hand. "They need to finish their mission."

"Which is?"

"Looking for God," Otto said it reverently.

They all stared at him for about two seconds, then the group burst into merry, high-pitched laughter, kicking in the air and slapping each other's arms.

"What?" Otto asked, but all that did was fuel more laughter until the harem guys were totally convulsed while their women, laughing just as hard, stood over them and tried to pull them up.

"Looking for God." Kenny wiped his eyes and held his sides. "Oh, that's too much, too much."

"What's so funny about that?" Otto was irritated.

"What a complete waste of time." Sam shook his head, patting the hand of the barbarian girl.

"Why is it a waste of time?"

"Simple." Jakto swept a hand over the landscape. "You don't have to look much further than this."

Otto followed his arc and saw the velocity stars and the two odd moons and heard a Desert Song and felt the beauty and yes, this could only be God.

So what? "They still need to go," he said.

The merriment abruptly subsided and all regarded him, silent; a mistral caressed his cheek and something eternal moved too far on the horizon and he looked in the direction Kenny had marked but could not see the silver needle.

"So that's what you were doing out there," Kenny said.

"Yeah." Otto saw no need to elaborate.

The others exchanged glances. "Okay," Kenny conceded, "no rocket. No train, either. We'll go after the Vikings."

"Now you're talking!" Moses jumped up and kissed a girl wrapped in a burqa, getting a good-natured slap in return.

Jakto snapped his fingers. "Why, I believe we could stay for that."

"Vikings?" Otto asked.

Chapter XVIII

The All-Encompassing Grace Of God

Yep, Vikings. A walled village of them, high on a sweeping fjord with a glacier, an actual glacier, tumbling down the opposite bank.

Otto pulled up, amazed. "Wow," he said. His horse nickered to get going but Otto had to stare. One minute, racing across sand dunes under ochre skies underscoring the hypnotic blue always threatening capture, then crest a bluff and, presto, Norway. Otto had never been to Norway but this was every postcard or travel documentary he'd ever seen about it: God-crafted rock rising in always-higher layers until frozen stone draped half the horizon, while sapphire waters bound the slope and cliff side. Just wow.

Jakto rode up next to him. "Coming?"

"This is magnificent," Otto said.

"Yeah." Jakto patted his horse, which smiled. "We like coming here. Better get moving, though, or you'll miss the action." He rode off.

Otto adjusted lance and shield, regarding his horse with ill-disguised suspicion. It was quite the practical joker, earlier undoing the saddle while Otto was occupied with the equipment. He'd mounted and immediately slid off, Chaplinesque. The horse considered that hilarious, as did everyone else. The horse then timed its movements so that Otto threw the saddle into empty air instead of on its back. Once that joke had played out, the horse went for low tree branches – quite a feat in the desert – leaving Otto hanging a few times while it galloped merrily away. Jerk.

"So, Flicka, what's on your mind now?" he asked.

The horse looked at him with an innocent expression but Otto didn't buy it. "Just don't throw me, all right? That hurts."

The horse nodded and looked expectantly down the hill where the rest of the Tartars, or Mongols or whatever, rode around the village whooping and gesturing with swords and lances. Otto spurred and the horse leaped into the air, almost throwing him, but he hung on and even made a respectable pass of the lance at one of the wall's defenders. Flicka brought him into a scrum a little farther down, ending up next to Sam, who grinned. "Isn't this great?" he yelled.

Otto had to admit it was exhilarating. He aimed the lance at a small, dark Viking standing on top of a rampart, knocking him off. "Cool," he said to Flicka, who whinnied agreement.

Whack! Otto's right side collapsed, on fire, and all his air blew out. He looked down at an arrow buried deep in his ribs. "*Bwa?*" was all he could manage and he suddenly felt sick and dizzy.

"I got it," Moses rode up, grabbed the arrow, and yanked it out. Otto screamed. "You'll be all right in a minute," Moses said and spun off, waving the arrow triumphantly over his head.

Flicka pulled him out of the horde, ears set in disappointment. Otto couldn't breathe, a roaring in his ears, the world going black. He was dying. Again. He wondered if he'd wake up face down on those same blasted cobblestones.

Oh, man, please, no Frank or Latchemondy reruns.

Maybe he'd pass to another Afterlife. Was God in that one? Or, maybe he'd go back home, reincarnated as some egg farmer on the Cape of Good Hope. That'd be different. But, after a moment, clear light came back and the pain in his ribs subsided.

Otto sat up straight and pulled up the tunic and watched the wound close, just like the coal on his leg. Man! A place of no more pain, huh, Lord? Or, more accurately, a place of great and severe pain that's over in about a minute. "Not sure this is an improvement," he muttered. Flicka pushed at him so he rejoined the attack.

It went on for about another fifteen minutes and Otto caught a rock upside the helmet but all that did was make him silly for about ten seconds and Flicka didn't even leave the pack. Things calmed down after a bit and Kenny and the Viking chief met in front of the gate and negotiated. They decided the Tartars failed in their attempt to breach the walls but the chief died heroically on the rampart, leaving the village grieved and leaderless. The chief would stay with the Tartars for a week then come back for a grand Viking funeral that everyone said would be a hoot. Naturally, while all this was decided, Flicka grabbed Otto's helmet from behind and flung it across the crowd. "Very funny," he groused and stalked through the laughing Tartars until he found it.

The Viking chief, giving everyone attitude, mounted a small, tough-looking pony and they all rode off with the chief in the middle, casually guarded. He looked like an extra in every Viking movie ever made: tall, white-blond shoulder-length hair, a scar across one cheek, brutally handsome and proud, staring at the Mongols, or Tartars, whatever, with a haughty air.

"Wow," Otto said.

"Yeah," Moses agreed, "he's something. A bit touchy, though."

Otto rode Flicka up to the Viking. "Excuse me," he said.

The Viking glanced at him sideways and the sneer deepened. He said nothing.

"I don't mean to trouble you," Otto kept his tone apologetic, "but are you a real Viking?"

The Viking turned his head and looked full at Otto, the challenge and offense deep in his eyes. Otto pulled up short. "Okay that answers that question," he said to no one in particular then spurred to catch up. "I didn't mean to offend, I'm just curious who you are."

The Viking said nothing for several moments and Otto figured he'd worn out the little welcome offered when the Viking grunted, "Erick."

"Not Erick the Red." Otto couldn't believe he'd be that lucky.

"No, I am not that one," Erick spat. "I am not a murderer."

"Huh?"

Erick glared at him. "You ask after the Red so you must know him. He was a banished man. He killed wrongly." Erick made a strange sign with his fingers.

"Sorry," Otto said, "I don't know him, not at all. I know *of* him, that he discovered Greenland. And his son discovered America."

Erick scorned. "The Red One did not mark Greenland. Gunnbjörn Ulf-Krakuson did. And Bjarni Herjolfsson found Vinland, not Leif. Leif tried to make a go of it there but was unsuccessful. He could not handle the *skraelings*."

"Not a big admirer of that family, are you?"

"No." Erick spat again, apparently a Viking trait. "They were contentious and liars. They were not honorable."

"*Hmm.*" Otto considered. "That's funny. They come down in history as pretty noble, you know, intrepid explorers and all that."

"History is wrong," and Erick turned back.

Otto had been dismissed, he knew, but curiosity still got the better of him. "So how do you know them?"

"I know of them. I did not know them. I did not wish to."

"So how did you know of them?"

"As anyone knows of anything. Do you challenge my word?" and there was flame in the Viking's eyes.

Definitely touchy, Otto decided. "Sorry," he said, hastily, "It's just I'm very curious about past events and I wondered if you were a contemporary."

Erick stared at him for a moment. "Recorder," he said with a modicum of reverence. Must be a respectable Viking occupation. "Yes, we were contemporaries, although I lived in Black Pool. I died at Clontarf."

Otto figured 'Black Pool' was a translation of some Viking word, but the other one ... "Clontarf?"

Erick eyed him suspiciously. "I thought you a recorder."

"I'm not a very good one." Probably the best explanation.

It was. Erick canted an "okay then" head. "The battle that drove us from Dyflin. I drowned in the surf. My armour was too heavy."

Dyflin? Skip it. "What year was that?"

"Year?" Erick's brows furrowed. "The year of Clontarf."

Great. Erick probably used a Viking calendar, which was

moon cycles or wolf howls or something. "Do you know what year it was on the Christian calendar?"

"Christian," Erick sneered, "that is weakness."

Otto blinked. "You mean, you're not a Christian?"

"Do I look like a woman?"

Otto was perplexed. "Then how did you get here?"

Erick looked at him with real distress in his eyes. "I do not know. I expected to stand in halls where swords clashed shields and heroes raised ale horns in a continuous shout to All Father. Feast with sires and brothers, my wife in the Vigrio and we would grapple in love. This ..." he swept a giant arm and shook his head.

"Yeah." Otto made a wry face. "It's not exactly how I pictured it, either. But, you gotta admit, it's pretty nice."

"It has its charms," Erick agreed, "but I know no one here. And Odin evades."

"Odin? You still believe in Odin?"

Erick whirled on him. "Do you not, blasphemer?"

Startled, Otto backed Flicka away from the Norseman's sudden fury. The guard pressed a little closer, muttering, but Otto waved them back.

"No," Otto answered firmly, "I don't. And given the evidence," he mimicked Erick's hand sweep, "I'm surprised you still do."

Erick's face worked into a thunderstorm and Otto figured one more smartass comment and he'd be in the middle of a Viking berserker attack, when the chief's brow cleared. He looked downright sorrowful. "That Odin turns his face away does not mean he is not here."

Now, that was interesting. Otto spurred closer. "You're looking for God, aren't you?"

"We are all looking for God."

"Do you know about the ship?"

Erick looked at him blankly. "The rocket ship," Otto explained, "the one to look for God."

"I know of it," Erick said shortly and turned away with a dismissive air. Otto rode next to him for a moment more, hoping to re-engage, but Erick remained stone. Otto faded back to Moses.

"Told ya," Moses chuckled.

"You know," Otto patted Flicka's head and the horse put an ear back in pleasure, "I don't get it. The guy's an obvious pagan, yet, here he is."

"Grace of God," Moses shrugged.

"What, God has a quota for pagans?"

"No, dummy." Moses gestured at Erick, "He obviously knows what Christianity is."

"Yeah, but he, just as obviously, rejected it."

"Maybe not when he first heard it. For about, oh, what, two seconds, he actually believed it."

There it was again. Pashtun had commented on the ridiculous ease of salvation. But, c'mon, nothing's that easy.

Is it?

"Dunno, Mose. Something doesn't seem right about that. Just a few seconds of believing in Christ gets you a ticket in?"

"Sure. You think God is petty?"

Well, no. Which could mean that interesting events and activities Earthside would not, as he'd supposed, affect one's chance for Heaven. "Wish I had known that," he rued, "I'da had a lot more fun."

Moses pointed at the Viking. "Does he look like he's having fun?"

Otto scrutinized Erick. Disdainful, with an aloofness easily mistaken as superiority. But there was another air about him, something Erick couldn't hide.

Loss.

"No," Otto said, "I suppose he isn't."

Chapter XIX

God And His Inscrutable Purposes

It was a good funeral: mournful Viking dirges, torchlight parades, and Erick set adrift in a grave-ship that was quickly ablaze under a cascade of fire arrows. Otto was fairly certain Vikings buried their royalty, dragon boat and all, so this wasn't authentic but, really, who knows? Kenny had suggested it and Erick didn't object, so it was either legit and Otto was ill-informed, or Erick was playing along with Kenny's muse. And willing to bleed for art, because he lay stoic while the flames took him. Had to hurt, but Erick didn't even blink. When there was nothing but ash on the water, he emerged on shore naked, magnificent. Two of the Mongol women immediately changed allegiances and went with him to his longhouse, followed by cheering retainers. Maybe that's why no burial inside of a dragon ship.

They stayed for a couple of days, feasting and memorializing the slain, and unslain, Erick. Otto remained apart, watching more than anything. A particularly fetching Viking woman tried to interest him, but he wasn't feeling communal.

"What's wrong with you?" Jakto asked as the woman violently shook her hip-length bright-blonde mane and stalked off, irritated.

"I don't know," Otto muttered, stirring embers.

"You need a good raid," Kenny said, slapping Otto's knee. Ensconced on a portable throne, he looked regal in a purple robe and gold chain, part of his tribute from Magyar peasants living next to one of the mountains.

"We just had one," Otto pointed out, gesturing with his chin at the still partying Viking settlement, clearly visible past the rampart.

"Can always stand another," Kenny said.

"I know what's wrong," Tabitha, a seventeenth-century French cheese girl who had died of the plague, said. Dressed in full Mongol leathers, replete with scimitar, she lounged next to Sam, oiling a dagger. "You're in love with someone else."

That brought a hoot of laughter from everyone. Otto shook his head, annoyed. "I am not."

"Yes, you are." Tabitha tested the dagger's sharpness on her thumb. "I know it when I see it."

Otto regarded her. "Really? How's that?"

She sat back smugly. "I was in love about 175 times before I died. And about 175 times since." She stroked Sam's cheek affectionately, which brought another round of hoots. Sam grinned. "She has a point," he said.

"Lust isn't the same as love," Otto said.

"Oh, how catty." Tabitha grinned at him good-naturedly. "Which seems to be the way of men from your century."

Otto's face flamed. "The statement stands."

"Then consider," Tabitha snuggled into Sam, "that one is an element of the other."

An admiring round of "*wooooo!*" came from the group. Otto glowered at her. "That's pretty insightful, Tabitha. Did you get that during the first 175 or the next?"

She clucked. "As I said, catty. And here, you learn a lot of truths. As you would, if you'd open your eyes."

"My eyes are open."

"But your brain isn't."

"All right, all right." Kenny held up a placating hand, "We're getting a bit confrontational."

He was right because Otto was at that moment measuring the French tart's mettle and wondering if he could take her. Probably not. "Sorry," Otto said.

She canted a dismissive shoulder. "It's okay. Love will do that to you."

"I'm not in love."

"So, who is it?" Jakto asked.

"I told you, I'm not in love."

"Right. Who is it?"

Otto waved an exasperated hand. "Okay! Since you guys insist, my wife."

That was met with loud and sustained catcalls and laughter. Otto took them in, surprised. "What? I love my wife."

"Too much." Moses wiped his eyes. "You're too much. That's not what we're talking about."

"Huh?" Otto was confused. "I love my wife! C'mon! What's the deal?"

"We all love our Life families, to some degree." Tabitha peeled a grape. "But that's Earth Love."

"Yeah-yeah, I've had this conversation." Otto flashed back to Ian.

"So then you know it doesn't work like that here."

"But I'm still wondering why not."

"Well, for one thing, there's a very good chance," Tabitha popped the grape in Sam's expectant mouth, "almost a certainty, that you'll never see your wife here. Ever."

"Thank God," Kenny blessed himself, spearing a bit of meat from the fire. Everyone laughed appreciatively.

"Okay, good for Kenny, but I'm having a hard time with that," Otto said. "It's not right. The Bible says we gather with our loved ones here."

"The scrolls said we will cross the sacred Western mountain and meet in Amenti." Jakto took a swig from a jar.

"Amenti?"

"It's an Egyptian thing. You wouldn't understand."

"Okay," Otto said, "so you've got the same concept. I'm betting we all do. That all of us, the entire human race, come together at some point."

"Sure," Moses said, "the Great Jubilee."

"The gathering at the river," Sam added.

"A toast!" Kenny suddenly shouted as he stood and raised a mug. "May the day of gathering never come!"

"Here, here!" and the others threw back the potent mare's-milk beer some entrepreneurial Mongols were selling from a cart over by the village. Except Otto.

"But ..." Otto spluttered, "they're your families!"

"Yes," Tabitha agreed, "and I remember my Earthly Love, er, Loves, fondly. And I know they're here somewhere, having as much fun as I am."

"You haven't seen them?"

A shake of the head.

"I've been here longer than everyone." Jakto's wave took in the group. "And I've never run into anybody I knew."

"Me neither," said Moses and the others chimed in agreeing.

"And don't forget." Jakto raised a finger. "When I arrived, there weren't a lot of people here."

"I know somebody who ran into his father," Otto countered. "In fact, I met two guys on the train who knew each other on Earth and hold regular reunions with a third."

Jakto dismissed that. "Glaring exceptions."

"But." Otto was not willing to let it go. "Your families were important to you, at least once. Don't you want to make sure they're okay?"

"They're okay," Sam said.

"Besides, that was then," Tabitha said. "This is now."

Jakto pointed around the fire. "What she means is this is your family now. This is who you love now."

They all looked at Otto. "Sounds like Ian," he muttered.

"Ian, the coach driver?" Tabitha asked.

Otto was surprised. "You know him?"

She smiled lasciviously. "Yes, yes I do. And in the Biblical sense."

That brought another round of appreciative hoots and Tabitha stood, curtseying. She settled back down. "So." She pointed a skewer at Otto. "Who is she?"

"I told you."

"Oh, stop it," Tabitha said. "It's someone here. Otherwise, you'd be playing horsey with that Viking babe."

Otto gave her a frown. "The mouth on you. And it's no one."

"I know who it is." Kenny paused for dramatic effect. "It's Claudia."

"Grendel's Claudia?" Sam asked and slapped Otto on the back. "You dog, you!"

Otto was amazed. "You know her?"

"Yeah." Jakto picked at a bone. "She comes out here a lot."

"To be with you guys?"

"Brings us ale. We like it."

Otto turned to Kenny. "How'd you know I knew her?"

"Moy Jin told me," Kenny said as he plopped next to one of his wives.

"How did he ... oh, never mind." Otto flipped a hand. "This place."

Tabitha grinned at him. "Yeah, this place. So, have you ..." and she moved her finger lewdly through an enclosed thumb.

The others roared. Otto gaped at her. "Man," he said, "you're single track, aren't you?"

She smirked. "It's what I like. And you do, too. But you haven't done anything with her, have you?"

Otto didn't respond.

"*Hmm*," Moses said, "Worship from afar." They all nodded at each other in approval.

"That acceptable?" Otto asked Tabitha.

"Whatever floats your boat," she replied. "Although you're wasting valuable Afterlife."

Otto *tsk*ed and sat back against the blankets and the conversation passed on to memorable raids and plans for future ones. He half-listened, watching the stars wheel past and the moons sit quietly. The others drifted away, Tabitha and Sam into the night, no surprise, Moses with a couple of Mongol girls, Kenny and his wives to the yurt. Jakto and he were left alone.

They both sat watching the flames. After a bit, Otto asked, "So what was it like?"

"*Hmm*?"

Otto waved a hand across the horizon. "This. Heaven. Amenti. Whatever, when you first arrived."

Jakto grunted. "Empty." His hand followed Otto's across the plains. "People stayed in their tribes. Took a while before the tribes mingled."

"Did they fight?"

"Eh," a waggle of fingers. "Sort of, but like how we do now."

"For fun," Otto concluded. "Doesn't that seem out of place?"

"No more than a wrestling match is."

"For sport, then. Okay. But, even then." Otto squirmed himself comfortable. "Seems out of place. It's aggression and conflict and attempting to best another. That's not supposed to happen here."

"Who told you that?"

"Well ... I mean ... no one specifically in those words but it's the conclusion you draw from holy writings. No more war, no more pain, the old things have passed away."

"And yet," Jakto threw another stick in the coals, "the scrolls are filled with war in Heaven. Even your scriptures speak of it."

"Yeah, but that's all pre-history."

"Is it?"

Otto considered. Perhaps he was reading it all wrong. The war between good and evil wasn't precursor but element, continuing *ad infinitum* and in all places and times, even in Heaven itself, but in a milder form as mock battles, reenactments. Which meant the urge to dominate and conquer was not expiated by death and subsequent arrival in this Afterlife but remained in the soul, carried like a wallet throughout these wondrous lands, and we form Mongol hordes and Viking villages and play war with our friends. But that was sinful.

Wasn't it?

"The City was different," Jakto said.

"In what way?"

"Stone. Mostly Egyptian and Assyrian, big palaces and courtyards and gardens that made those in Babylon look like a backyard. You should have seen the fountains. Magnificent." Jakto shook his head in wonder.

"When did it change?"

"Better question is how. Gradually. Hardly noticeable at first, but then Roman and Han Chinese architecture appeared, a lot of it side by side. The two great empires. Then medieval ones, Renaissance, and now ... I don't even know what to call it now."

"Post-Asimov blended with neo-Tolkien."

Jakto looked at him quizzically and Otto waved that off. "So why is that?"

"Why is what?"

"The changes. It's the Eternal City and should have held its present form since inception, but it morphed. Eternity should not morph."

"Why not?"

"Because that belies the concept."

Jakto chuckled and poked around in the coals. "I see. You

expected a static eternity."

Otto hunched closer to the fire, doing his own stick poking. "Yep. I guess I did. Heaven, a place where nothing happens."

Jakto raised a finger. "Wait. I know that one. Talking Heads. Good song, but 'Animals' gets me dancing."

Otto gave him a "what the heck?" face, and Jakto reached into a fabric bag and pulled out a Walkman and held it up. Otto read "Fear of Music" through the window.

"How the—" Otto threw a hand up in surrender. "Never mind, just never mind."

Jakto laughed, replaced the Walkman, and humming "Life During Wartime," tended the fire.

"Further proof," Otto said.

"Of?"

"That all this is happening in my head."

Jakto showed mild amusement. "Or, that things progress."

"How do you mean?"

"Stone and Assyrian buildings when I arrived because that was the pinnacle of human engineering. Then, Romans showed up, then people who know how to build with composites."

"Except that it's not," Otto countered. "There is no way even the most genius of most recent Earth architects could build buildings like that. It's well beyond our capability."

"So God enhances."

Otto stared at him. "What? You're saying God interviews new arrivals then puts their concepts into action?"

"No. God blesses the progress."

"That doesn't make any sense. And where is God, that He does this blessing?"

Jakto said nothing, quietly concentrated on his fire and Otto waited but the silence expanded; there wasn't going to be an answer, so he sighed and wondered how he'd concocted a Talking Heads-loving Ethiopian – er, Axumite – warrior. How had he concocted a Mongol horde, largely made of Tartars, for that matter? Wild imagination given free rein, and this is what happens.

"You have other purposes," Jakto said as he stirred embers.

"*Hmm?*" Otto roused from his musings.

"Besides this." Jakto pointed at the camp. "You want something else. I've seen it before."

"What have you seen?"

"Others like you." He pulled a small piece of rib from the fire and tasted it. "Seekers."

"Seekers of what?"

Jakto smiled. "Finality."

"I thought I was seeking a static eternity."

"Static, final, whatever word best describes it, you are seeking something else."

Otto thought about it. "Is that wrong?"

"No." Jakto got a flame going. "But it's pretty rare."

"How rare?"

"I think I've run into three of you, including you, since I got here."

"Only three of us, huh?" Otto settled in. "What happened to the other two?"

"Well, believe it or not, one of them is working on the rocket. Some astronomer named Marc."

"Yeah, I know him. How 'bout the other?"

Jakto thought for a moment. "Don't really know. Lost contact. He was a monk from twelfth or thirteenth century Europe. Wrote poetry." Jakto spitted a piece of meat and set it to the fire, where it sizzled. "Bernard, yeah, that was his name."

"So how is it, Jakto, that, of all the people here, only three seek finality?"

"It's a bit more than three, but the reason is simple." He waved his dinner across the horizon. "As you've already heard about a thousand times, this place is its own proof."

"Of?"

"Of God's existence, of His benevolence, of His love. See," Jakto roughed some blankets, getting comfortable, "everyone here, most everyone, anyway, figured they were in for some kind of retribution because of the stupid things they did on Earth … lying, cheating, that stuff. So, they get here, they are well taken care of, they're having a good time …" He raised a palm in conclusion. "They're grateful."

"So leave well enough alone."

"Yes."

Otto frowned that away. "There's something singularly wrong about that."

"For you, not everyone."

"Well, it should be. Or shouldn't be, I don't know." Otto threw a stick on the fire. "We're all supposed to get the answers here."

"Answers to what?"

"The big questions. Who are we? Who is God? What is the purpose of life?"

"The purpose of life is to find God," Jakto said.

Simple. Direct. And dead-on. So to speak.

"Exactly!" Otto pointed a finger at him. "I knew you'd understand."

"But *what* I understand," Jakto eyebrowed the horizon, "is that you can't get much closer to finding God than this."

"Sure you can. You can face Him. And ask directly."

"You know," Jakto opened a hand, "we're all going to face God eventually."

"Yeah, I do know, the end of time, which Kenny and the rest of you don't want to happen. So, when exactly is that?"

Jakto chuckled. "You mean, tell you, in terms of time, when time ends?"

"*Ach*! Metaphysics!" and Otto slapped hands to the side of his face. Jakto laughed.

"So," Otto said, "you're telling me to just wait for the Apocalypse. Or Ragnarok, as Erick would put it."

"The eye of Ra sent as Hathor to purge the world of evil, but Ra made her drunk with blood-red beer."

"I have no idea what you're talking about." Otto fished around for a skewer.

"Another version of the End Times. For the interim, we're to enjoy ourselves."

Otto blew a breath. "I don't know, Jak. I'm not so sure I can wait that long."

"So, then, why aren't you back at the rocket?"

"Kenny seems to like my company."

Jakto smiled. "Kenny likes everyone's company. If he had his way, the whole Afterlife would be one big raid."

"No doubt." Otto slipped a rib on the skewer and into the fire. "In truth, I don't have enough credits to go back to the rocket."

"So you need to earn some."

"Yep."

"Providing, of course, that you actually want to go back."

Otto considered. "Yes," he said softly, "I do."

"Okay. What does the rocket need?"

"Two more people. One, if I get there in time." Otto grimaced. If.

"Who's the other?"

"Clueless."

"You sure?" Jakto kicked at a stray ember. "I mean, when we took a boat down the Nile, everyone rowed, but everyone had specialties. I was an archer. We had a hunter and a woodworker, a man gifted in weaving, a steersman, a butcher, a fisher ..."

"... and a candlestick maker." Otto could not resist.

Jakto frowned. "Uh, yeah, in a sense, but we used oil lamps. My point is, everyone had a function besides running the boat."

"And?"

"What function is the rocket missing?"

"Heck if I know, Jak. I don't really understand why they accepted me."

"What'd they tell you?"

"Said I had the ability to see relationships between separate bits of info."

"*Hmm.*" Jakto approved. "That's pretty vital. Could keep you out of trouble. What else do they need?"

Otto threw up his hands. "Who knows? A chief cook and bottle washer. Someone to shovel the coal. A navigator—" Otto stopped, frowning.

"Go on."

"Someone, who ..." Otto struggled for clarity. "... who's used to unknown places, creating reference points for further exploration. And for finding the way back."

"Know someone like that?"

Yes, he did.

Ferdinand.

"As a matter of fact ..."

Jakto pushed some coals in the fire. "Then it seems to me that you'll earn your credits by getting this person on the crew." Jakto raised an eyebrow.

Otto's gaze narrowed suspiciously. "Jakto, that's pretty insightful."

"Thanks."

"No, I mean, that's really insightful way above the norm for insightful. Know what I mean?"

Jakto said nothing, just fooled with the fire. "Who are you?" Otto finally asked.

Jakto mouéd. "Like you, another resident. I've been here longer than most, though. And sometimes you get to know things, sometimes you get asked to do things, and maybe we should leave it at that?" Jakto looked hard at him.

Otto held up his hands. "Okay."

Jakto watched him for a couple of heartbeats and then pointed off in the distance. "The train is that way, about two river units."

"River unit?"

"Oh, sorry, Egyptian measurement. We used them. Everyone did." Jakto did some fast calculations. "Say twelve miles."

"Are you saying I should go?"

"Everyone's asleep. Or whatever. True to the Mongol tradition, no one will get up before noon. You should be on the train before Kenny misses you."

"I can't get on the train, remember? You guys took my ticket."

Jakto dismissed that. "I'm sure they'll get it to you."

"Who's 'they,' Jakto?"

Jakto went blank. Otto waited but the silence was stone. "Twelve miles?" he finally said, breaking it.

Jakto pointed again. "That way."

Otto stood, dusted himself off, and looked in the direction of Jakto's point, uncertain. "So I guess I should get going."

"I guess."

"Twelve miles, did you say?"

"Thereabouts."

He stood, hesitant. Jakto played with the fire, a rib-eating smirk on his face. "Jakto," Otto said.

"*Hmm?*"

"I'm actually going to miss you guys."

"We do grow on you."

"I mean, really, you guys are about the only friends I've got here."

"Want a hug?"

Otto threw out a hand. "Stop it." Jakto grinned. "So," Otto resumed, "am I going to see you guys again?"

"Doubtful."

Otto nodded and gazed off toward the train.

"Send a postcard," Jakto said.

"How do you know what a postcard is?"

"We Axumites are more sophisticated than you think."

Otto laughed. "Okay. Finish that rib for me, will ya? Later, dude," and he turned and walked away.

Otto skirted the Viking settlement. A guard waved a cheery hand and Otto waved back. He stepped up the berm and had a good double-moon view of the estuary. A couple of dragon boats floated down there unattended and Otto wondered if he should liberate one for the trip. Right, one guy trying to maneuver a fifty-foot pile of wood down the fjord. And who knew if the river met the tracks anywhere.

A large shape moved in the darkness below him, disturbing the sand and rock. What's that, a giant? Otto's breath caught. A giant would not be out of place here. Let's just hope it's the friendly kind. "Who's there?" he called.

The shape stopped and flowed in his direction, picking its way up the slope. Otto prepared to run but then the shape gently whickered.

"Flicka," Otto said. "What are you doing here?"

The horse tossed a look in the direction Jakto had pointed. Otto raised eyebrows. "Who saddled you?" he asked. Flicka winked at him.

Otto considered. "Well," he said, approaching Flicka's side, "who am I to look a gift horse in the mouth?"

Flicka stared at him and then grabbed his helmet, vaulting it over the berm. Otto *tsk*ed, annoyed, and scrambled halfway up to retrieve it but stopped. No longer necessary. He slid back down and mounted. "'S'go," he said and Flicka lurched, keeping a half-trot, half-run cadence. The moons settled on Otto's shoulder and he clearly saw the scrub and woods and low hills that made up this strange portion of desert and ocean. The way they were going was open and flat, like a road, beckoning.

Like the guiding Hand of God.

Chapter XX

Divine Conspiracy

Within a day, the train was back in the City. If schedules remained consistent, it would be at least two more days until Otto got back to where he first boarded. But who knew with this place? Could be two weeks.

Otto assumed where he got on was where he should get off. 'Course you know what happens when you assume ... given all the weirdness, his stop could be in an altogether different place light-years, or dimensions, away. The City might constantly shift, like New York in *Doctor Strange*.

"I'll let you know," the Hawaiian conductor said and walked away, so, okay, don't worry about it.

Otto spent the time idly watching the City drift by. It was all he felt like doing. Doc was probably a step or two away with a ready hand of poker but, no thanks. Best hold on to the credits he had.

Out went quickly, the scenery whipping back and forth between desert and mountain and forest primeval before instantly turning into buildings and streets ... "forest primeval". Otto chuckled. A classic bar joke about the naming of one's privates popped into his head. He wondered if Longfellow knew the abuse his name suffered over the decades. Be a hoot to get his reaction.

Be a hoot to get a lot of reactions, including ones from Miles

Standish and Priscilla and Hiawatha, whoever that was. Otto could spend a very happy eternity tracking down such sundry celebrities. Given distances and the difficulty, it'd probably *take* eternity. Shouldn't; should be a Google search, pop open those Celestial Yellow Pages and then dial 'em up: "Hello, Mr. Lincoln? Say, you don't know me, but I studied you in college and I have a few questions ..."

Why wasn't it that easy? He wasn't buying Ferdinand's "considerations" or Tabitha's difference between Here and There. No, this was deliberate. God was purposely keeping people from finding each other and Otto couldn't, for the life of him, figure out why.

One of the questions to ask when he got to the Throne Room.

One among many questions.

"Here you go," Moy Jin said, handing Otto's ticket through the grate as Otto leaped off Flicka's back and vaulted into the station.

"Where'd you find that?" an astonished Otto exclaimed. Moy Jin shrugged and went back to shuffling papers.

"Better get moving!" Pashtun, standing in the back portal, called out as the train rounded the loop.

"What are you doing here?" Otto asked but Pashtun pointed meaningfully down the platform where the train was slowing. "How did you guys know?" he shouted as he rushed toward the waiting Hawaiian conductor. "Have a good trip!" Pashtun shouted back and Otto jumped aboard, helped by the conductor, who eyed the Mongol get-up and asked, "Have fun?"

Obviously, all this had been orchestrated. Prearranged. Set up. But why? Was Otto the duped player of some cosmic grift, or was Someone merely amusing Themselves? Otto flashed on that Michael Douglas movie, *The Game*. He hoped there was no plunge through a skylight in his immediate future. 'Course, wouldn't be any weirder than anything else so far.

"Mind if I sit here?" a voice broke into his thoughts. A short, grey-bearded man dressed like a San Francisco hippie, tie-dye shirt and all, stood next to the row, expectant.

Otto glanced about and noted the many empty seats stretching down the car. Obviously the guy wants company, even if Otto didn't. But let's be nice. "Sure," he said and moved his feet.

The hippie smiled gratefully and slid into the seat facing him, then took in Otto's get-up. "What are you supposed to be?" he asked.

"Tartar."

"Oh," he said and extended a hand. "Name's Jacob."

Otto took it, eyeing him suspiciously. "Not *the* Jacob, husband of Rachel? Wrestler of God?"

The hippie laughed. "No, not him. Jacob Schiff, of New York City."

"Otto Boteman, of northern Virginia."

They shook and Jacob smiled. "Why'd you ask me that?"

"Been a strange few days."

Jacob nodded. "I get that. And funny you went in that direction. Are you a Talmudic scholar?"

"No, just reasonably well informed."

Jacob approved. "You do seem to know your Pentateuch. Don't forget Jacob was also the husband of Leah."

"Oh, yeah. Wasn't she the one he was tricked into marrying?"

"The very same." Jacob settled and gazed happily out the window.

"Nice love beads," Otto said, pointing at the red-dyed almond husks strung around his neck.

Jacob chuckled and patted the beads affectionately. "Silly, isn't it? I've got some kind of attraction to this get-up. So opposite to what I'm used to."

"Let me guess." Otto studied his groomed beard, moustache, and portly figure, "Victorian?"

"Good guess. How'd you know?"

"You have the look."

"So you can imagine why I find this present style attractive. When you spent your whole day sewn into a waistcoat," (he pronounced it "westkit,") "well, this is liberating."

"I can imagine."

"If you know these are love beads, then you must be from the era?" Jacob raised an eyebrow.

"Survived it."

Jacob laughed. "Yes, I've heard it was a bit unsettled."

"I thought 1968 was the end of the world. King and Kennedy shot, the riots, Vietnam. But, then we had that extraordinary

Christmas, Apollo 8 circling the moon."

"I would like to have seen that." Jacob was wistful.

"So you're what?" Otto waggled a hand. "Eighteen-sixties, eighteen-eighties?"

"A little more recent. I was eighteen in 1865. Died in 1920."

"*Fin de siècle* and all that. Did you fight in the Civil War?"

"Just missed it. I arrived in New York after it ended."

"From where?"

"Germany."

"One of the huddled masses, hey?"

"Yearning to be free." Jacob smiled. "And you?"

"It was twenty-nineteen when I left."

"It was?" Jacob leaned forward, his face anxious. "Tell me, does Israel still exist?"

"Well, yeah, they do, having big problems, as usual."

"Thank God," Jacob breathed, sitting back. "Not for the problems, for the existence. I get such spotty news. The last I heard, they were in some big war with Egypt."

"Yeah, they won that one. Pretty handily, too. In six days."

"Six days?" Jacob whistled. "The time it took Jehovah to restore the world."

"*Hmm.*" Otto considered. "Never thought of it that way. Are you Jewish?"

"Yes."

"Then, and please don't take this the wrong way," Otto added hastily, "what are you doing here?"

"I could ask you the same question."

"You could," Otto agreed, "and you're right to do so. But everyone I've encountered here so far had some kind of Christian belief. I mean, if you were an Old Testament Jew, I could understand it because of pre-Christian promises and all that. But you're not."

"And what makes you think I haven't had some kind of Christian belief?"

Otto thought back to his conversation with Pashtun and the later one with Moses. "Okay, I'm just about willing to accept this notion of momentary conversion. Do you know if you had such a moment?"

"No. I never did. Of that I am quite sure."

"Then I don't get it."

Jacob regarded him. "Are you aware of the Pentateuch descriptions of Paradise?"

"Well, yeah, sort of. I always thought them allegorical."

Jacob shook his head "No, they're not. They were accurately conveyed by Jehovah to impart hope in the People. And He made a stark distinction between Paradise and Heaven. God is not in Paradise."

Otto reflected. "S-o-o-o ..." he took time with the concept, "... that God is not here makes this place a good candidate for Paradise, not Heaven."

Jacob nodded. "Yes, it does. Except for the presence of all you non-Jews."

"And except Paradise was emptied on the day Christ rose. Or died. I forget which."

"According to your beliefs."

"And according to yours." Otto pointed out.

"We do not accept Christ as the Messiah."

Otto grinned. "And yet, all these damn goyim stinking up the place."

Jacob grinned back. "I wouldn't have put it that way, but since you have ..."

"No offense taken." Otto waved an airy hand. "Because, Jacob, it looks like all of us got it wrong."

"There, you are absolutely right. I see elements of everyone's Afterlife here. Even Buddha's Nirvana. I found some Japanese monks sitting on a hillside in a state of complete tranquility and meditation, not moving. Some of them haven't moved for a thousand years."

Otto furrowed his brow. "How's that? If there's one theme around here, it's some kind of relationship with God, Jehovah, what have you."

Jacob spread "who knows?" hands.

Otto pursed his lips. That didn't fit at all, unless Cyril and Theodore had gone to Japan, too. "Where'd you find the monks?" he asked.

Jacob pointed toward the back of the train. "In Out. A mountain range sitting by itself."

Otto cocked his head. "What were you doing in Out?"

"I travel there quite frequently."

"Do you know Kenny?"

"The barbarian?" Jacob laughed. "Oh, of course. Delightful fellow, if a bit addled."

"That's him. He gave me these nifty clothes." Otto smoothed a crease. "Is that why you go to Out, to see him?"

Jacob became guarded. "Among other reasons."

"Such as?"

Jacob leveled a gaze. "Persistent, I see. Well, without going into long explanations, I'm involved in a project."

"Which is?"

Jacob's eyes narrowed and he examined Otto for several uncomfortable moments. "Are you an agent?" he blurted.

Puzzled, Otto said, "Well, yes. I mean, I used to be. I was an agent back home for a while. All I'm here, is confused. What gave it away?"

"You, then, are not one of their agents?"

"Whose?"

"The Opposition's."

Yep, puzzled. "What in this Bizarro World is that?"

Jacob regarded him then visibly relaxed. "You are not lying," he said as he gazed out the window.

Otto didn't know enough to be angry, so he settled for bafflement. "No, I'm not. And why would you think I am?"

Jacob held up a placating hand. "I had to be sure. An agent, when asked directly, cannot lie, or he falls to dust."

"Falls to dust." Otto wasn't sure he heard that right. "Like Tinker Bell?"

"Who?"

"Never mind. Think I got the reference wrong, anyway. So, why don't you tell me what you're talking about? Like, who are these agents?"

"Those who oppose our project."

Well, that certainly clarified things. "You know, I'm fairly certain I left all that cloak and dagger stuff behind."

Jacob sympathized. "I know. But human and Divine natures remain true."

"I have no idea what you mean. And what is this project, anyway?" Confusion gave way to curiosity.

Jacob leaned forward, looked around cautiously, then whispered, "To find the Throne of God."

It was, suddenly, clear. "The rocket," he said, "You have something to do with the rocket."

Jacob's eyes widened. "You know of it?"

"I'll say. I'm a crewman. Or a potential one."

"By the prophets of old, if this is not proof of Divine Guidance ..." Jacob fell into a closed-eye reverie that was probably prayer, then without warning, glared at him. "So what are you doing here?" Rage clouded his face. "You jeopardize everything!"

"Whoa, whoa there." Otto held up a restraining palm "What are you talking about?"

"I am talking about the Opposition!" Jacob hissed. "You expose yourself. You put us all at risk!"

"First of all." Otto, feeling combative, leaned into Jacob. "You're the first person to mention this Opposition and agents and people turning to dust, anything like that. I'da thought Amelia would have clued me in."

"She didn't have to. You would have been safe at Star City."

"Yeah? Well, news for you, Jacob, old buddy, they sort of turned me out."

Jacob was startled. "Why'd they do that?"

"I didn't have enough credits for the necessary supplies."

"Oh." Jacob sat back stricken. "Then I failed."

"Okay." Last straw broken. "Someone really needs to tell me what's going on."

"That you didn't have the credits is my fault." Jacob looked apologetic. "See, that's my part. I gather loose credits and give them to Konstantin."

"So, you're a financier."

"Yes."

Otto eyed him. "I thought Pashtun was Star City's only outside contact."

"He is their regular contact, true, the only one everyone knows about. There are a few others, here and there, working covertly."

"Covertly. Because of this Opposition."

Jacob nodded.

Otto considered all of this for a moment. "Are you," he quietly asked, "and everyone associated with the ship, out of your flippin' minds?"

"No, we are not."

"Then, you'll have to give me a little more. Like, what is this Opposition?"

"It is what it has always been."

"Huh?" Otto cocked an eye. "You mean, good and evil? Right and wrong? God and Satan?"

Jacob nodded.

For a moment, Otto was speechless. Then, he burst out laughing. "Okay, okay, you got me. You do. This is pretty good. Pulling the leg of the new guy. Right, got it. Good. Let's get a beer and chuckle over it."

"I am not kidding."

The look in Jacob's eyes underscored that. Otto studied him. "Jacob," he said, "I've already had this conversation, with, believe it or not, one of the Queen of Sheba's Ethiopian – er, Axumite – soldiers."

"Jakto."

Otto's combat blood rose again. "How did you know that?"

Jacob looked out of the window. "We're coming to my stop," he said. Otto followed his gaze. They were in a rather bustling portion of the City; must be a market or something nearby. Jacob shifted, getting ready to leave.

Otto pitched forward and grabbed his elbow. "What's going on, Jacob?"

Jacob patiently, and with a lot more strength than his hippiness intimated, peeled Otto's fingers back and stood. He focused on Otto. "The Opposition," he said, "has successfully delayed the launch for some time now. Removing credits here, diverting a part there, sending crewmen off on wild goose chases." He bore down. "I do not know if you're on one of those chases or if God's Own Hand guides you. How your mission comes out will determine it. Keep your wits about you and your eyes open." He pushed down the aisle.

Otto's confused face followed him. "Claudia?" he asked.

Jacob stopped, regarded him. "One of us." Momentary pause. "Good luck," he said, and walked away.

Otto watched him walk through the car and out of sight. The train slowed, stopped, and then picked up speed again. He peered out of the window to spot Jacob but the crowds were dense and the traffic denser and maybe he'd gotten off on the other side. Otto flopped back, completely flabbergasted.

Jakto ... "sometimes you get asked to do things."

Otto couldn't get his head around it. His little lark in the desert had turned into a John le Carré novel, which was fairly typical of the genre so what was this? His coma-wrapped brain delving into the espionage stories he loved? Mix in elements of *Dungeons and Dragons*, with God and Satan vying for control of a fabulous fantasy world of hordes and Nirvana and British fleets ... maybe this was *Baldur's Gate 4*. Otto glanced around, expecting to see a Dark Elf, hoping to, because that would finally convince him this was all him, just him, generating all this.

The new passengers waved or smiled and then settled into their business. Otto wondered which of them were agents.

Great. Now he was paranoid. Thanks, Jacob.

Chapter XXI

Man And His Symbols

"Ride, sir?"

Otto looked up. "Ian." Of course.

"Ah! Good day to you, sir, good day! George, say hello to our constant passenger!" George looked back, winked, and whinnied.

"George," Otto asked, "do you know Flicka?"

George nodded.

"What's the deal with her?"

George snorted and shook his mane.

"Yeah," Otto said, "my thoughts exactly." He clambered up and sat back against Ian's plush leather seats. And then sat back again. "Man, comfortable. More so than usual."

"Indeed." Ian smiled. "I had them re-stuffed this morning. You are the first to try them and I can tell by your reaction they were credits well spent."

"Definitely. You could offer nap rides."

"Nap rides, *hmm*." Ian and George exchanged glances.

Otto settled. Tricked-out cars and carriages and skaters and bikers flowed merrily by the station exit as the train – the Hawaiian conductor waving from a window – zipped away. Otto waved back and quickly acquired a sense of well-being.

"So." Ian cast a critical eye at Otto. "Your outfit suggests you had a good time. I am guessing you wish to continue that.

Grendel's, then?"

Otto considered. A delicious ale, served by the delicious Claudia (now linked to him in a planet-wide conspiracy, which made her doubly delicious), could be just the ticket. Especially since he was now dressed like the staff and could start slinging pitchers under Claudia's direction. Wonder how she was as a boss. Bossy? He smiled evilly. Okay, boss me, baby, all night long. He savoured the possibilities but, maybe, instead, he should keep momentum and go straight home. Crewman to recruit, rocket to launch, God to find. Still, these are some really nice cushions; let's relax a bit first. "Just drive around for a while, Ian."

"Certainly." Ian clucked to George, who tossed his head and yanked the carriage right into a bike pack, scattering them. George grinned and Otto figured there was a bit of trickster in every horse.

"Tell me," Ian asked, "did you find your rocket?"

"I did."

"And?" Ian turned a speculative eyebrow at him.

"They threw me out."

"Oh," Ian commiserated, "I am most sorry to hear that, sir. For what reason?"

"I didn't have enough credits."

"Truly?" Ian consulted a clipboard. "You seem to have more than enough now."

"I do?" Otto leaned forward and scrutinized the papers, but it was still columns of meaningless numbers. "How many?"

"As when we first met."

"You mean, it's all back to normal?" Which, Otto realized, was now a relative term.

"It would appear so."

Otto sat back. "Well, that was ... quick. I spent the last three or four days riding the train because I had to replenish credits and presto change-o, there they are." Otto, amazed, shook his head. "Okay, Ian, I guess that means you can take me right back to the station and I'll start this whole silliness again."

"Are you sure, sir?"

Otto blew a raspberry. "Yes. No. I don't know." He made a frustrated gesture at the long-gone train. "Thought I had to go do some things around town first ..." like recruit Ferdinand, "... but I guess that's no longer necessary." The replenished credits were a signal to get on back here and let's get to launching. Apparently, the next-to-last crewman had arrived. No need to bother Ferd.

Right?

"May I venture an opinion?" Ian said as he took a spot in a long line of stereo cars blasting Beethoven's *Ninth*. Actually pleasing. "I would say this restoration of your credits is a sign you are now back on the right track."

"I believe you're right. And, speaking of tracks, let's get on back to the station."

Ian smiled. "A pun, my word! But that's not what I meant. Heading back is the last thing you should do."

"Why not?"

"Because you will immediately lose all your credits. Again."

Otto eyed him. "Think you may be wrong about that, Ian. They told me to come back here and recharge and lookee here, recharged so ..." Otto made a sweeping palm back toward the station.

Ian dismissed that. "That is not it. You're 'recharged' because you are now corrected. Whatever drove you to see the rocket was wrong and, now that you're done with it, you are fully restored."

Otto stared at Ian's back. "That doesn't make any sense. Based on what's just happened, the opposite is true."

"Think about it." Ian adjusted the carriage's drift. "You went off on this mission, and you lost your credits. When you abandoned the mission, your credits were restored." Ian gave him a significant look. "Seems a pretty clear message."

"But ... I haven't abandoned the mission. I'm still on it. It's why I came back. And, abracadabra, the credits are restored. That seems a pretty clear message, too, Ian."

"You mean you had to come all the way back, as far as one can get from your rocket, just to get back to standard?" He gave Otto another significant look.

Otto felt some of the air go out of him. Ian could be right. Maybe this *was* a wild goose chase. Otto'd hop the train and bounce into Box's place and pile up supplies and reach into his wallet and ... broke again. Back to the City, replenish, back to Box's, busted. Over and over forever and ever because the rocket was, simply, a joke.

No. It wasn't.

"I get your point, Ian, but that's not it, not at all. I never felt more right in my life when searching for the rocket. I was on a mission. On target. Focused. I mean, I met the crew. Amelia friggin' Earhart is the captain, can you believe that? I even met some periphery actors like Jakto and Jacob—" The light bulb went on. "Jacob! It was Jacob."

"I'm sorry?" Ian raised an eyebrow.

"My credits weren't restored. Jacob got them to me." He paused. "Somehow. I think."

"Is this what you were told?" Ian said, "Because no one, no person, can restore credits."

"Well, then, where did they come from? Or, more accurately, come back from?"

"Intent," Ian said and guided George away from the stereo line and through a very pleasant park.

"'Fraid you're going to have to explain that one, Ian."

"Certainly, sir. As your inner nature asserts itself, the hidden thing, the propensity you never knew, emerges, like George and me, here." Ian leaned forward and affectionately patted the horse's rump. "Then you are delivered the means to achieve it. The credits, other things. Not all at once, mind you, for we all must have a challenge, but as you approach your target. It's incremental."

"I thought you woke up one morning and there was George."

"Indeed, sir, but it was a while before that morning came."

"So what happened in the interim?"

"Sir?"

"While you were waiting for George. What did you do, or realize, or get through the mail or whatever?"

"Oh. Well." Ian hesitated. "I can't really explain."

"What do you mean, Ian? You're the answer man."

"Yes, but ..." Ian raised his hands in helplessness. "It's a personal thing that only you can recognize. I saw things and opportunities on the way, but they meant something to me only."

"Did that include credit replenishment?"

"Well, no, not exactly. Just ... there were enough for the moment, or the thing I was contemplating."

"The thing you were contemplating, like, what, a leather and diamond encased whip?"

Ian laughed as George gave them both a worried look. "No, no, not something so obvious. Just, everything came together at the right time."

"But, Ian, that's how I feel now. I know what I have to do. And that's ride the rocket."

"Are you sure, sir?" Ian cocked his head. "Or does your rocket urge stand for something else?"

"Such as?"

"You must remember I was an engineer and not one to muck about with philosophy but there are theories of archetype and symbolism."

"Jung."

"Young, sir? Are you commenting on my innocence?"

"No, Jung. J-U-N-G, deeply weird psychiatrist from, I think, the thirties."

"Oh, yes!" Ian exclaimed. "That guy."

Otto looked around. "You think he's here?"

Ian flipped a rein. "Probably, sir. I seem to recall he contemplated divinity, or at least eternity, things along those lines. No doubt while doing so, he slipped into momentary belief and, well, there you are." Ian spread his hands.

"Right, right." Otto waved that away. "If I'm following you correctly, then you're saying my urge to go on the rocket isn't really about the rocket at all."

"I can't say, sir, but it seems to me that were you meant for it, you would now be on it."

"But I will be. If I get this thing done. Quickly."

"What thing is that, sir?"

"Bring back another crewman."

Ian, surprised, shoulder-glanced him, swerving toward an approaching carriage, but George pulled up. "And who would that be?"

"A neighbor of mine."

"This neighbor has expressed an interest?"

"Well." Otto shifted. "No, not really. He's quite content with his current life."

Ian cast a skeptical brow. "And you believe you can talk him into a rocket ride?"

"Well, yeah. I think."

Ian said nothing, just shook his head and tended George. Otto frowned. What, exactly, *was* he thinking? March straight into Ferdinand's place and say, "Hey, Ferd, how 'bout you give up your shops and prosperity and head out to the desert with me where a crazed pack of pseudo-Tartars will try to make a Costco rotisserie chicken out of you? Then, if we get away, you and me strap ourselves into a patched-together heap of metal which will probably blow up on takeoff. Sound good?"

Ferdinand's most likely response: "Otto, old boy, are you out of your mind?" Then he'd either run Otto through with a sword or give him the bum's rush out of the door, and Otto'd slink back to his condo, raise a glass to Deng, and wonder how he'd managed to get so deluded.

Was he?

A tidal wave of doubt rushed over him. Untested rocket, untrained crew, no idea where they were going or how to get back – pretty foolish. It's like a bunch of kids building a fort in the backyard, except the fort had real cannons. Gonna do a lot of damage to a really nice neighborhood. Maybe Ian and Sam and Tabitha, and just about everybody else, were right: the rocket was nothing more than a giant, metal-clad middle finger aimed at God, basically telling Him that His Heaven isn't good enough ...

... No, that's wrong, no one's saying that; no one in the crew, anyway. There's no ingratitude here, quite the contrary: we want to thank the Architect. The urge to find God isn't foolish, nor an insult; it's the demi-urge of every created being. Or should be.

Yet here, on this planet of All Souls, only a handful made strides in that direction. And all *they* had, after thousands of years, was a half-mad Russian's half-baked scheme to get a theoretical space vehicle off the ground.

Otto, old boy, are you out of your friggin' mind?

Maybe Ian was onto something. Maybe everything here worked on a purely symbolic level, like mescaline-induced visions, and God woven into them. Heaven as a mushroom dream. So, then, the rocket stood for ... escape, exploration.

Phallus.

Otto chuckled at that one. From Jung to Freud in a matter of nanoseconds. Yeah, this was all about sex. The rocket was a penetration metaphor and the Father was some Oedipal or Electra demi-urge and if Otto would just get laid ... he thought about Claudia for a lascivious moment and then, wholesale and with no further consideration, dismissed the entire argument.

Because God is not obscure.

"Ian, I don't think God works through symbols. He's pretty straight up."

Ian clucked a direction to George. "That may be, but there is only so much the human brain can comprehend, and symbols convey volumes. That's why we use them in math."

"Then you're saying that symbols are the only means of grasping the infinite. I don't think so."

"No, I'm not saying that because I don't believe that, either. Ach!" He whipped the reins, something George didn't appreciate. "I'm not good at explaining this. But I know someone who is."

"Who?"

"A man of wonderful perspicacity."

"More than yours?"

Ian laughed, "Well, thank you, sir, but yes. He's the philosopher, Rousseau."

Otto wasn't sure he heard that right. "Rousseau? *The* Rousseau?"

"Yes, sir."

Otto blinked. "What's he doing here?"

Chapter XXII

In Which Otto Meets The Rational And An Agent

"The very question I ask myself," Rousseau chuckled, bent over a small work table with a recessed concave dish spinning in the middle by means of a foot pump. He rode a black stone, waxed to a stick, along its edge. Sparks flew. Rousseau pulled out the stone, gently blew on it, eyed it critically, and then placed it back in the spinning dish.

Otto had found him in a thatched workshop at the rear of a dirt-packed courtyard, dominated by a plaster-walled straw-roofed cottage with flowering vines draped all over it. Very seventeenth century, as was the huge wooden-and-iron padlocked gate set in the middle of thick, medieval rock walls surrounding the courtyard, just off the street where Ian had dropped him. Guy liked his privacy, Otto decided, and looked for a pull rope or a bell or something and then discovered the padlock was open and, with a little effort, pushed his way in. Guy likes his ambience. Several women in long dresses strolling around the substantial grounds, carrying baskets of cheese and bread, directed Otto through the complex to the workshop.

Otto stood at the end of the table watching for a few moments, then asked the next obvious question. "So ... do you have an answer?"

"Very simply, the grace of God." More sparks, more blowing. "Are you familiar with my writings?"

"Not really."

"Oh," Rousseau sounded disappointed, "Yes, well, judging by your outfit, I doubt reading was a pastime."

"This is just my Mongol get-up. I'm from twenty-nineteen and read quite a bit."

"But nothing of mine?" Surprised, Rousseau stared at Otto while holding the stone against the dish, apparently a little too long because he said, "*Merde*!" hastily pulled it out and looked at the result, frowning.

Forced to read a few of the guy's essays in college, Otto found them insufferably patronizing and enough dreary windbag commentary for one lifetime. Wouldn't be quite politic to mention that, though. "Uh, no."

"May I ask why not?" Rousseau seemed more irritated by Otto's answer than the stone's damage.

Otto feigned unconcern. "Not interested."

"Not interested?" Rousseau was downright astonished. "Why ever not? I dealt with the most profound issues of human existence, the nature of our very souls' love, the raising of children ..."

Great. An egotistical author. Was there any other kind? "Because," Otto kept his voice flat, "in my lifetime, there were lots and lots of books to read. I mean, lots. And that's just the printed books. Don't get me started on E-books. Which are pixels. Don't ask what a pixel is, I don't really know. Point is, I simply ran out of time."

"So who did you read instead of me?" Hurt tone in the voice.

"Contemporaries."

"Ah," Rousseau said, knowingly, "I suppose that makes sense. Despite the universality of my arguments, the way they transcended time, one would naturally be attracted to the popular press of one's age."

Insufferably patronizing. "Yes, I'm a bourgeois little shopkeeper."

Rousseau waved an apology. "I don't mean to offend. It's just that I treated so many important subjects, it grieves me to find I was largely ignored."

"You weren't." Otto pulled up a stool. "You were well known. The whole concept of the Noble Savage is attributed to you."

"Truly?" Rousseau's eyebrows rose. "*Hmm*, well, that's something, although it was an offhand thing with me, you know. I thought my concepts of the general will would do better."

Otto settled. "Not familiar with those."

"Would you like to discuss them?" Rousseau looked hopeful. "I'm sure you'll find it most stimulating."

Do we have to? Otto almost asked. "Actually, I'm here for a different purpose."

Rousseau made "go on" moves. Otto continued. "I need some advice." He paused. Given the level of ego displayed here, might be good to prime this pump. "Ian tells me you're one of the smartest guys around here and, of all the people in the City, you can help me the most."

Apparently, the right thing to say. Rousseau flushed, looking pleased, and put the stick down. "Well, Ian is a forthright man but tends to exaggeration." The modesty was so obviously forced, Otto almost laughed. "I'll listen to your issue, but, please, don't expect too much."

No problem there, Chief. "I was supposed to take a trip on a rocket," Otto said.

Rousseau's brow furrowed. "A rocket?"

"Yeah, you know, a rocket. Outer-space travel." Otto reviewed his hazy knowledge of seventeenth-century French science for the proper reference. "Like a big balloon but goes to the stars instead."

"I know what a rocket is." Rousseau looked insulted. "I have after all, kept up."

"So you know about twentieth-century space travel. Okay, good, because that's what I was supposed to do."

"What were you supposed to do?"

Otto made a helpless gesture. "Get in the rocket. Go up." He paused. "To find God."

"Oh, *that* rocket." Rousseau picked up the stick again, examining the stone. "So why didn't you?"

"Didn't have enough credits."

Rousseau chuckled. "As if that constitutes a proper excuse. No." Rousseau put the stone back. "You were not supposed to go. And for good reason."

"Why?"

"The rocket stands between you and God."

Otto arched a brow. "Excuse me?"

"Instead of finding God, you found something that prolongs your separation from Him."

"What?" Otto sat back. Dangerous move on a stool. "That's not true. The whole purpose of the rocket is to unite us with God."

"So you think." Rousseau raised a finger dramatically. "But the rocket has blinded you. See." The finger wagged. "You still carry in your mind Earth-taught images of God. Golden throne, white beard, big mace in one hand, angels and saints throwing crowns hither and yonder. Very popular." A dismissive flick of the same finger. "And because you seek that, you miss the God that stands before you."

"What God?"

"This." Rousseau swept a hand courtyard wide and Otto knew he meant the miracle of the City.

Otto frowned. "I don't know."

"Of course you don't." Rousseau examined the stone again. "You still retain the technologies of your mind. That is what separated man from nature, you know. We placed our inventions before us, self-made gods, and we missed God Himself."

"But—"

"No 'buts'!" Again with the raised Finger of Drama. "What happened is simple – God has saved you from yourself. You are not lost in some absurd ether beyond the moons right now because God had the sense to take your credits away. You should be grateful. Now." He patted Otto's knee paternally. "Go out, in this wonderful new world He has given you, and *really* find Him." Rousseau returned to his stone.

Dismissed. After a moment, Otto slipped from the stool and out of the door, crossed the courtyard, waved to a couple of the women who cheerfully waved back, then out through the big gate and back into the modern world, cars and bicycles and tall, wondrous buildings that led up to that wondrous sky ... Otto jerked his head down, deliberately staring at the curb and the wheels of a carriage pulling up.

"Ride, sir?"

"Ian." Otto chuckled. "I might have known."

Ian grinned. "I anticipate the needs of my customers. So off to home, then?"

"I suppose." Otto settled into the cushions and Ian clucked to George, who high- stepped in front of a three-person bicycle, the driver of which good-naturedly sounded a bulb horn.

Ian looked back at him. "So?"

"He makes excellent points, I gotta give him that."

"And what is it he said?"

"What you said. Symbolism, pretty much. What we expect is a type of what is actual, so reality blows right by us. Very 60s."

Ian laughed, "Well, he was the first hippie. So, what do you think?"

"I don't know what to think. Tell you the truth, Ian, I'm feeling a mite disappointed."

"Indeed, sir?"

"Indeed." Otto watched a DeLorean driven by a gigantic black man with an even more gigantic Afro keeping pace with the carriage. Otto gave him a thumbs-up and the giant reciprocated. "If Heaven is a place without God, I'm thinking it's not much of a Heaven at all."

Ian reeled a bit. "Oh, sir, so much like blasphemy that sounds. You see God in everything here."

"I know, I know." Otto offered a 'forgive me' palm. "But, Ian, the Heaven I'm comfortable with isn't a place of symbols. There's nothing between you and the Throne Room. You can see and petition God directly."

"Perhaps, sir, that is a human construct. Perhaps God always intended to remain aloof."

"Deism, huh?" Otto mused, then tossed it. "I don't buy that model. My sense of God has always been His vitality."

"There is nothing more vital than this." Ian's gesture took

in the street.

"Yeah-yeah, but now you're back to symbols." Otto shook his head, "I swear, Ian, these last few days or weeks, or whatever they are, have really thrown me. It's like I'm under attack."

Ian scoffed. "By whom?"

"The Opposition."

"Excuse me, sir?"

"Something I heard on the train." Otto looked at him and said, half-jokingly, "You're not an agent, are you, Ian?"

"What? An ... agent? I'm a carriage driver."

"Yeah, but are you an *agent* carriage driver?" Still the half-joking tone.

Hesitant, Ian gave Otto a blank, "what are you talking about?" look that was pure denial, then particled and collapsed like a sand painting hit by the tide.

"What the hell?" Otto yelped and bolted forward, grasping the exquisite leather backboard and staring at the driver's seat, now covered with fine white ash. He was almost thrown over the front as George skidded to a halt, looked back, and screamed.

"What the hell?" Otto said again and tentatively ran a finger through the ash, some of which collected on his finger then vanished. George lifted his head straight to the sky and howled. Otto gawked at him. He didn't know a horse could do that. George turned and glared at Otto, the malevolence in his eye clear and white-hot.

"Uh-oh," Otto said.

George lashed two copper-clad rear hooves straight into the carriage, smashing through the front and distributing Agent Ian's ashes all over the street. The hooves almost reached Otto and he threw himself back as the next set of kicks destroyed the driver's seat completely. George reared back again and Otto rolled out of the side as George unloaded a hoof, barely missing Otto's head. He spun on the ground and found himself under the carriage, temporarily safe.

Chaos. The bicycles and taxis and jet cars behind him were a mishmash of crashed bumpers and yelling drivers. Horns, from *aoogah* to air, sounded continuously. A traffic jam in

Heaven. Go figure. Otto checked George and concluded from the thrashing about that the horse was almost free of his trappings. This meant he'd be free to pound Otto into pulp.

Quickly, Otto rolled out street-side, away from George's head, and scooted under another wagon that had locked with Ian's back wheels. Not the brightest idea because *its* horse, coal-black and fire-eyed, caught George's mood and peered under, teeth showing. It aimed a fast hoof, just as copper-clad, at Otto. If it weren't for the "Here, now!" of whoever was driving and a yank on the reins, the horse would have pumpkin-smashed Otto's head.

Otto rolled clear again and found himself in front of a low-rider Honda with a front suspension barely an inch off the pavement, its driver and hundreds behind desperately untangling bumpers and traces, the whole mess pushing Otto along its merry way ...

... right back to George, who had thrown his reins looking around for someone to kill.

Guess who?

Screw this.

Otto jumped to his feet and dashed ahead of the Honda, ducking to the left. George spotted him and roared, just roared, a terrifying sound that gave Otto urgency as he bolted, the slap of copper hooves accelerating toward him. About a half-block away, the DeLorean idled next to a clothing store and Otto beelined for it. So did George and Otto judged the sound of his approaching hooves and angry roars perfectly, slipping to the left along the sidewalk as George's front legs crashed down where he'd just been standing. George slid past, gnashing at him with demon teeth Otto never knew horses had, careening through the plate glass window of the store. Glass and screaming customers flew everywhere, George's angry shriek clear above everyone else's.

Otto gripped the DeLorean's gull-wing passenger door and pulled it up. The giant black man stared at him in surprise as he jumped in. "Get me out of here."

The black man shrugged and smiled. "Sure."

He shifted and floored and with smoke and the screeching of tires, they were fishtailing across five lanes of traffic and airborne and in a park, scattering walkers and runners and dancers like bowling pins as they shot through the center of the green.

Otto looked back and saw George's legs flailing in the window, seeking purchase. "Faster!" he yelled.

The black guy grinned and gunned it and they raced down a dark alley of trees linked overhead, flying past astonished picnickers, and Otto wondered what would happen when they reached 88 mph. Maybe he'd finally wake the hell up.

Wake the hell up. Please.

Chapter XXIII

Kids And Coincidences

The DeLorean slipped quietly down a particularly fetching street lined with shops of crystal and diamond. "Wow," Otto marveled.

Unathi pointed at the most fetching shop of all, its display windows filled with sparkling crystal stemware. "That one's mine."

"Wow, again."

"Thanks." Unathi swelled with pride. "It's how I bought this car," and he slapped the wheel affectionately.

So capitalism does reign, at least the profit aspect of it, but wait, thought it was one's value that determined wealth, or something like that. What exactly did Ferd say? Oh, heck, leave it alone. "You're quite the guy, 'Nath. So, you're sure this is okay?"

"More than okay. The others will get a kick out of you. An honest-to-God Tartar."

"It's just a costume. And, do you mean, the others will kick me?"

"*Ha!*" Unathi had a spine-shattering one-note laugh, very pleasing. "They may! Small price, don't you think?"

"Got that right." Otto looked back for the thousandth time to see if a mad George was still pursuing. They'd lost him in the park and Unathi ensured they stayed lost by careening madly through streets and alleys. It was like a Bruce Willis movie, with Otto as the geeky sidekick, and he expected police cars and helicopters to converge on them at any moment. But nothing, except pedestrians flying here and there and a couple of overturned carriages and bicycles. Otto wondered if anyone was hurt.

Probably. There's a whole lot of getting hurt in this Afterlife. Between a mad-eyed George, a dissolving Ian, and Kenny's random stabbings, the opportunities to lose an eye were certainly greater than advertised. Sure, it'd grow back, but there's a principle. And nobody with a badge had showed up to restore order, either: cuff a few miscreants, pistol-whip a loudmouth, put a halter on a crazy horse. Where was Mr. Latchemondy when you needed him?

Good question.

Infrastructure ran smoothly, trains and cars and streets swept clean of all that dissolved agent dust, so somebody was in charge. But hijinks remained unpoliced. What was one to conclude? On the upside, everybody does pretty much what they want, with the occasional lost eye a mere inconvenience, quickly remedied. The downer: everybody does pretty much what they want, including agents of Lucifer or Ashtaroth or the Democratic Party, whatever, who fall to dust when asked their party affiliation and, for reasons still indiscernible, actively seek to dissuade Otto from getting to the rocket by doing things like, oh, say, siccing crazy horses on him. Otto looked back again, nervously.

"Relax," Unathi said and whipped into a garage on the ground floor of a stunning townhouse behind the crystal shop. "We're here."

"You still sure this is okay?"

"Yes." That big grin again. He turned off the motor and released the doors. "Come on."

The gull-wing rose and Otto used a handle to haul up, looking over the car's top as Unathi unfolded. And unfolded. Otto figured Unathi was a big guy, but Goliath himself stood next to the car, gently closing his gull-wing and then patting it. Otto goggled. Guy had to be almost seven feet tall. "How the heck do you get in there?"

"*Ha!*" That laugh again. "It's a talent, especially with this."

Unathi pointed at his 'fro, which had to be seven feet in its own right.

"Beautiful," Otto admired.

"Thank you. Cetshwayo kept our hair shorn, so when I met some Black Panthers sporting these, I had to try it."

"Cetshwayo, the Zulu chief?"

"The very one."

"You're a Zulu?"

"Born and bred," Unathi responded, proudly.

Otto was pleased beyond belief. "That is so cool. Where did you meet Black Panthers?"

"Around." He gestured toward a set of French doors. "Follow me."

Unathi stepped inside and bellowed, "I'm home!"

Otto, behind him, heard a flurry of movement and excited voices. "Are those kids?" he asked, surprised.

They certainly were. About seven came blurring out from a side hallway, polished pale marble floors ensuring they slid, more than ran, over to Unathi and Otto. They ranged from seven to ten years old and different colors and races – a Chinese girl, lithe and giggling; a black boy, beaming and handsome; a couple of red-headed Irish kids ... even an Eskimo.

Do they say "Eskimo" anymore?

Otto stepped back as Unathi formed a scrum with the shrieking kids in the middle of the floor. The giant roared and tickled and wrestled and pummeled and the kids did likewise, the cries and screams in crescendo, and Otto laughed his head off.

"They are funny, aren't they?" a quiet voice said. Otto turned and his eyes widened. Probably the most beautiful woman in the Universe stood there – at least six feet tall, with absolutely flawless, coal-black skin, perfect small teeth and the most expressive sloe eyes. She had the kind of figure that dropped most men to their knees. It was all Otto could do not to fall to his.

Claudia who?

"Ah ... *bwa* ..." was all he could manage, then composed himself. Somewhat. "Sorry for being a chauvinist pig, but you are just stunning." She dimpled in appreciation.

"Hey, leave my woman alone!" Unathi called from the scrum and Otto turned guiltily but the big man was grinning, still buried in children. The woman laughed a bell tone that caressed the ears. She held out a hand. "I'm Grace."

Otto took it. "You certainly are." She laughed again and Otto was thoroughly charmed.

Someone tugged Otto's jerkin. He looked down at the Chinese girl, all big eyes and solemnity. "Come play with us," she insisted. Otto scooped her up, shrieking, and leaped into the fray, where Unathi and he were beset by a renewed wave of children. After a few minutes, they had the kids rounded up and tangled together.

"Surrender!" Unathi ordered and met with shrieks of protest, so he sat on the pile until they submitted.

"Dinner," Grace said.

Several small hands grasped Otto's arm and pulled him down the hallway from which Grace had emerged. The same pale marble led down a dark wooded passage that opened into a narrow but high-ceilinged dining room with a long, skinny table in the middle and high-backed wooden chairs set against it. It looked like a room in an English manor, dangling chandelier and all. Plain white dishes, probably Corelon, ranged around a huge tin pot of ...

"Basghetti!" one of the Irish kids yelped in pleasure and echoed by the others who flowed through the room, excited, grabbing seats. "Sorry, but that's the entrée," Unathi said to Otto. "With kids, you gotta economize."

"You kidding?" Otto replied. "I love basghetti."

Unathi chuckled as he passed toward the head of the table. The Chinese girl took Otto's hand. "Sit here," she ordered and he obeyed as she took the chair next to his while the Eskimo child took the other. Grace sat at the end, opposite Unathi, who waited until his brood sat then placed his hands in prayer. The children quieted and followed suit, as did Otto. "Lord," Unathi's voice boomed, "bless this food You have provided for us. Amen," and there were echoes of "Amen" from all, including Otto. Unathi and Grace stood and met in the middle as kids pressed them with plates, demanding double portions. "Our guest first," Unathi said over the whines of protest as he handed Otto a steaming, high plate of noodles and red, rich meatball sauce.

Otto took it and savoured the odor. Unathi and Grace looked

at him expectantly, as did the kids, so Otto tasted the sauce. "Wow," he said, eyebrows raising appreciatively, "Just wow."

Grace inclined her head. "Thank you."

"I mean it. Wow!" Otto adjusted his plate for attack while Unathi spooned portions to the impatient kids. "I always thought my wife made the best sauce in the world, but this is better. Don't tell her I said that."

Grace laughed, "I won't."

"So where'd you get the recipe?" he asked around a mouthful, joining the kids in enthusiastic eating.

"St. Louis."

"Really? Funny, I never thought of St. Louis as a gourmet center."

"We invented the hot dog. And the hamburger."

"You think of those as gourmet?"

Her eyes twinkled. "Most do."

As Grace and Unathi resumed their seats, Otto fell to it, enthusiastically mimicked by the kids. Intrigued, he focused on the Chinese girl, who winked at him from time to time. "You know," he said to Unathi, "other than a crowd of shrieking pint-sized barbarians trying to kill me in the desert, these are the first kids I've seen. Real ones, I mean. Not murderous little trolls."

"Unsurprising." Unathi licked his fingers. "There are very few here in the City."

"Why is that?"

The giant pointed. "Ask them."

Otto raised an eyebrow at the Chinese girl, who was in the throes of a major noodle slurp. "Because," she said simply.

Otto elevated the eyebrow and the girl snorted, "We like being kids."

"Everyone does. So why aren't there more?"

"I dunno. Maybe because they got to grow up."

"You didn't?"

"No." She daintily wiped her mouth with a half napkin. "I was a girl child. I was left on a hillside to die."

"Good lord," Otto summarized.

The Eskimo kid pointed at himself. "Stillbirth."

"Thrown up on an Ottoman's pike," an Arabic-looking kid volunteered. "I was eighteen months old."

Otto was suitably horrified. "Man!"

The kids exchanged satisfied glances and returned to dinner. "So," Otto continued, "none of you made it very far, for mostly terrible reasons. Okay. But that happened to a lot of kids – in fact, I know one – so why aren't there more of you?"

The Chinese girl slurped a forkful. "Choice."

"You mean, kids can choose to be adults?"

"Yes."

"And, in converse, choose to remain kids?"

The girl raised a fork in affirmation. Well, waddya know, another oddity of this odd Afterlife. Otto wondered what the mechanism for adult-to-kid conversion was: fervent prayer, contributions to your favorite City charity, or simply ask for it? To be a child of God in the City of God, forever ... "You'd think more people would do that," he murmured.

"You'd think," Unathi echoed, "but the same rules apply. You must have parents and there are restrictions and schooling and bedtimes. Would you like that?"

"*Hmm*," Otto mused. "No, probably not. Once you've tasted adult life, it's hard to go back. But I guess if you never did ..." and he looked at the girl who waggled her eyebrows and fell back to her meal. "But, still, given the demographics, especially child mortality in the earlier centuries, there should be a lot more of you guys running around."

"What's the one thing every kid always wishes for?" The Chinese girl asked while still focused on her plate.

"A pony?"

"A pony!" a little pigtailed ten-year-old blonde girl across from him, who had "Scandinavia" written all over her, clasped hands excitedly.

"How 'bout not giving them any ideas?" Unathi grumbled and Otto raised shoulders in apology.

"No, silly." The Chinese girl playfully slapped his forearm. "Not a pony, although ..." She gave Unathi a sideways glance, which he ignored, "To be older."

That was true. How many times, when he was ten or eleven or even eighteen, had he wished to be a full-blown, rights-wielding, car-driving, apartment-renting grownup? And then he was, and how many times after that had he wished to be a kid again? "Do any of them ever revert?"

The Chinese girl returned to her dinner and Otto supposed there were instances of kids to adults and back to kids again, with a whole host of attendant issues at each transformation, such as the transformation itself.

How, exactly, did that work?

"So how'd you guys end up parents?" Otto asked Unathi, "I mean, it wasn't like ... you know, in the regular way. Right? I mean ..." He made a helpless gesture at the kids. "Can you get pregnant with a soul that already exists?"

Grace and Unathi exchanged chuckles. "No, you can't," Unathi responded, "and you can't create new souls here, either, so no one gets pregnant. As to how we ended up with these criminals" – he surveyed the children with fondness – "can't really say. It just happened."

"We both like kids," Grace summarized and that was probably it. If there was one thing Otto had figured out by now, full and comprehensive explanations of Afterlife phenomena never came.

"Frank chose to be an adult," Otto offered.

"Frank?" Unathi asked.

"The guy I knew when I was a kid. He was one of the first ones I ran into here, believe it or not. His mother beat him to death with a baseball bat. So I guess adulthood looked better."

The Eskimo kid leaned forward. "Is he a short guy, Asian-looking, kind of slight?"

"Yeah!" Otto, surprised. "Yeah, that's pretty accurate. You know him?"

The Eskimo turned to Unathi. "Greeter," he said, and Unathi and Grace swapped glances.

"What's that?" Otto asked.

"Greeters are a bit of an unknown," Grace said, "you're not sure who they work for. A lot of them are Opposition."

"You said that with a capital 'O'."

She smiled. "You really are new here, aren't you?"

"Yeah, and I'll be all right. What exactly is this Opposition?" If Jacob couldn't explain, maybe these people could.

The atmosphere turned chilly, the kids guarded. Unathi's eyes hooded and Otto had a sudden and keen sense of personal danger.

Great. As usual, he had said something offensive, the kind that led to beat-downs. Or murderous horses chasing him through parks. He calculated. Unathi was a handful, probably couldn't take him, so had to use the kids as blocks, maybe get to Grace and hold him off. "What's going on?" Otto asked, putting danger in his voice, signaling that he would not go quietly.

"What happened between you and Ian?" Unathi retaliated, his voice as hooded as his look.

"You know ...er, knew ... Ian?"

"I was keeping track of him. So, what happened?"

"Keeping track?" Otto pushed back, wary, got to his feet, the atmosphere now electric as the kids moved into defensive positions. Otto mapped escape routes and the proximity of weapons: chairs to throw, knives to grab. Unathi had not moved but Otto saw the shift in his balance. Preparation.

Grace put a hand up, staying the giant. "He doesn't know. He doesn't." With that, the tension spilled out of the room. The kids all sighed and went back to eating, no longer concerned. The combat left Unathi. Grace turned to Otto and gestured at the chair. "Please," she said.

"I'm not so sure." Otto eyed the Zulu.

"Please," she repeated, and there was so much sincerity in her voice that he had to comply.

He settled into the chair. "What's going on?"

She was sympathetic. "The same thing as ever. There are purposes, and those who want to thwart them."

"What purposes?"

She gave him a meaningful look. He flashed on the rocket. "Okay. What's this Opposition?"

"What it's always been."

"That's what Jacob said. Didn't make sense then, either, and, frankly, I am getting really, really tired of all the riddles."

"What riddles?" one of the Irish kids piped up. "You read the Bible, didn't you?"

Otto cast a brow at him. "Well, yeah, but I've found pagans and heathens hereabouts and been told of Buddhists running around, so it seems just one of many acceptable texts."

"Regardless of text." Unathi dabbed at his mouth. "The conflict remains the same."

"What, good and evil?"

The other Irish kid nodded. "You got it."

"But, we're all dead. Right?" and he looked around the table for confirmation because, well, who knew anymore?

"Oh, sure." The Arab kid waved a hand. "If you're talking about the transference from Earth."

"I am," Otto said, "And that ends it. No more struggle."

They all burst out laughing – genuine amusement at what he said, the Chinese girl even pinching his arm in appreciation. Otto didn't join in. "All right," he said, "This is annoying."

"No one ever said it ends, you know," the first Irish kid said, trying to get a meatball from the second.

"If anything, it gets more intense." The Arab kid smacked an appreciative sauce- smeared lip.

"Welcome to the Afterlife." The Chinese girl returned to her meal.

Otto gazed at each of them in turn, then said, "Now hold on ..." then stopped, groping for the right words to put all this nonsense away, because, in the face of mounting evidence, Otto was endeavoring to assert an image of Heaven that, frankly, was unverified. But the words didn't come. The Bible spoke of Heaven in terms of what it wasn't: no more pain, no more sorrow, the wiping away of tears. But he'd experienced pain, albeit temporary, and he was in sorrow ... well, no, not really, frustration, yes, that was more accurate ... and there were tears, but figurative ones, based on the temporary pain and frustration. So, if he really thought about it, the Bible's description was accurate.

And no help.

The seventy-two virgins ... he'd never bought into that, anyway, so he'd never expected to see them lined up in diaphanous material outside his big tent. But, think of it, there were distinct pleasures and great delights here so, allegory? Metaphor? Maybe. How 'bout Nirvana, the losing of yourself and Oneness with the Godhead ... sounded more like a coma than Heaven, so he'd rejected that, too, but go outside Otto, stare up, and see what happens.

"Coney Island," Otto said.

Grace cocked her head. "You know," Otto gestured at her.

"All the posters and expectations and you finally get there and, well, it's not quite what it's cracked up to be." He frowned. "Bit of a letdown, in truth."

"Why?" she asked. "What delighted you about living?"

"Well ..." There was no short answer to that question. "I guess, just being alive."

"Yes." Grace lifted a finger. "And that's what it always came down to, especially when you were doing something you loved. Like, I'd be in the kitchen car swirling the brandy eggs and the train would lurch but I'd catch myself and laugh—"

"Wait a minute," Otto interrupted. "Kitchen car? You worked on trains? In St. Louis?"

"Yes."

"Did you know a porter named Sam, died when stuff fell on him?"

Those lovely eyes popped open. "Yes! He was my husband!"

Otto shook his head in amazement. "I'll be."

"Where'd you meet him?"

"In the desert. He was running with a guy named Kenny—"

"Kenny the barbarian?" the Eskimo cut in.

Otto turned to him, a bit stunned. "You know Kenny?"

"Harmless. A little nuts," the Eskimo said to Unathi as he made the spinning-finger-near-his-ear sign.

"That's him," Otto acknowledged, and he looked slowly around the table. "What," he asked, "is going on?"

"What do you mean?" Unathi responded, wiping his mouth.

"What do you mean, 'what do I mean?'" Otto threw up his hands. "No one's supposed to know anyone here, no one runs into their Earth families or friends, and, right here, we all know the same people. How's that possible?"

No one said anything. They all turned to their meals, not looking at Otto, who swiveled from one to the other in bewilderment. The kids got up and cleared the table and there were endearments between them and their parents of the "have a good night" variety and the Chinese girl patted him on the arm and kissed him on the cheek. "You'll be all right," she said and trooped out with the others for games and homework and bedtime stories, like normal kids. Like Earth kids.

"Well?" Otto asked Grace as everything subsided and she

took a chair opposite him, pouring herself a glass of wine. She offered him one and he took it. "You know everything you need to know," she said.

"Huh?"

Unathi tested his own glass and smacked his lips in satisfaction. "We need to get you back, I think,"

Otto waved him off. "One thing at a time." He turned to Grace, "What do you mean I know everything I need?"

"Think of it." She toyed with her glass. "Back on Earth, wasn't that true?"

Otto brushed that away. "No, it wasn't. We didn't have any answers at all. The origin of life, all the purposes, the reason for evil, that stuff."

Unathi brushed *that* away. "Yes, you did. All those were summarized somewhere. And you knew, whether you wanted to admit it or not, what was right and what was wrong."

"It's the same thing here," Grace said and she and Unathi raised glasses to each other.

"But ..." and Otto lost the argument. "You know," he said, "that's damned dissatisfying."

"Then," Grace retorted, "find the answers." Her look was steady and challenging and there was nothing more to say.

Unathi shoved back from the table. "Let's get going."

"Where?" Otto asked.

"You have a mission to fulfill." Unathi stood and gestured back to the garage. "Shall we?"

Chapter XXIV

Steve Mcqueen's
Gotta Be Around Here Someplace

It was a milder exit than arrival because Unathi and Otto pushed the
DeLorean out of the garage and down the street as the giant peered
right and left, examining the neighborhood. "What's got you
spooked?" Otto asked as they both jumped through the open gull-
wings at a full trot.

"Nothing. Just taking precautions." Unathi nonchalantly steered
the car, lights off, down the hill.

"Against what?"

"Nothing." Another shrug. "Just my nature."

"Oh, come on. Is George around here someplace?" Otto glanced
anxiously about.

Unathi grinned as gravity slid them around a corner and he
started the car, gunned it, and whipped them around more corners,
checking his mirror at each turn until he grunted with satisfaction.
"There."

"Is George following us?" Otto asked, in full anxiety mode.

Unathi laughed that off and Otto blew a breath of exasperation
as Unathi zipped through neighborhoods of rather extraordinary
architecture. It was night and the stars whirled by and the moons
were up. Under any other circumstances, magical. "I didn't sign up

for this," Otto muttered.

"None of us did." Unathi swung into a main thoroughfare and settled behind a steam car merrily chugging away. The guy driving it was dressed in an 1820s get-up replete with bowler hat and waved cheerily at Unathi, who waved cheerily back.

"I mean, now I think I should have stayed in the condo." Sipping Ferd's wines and sampling the pipes, saluting Deng, naming constellations ... would that be so bad? Otto watched bowler hat clamber around the back of his contraption, furiously shoveling coal into the boiler. Looked like he was having a good time. Otto could be having a good time, too.

"Yeah?" Unathi eyed him. "What'd you do on Earth?"

A rather startling change of subject but, okay. "Lots of things. Just before exiting," – Otto smirked at that – "an analyst."

"What's that?"

Otto explained.

Unathi grunted. "That's a job? Things seem to have gotten a bit complicated down there."

"'Down there'?" Otto picked up on it. "Is that a geographic reference? Are we really up in the sky, at least, what we took for the sky?"

"No idea." Unathi peered at the rearview mirror. "It's just convention."

"Oh."

"But, back to the point." Unathi cut down an alley, scattering a crowd of women carrying baskets filled with flowers standing around a market stall gabbing. They yelled at him good-naturedly and he waved a hand out of the window. "This analyst work you did was in response to events, right?"

"Well, yeah. Everything pretty much is."

"Right, so it's pointless to say you should have stayed in the condo. Events create a response, even here. You're involved, whether you want to be or not. Especially if you're one of the good guys."

"Are we the good guys, 'Nath?"

"Stupid question," he said and slowed into the traffic pattern of another street, filled with more bicyclists than anything. "Why do you think you're having so much trouble?"

"Bad guys think they're the good guys too."

Unathi snorted, "No they don't. They know they're being jerks. Good guys know they're doing right."

"Hitler thought he was doing right."

"Who's Hitler?"

Otto flicked a hand. "After your time. And probably not here, if there is any real justice left in the Universe."

"There is." Unathi set his lips grimly and whipped down a side street, checking his mirror again. "And we suffer because of it. Are you familiar with British colonial expansion?"

"Got an excellent briefing from an Indian guy named Pashtun." Otto fish-eyed Unathi. "Know 'im?"

"Yep," Unathi said, and no more.

Otto shook his head. "Of course you do. So, yeah, I got the highlights – sun never setting on the Empire, Maratha, Boer War, all that. Why?"

"How can a war bore?"

"No, no." Otto waved a hand. "B-O-E-R, not bore. They were Dutchmen living in Africa. Or Germans, something like that. The Brits fought them around 1900 or so. And why did you hear the word 'Boer' instead of its equivalent in your language?"

"Ah, you mean *abathakathi*, the Voortrekkers. And I heard 'bore' because I speak and understand English quite clearly."

"So you know that war."

"No," Unathi said, "I know the war before that. And my own."

"There was a Boer War before the Boer War?"

Unathi remained quiet as he navigated yet another side street, then said, "The British were pushy, always coming at everyone. They fought the Voortrekkers, your Boers, which was fine until they pushed at us. Like every other Zulu, I wanted to push back, but Cetshwayo told us, 'No, be patient' and, you know, that turned out a wise policy, bought us time. I mean, wise for the nation, not so wise for me."

"I'm not following."

Unathi smiled grimly. "Because I ended up dying for the British at Isandlwana."

"Wait." Otto raised a finger. "You mean, Rorke's Drift? You were at Rorke's Drift?"

"No, Isandlwana. Rorke's Drift came later. I might have survived that one."

"Okay, but you died fighting for the British."

"Yes." Unathi's eyes were unreadable. "At the hands of my people, dragging me through Umgungundlovu and throwing me at Cetshwayo's feet. The last thing I remember was the contempt on his face. My brother," he whispered.

Otto knew a hard moment when it showed up, and he turned back to the street. They were now on the tail of what looked like a tandem club, thirty or forty two-person bicycles sporting tall orange spotter flags on the back, all the riders wearing orange T-shirts and shorts. They had the whole street and Unathi stayed a few car lengths away from them. Lots of cyclists in this here City ... Otto peered at the sky. On a night like this, why not? The cyclists were laughing and high-fiving and passing bottles of wine back and forth. More fun.

Decent moments passed. "How did you end up with the British?"

"I heard the words of Shembe and turned away from Nkulunkulu and embraced the One Living God, and that made me outcast. I had no choice but to seek a place among the hated British, serving them as scout and interpreter. They treated me little better than a dog, but that did not matter. Not at all." He looked fiercely at Otto. "Because the Word was among them. I endured for that reason. For that reason, my name is a curse among my people but, here I am." He flourished a hand across the City. "And that is universal justice, the most important thing in Creation, and that is why" – Unathi suddenly whipped the DeLorean into an alley and slid between two parked wagons – "you must go on the ship."

"But ..." Otto wanted to ask if Unathi'd run across any of his former Zulu pals around town, which should have a deleterious effect on his concept of universal justice, but was given no chance.

"You. Must. Go!" Unathi seized Otto's leather jerkin in his giant, powerful hands and Otto felt the strength there, but that was nothing compared to the resolve on Unathi's face. The big man smashed him against the door as the wing rose and Otto was suddenly sprawled on the sidewalk, staring up at him. "What the hell?" he yelped.

"Run! Run now!" Unathi pulled the door down and floored it. The DeLorean, tires smoking, one-eightied back to the avenue, fishtailed and was gone. Otto gasped because, right behind it, shadows raced in pursuit.

Was that George and a couple of his friends? Otto rolled to his feet and sprinted to the corner and peered around the brick. At the far end of the block, the tandems sprawled, upended and tangled together, their wheels spinning crazily in the air, flames among them – which was weird, unless the tandems had been fueled somehow. The DeLorean sat sideways in the midst of the wreckage and Unathi stood next to it, silhouetted by the flames, huge, terrible, and facing ... not George, but three or four tall, thin men wearing suits, features lost in the flickering light, threatening.

But so was Unathi, and the Suits hesitated. Formidable, he could reduce them to piles of blood and bone with just a squeeze of his hand, or to dust by merely asking for their agency. The circumspection of the Suits was understandable. Not understandable was how Heaven, the Afterlife, whatever this was, had suddenly turned into an action movie.

"Not supposed to be this way," Otto muttered.

One of the Suits turned and stared right at him. Uh-oh. What to do? Jump out and join Unathi in a fight he didn't understand against an enemy he didn't know? Or, as Unathi commanded, run?

No contest.

"Hey, jackasses!" Otto yelled as he stepped into full view. "You're messing with my pal there!"

Instead of a look of relief as the sidekick showed up in the nick of time, Unathi's face turned to incredulity and desperation. "Otto, you idiot!" he yelled. "Run! Run now!" and he reached out a giant hand and grasped the jacket of one of the suit guys who had turned toward Otto ...

... and the suit backhanded Unathi over the top of the DeLorean.

"Holy crap!" Otto yelped. Skinny suit boy slapped a five-hundred-pound warrior thirty feet in the air! What kind of badasses were these guys?

Want to stay and find out?

"I am not running away, I am not running away," he chanted as he ran away, sprinting full tilt down the alley toward the lights at the far end. He dodged obstructions, little piles of cardboard or crates and trashcans, superfluous in Heaven you'd think, and he wondered briefly if the alley had been deliberately dressed for noir. He glanced back, thought he saw movement and doubled his efforts.

He spilled onto a street, surprising a knot of minstrels dressed like fourteenth-century court jesters strumming lutes and hand harps and fingering recorders. They stopped mid-tune, which Otto recognized as "Whiskey in the Jar." Didn't Metallica cover that?

"Y'all right?" one of the jesters, a portly one with a redneck accent, called out.

"Yeah-yeah, I'm good." Otto straightened his leggings and brushed at them, but pointless, there's no dirt there. The redneck jester gestured to the others and they picked up where they left off, dancing some odd little jig back down the street as they played. Otto watched them over his shoulder as he headed the opposite way. Weird. There was a sudden ripple in the jesters' ranks and a bit of uncoordinated jigging and Otto saw, in the middle of them, two very tall and thin men dressed in suits. Staring at him.

Time to go.

Otto had been to Escape and Evasion school during his street agent days, which he'd thought funny at the time because, c'mon, when was he ever going to be in a position to use it? It's not like his job involved jumping out of perfectly good airplanes, but his boss said, "We have slots, so you're going," and the course was every bit as miserable an experience as Otto figured it would be (had to eat worms) and sure came in handy now. Otto took an angle directly at the Suits then dashed back the other way, weaving among a convoy of orange VW camper buses with hippie flowers painted on their sides. The idea was to make the Suits react, because reaction was slower than initiative, and it seemed to be working; that is, until the Suits split to flank him. Whoops. Otto sprinted around a calliope which was playing "Take Me Out to the Ball Game," marked another alley, and ran pell-mell down it.

Don't circle, segment.

He turned right at the end and ran for a block then crossed the street and left down another alley, then right and a block and then left – don't get into a pattern! – so he ran straight through three more alleys then left and straight down a side street then right. He tore through crowds that ranged from English guys in top hats and tails to a bunch of Romans in togas and armour. At least he thought they were Romans: could be Lithuanian bocce ball players having it on. Every crowd met him with a "Hey!" as he scattered them, then applauded as he bounded away, his progress traceable by the rise and fall of handclapping, dammit. The Suits were still with him, as a result.

He careened into a broad avenue and skidded to a halt, amazed. The street was a glittering diamond of light and color, a combination of Broadway and a Hollywood première with the best of French *Moderne*, but without any flashing neon of any kind – glowing stained glass, instead, so tasteful and beckoning that he had to take a minute, catch his breath (why did he have to catch his breath? Shouldn't he be able to run for years here?) and admire it. He'd get back to fleeing in a minute.

Right dead in front of him was a plate glass – no, plate crystal – window, with hundreds of leather-bound books arranged behind it in an ever-deepening spiral of lights and rows and shelving, lost in the distance. Otto pressed his nose against the crystal. Warm, welcoming. He looked at the most prominent book, the one beginning the spiral: Newton's *Principia*. He gasped. Not a copy, he instinctively knew. The original.

Something dangerous and otherworldly and filled with ill intent pursued him. He had no backup, the persons he counted as allies either unconscious behind a DeLorean or otherwise unavailable. He was exposed and vulnerable, as he'd been so many times during his Earthly life. But where had he always gone for peace of mind?

To a place of books.

He turned the knob (a cut diamond, he was sure) and walked through the oaken door inlaid with glowing glass. A little golden bell over the jamb rang as he did so and the door closed silently behind him.

Chapter XXV

Rare Books And Proto-Hippies

Ah. That smell – leather and pages and dust, the perfume of every library he had ever got lost in when a kid. Otto closed his eyes and took in a deep breath, savouring it ...

Eleven years old, Ft. Rucker Post Library. Mom had dropped him on the way to the Commissary and there he was, sitting at a back table with books he'd yanked from the shelves piled in front of him: *A Wrinkle in Time*; *Marooned on Mars*; *The Forgotten Door* ... yes! Days (hours) later, Mom dragged him out of there trailing checkouts while his brother and sister teased, "Bookworm!" and they hand-fought all the way home, laughing, Otto guarding his cache against their Hershey-bar-stained fingers. Then baseball and tag and sprinkling with the hose and spinning till dizzy and falling on the lawn and staring up, up, at sunset-tinged clouds and the first star and the "Wish I may, wish I might" and the second star, straight on till morning. Then upstairs and hunched over Bradbury or Bova or Knight, pages turning so fast.

Heaven.

After Dad's Huey ate a rocket over an unnamed Vietnamese hilltop, Mom sold the house and they moved in with her severe Baptist parents, all crammed into a little Dutch saltbox on the main street of Perkins, NJ. Mom took up with some local guy,

Otto's sister ran away, and his brother became a drug dealer. Otto became a gypsy, moving between hideouts to evade Gramps's 8:00 p.m. bedtimes and constant preaching against girls and booze and anything else that provided a modicum of entertainment. The Perkins Library, housed in a quasi-abandoned, falling apart and leaking, former high school, became his number one refuge, stuffed with the latest books and magazines and honeycombed with good places to secrete himself after hours.

He filled his lungs with refuge air. "I love the smell of libraries in the morning," he whispered in his best Duvall, "Smells like ... sanctuary."

"May I help you?" a quiet, cultured voice asked.

Otto opened his eyes. A guy dressed like the Quaker Oats logo, but without the hat, stood in front of him. Hook nose, cavernous eyes, wispy hair falling carelessly about his skull, maybe thirty-five or something, with the severity of expression and set of jaw that marked Gramps's idea of the righteous man.

"Puritan?" Otto asked, ready to bolt.

The man smiled and, instantly, the severity was gone. "Hardly," he said, "Sandemanian, but I gave that up."

"Sande ... what?"

"A rather extreme form of Evangelicalism, if you are at all familiar with English theological disputes of the eighteenth century. Judging by your appearance," the man gave Otto the critical eye, "I think not."

Otto flourished hands down his costume. "This old thing? Just my Tartar duds, for the desert."

The man cocked his head. "You have been Out?"

"Yes. You?"

"No, but I have heard many tales of it, mostly from a charming acquaintance of mine, a Maratha warrior who drives a taxi out there."

"You can't mean Pashtun."

"Indeed. You know him, then?"

Otto slowly nodded his head. "Yes, I do. Which is amazing. Even more amazing is that you, a random guy in a random shop on a random street, also know him."

"Not really." The man dismissed that. "There are far more fortuitous chances here than 'randomness,'" he made air quotes, "dictates. And now that we have discovered a mutual acquaintance, let us be introduced." The man held out his hand. "William Godwin, at your service."

"William Godwin." Otto furrowed his brow as he took the hand. "Your name is familiar."

"In what way?"

"I ... really don't know."

"No surprise," Godwin said, a touch of sadness in his eye, "I had my moment, but it passed. Rather quickly, I might add."

Otto chuckled. "Don't they all? So when was your moment?"

"The French Revolution. Shortly before, actually. I wrote several tracts and books espousing a rather radical social construction sympathetic to the Revolution's ideals, but quite at odds with the monarchy. It made me a controversial figure, especially when the Revolution took its bad turn." He grimaced. "I was not a popular person after that."

"I can imagine. That whole *Fraternite Egalite* thing turned into quite the cock-up."

"Y-e-e-s," Godwin drew the word out, tapping the bottom of his chin. "As did my fortune. I lost my business, my social standing, all my friends deserted me. The worst of it, I lost my wife."

"Left you?"

"Died. In childbirth."

Otto didn't know how to react. Mere moments before, he'd had been running for his life from some weird alternate life form and now this stranger relates a history of sudden and unexpected hammer blows, the sting of them still fresh after all these centuries.

This is Heaven?

Godwin poked around in a nearby shelf and pulled out a huge, leather-bound volume. "This is hers," he said reverently, handing it over.

"Whose? Your wife's?"

Godwin nodded.

Otto hefted it, deciphering the ornate cover: *A Vindication of the Rights of Women* by Mary Wollstonecraft. "I thought your name was Godwin."

"It is. She retained her family name."

"Really. In the 1790s?"

"Seventeen ninety-two." Godwin tapped the book. "That's when this was published."

"Far-left hippy Democrats all the way back then, huh? Who'da thunk it?"

Godwin narrowed his eyes. "'Far back'? In what year, exactly, did you succumb?"

"Twenty-nineteen. I said it was recent."

"It's that year already," Godwin said, mostly to himself. "Tell me, have your kingdoms fought their Armageddon and ushered in a worldwide polity of peace and justice?"

"Uh, no," Otto said, "Things aren't too much different from when you were around. America's gotten to be huge."

"So I'd heard," Godwin drifted off a bit then snapped back, full attention on Otto with a look so intense Otto took a step back. "Have you ... seen her? Met her, perhaps?"

Otto was a bit flustered. "Who, your wife? Uh ... no, I don't think so. No one by that name, anyway."

Godwin seized Otto's vest with a grip of iron and propelled him around a corner, Otto almost on tiptoes. "Hey!" he protested.

Godwin threw a shaking finger at the far wall. "Have you seen her?" he insisted.

Otto followed his point to an oil painting hanging on the wall, soft and diffused in the filtered light, a brown-haired, brown-eyed woman, regal more than beautiful, with a regard in her eyes that spoke of wisdom and pain and hope, the look of brilliance and compassion. Otto was taken with it. "No." Otto said softly. "No. I would have remembered."

Godwin made a grieving sound deep in his throat and detangled his fingers from Otto's leathers, taking the book from Otto's hands and quietly back around the corner with it.

"Why did you think I had?" Otto called after.

"Those fortuitous chances," was all Godwin said.

The tragedy of the reply said everything. Otto had confirmed Sam's presence to Grace, so the fortuitous chances were real. But that was ... inadequate. Loved ones, longed-for ones, evaded. The best you could do was hope some stranger would tell you of a fleeting encounter or experience your own fleeting encounter, like Ferd and his Dad. But Godwin still burned with an obvious and overwhelming love for his lost wife, and keeping them apart was unnecessarily cruel, downright malicious.

This is Heaven?

Otto stepped around the corner where Godwin fussed with some other volumes. "You've been here three hundred years," Otto observed.

"Give or take." He remained focused on the shelves

"In all that time, you could not find her? She could not find you?"

"No." Short. Grief-stricken.

The moment grew. "I'm having a very hard time with that, William."

He turned the sad, slight smile back in place. "As are we all."

The moment swelled between them: a man yearning for a love lost centuries before, another man with a growing disquiet that this Heaven, this Afterlife, was less than advertised, less than expected.

Less than wanted.

Godwin shook himself. "But, where are my manners? You are a patron and here I am upsetting you. Would you like some tea?"

"No, I'm good," Otto said, "And you're not upsetting me. You're ... teaching me."

A kind, but sorrowful, look filled Godwin's eyes and he bowed slightly. Otto opened his hands, taking in the shelves. "I gotta say, this is a nice shop."

"Well, thank you, I do try to make it a pleasing experience. Are you sure about the tea? Darjeeling, quite an exquisite leaf."

"I'm good." Something occurred to Otto. "Did you, by chance, get the Darjeeling from Ferdinand?"

Godwin nodded. "I did. His shops carry the best of everything."

"So he told me. Did you get your inventory from him, too?"

"No. My acquisitions are made here and there. I specialize in first books, ones that set tone or proposal or precedent. For instance, this," Godwin pulled out a bound series of printed pages with 'Nicolai Co' in bold across the front. "Copernicus. The one he handled as he died."

"How in the world did you get that?"

Godwin smiled. "The world, sir, has no bearing."

"Things beyond our ken, right?"

"Precisely."

Otto ran his eyes over the shelves disappearing up the murky ceiling. The books ranged from the expected vellum-bound masterpieces of medieval binding art to scrolls and even some cheap-looking paperbacks. "Books that set tone, huh? How do you determine that?"

"By what follows their publication." He flourished the Copernicus. "This one changed our position in the Universe."

"Ah." Otto got it. "Like Tolkien's *Lord of the Rings* changed the fantasy genre."

"Well ..." Godwin frowned a bit. "Not so ... limited. More widespread effects."

"Okay, then, like Galileo ..." Godwin nodded and made a vague gesture to some back shelves, "and Asimov's *Law of Robotics* ..." another nod "... and *Frankenstein*."

Godwin looked as if he'd been slapped. "Pardon me?"

"You mean, you don't consider *Frankenstein* groundbreaking? It was the first real science-fiction novel. And written by a woman, no less."

"*Frankenstein*, or *The Modern Prometheus*. By Mary Shelley." Godwin's voice was ice-cold.

"Yeah, that's it. So you know it. So ...?" Otto made a 'well, then?' shrug.

"Are you trying to bait me?" Godwin was genuinely offended.

"Well, no!" Otto was genuinely baffled. What'd he say? "I thought we were having a rather pleasant conversation!"

"Mary Shelley is my daughter."

Stroked Otto with a hammer. "Ah," he said. "Oh, right. I think I knew that once. I just ... forgot."

Godwin held his gaze and there was something, a shade, deep in his eyes. Otto raised his hands in lame apology. "Didn't she marry Percy Shelley?"

The shade deepened, as did Godwin's frown, and with a sharp headshake conveying a level of disgust – what's that all about? – he turned to the shelves and replaced the Copernicus and maybe it was time for a change of subject. Otto pointed at the manuscripts. "I'da thought these would be in a museum somewhere."

"There are no museums here." Short and curt.

Yep, guy is torqued. Percy Shelley must not have been the best son-in-law. "That so?" Otto tried to sound sincere and interested and knew he was failing, but keep it going. "Okay, makes sense, the guys who get put in museums are probably walking around. A library, then."

"Have you been to a library, sir?"

"Here? No."

Godwin pursed his lips. "Then you should go to one. You would immediately know the difference."

"And what is that?" Otto asked, but Godwin was looking past him, his brow furrowed, a look of concern on his face. "Oh, my," he said.

Otto turned, peering through the front crystal window. There was an odd stirring, a wind that wasn't quite right, a shadow where it shouldn't be. Otto's hair rose.

"Are they looking for you?" Godwin asked quietly.

Otto was a bit surprised. "You know about them?"

Godwin nodded and Otto watched as the shadows converged on the shop. Goosebumps now.

"If you walk down the center aisle, about twenty yards," Godwin whispered, "you will see a small cut-out to the right. Go that way."

Otto looked at him. "You're helping me?"

"Yes," Godwin swept a hand in urgency. "Go now."

"You know about the ship?"

"I know of no ships. I do know that whatever calls you, if it brings them," he waved toward the window, "it must be important. So go. Please. Now."

There was a fright in Godwin's voice that enhanced Otto's dread. "Who are those guys?" he asked but Godwin did not respond, instead turned paler, and that was enough. Otto sprinted past him and down the aisle, frantically looking for the turn and almost missing it, well hidden behind stacks of vellum as it was. As he ducked right, he heard the bell. "May I help you, gentlemen?" Godwin said.

Crash! The sound of crystal and glass exploding. Godwin

yelped and a tornado of torn books and broken shelves whipped past Otto's hiding spot. "Good God!" he said and the combat urge overtook the dread. Otto stepped back to the cut-out's turn, ready for battle.

The air touched him. So cold. So bereft. He gasped.

The sounds of struggle crescendoed and more debris rocketed past Otto's position. Godwin shouted, but not for help, "Go! Go!" and Otto felt the cold reach around the corner, seeking him.

He ran.

Chapter XXVI

Alleys And Doubts And A Kiss Made Of Heaven

Otto crashed through a crash door at the end of the aisle, falling into an alley of neatly stacked open boxes jammed with manuscripts. Holy Trove, Batman, exactly how many precedent-setting books *were* there in the world? Otto considered a quick rummage but a crack of wood somewhere inside the store got him to his feet and flying down the pavement.

He spilled onto a street of garish neon, like Chicago in the 50s. Restaurants, bars, taverns, diners, you name it, all jammed together and blinking fiercely to get his attention. Hordes of people roamed the sidewalks, piling in and out of each neon-lit door. There were seventeenth-century fops and 50s beatniks and toga-d Greeks and chaps-wearing cowboys and mass and crush and the roar of good cheer.

Perfect.

Otto slipped into a knot of masqued Venetians who hail-fellowed and slapped his back so much it hurt. He moved to the middle and glanced back surreptitiously. The air around the alley stirred, questing, and Otto knew it was only a matter of time. He ducked below eyesight and followed along. "Wine!" One of the masquers handed him a leather skin and Otto took it, grateful.

Man, good stuff. "Where'd you get this?" he asked.

"Grendel's," the masque, a raven with a long beak, rolled the 'r.'

Grendel's. Claudia. Safety.

"Where's that?"

"Ah, sir!" Raven-beak was rhapsodic, "You do not know of Grendel's, that wondrous haven of cheer and fellowship and the bewitching Claudia, her of the deep, dark ales and now!" Raven-beak flourished the skin. "The wines of Andalusia! Well, then ..."

Otto threw up a 'halt' palm. "Yeah, I know it, bub. I asked 'where,' not 'what.'"

"Oh," Raven-beak said, "Well, my apologies, carl, I mistook your meaning. But, surely, you know all you need do is hail a cab?"

"Name's Otto, not Carl, and I'm feeling like a walk." And not running into another Ian. Or George.

"A walk?" Raven-beak threw an arm across his mask in mock horror. "How absolutely pedestrian!" He turned to the others as they roared with laughter.

This guy needed a punch in the beak. "Where?" Otto let his tone convey that.

Beak was undisturbed. "Oh, well, if you insist." He vaguely waved a ruffled hand toward a set of neons that wriggled and danced into two red dragons. Chinese food, probably. "You'll find a small alley there. Just go through it."

"Right there?" Otto pointed.

"Yes, yes, Otto the carl, your sense of direction is quite to be admired. So go, walking man." Beak flourished fingers dismissively. "Go."

Yep, definitely a punch was due. But later. He stepped through the Venetians and ducked behind a set of scooters driven by gorgeous Amazon warriors. Love to get the story behind that but the air flowing into the street was probing the crowd, so best get moving. "Tell Claudia," Beak called as Otto found the small opening, "that Admiral Zeno says hello!"

Admiral Zeno? That Captain America villain? Or something like that? Probably not and Otto pushed through. Dark and narrow. Man, not good. He peered into the murk. Exactly the right spot for tall things in nice suits to be waiting in ambush. And Beak wasn't coming off as the sincerest of guys, was he?

No choice. There was real danger behind. What's ahead can't be any worse.

Can it?

Taking a deep breath, Otto plunged.

The alley was a lot longer than it should be and narrowed as he pushed along, and became darker. Otto probed with his palms and toes and knew he had made a big mistake. Never see the ambush coming. He'd finger-brush an ice-cold face and, startled, jump back and stumble over loose bricks and go down and they'd be on him and no one would see or hear or help.

Except God.

Otto stopped. Again, once again, like so many, many times throughout his life, he was in a situation where only God could help. Mom, on the floor choking on her vomit, drugged and boozed and crying over her lost husband and the guy who'd just deserted her and they didn't have a phone because Gramps didn't believe in them so it was up to him and he'd whispered "God, help!" to a God he doubted and, somehow, got her throat cleared and her breath back but it merely delayed the inevitable, the later night when he found her stiff and cold. The cry to God had worked, though. And it worked the time he and his team entered a house, guns drawn, and there was a noise upstairs and he knew, just knew, a shotgun would lever over the banister and eviscerate him so, whispered, "God, help," to a God he no longer doubted and he reached the top and found the bomber and his girlfriend painting a wall. Didn't even hear Otto and his squad come in.

And such mundane, everyday Earth situations didn't even compare to this one. Heck, he was in this alley, in this dangerous situation, because he was looking for God, so this merits immediate Divine assistance.

"God," he whispered. No. That was wrong. "Father," instead, more reverently.

Nothing.

"Father!" he implored again.

And again, nothing.

Which made no sense. If he got half-assed responses back on Earth, he should get full-assed ones here. After all, the intervening space had been somewhat shortened. In theory.

But, what if it wasn't? And what if the standard protocols of Earth intervention were obviated here, replaced by new ones, different ones? Ones he had no clue about.

The dark thickened, if that was possible. C'mon, God, at least snap on a streetlight or something. But no, the dark grew a magnitude worse as he watched. "Ya know," he addressed the dark, "I'm beginning to have me doots."

Added to every other bizarre thing that had happened to him since he'd arrived here, such as the absence of God and loved ones and the danger and fear and seriously lethal bad guys, this dark was a bridge too far, a straw too much, an alphabet block too high. The tower shuddered, and teetered, and fell.

This. Is. Not. Heaven.

Certain thoughts freeze and drain, radically changing life's course. Like back when he and Sherry were living together and he took her over to Tree's apartment and the place was packed, black lights on and posters glowing and Chuck and Jonny Boy and the Pine girls were screaming and running and wild-eyed and Otto said, "Tree, what the hell?"

"Dude!" Tree's eyes were spirals, his grin hooked to each ear. "The punch, man! The punch!" and he spooned a frantic glob into a cup and shoved it at Otto. "It's speed, man, speed! Get with it!"

Sherry had spun on her heel and walked out as Otto stood paralyzed, his love for Tree and the wild life of 70s New Jersey suddenly gone. He smacked the cup out of Tree's hand and said, "You're crazy, man!" and left and found Sherry sitting on a neighbor's porch.

"We have to get out of here," she said. "Not the neighborhood, here. This life."

He married her the next day, joined the Air Force the day after, and never went back.

Or the time he stood on the frozen flightline of Kunsan AB, Korea, shivering in his parka and Floyd Tressick, the weather forecaster on duty, stood with him and said, "God laughs and the snow flies," and Otto asked what he meant; quietly, firmly, Floyd had explained a God of grace Otto had never heard of, so radically different from Gramps's God of hellfire and anger and, right then, at that moment, he believed and his whole perspective changed and he became an agent, a fighter, a defender of the only nation that had as its basic premise the grace of God.

And if this was not Heaven, and the God he looked for and called for was unreachable, then he had wasted his entire life. Well, at least his life from the Kunsan flightline on.

Otto rocked a tad, the only visible sign of the psychic fist that had just rammed into his stomach. He was in an Afterlife nothing like promised, nothing as expected, in peril and fighting against forces he did not understand, the pains of Earth continuing but now without the hope of something better. There's nothing beyond the Afterlife. There's nothing here. He was lost.

But lost, where?

Maybe this ... place ... was not where the soul goes for its much-deserved rest, the place of joy or judgment the many religions promised; such a place is non-existent and this ... place ... is merely where the accumulation of electrons and protons and whatever else constituted his soul settled after losing its earthly host, because energy cannot be destroyed and the energy of our thoughts simply, move. Maybe off to some pool of dust and gravity somewhere on the other side of the Orion Nebula spiraling into the core of a new star as he, whatever this glob of thought and memory that constituted "he," spun imagined entertainments and all this ... hallucination ... would one day burst forth in nuclear glory, noted by some future astronomer and given a category number, and "he," all "he" thought and felt, would simply evaporate.

There is no Heaven. Only physics.

Something stirred behind him, the air dropped a degree, and Otto knew the thin men were closing. He could stay here and fight and lose, or he could keep going and lose later. There's at least a modicum of a chance in that, even if this is mere physics. Even if this is actually Hell and at the end of the alley broods Lucifer, red and sulfurous, on a throne of skulls, his jaundiced eyes gleaming with amusement and his fangs blooded. "Mortal fool! I feed on your hopes!" and hands without end with nails without life reach and tear Otto's soul from him and devours it.

Now there's an image.

Otto chuckled, despite everything, and felt better and what the hell, haha, no pun intended, this is where we are and this is what we're doing, so let's see what happens next. Face the despair of losing God later. He stepped purposefully, ready for the ice-cold face that was surely there and stepped again and no, nothing, and he was ten, twenty steps into the murk when, listen:

What was that?

Otto cocked his head. Music? Yeah, dopplered, like someone

opened and closed a door.

... and it's no, nay, never (clap clap clap clap) ...

Otto bolted down the alley, bricks and ice-cold faces be damned. There was a greying in the distance, the end of the alley, and he whipped through it, almost bowling over a small Incan-looking woman dressed in a kimono. She *ah*'d in surprise and then howled with laughter, pleased beyond anything at Otto's sudden appearance. He grinned at her while quickly looking around. Yes, there, the shop of crystal structures, the pre-Colombian restaurant, and in between, the dark door.

Doubts, suddenly, gone.

A cold stirring of wind behind him caused the braying woman to stop, stare bug-eyed down the alley, and then shuffle hurriedly away. Otto leaped for the door and plunged inside. The same Norse décor, the Viking clientèle and there, behind the bar, hefting four giant overflowing steins …

"Claudia!" Otto yelled.

She gaped at him, her ice-blue eyes widening. She glanced at the entrance and back at him and then dropped all four steins on the bar, gesturing feverishly at one of the staff to take them.

"Come!" She frantically waved him over. Otto pushed past a couple of Umbrians, getting a good-natured "Watch it!" for his trouble, and ducked under the waiter door, sliding to her feet. She grasped his hand and pulled him up, surprisingly strong, surprisingly warm. "Play!" she yelled at the Celtic band. They immediately changed from the round to a reel, loud and stomping and the whole crowd, all four hundred thousand of them, cheered and jumped to their feet and began the most frenzied, claustrophobic clog Otto had ever seen.

Cover.

"This way!" she said, pulling Otto through a back door and down a paneled hall. They were at full tilt, turning here and there and Otto wondered how such a long, narrow hallway fitted into the building, but space was relative here, wasn't it? They clattered up a set of rickety stairs and then down three flights of even more rickety ones before pulling up to a small wooden door with a big iron knob on it. She twisted it and smashed her shoulder against the wood, the effort making her cry out. Otto reared back and applied his shoulder and, after a couple of rounds of mutual effort, the door flew open.

"Quickly!" she said and pulled him onto the landing of a set of even more rickety stairs that dropped out of sight into darkness below.

He hesitated and she pulled harder, insistent. "Now!" Okay, no choice, and fell in behind as they raced down. She stopped, lit a torch with a match, which revealed another torch ahead, and she lit their way down a stone hall that suddenly emptied into a huge storage area. Racks of hogsheads piled up to the ceiling. The piercing odor of ferment and peat made his head swim.

"What's this place?" he asked.

"The whiskies," she said as she fumbled behind a rack that was against the far wall. Otto inhaled deeply. "Man," he said.

She stooped over, her hands busy behind the lowest barrel, but she looked pleased. "About another hundred years," she said.

"I think they're ready now. And Admiral Zeno says hello."

"That one," she chuckled dismissively, "And no, they're not. Ah," she said and stepped back. There was a click and a whir and the slow sound of grinding stone. A crack formed down the wall, which slid to the left, taking the stack with it. Otto craned his neck. There was a long, torchlit passage stretching to the distance. Torchlit? How'd that happen?

Silly question.

Claudia pointed. "Go this way."

"Where will it take me?"

"To your purpose," she said and wrapped her hands behind his head and pulled him to her and kissed. And kissed.

Otto savoured two kisses in his life. Not the first one he ever had, when he was twelve and fumbling with Linda Allison on her back porch in Alabama and she had henpecked his lips rather quickly, but the one he had when he was fourteen on the dance floor with his first true girlfriend, April, and she had kissed him with longing and depth and time stood still and about four or five songs went by before he even remembered his name. And the first one with Sherry, standing by her car at midnight outside her house in Mt. Holyoke, New Jersey, after having spent the last four hours doing nothing but talking, exclaiming in amazement over how much they had in common. A kiss that made the stars whirl and summer extend forever and kept him eighteen and alive and roaring with the passion of it.

Claudia's kiss beat both of those all to hell.

Transport. Best word he could use. He was no longer Otto but a spirit on the wind, reaching every corner of this Afterlife and what preceded and what came next, all in an instant. He stood at the apex of the Universe and commanded stars to dance, galaxies to pulse, planets to whirl. Deep within him a surge of electricity and want roared and solidified into diamond and fire throughout his being.

She pulled back, breathing hard.

"*Bwa?*" was all Otto could manage.

"You. Must. Go!" she managed to gasp between breaths, her flush receding, the light of her blue eyes settling. Must have been good for her, too.

"You're kidding, right?" The diamonds in his blood raced and he reached for her.

She took his hands, trembling, and held them. "No," she said, shakily, "You have to go. They'll find you."

He was torn completely in half, the sense of danger competing with the sense of want. He gazed at her and danger was losing.

She placed a warm, blood-driven hand on his chest. "In time," she whispered.

Yes. In time.

He pulled her to him fiercely, a tight, wanting hug that she reciprocated, strong, almost cracking his spine, but enough and they released and stood staring at each other.

"Please," she said.

He nodded, turned, and ran down the passage. He looked back when he heard the stone grinding. She stood in the rapidly closing portal, lit by torches, a thousand years in her eyes and an eternal message in her stance.

In time.

Chapter XXVII

These People Shouldn't Be Here

Torches lit the passage every twenty feet or so, like in some old video game. *Hexxen*? Yeah, that one, which meant ogres should jump out any minute swinging axes, and him without a firewand. Otto braced, but nothing happened.

Thank God. This was weird enough.

He ran straight down the passage for about ten minutes before it sheared off at a whole new angle. Ten minutes down *that* and then another angle and then three more angles over the next thirty minutes and Otto's sense of direction evaporated. He kept on, trusting the passage was taking him to safety, else why would Claudia throw him in here? Unless she was an agent and he was heading into the arms of suited thugs. "We've been waiting for you, Otto. *Bwahahahahahaha*!"

After that kiss?

Otto almost came to a halt – very hard to run when a stupefying wave of desire weakens the knees. He had an urge to turn back and find her, but what a dumb move; the Suits'd get him and, worse, he'd have spurned her gift of flight. Buzzkill. So, no, dude, keep going. Somewhere at the end of the Labyrinth, Ariadne waits.

Where, exactly, *was* the end?

No idea and, after what Otto figured was another half-hour or so and three *more* angles, he slowed to a walk. Not that he was tired; to the contrare-e-e, he was delightfully flushed and bursting with the thrill of it all (especially that kiss, yes). *Hmm.* Fleeing in terror, he got winded, fleeing after Claudia's smooch ... well. Put a whole new twist on pre-marathon warm-ups around here, didn't it? Otto took a deep breath and ran his fingers along the stonework ...

There appeared to be gaps.

Otto pressed his eye against one and saw distant light. He ran a hand experimentally along the wall and pushed. Nothing, so he placed both hands and pushed again, but still nothing. Otto studied the wall. Some of the stonework at the bottom was a bit off, so he stooped and fumbled along the lines. The stones depressed, throwing him off balance and almost face first into the wall which swung toward him with a grinding noise and he scrambled out of the way. It stopped, a stone door halfway open. Otto peered behind it. Steps, going up.

How 'bout that?

He ascended, cautious, expecting a suit to jump him but the top opened onto an empty street. A quiet one, lit by old fashioned gas lamps, and, hey, down at the other end – was that a guy carrying a long-handled match? Sure was. Otto watched as the man, dressed in a top hat and tails, put down a stepladder, gingerly climbed it, lifted the glass on a lamp and applied the match. A flare and crack and the hiss of lit gas, perceivable even at this distance. The man climbed down, tucked the ladder under his arm, happily waved the match at Otto, and strode around the corner.

Otto smiled. Chim chim cheree.

All right, let's get going, before the Suits show up and harsh my mellow. So, how to get home from here?

Forget summoning a carriage – Suit Boy, Inc. probably owned the franchise. Could run down the street, grab the gas man and ask directions but, no doubt, that conversation would turn into metaphysical doublespeak:

"Can you tell me how to get home?"

"Certainly, just go."

"But, where?"

"Home."

"No, where is home?"

"Where home is," and then Otto would splutter and Gas Man would laugh and say he'd be all right and Otto would punch him.

Let's not do that.

Otto didn't recognize the street but that was nothing new and he took its measure. Quiet set of New York brownstones, residential. Nice. Innocuous. Probably filled with Suits bent on dismembering him. Okay. Select a direction and stroll along until some opportune sign made itself apparent. He stepped off the curb and casually looked at the building across from him, the word "Library" posted unobtrusively in gold script over its doorway.

Opportune sign making itself apparent.

Otto mounted the granite steps two at a time. Stone lions flanked the entrance. Perfect. He patted one of them on its head as he passed through a pair of frosted glass doors more appropriate to a restaurant than a library. A long, bare hallway, wrapped in rich, dark paneling with sconces on the wall giving off a half-light, extended to another set of frosted glass doors. There were no paintings, no signs, not even a "This Way" arrow. Reminded him of a funeral home and Otto dropped into "be-ready-for-anything" mode. He peered through the second set of door glass. There was light on the other side, but no movement. He turned the crystal doorknob and entered.

It was a larger room, similarly paneled and sconced, but with a long, nondescript desk facing the door. A nameplate, "Librarian," sat precisely in the middle of the desk, aligned with the front edge. A brass reader's lamp illuminated a scattering of parchments that a man, sitting at the desk, studied with a hand magnifier. Otto scrutinized him. Older, late sixties; a long, rather messy, flowing beard contrasted with his bald head and neatly pressed Victorian-style jacket.

Swear the guy looked a lot like those old photos of ...

"Charles Darwin!" Otto gasped.

The man looked up in surprise. "Why, yes. Have we met?"

"You're Charles Darwin!"

"Quite," Darwin put down the magnifier and regarded Otto coolly. "We have established that. And you are?"

Otto was still too stunned to revert to manners. "But, what are you doing here?"

"I am working, sir."

"You, of all people!"

"Ah." Darwin's face cleared. "I see. Given your outfit, I presumed you were of the medieval steppes, but you know of the controversies so you must be more recent."

"This is just my Mongol get-up. And yeah, I know about the controversies. Scopes Monkey Trial? Creationism?"

"Scopes I have heard about. 'Creationism.' That is new to me. Your use of the word indicates a theory developed around the Genesis story?"

"No, not a theory, a belief. A world view."

"*Hmm.*" Darwin sat back, fingering his beard. "A world view in opposition to my theory of evolution."

"Yep."

"What year were you?"

"Twenty-nineteen."

Darwin let out a long sigh, "After all this time, still misunderstood."

"I don't think you were misunderstood. You did propose evolution, right?"

"As a mechanism. Nothing more."

"Okay, fine, but you had to know what it was going to do."

"I did."

"And yet," Otto flourished hands, "here you are."

An amused smile crossed Darwin's lips. "Do you equate heresy with damnation?"

"Doesn't everybody?"

"Only the ill-educated, who have small understanding of our Lord's Grace."

Otto steamed. So, Darwin wants to make this personal. Fine. "Yeah, okay, I've heard all that but you're like the poster boy for atheism, you know."

"Poster boy?" Darwin's brows furrowed, "You mean someone going around pasting up theater bills? I fail to see the point."

Otto flipped a hand. "It's an expression. Isn't the Universal Translator making that clear?"

"We are both speaking English, sir."

"Well, versions, I suppose. What's that quote? England and America are countries separated by a common language."

Darwin chuckled, "That's good. Who said it?"

"I think it was Churchill."

"Who? Lord Churchill? I didn't think him that erudite."

"Not that Churchill, the other one. Or maybe it was Shaw."

"Shaw. Is he a peer? Don't believe I know him."

"No. Run Run Shaw, and he's a god." Otto smiled inwardly at the joke and Darwin's obvious confusion. "So, what are you doing here?"

"As I have already stated, I am working, sir."

"Yeah-yeah." Otto waved that away. "But that's not the question and you know it. So, Mr. Evolution, Mr. There-Is-No-Soul-We're-All-Just-Apes, ends up here." Otto leaned forward. "Must have been a bit of a surprise, wot?"

Darwin frowned as combat lit his eyes. "Sir, I have never, ever said there was no soul and I am sure my surprise was no less than yours, considering you are an ignorant, ill-mannered oaf who should have been excluded from the City on that basis alone."

"Ignorant, ill ..." Otto spluttered and took a threatening step. "I'll show you some oafiness, hairball! How's *this* for oafiness?" And he raised fists.

Darwin sprang to his feet. "That you have already," presenting his own fists. They both shuffled into ready stances, growling at each other.

"Gentlemen! Enough!" a voice rang out, clear, bell-like. Otto and Darwin turned.

A man stood in the near set of doors, dressed in jeans and sandals and a plain white T-shirt, but wasn't a hippy. White-haired and craggy, built like a bull, with a huge hook nose. "Emerson!" Darwin said in an exasperated voice.

"Emerson?" Otto started. "You mean, *the* Emerson?"

The man looked at Otto with a twinkling eye. "It depends, Mongol, what your 'the' implies."

"Tartar. And, you know, Emerson."

Emerson broke into a broad smile and Otto saw genuine joy infusing the man. "Indeed, I do. And I am highly amused to see you, young man, about to engage in a brawl with him," and he made a contemptuous gesture at Darwin.

"Stay out of this, Ralph," Darwin snarled. "This pup needs a lesson."

"Pup?" Otto shook a fist. "I'll 'pup' you!" and he grabbed at Darwin's lapels.

Emerson moved quickly, interposing between them. Rather agile for an old guy pretending to be a hippy. "Gentlemen," he warned, "none of that."

Otto and Darwin glared past him at each other but were more than arm's length away, so could do no damage.

"Now then." Emerson looked them over. "I couldn't help overhearing your, uh, disagreement." He turned to Otto. "You, sir, seem to think Darwin's theories, as late as they were," – here Darwin snorted – "render him ineligible for this place. You," he said to Darwin, "are incensed that an intelligent man would properly conclude 'your,'" air quotes, "theory is flawed, especially given our present circumstances."

"Waddya mean by 'late as they were?'" Otto asked.

"And what do you mean by 'your' gestured in such a dismissive manner?" Darwin challenged.

"Merely an observation that evolution had already been considered years earlier," Emerson said to Otto, then raised an eyebrow at Darwin, "and that someone else actually developed it."

Otto gaped at Emerson. "Who? You?"

"Of course not him!" Darwin yelped.

"Very true," Emerson said, "Although I found nothing new in that book." Emerson waved Darwin off. "There is evidence its origin," here Emerson chuckled, "came from elsewhere."

Darwin scowled at Emerson. "Sir, the taking of a raw idea and developing it to the point of palatability and understanding is not intellectual theft. Unlike the presentation of half-thought-out homilies as a logical method."

"Homilies?" Emerson's brows lowered, threatening to affect weather in China.

"You're talking about Transcendentalism, right?" Otto was proud he remembered that.

Darwin made a disgusted face. "'Transcendentalism' indeed."

"Maybe there's another young pup here in need of a lesson,"

Emerson said, taking a step toward Darwin and raising his fists.

Otto stood, amazed. He was about to witness a fistfight between two of the nineteenth century's biggest icons. Too much.

"Enough of that!" a woman's voice shrieked. Startled, all three turned to the door where a large ornery woman with white hair cut to the ears stood. She pointed a claw at Otto. "The Tartar's not here to watch you two idiots fight!"

"Mongol. And no, let them," Otto said, leaning forward in anticipation. God, could this get any more surreal?

The scrappy woman shoved Otto in the chest, sending him sprawling. Strong, that one, and Otto pulled himself up the wall. "Now." The woman grimaced at Emerson and Darwin. "Why don't you two knock it off and attend to the patron?"

"I think they are," Otto said as he straightened his jerkin. "I'm guessing a patron shows up, you guys offer help and then have a fistfight over the privilege."

Scrappy woman's lips compressed. "The first part, yes," and she gave the other two a significant look.

Darwin gestured at Otto while straightening his jacket. "He started it."

"And you certainly prolonged it," Emerson accused as he picked at his T.

"All right!" Scrappy silenced them. "So, patron, how can we serve you?"

Otto considered. "Well, actually, I was finding my way home and saw the Library sign and someone told me I should check it out ..."

Darwin was dismissive. "You can't check out the sign."

"Indeed," Emerson piped up, "It's permanently affixed."

Otto, baffled.

Scrappy blew out her cheeks. "That's not what he meant. He wanted to see what the library offered." She paused, gazing at Otto curiously. "Are you from the later centuries?"

"Yep. Twenty-nineteen." He extended a hand. "Otto Boteman."

The old lady beamed, a frightening stretch of face into a smile that almost made Otto jump. "Well! Nineteen-ninety-five, for me. Madalyn Murray O'Hair," and she took his hand like she wouldn't give it back.

Otto yanked it away, thunderstruck. "What?"

She grinned. "Figured you'd know me."

"What's to know?" Emerson looked up, curious.

"How?" Otto swept a hand to include all of Heaven. "I mean, just how?"

Madalyn shrugged. "Apparently, when I was a kid, I believed." She grinned big again, to the point of terror. "Bit ironic, I'd say."

Otto threw palms skyward. "I don't get this; I don't get this at all. Who's next through the door? Hitler?"

"Who?" Darwin asked.

Madalyn frowned. "I wasn't that bad."

"Not that bad ..." Otto, incredulous, turned to Darwin. "Sorry I called you the poster boy. She," – and he pointed an accusing finger – "is the freakin' runway model."

"'Runway model'?" Emerson's gigantic brows flooded the Yangtze. "Is there some standard for running now?"

"Look it up." Otto scowled at the woman. "What the hell, Madalyn? You, almost single-handedly, destroy America's faith in God, and here you are?"

"I didn't destroy anything!" Madalyn snapped. "The Bible shouldn't be read in school, that's all."

"Excuse me." Emerson cocked his head. "Why not?"

"Why?" Darwin countered. "That's what church is for."

"Exactly!" Madalyn gave him an appreciative glance.

"Oh, great." Otto threw up wider hands. "Let's get the Warren Court back together, why don't we? They should be here any second," and Otto tapped his foot, staring at the door.

"Look," Madalyn snarled at Otto, "it's not my fault the country fell apart. It was heading that way, anyway. Besides." She rubbed her neck ruefully. "I think I paid."

"Paid?" Otto was incredulous. "How? You're here!"

"I didn't arrive under the best of circumstances, okay?"

"*Pshaw,*" Emerson razzed "Who did?"

She turned on the philosopher. "What'd you do, die peacefully in your bed? You wanna hear what happened to me?"

"Deserved, I'm sure," Darwin commented dryly and now another set of raised fists as Madalyn fell into combat stance. Emerson, in one swift movement, picked up Darwin's chair and smashed it across Madalyn's chest. The chair splintered and the big, tough woman fell back hard, driving Otto into the wall. "*Oof!*" they both said at once, although Otto was convinced he got the worst of it. Darwin grabbed Emerson in a headlock and Madalyn, screaming, launched herself off Otto (prompting another oof), scooping a big book off the desk and slammed it into the side of Emerson's head. Darwin kicked her viciously in the knee while strangling a yelping Emerson and she fell back hard against Otto, driving him into the wall again.

"*Oof!*"

Otto fell to the floor and crawled along the baseboard. Books and furniture and fists flew over his head as all three of them shrieked and pummeled each other, in an eye-scratching scrum, all around the room. He kept his head low but the occasional splinter or elbow cracked him.

Man, this hurts. Time to get out of here. He looked back at the entrance. Suit guys were probably gathering there, attracted by the commotion, so forget it.

Peering along the baseboard, Otto saw an indentation on the far side. He scrambled, dodging a lamp hurled by Darwin. He hunched at the indentation and followed it up.

Yep, a door.

Reaching quickly, he grasped a small knob, turned it, and fell through. Rolling along, he kicked the door shut behind him, the sound of battle instantly cut.

"Shh!" someone said.

Otto pulled himself up. Then stared.

Oh. My. God.

Chapter XXVIII

Big Bangs

He stood in a hall of colossal dimensions, Brobdingnagian, Godzillian – pick an exaggeration – receding into a distant fog of light and lines. Hundreds, no, thousands of brass and crystal chandeliers – half of which supported lit candles at least three feet high, the other half, football-sized globes of electric arc – hung from iron poles dropped from a ceiling washed out by the glare. The effect was pleasing, not painful. Gigantic ceiling to floor windows, paned in lead and stained glass and framed in golden woods, ran blazing down both sides of the hall, shrinking to nothing in the far fog.

Otto cocked his head. What's lighting the windows? Last he checked, it was dark outside.

Twenty to thirty rich blond-wood bookshelves at least fifty feet tall but ending well below the bottom of the chandeliers stood between each set of windows on both sides of the hall, all marching to the same far distance. About five yards separated the bookshelves from each other, and Otto attempted a quick calculation of how many bookshelves per set, assuming 100 yards between the windows, and quickly gave up. A lot, that's all.

Golden tags with script glowing in the same mysterious manner as the windows hung on the ends and along the separate shelves holding thousands of bound volumes and unbound manuscripts.

Long tables of dark wood, candelabras scattered across their surfaces illuminating more volumes and unbounds strewn haphazardly across their lengths, stretched from the bookshelves on either side to a center aisle dividing the room and running as far as Otto could see. People, some robed, some not, some pantalooned and hatted, some toga-d or waistcoated, sat on tall, ironwood chairs pulled up hard to the tables, notebooks beside them, writing furiously as they consulted the documents. An odor of vellum and parchment and binding washed over him – Eau de Library – once more. He leaned back and inhaled noisily, a stupid grin on his face.

"*Shh!*" again, and Otto located a pretty woman sitting nearest him dressed in a wimple and holding a severe finger to her mouth.

"Sorry," he said.

She glared at him, annoyed, and returned to her manuscript, which appeared to be Latin. He flashed on a teenage memory: his best friend Don and he standing on the frozen shore of Mirror Lake, a January midnight, the stars overhead eclipsed by their frosty breath and the smoke of a joint they were polishing off and Don, laughing, pointed up, "Heaven, man, it's one big library."

"Don, you were right," he whispered.

Bam! The wimpled girl slapped her notebook closed, grabbed up papers, and stalked away with a backward, murderous glance. Otto mouthed a "sorry!" after her but that did no good.

"She's a bit testy, that one." A man, looking up from a folder filled with what looked like printouts, smiled.

"A bit. You know her?" Otto asked.

He shrugged. "Not by name. Fifteenth-century Russian nun, I think, researching proofs of Divine Infallibility."

Otto's eyebrows rose. "That's here?"

The man's swept hand took in the expanse. "Somewhere."

"How do you find it?"

"How do you find anything?" Another hand sweep. "By looking."

One of life's eternal truths Otto concluded, and flopped in a chair opposite the man, examining him. Boyish, exuberant, a smoulder in his eyes that spoke of genius. Just the right kind of guy to explain the library's workings. Otto leaned over the acre-wide table and stuck out his hand. "Name's Otto Boteman."

"Georges LeMaitre." They shook as LeMaitre took in Otto's

leathers. "What are you supposed to be?"

"Mongol. Or Tartar, take your pick. So, what are you looking for?" Otto asked.

"Singularity."

Otto's blink prompted another smile. "I'm trying to perfect the formula that reduces the Universe to its single, original point."

"There was a single, original point?"

"Seems so." LeMaitre thumbed through several scribbled sheets dense with mathematics and held one out to Otto. "Tell me what you think."

Otto politely declined. "I suck at math."

"Oh." LeMaitre, sympathetic, explained. "Essentially, this is a recursive formula that draws all of matter down to its first point. I'm just having a hard time locating the point."

"And what's the point of that?"

LeMaitre grimaced. "That's a pun in English, isn't it? Doesn't hold up so well in Flemish, but I get it. Ever hear of the Big Bang?"

"Well, yeah."

"Thought so, you seem modern, despite the outfit. Good term. Hoyle came up with it."

"The guy who wrote the game books?"

LeMaitre grinned. "No, that was Edmund. Fred Hoyle was an astronomer." He craned his neck, "I think he's down there somewhere."

"Who? Edmund or Fred?"

"Fred. Edmund's running the City-wide backgammon tourney."

"*Hmm.*" Otto considered. Might want to get in on that. "So, Big Bang. First, nothing, then, everything. Fits right in with all this, doesn't it?" Otto's wave took in the City.

"I'd say," LeMaitre agreed, "and there's poor Fred, still trying to prove steady state." They both chuckled, although Otto had no idea why.

"So." LeMaitre shuffled his papers. "What's your project?"

"Uh, what?"

"Why did you come in?"

"Well …" Otto hesitated, not sure how "ducking suits" would go over as an explanation. "I sort of happened by."

LeMaitre raised an eyebrow. "Just browsing? You'll never leave, you know."

Otto looked at the shelves closest to him, the end tags brightening as he did. The letters moved, first into Dewey decimal classification, the 900s, then into words, a lovely Gothic script: *Histories of the Various Nations.* "Whoa," he said.

LeMaitre followed his gaze. "Worthy project," he approved. "Everyone here likes a good story."

A good story. Another one of life's eternal truths. Something stirred deep in Otto's stomach and he shifted to get a better view of the scrolls and loose sheets. "I'm bettin' that shelf contains a little more than standard timelines."

"Indeed," LeMaitre said, "You'll find testimonials by people who were there at whatever period you're researching. Not just the folks you've already heard of, like Columbus, but Columbus's cook and the guy who swabbed the decks, for instance." LeMaitre arranged his materials. "And it's all recent stuff, written after they got here and from perfect memory." He gestured. "Go take a look."

Otto peered at the shelf. Man, think of it: Chief Joseph's right-hand man giving a first-hand account of the Nez Perce war; a '49er talking about the trek to California; a '48er's flight from Europe to the New World. Myths busted, suppositions disproved, all by getting up and grabbing a few random papers.

Lovely. But, ultimately, dissatisfying.

"I think," Otto said, "I'm interested in a little more than that."

"Such as?"

"Original source material."

"What do you think all this is?" LeMaitre said, somewhat puzzled as he nodded at the stacks.

"It's still secondary, no matter how well written. I mean real origin. Before singularity. *The* Origin."

It took LeMaitre a moment, but then he sighed wearily. "You mean God."

"Bingo."

LeMaitre eyed him then said, "Why don't you reinvent the wheel, while you're at it?"

"What?" Otto sat back. "You've found God?"

"I found Him long before coming here." LeMaitre flipped some of his papers. "As you must have, too."

Otto made a helpless gesture. "I mean ... in Person."

"I know what you mean." LeMaitre glanced up sharply. "Most

of us don't need to."

"Okay, yeah, I know, I've heard that argument and this," Otto took in the library, "seems another in a long string of overwhelming proofs. But I—"

"Need to see," LeMaitre interrupted. "Crewman?"

Knocked Otto back a bit, that did. "Well, yeah. How'd you know?"

"Most unfortunate for you," was the only reply.

Otto would have loved an explanation, especially since LeMaitre's lowered brows and sudden belligerence hinted at something untoward, but he didn't get the chance. *Blam*! A tornado of wood and brass and books suddenly blasted him right out of the chair and into the shelves.

"*Oof*!" he yelped, for about the dozenth time tonight.

"*Oof*!" echoed LeMaitre, who had been blown right beside him.

The bookshelf creaked and shifted and slowly toppled, smacking into the one behind, the next sets dominoing down the hall. Pushing himself up from the pile of papers and volumes and broken furniture, Otto watched in amazement as the shelves picked up momentum and crashed into each other, an avalanche of massive wood.

Bedlam.

Chairs overturned and tables upended as scholars shrieked and poured out from the spaces between the shelves and into the center aisle to avoid a crushing and fell over each other. Chandeliers swayed and one crashed down on top of a table, blasting the books piled there like a grenade and sending other scholars flying. Two windows blew in, bathing the hall in glass shrapnel.

Otto turned.

The door he had previously rolled through now a fragmented, gaping hole, a lot farther away from him than it should be, about a football field's distance. What the heck? Otto would have loved to contemplate the physics of that, but three Suits stood there looking over the wreckage with expressions of satisfaction as the chaos multiplied and the library dissolved into riot. One of the Suits looked directly at him.

"Uh-oh," he muttered.

"Brought them on us, did you?" LeMaitre snapped as he pulled himself out of a book pile and brushed off wreckage.

"What are they?" Otto shrank against another pile of wreckage but it was useless, they had him.

"Stupid question." LeMaitre stepped over and pulled him up. "I assume you will want to get out of here?"

Wham! The window closest to LeMaitre and Otto exploded, knocking them both flat under a wave of glass and lead and frame.

Man, that hurt!

Otto reeled to his feet. The Suits crashed through the wreckage as if it were mere dandelion puff, throwing scholars bodily out of their way as they marched toward him. Oh crap. They'd be on him in seconds.

"There!" LeMaitre gasped from the floor. Otto followed his pointing hand. The shattered window revealed the City, in all its night-time glory.

Ah, so the light was generated by the windows themselves. Otto would have loved to contemplate the physics of that but now wasn't the time.

"Go! Go now!" LeMaitre leaped to his feet, pushing Otto toward the opening. A broad avenue stretched away from the window wreckage. "Get to the ship!" LeMaitre turned, heaving up a broken table and hurling it at the oncoming Suits, who scattered.

"How do you know all this?" Otto shouted at him.

"Just go!" LeMaitre roared and leaped at the closest suit, grabbing him by the throat. The other two piled on top and Otto did not hesitate: he jumped over the wreckage and through the window and pelted down the avenue, the sounds of battle and breakage gathering behind him.

Chapter XXIX

Pastries Made Of Lotus

"I am NOT running away!" Otto announced as he ran away. He spotted a promising alley and windmilled to a halt opposite it, looking back. Flames belched from the library windows as groups of yelling people on the sidewalk helped patrons escape. The flames whipped to the side as though a wind tore through them and Otto glimpsed figures inside struggling with each other. A suit loomed in a window, staring in his direction. Otto flattened against the bricking, then the flames came back and the suit disappeared. He fled down the alley.

It turned into another twisty endless tunnel, go figure, and Otto raced down it for what seemed like hours. The alley came back on itself a couple of times and Otto again lost all sense of direction. The streets it followed must be pretty convoluted. He fell into alley coma and, after a couple of days or hours or years, spilled onto another broad avenue, flailing his arms like Daffy Duck, convinced he had blundered into a trap. But, nothing happened.

It was getting lighter. Dawn. So he'd been out all night. 'Ey? Otto watched the sun break the horizon and the sky turn into that forever, deep, endless blue ...

Snap out of it!

Otto wrenched his eyes down, focusing on a cobblestone.

Cobblestone?

Otto looked around. He'd seen these buildings before, and off in the distance ... yep, the parade of crazy vehicles.

This was where he'd first arrived.

Otto instinctively fell into combat stance. Had to be a setup, had to be. He stood ready to fight as sunlight flooded the street with gold and the night people joined day people emerging from the various apartment complexes, everyone strolling about cheerily, exchanging greetings. Not a very threatening scene. Nervously, he looked back down the alley. No stirring of the wind, no sense of despair. Must have shaken them. For now.

Moments passed and still nothing happened except a lot of amused glances, so Otto stepped out of cat stance and relaxed. "Lord, I sure hope You're enjoying this," he sighed, eliciting an appreciative grin from some guy wearing an extraordinarily loud Carnaby Street get-up. As if Otto, adjusting his leathers, had room to talk. Nervously, he checked the alley again and figured standing around here playing switch was a sure-fire way to let the Suits catch up. LeMaitre said get to the ship. Everyone said get to the ship.

Maybe he should get to the ship.

But first, things to do and people to see, and that required credits. Did he have enough? Ian said so, but that guy had other motives. Well, one way to check – buy something. And, if memory served, there was a pretty good pastry shop nearby ...

"That one," Otto said, moments later, pointing at a cheese Danish. The barista flashed his gold and diamond smile, flipped his gold and green tunic, and said, "Welcome back, new guy!" as he handed Otto a plate.

"You remember me?"

"Of course!" the barista nodded enthusiastically. "That was a memorable day."

"More painful than memorable."

The barista shrugged. "Maybe, but stirrings of old memory are refreshing."

"Old memory?" Otto blinked at him. "You mean of Earth?"

"Of course," The barista gave Otto a napkin. "But, here, it becomes background. After a while."

"How long have you been here?"

"What year was it when you left?"

Otto told him. "Ah." The barista did mental calculations.

"Around 500 years."

"Really?" Otto was impressed. "So, what, you came out of some slave hellhole?"

"Oh, no." The barista waved that off. "I was a mariner, sailed with Dias around the Cape. Had a good life, a family in Dakar, another in Lisbon." He grinned his jeweled grin.

"And you don't miss it?"

"No. I don't think of it. What with all this," and his nod took in the City. Another grin. "Anything else?"

"No. Wait, yes. How much is my credit?"

The barista consulted the ever-present clipboard. Otto craned his neck but couldn't see. "You're okay." The barista slapped the clipboard down behind the counter.

"In what sense?"

The barista pointed at Otto's plate. "You're covered."

"And what else?"

"What else do you want?"

Otto took a stab. "To get to the ship."

Wrong stab. The barista cocked a puzzled head. "What ship?"

"Never mind." Otto sought a table in the back, away from the other patrons. He ate the Danish and ordered another, which the barista cheerfully brought without further questions, and Otto watched for a while as he served others.

So, memory fades. Or becomes secondary.

Lotus-eaters.

After a few decades of this place, how could you not be? An eternity of fun and hoo-ha and runnin' around. God? Eh, He's around here somewhere. Don't worry about it. Have another Danish.

Was that so bad?

Otto scooped up the last crumbs and stared out of the window. Spend a thousand years studying the architecture of those extraordinary buildings, a thousand more sampling the restaurants, two thousand doing it all over again and then five thousand in the libraries. Maybe he was running all over the City for no reason. Maybe the Suits were well-intentioned, actually trying to save him from a huge mistake. Their methods were a bit extreme but, given the issues, could be justified ...

Yeah, right.

Violence precludes altruistic intents. If the ship was metaphysically wrong, then the Suits would merely sidle up and whisper, "Hey, buddy, you're on the wrong track," not blow libraries apart. Their murderous persistence spoke volumes. But, about what? Why were Suits and their agents so adamantly opposed?

That depends on the nature of the Suits.

Otto toyed with the plate. Were they angels? He didn't think so; angels were supposed to help humanity, not hinder it. Demons? Sure acted like 'em, but if this is Heaven, what are they doing here?

Because it's not Heaven.

Yeah-yeah-yeah, and not Hell, either, or, at least, not as advertised. Otto confirmed that with a last bite of Danish. Doubtful there's one this savory in the Burning Lake, unless some florid demon was teasing the damned with bear claws. Homer Simpson and the Donut Machine. Where was the Department of Ironic Punishment?

Otto flashed on Latchemondy's little demonstration and shuddered. Now, THAT was Hell. The price of rejecting God in time was separation for eternity. Everyone focused on burning forever and being stabbed with pitchforks, but that wasn't the point, no pun intended – it's that the created never behold the Creator ...

Never behold.

Otto stopped mid-chew. We never find our Parent. Lost in Disneyland, surrounded by all the pleasures but terrified because Mom and Dad are gone and you wander about, vulnerable, scared, bereft. Otto peered at the other patrons. Sure didn't look bereft, looked, instead, like they were having a good time.

Not knowing.

The words came unbidden to his mind. Said years ago by a night-school friend, a particularly intense guy who contended with everything, what was his name? Drew, right, yeah, only knew him a year before he dropped out and God knows what he went on to since he hated everything so much. Once, out late, deconstructing the world: "You think God punishes with disease and poverty?" Drew snorted. "No way. He punishes with not knowing."

Living an entire life under delusion, completely wrong about every single thing and blithely unaware of it – that's what Drew meant. All the energy of life spent on a mistake, ending up, fifty years later, exhausted, bitter, and wasted. Then death, and now in a similar situation, believing this is God's Afterlife; but God is an absent dad, just sending in the support checks while you eat great Danishes, have fascinating conversations with Third Century Chinese nihilists and drink the best of ales until dawn. Not Heaven but a lesser version, a way station, but the train never arrives.

An eternity of not knowing.

He really, really, had to get back to the ship.

Otto finished and stood up and the barista offered another Danish but he shook his head and walked outside. The sun was full and warm and inviting an upward glance but Otto deliberately kept his head down. Cheerful people walked by, "Good morning!" and Otto swore they were the same beautiful people he'd seen on first arrival, which made sense because they probably lived around here. Beautiful people, beautiful place, come, sit with us, take in the health of the day and gaze on the lotus sky and sip these fine waters and eat these fine fruits and we will be indolent and peaceful and soporific. No strife. No anger. No struggle. Bliss.

Was that so bad?

Little chance of boredom. Even sitting around his apartment wouldn't bore. If push came to shove, he could go out and do odd things, like lie in the street and let automobiles run over him. No problem. Go to the office, don't go to the office. No fear of failure, no sexual tension. Challenge everybody or nobody, talk to wonderful people and study intriguing subjects, an eternity of exploration and role-playing. No pressure. No expectations.

No God.

Forget it.

Otto didn't spend his life fighting evil just to spend his eternity without ever seeing the Boss. While he appreciated the gifts, the Giver was more important. He had questions. He had complaints. He had every concern of every human who was ever born, and he wanted answers straight from the Horse's mouth, not from libraries. He wanted to gaze into the eyes of the Father. And he wanted to be sure, absolutely sure, that he had spent his entire life knowing, instead of not knowing.

So, let's go, shall we?

Otto looked toward the line of cars and headed that way, reaching the corner in about ten minutes. He smiled as a three-person bicycle rode by, the riders dressed like circus clowns. They cheered Otto as they zipped past and he waved.

Gotta admit, this is a fun place.

He turned back to the street and was nose to nose with a horse. Pulling a carriage.

Uh-oh.

"Ride, sir?"

Startled, Otto looked past the horse at the top-hatted driver. Not Ian. Not George, either. Still. "You an agent?" he asked, prepared to flee.

"An agent?" the driver, beetle-browed and portly, frowned. "I was a factor. Is that the same thing?"

"A factor in what?"

"The tobacco trade."

Otto suspected they were not talking about the same thing, which meant they were speaking different versions of English. But the driver had not floated away in ash and the horse looked at Otto rather benignly, so he got in. "Do I have enough credits to ride?" he asked.

The driver flourished a clipboard. "Yes, sir. Where to?"

"How many credits do I have?"

"Enough."

"How much is that?"

"Enough."

Drat. "Okay, take me home," Otto said and sat back.

It was a standard ride but Otto was hyper aware of all the cabs they passed, certain George and a reconstituted Ian would pull up alongside and renew the battle. "Chuck you!" the driver called to an approaching carriage; "Chuck you, too!" the receiving driver called back and they both laughed.

"What's that about?" Otto asked.

"We are," the driver snapped a playful whip in the air, "the City Hanson Cab Union, CHCU, pronounced 'chuck you,'" and he smirked.

Ah. Inside joke. Otto wasn't amused.

Ten minutes and three turns later, the carriage stopped in front of the building. Of course. "There you are, sir," the driver got out and helped Otto down. "Name's Ebenezer, Ebenezer Cooke. I ply this area, so if you need further assistance?" and he raised a beetle brow.

"Thanks. Did you know Ian? Or George?" Otto got ready to run.

"Ian or George, Ian or George," Ebenezer tapped his chin thoughtfully. "No, can't say I do. Or did. You speak of them in the past tense. Were they Earthers?"

"Earthers?"

"Persons of shared acquaintance while alive."

"No. City folk." Otto paused. "Afterlifers?"

Ebenezer smiled. "Neighbors."

"Neighbors." Good term. He looked at Ebenezer. "So, what's a factor?"

"An agent," Ebenezer said. He got back in, flicked the reins, tipped his hat and rode quickly down the street. Otto shook his head – definitely not talking about the same thing. He turned for the door but pulled up, surprised. A tall, skeletal man, dressed like a Beefeater (sans pike), blocked his way. "Help ya, bud?" he asked.

"Well, no. I'm just going in."

The Beefeater produced his own clipboard. "Name?"

"Excuse me?"

"Your name," the Beefeater tapped the clipboard impatiently.

Otto blinked. "When did this start?"

"What?"

Otto pointed. "You. We didn't have building security ..." and Otto intended to say a measure of time, three weeks, a month ago, whatever since he left, but didn't know. His voice tailed off.

The Beefeater shrugged, "Change in policy. Name?"

"By who?"

Another shrug. "Management. Name?"

"Management? Whose management?"

"Management is management. Name?"

"No, no." Otto waved impatiently. "What management? The building, the street, the City?"

The man peered down at Otto. Man, he was tall. "Management," he said slowly, as if talking to a particularly stupid child. "You gonna be difficult, bud?"

Otto glowered at him. "You'll get my name when I get yours."

The tall man glowered back. "It's Carlton."

"Carlton. The doorman. You're kidding, right?"

"No, I'm not kidding. That's my name." Carlton frowned and

anger lit his eyes. "Why'd you say it like it's a joke or something?"

"It is a joke. You're a joke." Otto thrust out a jaw.

The clipboard came slowly down to Carlton's side and his eyes narrowed and he drew himself up to full height, which topped Otto by at least four or five inches. His shoulders straightened and his knees flexed, aspects of a seasoned warrior.

Gulp.

"Joke, huh?" Carlton bore down on Otto, who took an involuntary step back. Fight or flight time. Otto measured Carlton and chose flight. He spun on his heel ... "*Ack!*" he gasped as Carlton dangled him off the ground.

"I'll show you what kind of joke I am!" Carlton bellowed.

Wham! Otto bounced off the building wall and dropped onto the pavement. "How much of a joke am I now?" Carlton roared as he scooped Otto off the sidewalk and hurled him effortlessly at the wall again.

"*Oof!*" Birds twittered around his head.

"Am I still a joke?" Carlton scooped him up for the third time and Otto knew this would be one throw too many.

"That's enough," a voice somewhere behind them quietly said. Otto felt Carlton's arm stiffen for the windup, then hesitate. His grip loosened and Otto fell heavily to the pavement. The birds had turned into a flock of screeching blue jays. He tried to sit up but had no balance at all and pitched over.

"Man," he said, the building reeling above him, "I thought you weren't supposed to feel like this here."

"By now, your preconceptions should be about gone," the voice responded and a figure moved into view. Otto forced his eyes to function properly. It took a moment. "I might have known," he said.

Chapter XXX

Factions Explained. Sort Of.

"Do you need assistance Mister ... Otto?" Mr. Latchemondy hovered, a slightly worried look on his face. Hovering behind him was a still-angry Carlton.

"Yeah, how 'bout calling off your—"

"Attack dog? Of course." Latchemondy turned on Carlton and did something Otto couldn't see. The big goon visibly quailed and shrank back to the front of the building.

Otto propped on his elbows and shoved a thumb at the doorman. "That guy works for you." A statement, not a question.

"Yes, he does," Latchemondy acknowledged, "and yes, his methods were excessive and, I assure you, unauthorized." He frowned at Carlton.

"Nobody talks to me like that!" the Beefeater shook a fist at Otto, who slid back on his elbows and then rocked to his unsteady feet.

Might have to run.

"That will be all, Carlton," Latchemondy's voice was clipped and threatening and the big Beefeater glared at Otto then turned and walked down the street, disappearing suddenly into another entrance. "I do apologize." Latchemondy bowed a contrite head.

"'Carlton, the doorman.' You being funny?"

Latchemondy's eyes twinkled. "Were you not amused?"

"Yeah, very." Otto rubbed his head then checked his hand for telltale blood because he had to have a skull fracture, had to. "Where'd you find that guy, anyway, in a—"

"Gladiator slave pit? And yes," Latchemondy raised a hand, stilling Otto's protest, "stop doing that. And no, not a gladiator. Carlton worked for a Mafia don as a bodyguard in 1950s Chicago. Appeared to know his business." Latchemondy stared ruefully at where Carlton had disappeared.

"You hired a hitman?"

"Yes."

Otto *tsk*ed. "They're not exactly the best candidates for doormen, you know. Temper issues."

"I tried to interest a Viking chieftain and an Ethiopian soldier, but they turned me down."

Otto's eyes narrowed. "Keeping tabs on me, Mr. L?"

"No, I'm not. I am reading your stances and expressions, as I have explained before."

Otto waved that off. "There's no way in ... Heaven ... after ... whatever ... you could read that from my face. Someone told you about Erick and Jakto. Admit it."

Latchemondy said nothing, and his face gave nothing away. Otto sighed. No use beating this horse. "So why'd you hire a doorman?"

"To let me know when you came back."

"You seem pretty informed about my movements, so why bother— Oh crap!" Otto froze because standing on the sidewalk, about twenty feet away, were two Suits, arms folded, skull-like heads regarding him with malice.

Latchemondy followed Otto's gaze. "Don't be concerned about them," he said.

"Don't be concerned?" Otto did a 360, wildly locating escape routes. "They're trying to kill me! Just like your idiot doorman!"

"They will not harm you."

"Yeah?" Otto shoved a belligerent face at Latchemondy. "Why, they work for you, too?"

Latchemondy backed away and coolly regarded the Suits, who had drawn closer and stood silent behind him. "They do not," he said.

Otto dodged, keeping Latchemondy between him and the Suits. "These jerks have been following me around, hurting people. Blowing things up!" Otto blazed at Latchemondy. "Ya know, for Heaven, this is a pretty violent place."

"That's because of your nature," Latchemondy said.

"Who? Me? I never went around picking fights!"

"But your species did."

"My species. Great. Fine. So this is one of those science-fiction books where the superior alien crapheads," Otto made a contemptuous gesture at the Suits, "imperiously decide we are too backward and brutal to be allowed entry into the Galaxy of Everlasting Peace and Humbuggery."

Latchemondy smiled slightly. "I so enjoy our conversations. Let me be clear, though, that we are not aliens. We are—"

"Another creation." Otto pointed to his face. "Yeah, see I can do that, too. And, right now, you are reading that I am not—"

"Buying it at all, as you would say. Yes." Latchemondy inclined his head. "I thoroughly understand. And, no, you are not in a coma."

"You misread that one, Latchemondy, old man. That was a wish, not a belief. So." Otto gazed at the Suits. "Who, exactly, are these guys?"

"Another faction," Latchemondy said. The Suits did not move nor blink nor give any impression they were anything else but a couple of very lifelike dummies.

"Another faction of what?"

"Creation."

"Demons?" Otto's eyebrows rose. "These guys are demons?"

"Demons?" Latchemondy's eyebrows matched Otto's and the two Suits actually moved, looking at each other with an expression of surprise and then back at Otto with amusement. "No," Latchemondy said, "no, definitely not. They're another faction."

"Of what?" Otto almost shouted his frustration. "And don't say 'creation,' dammit!"

Latchemondy said nothing. He stood, arms folded, as did the Suits.

Otto let out a long breath. "All right. Somebody owes me an explanation, and not one of those metaphysical ones, either. Especially after what I've been through." He glared at the three.

"Without belaboring it," Latchemondy said, "there are some," he nodded toward the Suits, "who firmly believe human presence in this Afterlife is sufficient. Actually, more than you deserve."

"Sufficient for what?"

"For God's grace."

"Huh?" Otto was perplexed. "What does that mean? That we shouldn't be here, that no human deserves an Afterlife?" He glared at the Suits. "Pretty friggin' arrogant, if you ask me."

Latchemondy nodded. "There are others who would heartily agree with you, Mister ... Otto. God's grace is His Own province. Nonetheless, there are always those who arrogate to themselves an understanding not shared by the majority." He looked at the Suits mildly. They looked at him balefully.

"So what's with all these blowings-up and agents and running me down? It's like they're trying to drive me out of the City. Out of the Afterlife, for that matter."

"They are not trying to drive you out," Mr. Latchemondy said quietly.

"You got that right. It's more like they're trying to kill me. Can you die here?" Otto asked.

"Well ... no, not in the sense you have."

"Then in what sense?"

"You can cease functions for a time."

"Yeah, I've seen that." Otto's mind flashed to Erick. "But I mean, permanent like."

Mr. Latchemondy considered. "It is possible but requires a lot of effort. You have to be in a rather hopeless situation."

"What? Such as in a place you can't heal?"

"Something like that."

"So, in a box filled with water or in a fire you can't get out of. Like a Lake of Fire. *Hmm.* Is that why Hell is nothing but fire?"

"We have already discussed Hell, Mister ... Otto," Mr. Latchemondy said, flatly.

Otto shuddered, remembering. "Yeah, right, okay, but is there a Lake of Fire somewhere?"

"I am not in a position to discuss the characteristics of potential places."

"Potential? It's yet to be built?"

Mr. Latchemondy said nothing. Neither did the Suits. Otto eyed them. "So, these guys wanna use me to stoke some future fire lake, huh?"

"No." But Mr. Latchemondy's expression left that open to doubt.

"Great." Otto threw up his arms. "Something else I gotta watch out for. What's all this got to do with the ship, anyway?" Otto scowled at the Suits, who remained impassive. Back to Mr. Latchemondy. "And why did you want to know when I got back?"

The three remained silent. Otto folded his arms and mimicked them, staring, expressionless, but his mind worked furiously. What, exactly, had he stepped into? Man, it was like a good case back home, start talking to some low-level punk who mentions a name and, there you are, in the middle of a big conspiracy with multiple levels of deception and hidden bank accounts and thugs chasing you all over the place—

It hit Otto like a hammer blow. "I'll be damned," he whispered, pointing a finger at the Suits. "You're afraid we'll actually find God!"

Their reaction was subtle, a bare flick of an eye, a slight shift, but it was enough. Latchemondy smiled thinly. "I believe you have something to do?" he said and glanced meaningfully at the entrance.

"You didn't answer the question," Otto said to him, "Why'd you use a doorman when you knew my movements, anyway?"

"It was important your entry into the building be delayed."

"Why?"

Latchemondy glanced at the Suits and then at Otto, who mentally smacked himself. Of course.

Bait.

"Not sure I like being the stalking horse, Mr. L."

Latchemondy half winked. "I understand. But, now, there is balance."

Otto regarded Latchemondy for a moment, and then regarded the Suits. Balance. In other words, Latchemondy had his back, at least for a little while.

Make the most of it.

"See ya 'round, boys." He saluted the Suits, pivoted on his heel, and walked through the double doors.

Chapter XXXI

If A Door Closes Then,
Often, The Window Closes, Too

Otto headed for the elevator, keeping an eye out for Carlton. Seemed like a guy to hold a grudge. He rode to the umpteenth floor. When the door opened, Otto peered around, expecting an ambush, but the hallway was empty. Okay. Sliding down the wall, he reached his condo and slipped inside, braced and ready, but no one was there.

Whew.

Otto stopped in front of the bedroom mirror. "So, what are you supposed to be?" he asked his Tartar image. Enough of this. He stripped the armour and leather into a pile at his feet and then flexed, naked.

Damn, was he buff! Hadn't looked this good since, what, seventeen? He grinned. One of the benefits of running around the desert smacking barbarians with lances. Or agents chasing him. That sobered him and he scanned the bedroom for assassins.

Wouldn't do getting jumped in his all-together, so Otto opened the closet and rummaged through the suits. As lovely as they were, he needed something more practical, like sweats, or even a dobok, although everyone would think he's a ninja or something. Were there ninjas here? Probably, but you'd never know it.

Otto's fingers brushed against something hard behind the suits. What the hey? He pushed the hangers to one side, revealing a chest of drawers set against the wall. Well, that's new. A folded OD duffle bag, like the one he'd been issued in basic, lay on top. Otto grabbed it and shook it open. Long, strong, and perfect for carrying all the gear an aspiring rocket man would need. Which can only mean ...

Otto yanked the top drawer open and found an array of jeans and work clothes. The other drawers held a one-man tent, cooking gear, tools, blankets, compass, canteen, freeze-dried food in packets, rope, a Pocketman ... and a Thompson Contender .44 with a box of ammunition.

"Wow," Otto said, and hefted the gun: heavy, big, designed for hunting. Hunting what? Dragons?

Otto studied it all for a moment then grabbed the clothes and, moments later, stood decked in jeans, chambrays, and boots. He packed the rest of the equipment into the duffle, Contender on top, unsurprised when the whole mess fitted perfectly. He stood the duffle on end – look at this: everything, and then some, he tried to get at Box's, gift wrapped and delivered credit free (as far as he knew).

Why?

Specifically, why all the rigmarole: dumped in the middle of the desert, kidnapped by a bunch of nutcase Mongol wannabes, chased through the City by murderous Suits or factions or whatever-the-hell when, apparently, all You had to do, Lord, was just drop a fully packed duffle on Otto's foot. He'd be floating around the crazy stars about now with Amelia and Marc and the gorgeous geisha. Heck, could already be hobnobbing with You, Big Guy. Everything else was a flippin' delay.

Why?

Well, Otto, old boy, you're a classic detective. Invoke the classic detective's follow-on question:

Who benefits?

The Suits, of course. For some inexplicable reason, they don't want humans to find God. Otto could assume, then, that all the delays, including the depleted credits that led to his unceremonious toss from Star City, were suit-induced. But, that meant the overcoming events, such as Pashtun giving him a ride and Kenny and the gang riding to his rescue (sort of), were Divine intervention.

Right?

Otto frowned. Not so sure about that; cantering around on Flicka and dinner with Unathi were more delays. But, then he'd met Jakto. And Grace. And, after a merry run through the City (highlighted by the Claudia Kiss of Eternity), here he was.

With a God-provided duffle and equipment.

Otto took in a long, pensive breath. Certainly went the scenic route, didn't we? Could have easily reached this point weeks (months?) ago by the aforementioned dropping of packed duffle on one's foot, Lord, or by merely having Otto stub a toe on the chest of drawers.

You and Your Mysterious Ways.

Otto heaved the duffle onto his shoulder, smiling grimly. Okay, Suits, let's see what else you've got. Maybe sixteen Prussian-costumed Nova Scotians speaking in limericks would waylay him right outside the door, needing him to reach behind a grate in an abandoned warehouse and retrieve the Jewel of Ophir, or some such nonsense. Buzzed by woad-painted Picts flying Sopwith Camels.

Bring it on, mofos.

Because, despite everything, he was still on point, and if he had to wade through sixty feet of velociraptor-infested Jell-O quicksand to finish the job, then, by the God he was looking for, he'd do it.

Before stepping out, he Carlton-searched and, satisfied neither doorman nor Nova Scotians lurked, walked six doors down and knocked. After a moment, Ferdinand opened the door, wearing the same red smoking jacket. "Why, Mr. Boteman!" he said, genuinely pleased.

"Get dressed," Otto said and then gestured at his own ensemble, "like this."

Ferdinand furrowed his brow. "Pardon?"

"And pack." Otto hefted the duffle. "You should find something like this, and all you need to put in it, in the back of your closet."

"There are no such items in the back of my closet."

"Trust me."

Ferdinand regarded him. "What is the purpose?"

"To find God."

Ferdinand chuckled, swirling a crystal goblet of shiraz, "I have already done that."

"Not like this."

Ferdinand took a sip, eyeing Otto over the rim. "Perhaps you should come in and we'll discuss it."

Otto shook his head. "No time."

"There is always time."

"Not in this case." Otto looked right and left. "They could be on us any moment."

"'They?'" Ferdinand looked suspicious. "What have you found yourself in, Mr. Boteman?"

"Otto, call me Otto. If we're going to be shipmates, we should be on a first-name basis."

"Shipmates?" Ferdinand's stance changed from annoyed amusement to sudden interest and Otto smiled.

"Yep, Ferd, ole boy, shipmates. The greatest of ships on the greatest of voyages, and all it needs is a navigator."

"I am not a navigator."

"Says the man who plunged up the Plata to see what was there."

Ferdinand considered that, looking down at his glass. "My shops."

"They'll be fine."

"But—"

"They'll be fine." Gangs of Suits will burn them to the ground, but no need to bring that up.

"Ship, you say?"

"Ship."

Ferdinand swirled the shiraz one more time, then tilted his head. "All right. It sounds interesting. But I reserve the right to come back at any time."

"Sure." May not be possible, Ferd, but that also didn't need mentioning.

Ferdinand gestured him in and Otto entered the living room as Ferdinand disappeared down a hallway. He walked over to the fireplace, which was lit, and patted one of its marble lintels. A replica had not appeared in Otto's apartment, nor had the alpaca chair, so maybe there was an efficiency at work here he didn't grasp. Since the Master Builder knew he was going to the crazy stars, why spend energy on features he'd never use? In a way, it was encouraging. But, in a way, he felt shorted.

He was examining the phantom windmill when Ferdinand

turned the corner, still dressed in the gown, still with the glass. Otto blinked. "Change your mind?" Oh no.

"No. But there is nothing in my closet resembling your ensemble." He pointed at Otto's clothes. "Nor any kind of outdoors equipment."

Otto frowned. "You're sure?"

"Quite."

Odd. If he, given his dearth of credits, had been provided with free dressage, he'd presumed Ferdinand would have it in bales. What to do? "Well, I guess we'll have to buy it," he concluded.

"Do you know where?"

"Yeah, a place called Box's. It's at the end of the line."

"Line?"

"The train line. To Out."

"Out." Ferdinand fumbled with the half-empty glass. "I don't wish to go there." He sipped.

"But that's where the ship is."

"Nevertheless," Ferdinand finished the glass and set it down carefully on the lintel.

A tremor of desperation spasmed Otto's stomach. "How can you not want to? You're the guy who mapped the Plata, beat back the Portuguese."

"On Earth."

Otto waved a hand, annoyed. "Yes, but that's still who you are. You must still have the urge." A flicker in Ferdinand's eye confirmed that and Otto grasped at it. "So here's your chance to do so again. On a much grander level."

Ferdinand looked toward the phantom windmill. "I admit that I have, on occasion, felt a desire to strike out and see what's there. I am convinced there are parts of this planet untouched by humans, even though we are so many. But then, I come to one of my shops and walk its storage bins and sample a product or two and speak to customers who tell me how much they enjoy their visits and I have this sense of such ... satisfaction." He considered. "And I firmly believe that any urge I have to ride the Plata is nothing but vestigial."

"After three hundred years?"

"Even if it was three thousand."

Otto stared at him. How in the world do you talk the satisfied out of their lives? Can't be done, just can't. Otto knew cops happy with the routine and surety and predictable results of small cases. He'd try to get them up and out, go run a dealer or a terrorist, but they'd give him the fisheye and shuffle a file and express how busy they were. It was frustrating because complacent and stolid didn't work in his profession. There was evil in the world and theirs was a priesthood demanding sacrifices of time and peace and effort to blunt it. It was their calling ...

Calling.

Otto straightened, then pointed an accusing finger at Ferdinand. "You are off mission."

"Pardon?"

"You're off mission."

"I don't know what you mean."

"It's simple. You've sold your birthright for a mess of pottage."

Ferdinand glowered at Otto, the offense deep and deadly in his eyes.

Good. Passion.

"You insult me? In my own house?"

"Think of it," Otto implored, "there you were, vibrant, alive, finding your very rightful place in a new world, striking your enemies and bringing knowledge to dark places, and then, like that," Otto snapped his fingers, "you were gone."

Ferdinand reeled as if Otto had struck him. "The Will of God is not to be questioned!" An emphatic tone.

"Exactly!" Otto's tone was equally emphatic. "It was the Will of God that someone of your great talents should be here available at the right time, to fulfill the greatest mission in the Universe." Dramatic pause. "To find Him."

"That is one interpretation," Ferdinand said coolly, "but there are many others. Such as, God intended someone else to rise in my place, take the rest of the Plata, seal it against the Portuguese, lead the viceroyalty to greater heights than I ever could." He paused. "I suppose."

"Or, taking the rest of the Plata is mundane compared with what you need to do here."

Ferdinand stepped back, silent, blinking at him, and Otto saw the indecision, the desire. "Ferdinand," he said quietly, "you know."

He did. It was obvious by the sudden spark in Ferdinand's eyes.

Despite his satisfaction, there was still an unresolved spot in Ferdinand's soul, the "what if" everyone carried with them their entire lives and, apparently, beyond. What if he hadn't contracted diphtheria? What if he'd lived another ten years? What if Otto had not idly thumbed through a list of government jobs and happened to spot the special agent description? The different lines a life could take, should a decision fall a different way.

And the beauty of this Afterlife, this Heaven, you can go see.

"Yes," Ferdinand said, decision made, "Yes. I will go with you." Otto's heart soared. "But," Ferdinand gestured at the duffle, "how critical is this equipment?"

"Critical."

"Then we must make sure we have it before departing the City."

"We don't have a lot of time."

"Why? Is the ship scheduled to leave?"

Could already be gone, but let's not mention that, either. "No. They'll wait for us." Hopefully. "It's not a time issue. We just can't go wandering around the City."

"That is due to the persons you mentioned earlier, I surmise."

"You surmise correctly."

"Who are they?"

Otto grimaced. "More like 'what' are they. I don't really know. They're damned strong and quite relentless. They don't want the ship to go. Really, really don't."

"And why is that?"

"I can only guess, but I think it has a lot to do with the age-old war between God and Satan."

"Satan?" Ferdinand was surprised. "That is not a name you hear."

"I know, and I'm only guessing, mind you."

Thoughtful, Ferdinand gazed at Otto's bag. "Then this is far more important than you have said, Otto."

Said with such dignity, such certitude, that Otto felt a jolt of how right that was. He could almost see the entire history of man whirlpooling to this moment. Somehow, if a motley group of misfits in an untested tube of scrap iron traversed an unknown and strange space to land at God's feet, then all of existence resolves. Adam, the Garden, the Wilderness, a ravaged man broken on a cross, all of it, thousands of years of slaughter and art, completed. Redeemed. Otto swayed with the enormity. He and Ferdinand stood at the linchpin of the Universe, the pivot, where all of existence was heading. The war would end.

No wonder the Suits were opposed.

Otto put a hand on the fireplace to steady himself. How was it that he, a former high-school idiot who'd heard a Gospel message sometime in his early twenties and converted and then, through a series of odd events, ended up a federal agent with a pretty good skill set, retiring after the requisite twenty and turning into a pretty good analyst with a pretty good wife and house and kid and life, innocuous, common, unimportant, was now charged with such an extraordinary mission? Who was he? No one, and nothing, just one of Your periphery guys, Lord. Did some things on the borders, kept the lanes clean, provided a service, then died.

So, why me?

Otto considered. Roles. That's what it came down to, assigned roles. In a chess game of a billion pieces, the move of the smallest pawn rippled across the giant board, sending signals, forcing recalculation, new strategies, new goals. A precocious child lost on a frozen moor, a bright young man drowning off the coast of Wales, a Minié ball tearing out the heart of a Civil War pastor, all changed the game. The pieces puzzled, wondering why one promising pawn fell so early while another not-so-promising ascended, but the Masters brooded, saw the sense of it, and altered their attack.

The smallest of pawns, the seemingly useless life, wasn't. It meshed into a common purpose leading to a silver tower in a giant desert on the oddest of worlds.

And two of the pawniest of pawns – an old nothing, no one, government analyst and a Platan explorer who died too young – were on the verge of changing the Universe.

It's enough to give one pause.

A vise gripped Otto's chest and throat. He gasped, wondering why a sudden realization of the moment would have such a devastating effect, when it became quite clear that he was literally caught in a vise. "*Urk!*" he said as the shirt tightened across his chest, the collar throttling him. Holy Hannah! His clothes were shrinking!

Ferdinand gaped at him, round-eyed. "What is happening to you?" he asked.

"*Uch* ... don't ... *urf*! ... know! Help me!"

Ferdinand jumped forward and, between them, they managed to unbutton Otto's Shirt of Strangulation and Pants of Boa Constrictor, as well as the Boots of Iron. And Socks of a Little Person. Otto lay on the floor, gasping, embarrassed. At least his skivvies were still the same.

Ferdinand, studiously ignoring an almost-naked Otto, held up the shirt, frowning. "This looks like ..." and with no further word, he slipped it on.

Perfect fit.

They looked at each other. "Do the rest of them," Otto said, and Ferdinand dressed in Otto's former clothes.

All a perfect fit.

Otto sat up, blinking. What the hell? Why in the world had his ensemble turned on him like a rattlesnake grabbed by the tail? It was as though he'd been thrown out of his own house.

And he knew.

Crewman Number 29 had arrived fully equipped, and all the ship needed was number 30 ...

The navigator. The one now wearing clothes that fitted him perfectly. Otto's clothes. Or, what used to be Otto's clothes.

Because he didn't need them anymore.

Otto's breath froze. Oh no. No. He was too late. He was.

But Ferdinand wasn't.

"Here," he kicked the duffle at Ferdinand.

"What are you doing?"

"Take it."

"What?"

"Just take it."

And Ferdinand did, standing there, duffle in hand, looking somewhat confused and squeamish because, you know, another man's clothes. But also looking ready: the explorer, the man on the verge of wilderness, resolved, intent. A man to cross deserts, scale mountains.

Find God.

Ferdinand was staring at him and Otto remembered his stripped status. "Wait here," the Argentine said and headed back to his rooms.

Otto looked down at himself. So, down to almost bare essence, he was. Naked came I ... where's that from? Oh yeah, Book of Job, another man of troubles.

At least God never tossed Job aside, as He had Otto.

Ferdinand turned the corner, holding out a pile of white cloth and braid. "Here."

"What's that?" Otto pawed it suspiciously.

"A Platan soldier's uniform."

"A what?"

"I found it here when I first moved in. It is the standard uniform of the garrison and what I wore on the river, but it is much too big for me. I never understood that." He eyed Otto. "Until now."

Otto gingerly took the bundle. "You can't be serious."

"I am."

Otto sighed and, a few moments later, stood before a mirror propped in Ferdinand's corner. The trousers were cotton and creased and buckled with bone buttons while the jacket was frogged in brown leather and had those mop-head gold epaulets so prevalent in bad opera. But it fitted perfectly and, Otto had to admit, was very comfortable. If ridiculous.

"Magnificent," Ferdinand said behind him, the admiration clear in his reflected face.

Otto turned. "I look like the street sweeper at the end of *Fractured Fairy Tales*."

Ferdinand was puzzled, but Otto said nothing more. The two men regarded each other. Ferdinand the Explorer, provisioned and ready for the borderlands. Otto the Soldier, charged with protecting the explorer on his journey. Roles defined. Ferdinand, the king on the chessboard.

And Otto, the dispensable pawn.

Chapter XXXII

A Good Reason Not To Come Back

"Ready?" Otto asked flatly as Ferdinand fell to his shoulder.

Yeah, Ferd, ready to go on the mission from which Otto, unceremoniously and with some contempt, was just dumped? And to which, insult piled on injury, he now escorts you? Maybe Otto could slip a letter to God into Ferdinand's duffle. It'd be a short one: Dear God, WTF?

WTF, indeed.

Otto cracked open the door and cautiously peered out. No one, so they made a mad but furtive dash to the elevator, Otto taking the corner as Ferdinand set the duffle in front. "Maybe we should use the stairs," Ferd said as the doors whooshed open.

"Are you nuts? We're what, twelve thousand floors up? Besides, what stairs? You ever see any?"

"Good point," Ferdinand conceded and they both stepped in and the doors closed and they descended, silently, smoothly. Should be okay. Shouldn't be any real trouble until they got outside.

Wrong.

"Knew you'd show up," Carlton grinned as Otto and Ferdinand stepped clear, two frantic seconds too late to catch the retreating elevator.

Otto swept the area, looking for escape. None. The only way

out was through the very tasteful marble-and-brass revolving doors that Carlton, armed with a cudgel like the one John Bull carried in those old British political cartoons, blocked. Kinda funny – Beefeaters carry pikes, dude – until Carlton slapped a palm with it.

Ferdinand's eyes bulged. "Is this one of them?"

"No, this is something personal." Otto measured the giant and calculated his chances. Not good.

"How many people have you managed to annoy?"

"A few."

Carlton gawked at Otto, brows furrowed. "And just what are you supposed to be now?"

"Like it?" Otto flourished two hands at himself. "Latest style."

"Look like a damn French admiral."

"Platan soldier," Ferdinand corrected.

"Dang right he's plottin'!" Carlton shook the cudgel at Otto. "And I'm gonna put a stop to it."

"And what would Mr. Latchemondy say about that?" Otto hoped the name served as a ward.

"Hang that guy!" Carlton dispelled the ward and dropped the cudgel sideways, bridging the space on either side of him. So much for running past.

"Excuse me." Ferdinand stepped before the giant. "What exactly is the complaint?"

"Not with you." Carlton nodded at Otto. "With that one."

"He has offended you?"

"Damn right."

"He does that." Ferdinand glanced at Otto meaningfully.

"Hey!" Otto protested, but Ferdinand turned back to Carlton. "One wonders, though, how much you let personal insult interfere with duty."

"Huh?" Carlton furrowed angry eyebrows at him.

"You seem an honorable man," at which Otto snorted, prompting a menacing rise of the cudgel, but Ferdinand ignored it, "and, no doubt, in your Earthly life, encountered situations where you forwent personal feelings for the greater good."

Otto threw out exasperated hands. "He's a gangster, for Pete's sake!"

"I'm gonna kill 'im!" Carlton took a menacing step toward Otto, but Ferdinand raised a restraining hand.

"Please, not quite yet," he said while shooting Otto a "shut up!" look. "You have, no doubt, quite justified grounds for doing so. But you will interfere with the boss's orders and it will hurt the entire organization if you indulge your anger."

Carlton eyed him suspiciously. "What boss?"

Ferdinand smiled slightly and looked to Heaven – er, upwards. "The Boss."

Springsteen, Otto thought irreverently, but Carlton didn't have the reference and what played across his face was something to behold. A roil of emotions, underscored by the surprise Carlton, no doubt, still retained from the first moment he opened his eyes in this wondrous City, expecting, based on his life's work, to be elsewhere. A face suffused with gratitude.

Carlton shook an unsure cudgel at Otto. "No way that guy is working for Him."

"It does seem unlikely," Ferdinand agreed, and Otto uttered another protest that Ferdinand shushed, "but I am sure, back home, you had similar doubts about others." He paused. "And yet, it turned out."

Carlton chewed on his lip, doubtful. "I knew those guys, though."

"True," Ferdinand said, "and you've had enough experience with our friend here to think him unworthy—"

"Hey!" Otto couldn't let that one go, but Ferdinand continued.

"—but apparently one other, this Latchemondy, has vouched for him?" Ferdinand raised eyebrows. Carlton swayed and gripped the cudgel and glared at Otto but there was resignation in it. "I will make you a deal." Ferdinand put a hand on Carlton's shoulder, quite a feat given the height differential.

This was Carlton's language and he looked expectantly at the shorter man. "What?"

"When we are done with our assignment." Ferdinand's shrug bespoke conspiracy, more of Carlton's language. "I will bring him back to you. You may pummel him for an uninterrupted hour."

"*Hey!*" Otto yelped but Carlton stepped back, evaluated them both, spat in one hand, and held it out to Ferdinand. "Deal."

Ferdinand, smiling slightly, spat in his own and they shook. Carlton moved out of the way and Ferdinand raised an eyebrow at Otto. "Coming?"

"Now wait just a minute—"

"Don't forget my bag." Ferdinand gestured at the duffle near Otto's foot.

"Yeah," Carlton chimed in, waving the cudgel for emphasis, "don't forget it. Bag boy."

Otto glowered at them as he grabbed the duffle and carefully slid past the giant until he had Ferdinand as shield.

Carlton grinned evilly. "A whole hour," he chuckled, slapping the cudgel. "That'll be worth the wait."

Otto almost said, "Be waitin' quite a while, Stretch," but then he'd have to explain the actual nature of the ship, something he shouldn't do within Ferd's earshot, at least right now. Instead, Otto rolled through the door, the Argentine in tow, eyed the street and found it clear, gave a backward glance at Carlton shaking his fist through the glass door, then stood for a moment on the sidewalk.

"Where to now?" Ferdinand asked.

"The train," Otto said. He looked at Ferd. "That was pretty good back there." Another glance at the hostile Carlton. "Despite my pending murder."

Ferdinand chuckled. "Thank you."

"You're a quick study, Ferd. Good in a crisis."

Ferdinand bowed imperceptibly at the compliment and Otto decided he'd join Kenny after dropping Ferd off and stay in the desert jousting with Vikings for ten thousand years or until Carlton forgot about him, whichever came first. He looked back. Carlton was swinging the cudgel like a baseball bat, big grin on his face.

Make it fifteen thousand years.

He absently tapped at some strange lump in a blouse pocket and pulled it out. Cigarettes, waddya know, the black ones Frenchies liked. Otto stared at the gaily decorated pack for a moment. Odd little provision, that. He shrugged—what wasn't? Never smoked on Earth 'cause those things'll kill ya He chuckled, lit one with the accompanying gaily decorated

Ronson—God provides—and offered another to Ferdinand, who took it without thought. A moment later, they were both wreathed in smoke, savoring the taste. Nice. Aromatic. And no choking.

Otto regarded the little Platan. Yep, a quick study. Just the kind of guy a rocket crew needs. An asset, a team player.

Unlike Otto, who tended to cause trouble. More and more, Ferd was looking the better choice.

Dammit.

"What are we waiting for?" Ferdinand said through a cloud.

"Our ride. Which should be ... yep!" The clop-clop of Ebenezer's horse announced the carriage's approach, the old guy smiling and doffing his hat. Otto threw the duffle in the back and they scrambled in. "Station," he said and Ebenezer doffed again and spoke to the horse which smiled, and they were off.

"I hope this is all worth it," Ferdinand said, meaning the scheduled cudgeling.

"Oh, it will be," Otto reassured and sat back and risked a glance at the capturing sky.

Yep, Ferd, when Otto stood on a desert hillside watching the rocket flame and shake and arc skyward, the winds of it pressing this silly uniform tight against his chest, waving as the rocket disappeared into that wondrous sky, God before them and Otto behind, alone, mission completed, of no further use, then maybe he'd skip Kenny and go straight to Carlton ...

... because an hour's cudgeling might actually console.

Chapter XXXIII

What Is It With Trains And Gunmen?

"What are you supposed to be?" Doc Holliday stared at Otto.

"French admiral," he said as he sat down.

"Platan soldier," Ferdinand corrected, taking the next chair.

Doc blinked, shrugged, and dealt the cards. "Stud," he said.

They played one hand and both lost and Ferdinand shook his head, "I don't know this game."

"What do you know?" Doc eyed him as he shuffled.

"Quadrille."

"*Hmm.*" Doc looked around. "We need a fourth."

"What's quadrille?" Otto asked.

"You'll like it," Doc said and waved at someone further down the car. "Kelly, wanna sit in?"

A big guy with a fat face shuffled over and yanked up a chair. "What's the game?" he asked.

"Quadrille," Doc replied and handed a set of chips to everyone. "Stake," he said, which Otto took to mean "ante" and threw in one. Doc put in four and Otto, obediently, grabbed an additional three but Ferdinand stopped him. "Just the dealer," he said.

"Oh."

Kelly grinned at Otto as he staked a chip, then threw out a hand. "Name's George. George Kelly."

"Otto Boteman" Otto took the hand and chuckled. "'George Kelly.' You wouldn't_be Machine Gun Kelly, would you?"

"You know me?" George's eyebrows rose and a very pleased smile crossed his face.

"Here we go." Doc rolled his eyes as Otto widened his. "You're *that* George Kelly?"

"Yep!" George sat back and hooked hands into his shirt, quite satisfied. "I am that George Kelly. Public Enemy Number One! How do you know me? Was it the Urschell job?" He looked at Otto expectantly.

Otto was wary. "Uh, no, no specific job. I was sort of a cop. Heard of you at some point."

Kelly was anything but wary. "No hard feelings, no hard feelings." He slapped Otto massively on the back and then regaled them with tales of kidnap and murder while Doc continued the eye rolls and Ferdinand gaped in astonishment and the game continued and Otto got lost in matadors, bastos and spadilles.

After three deals, and losing thirty of his 700 chips, he rubbed his eyes. "I've got a headache."

"Headache? Naah!" Kelly smiled broadly. "Not here. Listen, it's not that tough, if you're the hombre, you can announce alliance or solo ..."

"Or *vole*," Ferdinand added.

"Yeah, vole," Kelly agreed. "Anyway, I like alliance because it makes the king trump my secret partner," and he nudged Doc, who glared at him.

Otto held up a hand. "Just stop."

"We got thirty-seven more deals," Doc said. "You want to play a dummy hand to round it out'?"

"That'd be appropriate," Otto said and stood the run while Doc actually played his hands for him, trying vainly to teach Otto the game. About four days later, or so it seemed, they dealt the last round and Ferdinand had done well. "Where do I cash these?" he said, stacking his chips.

Doc gathered the cards. "Turn 'em in to me if you want, they're credited. But we're doing gleek, after a break."

"What's gleek?" Otto asked.

"Three-handed version of what we just played," Doc replied,

emphasizing the number.

"Fine with me." Otto waved off, stood, and walked to the window. Still in the City, although the buildings might be thinning out. Hard to tell. If he recalled the last trip correctly, Out was suddenly there, an unexpected emptying of the landscape.

Like right now.

The prairie rolled away in gentle waves of dust and sand and brightness, the distant mountains underscore to the hypnosky and Otto kept his eyes locked on a snowcapped peak in precaution. So, here it was, the rapidly approaching end of the most wondrous journey of his entire existence. He felt a rising in his chest, a sense of crescendo, like sitting in a car in some parking lot waiting for the beeper to sound then rush through the dark and kick down doors and shove guns in faces, kilos seized and bad guys hauled and all the work and prep and danger, over.

Over.

Maybe he should practice some goodbye waves so he wouldn't look too pathetic as the rocket rose and left him standing there. He raised his hand and made a faltering twitch of the fingers. Yeah, something like that, a pose of heroic resignation, wry, accepting, you boys behave yourself, send a postcard, hear? Maybe Claudia, looking down, would seal his sacrifice into her heart, forever. Maybe, some 200,000 years from now, he'd see her coming back, riding on clouds at the right hand of God, exalted, transformed, and granting him a bare smile of acknowledgment. In the meantime, he should find something to do. Drink a lot. Become a Cossack. Work for Carlton.

"What are you doing?" Kelly called from the table, amused.

Otto didn't turn. "Saying goodbye."

"Ya know, the train goes back," Kelly chuckled.

"True." Otto did turn. "But never to the same City."

"Sounds like philosophy," Doc said as he spun out cards and then, "yours," to Ferdinand who looked at Otto for a moment and then nodded. At least he got it, if not for the right reasons. Yet.

"Eh." Kelly was big and expansive and jovial and not the kind of guy to waste thought on shadings. "It's still the same. Find yourself a good bar, good company, good card players," he jostled Doc, who didn't seem to mind, "and you got this whole place covered."

"True words, friend," Doc looked at his cards and then at Otto. "You might take consolation from them."

Otto regarded him. That sounded dangerously close to his own thoughts. What, exactly, did Doc know?

"Out! Coming to Out!" the Hawaiian conductor burst in, grinning, and slapped Otto on the back, almost killing him. "I believe this is your stop."

Otto put his shoulder back together while Ferdinand dropped his cards. "Gentlemen." He bowed to Kelly and Doc. "It's my stop, too."

Doc stuck out a hand. "Been a real pleasure," he said and Ferdinand smiled and took it. Kelly stood and bear-hugged Ferdinand, absorbing him. "Yeah! You play some mean quadrille!"

"Let the man go, Kel," Doc said quietly and Kelly laughed and peeled off a somewhat flattened Ferdinand, and Otto chuckled and reached for the duffle ...

... hurling across the car, face first at about a thousand miles an hour, straight into a set of wooden chairs.

"*Oof!*" as he crashed through them, chairs flying everywhere, his flight ending when he slammed into the bulkhead, his nose squashing against it. Holding his face, he kicked a chair away and sat up, watching a tangle of Ferdinand and Doc and Hawaiian conductor untie each other's legs while Kelly threw suitcases off himself.

"What the hell?" the gangster roared.

Another hard lurch, this time in the opposite direction, and the whole pile of them slid along the floor and crashed together, some of the chairs flying through the windows. There was a rumble and a sharp *crack!* of an explosion and the car canted upwards then crashed down hard, all of them tossed into the air and then slapped into the floor, Otto, naturally, on the bottom, with Kelly's foot planted across his already aching nose.

"Get off!" he yelped and all of them grasped and pulled and hauled each other up to sitting and standing positions.

"What's going on?" Kelly, bewildered, yanked part of the card table off his legs.

"We're under attack." Doc stood, brushing off roof insulation.

"By whom?" Ferdinand scrambled out from under a pile of seats, helped by Kelly.

"That damn Kenny!" Otto kicked a portmanteau away and struggled out of the wreckage.

"Who's Kenny?" Ferdinand asked.

"Not Kenny," Doc said quietly and Otto turned. Doc was facing the front of the car, calm, balanced, arms swinging easily, the moment before one of the most famous fast draws in history. The whole car shook as if it were running over rough track, except they weren't moving, and cracks appeared along the walls and floors as Doc, stoic, watched.

In a scream of metal and destruction, the front of the car peeled and flew away, as if someone had broken it off and tossed it. The Out sun poured in, as did dust and smoke. The rest of the train crazy-angled away from them, a zigzag of crashed cars. Otto caught at a still upright chair as the floor rocked violently but Doc was steady, watching. Three Suits stepped up at the end of the open car.

"Uh-oh," Otto said.

Chapter XXXIV

Flintlocks And Arrows

"Kelly," Doc said quietly, unmoved, watching the Suits, "Gonna need some help."

"I'm with ya." The big man crashed through the wreckage and stood at Doc's side, tough, belligerent, ready.

Otto gaped. Machine Gun Kelly and Doc Holliday were gonna take on Satan's or whoever's legion? "Unbelievable," he whispered, and cast about. Ah, there, the duffle. He pointed. "Ferd, you should probably get that."

Ferdinand scrambled over the remaining chairs, pulling the duffle to him. The Suits watched this, looked at each other, and took a simultaneous step forward.

"Don't think so, friends," Doc held up a warning hand. The Suits regarded him. The one on the left raised a palm, some object nestled in it.

Doc's hand whipped through his jacket and there was a pearl-handled Colt, up and leveled. He fired twice. The leftmost suit was thrown off his feet and out through the hole, some odd purple beam lancing from the object and cutting through the ceiling over Doc's head.

Otto gasped. A combat laser! Where'd they get that?

"You bastards!" Kelly roared and pulled, from out of nowhere, a Thompson submachine gun. The two remaining Suits dove to either side as Kelly aimed ...

Dien Bien Phu all over again.

"Mother of God!" Ferdinand yelled as Kelly blasted the whole front of the car into oblivion, laughing and screaming while Doc, now with two guns blazing, supplemented. Otto yanked Ferdinand down behind a table fragment as glass and wood and metal and carpet shredded and shrapneled through the whole car while the Thompson sang and the Colts roared and all the furies of war gathered and shrieked their approval. An occasional purple beam cascaded wildly through the air, slicing hunks of metal, and there were glimpses of flapping Suits at the front, lost in the smoke and fire and chaos. The roar battered through the remaining car walls, hammering at Otto and Ferdinand, as did stray pieces of flying metal.

"What a weapon!" Ferdinand enthused. "What I could have done with that against the Portuguese!"

"Yeah, well." Otto pulled his head down as a purple beam arced dangerously close to it. "Those lasers aren't slouches, either."

"They ain't that good." Doc was standing above them, reloading. "No accuracy and about ten seconds between shots. Gotta build up or something." He snapped the gates closed and then spun both nickel-plated Colts in his fingers, smiling. "Arrows against flintlocks," and he stepped back to Kelly, who had dropped a cylinder and replaced it with another.

"Ah," Ferdinand said, peering over the table. "I know your meaning. The Indios would wait until we fired and then overwhelm us with darts."

"And yet, you won," Otto pointed out. Ferdinand raised an eyebrow and Kelly raised the barrel and grinned at Doc. "*EeeeHaaaaw!*" he called as the Thompson sang again and Otto hit the deck because Kelly was blasting from left to right and even Doc had to scramble back a bit as he cut loose with the Colts. More shrapnel and concussion, and Otto pulled Ferdinand out of harm's way as Kelly EeeeHaaaawed and raked while bullets ricocheted and purple beams slapped through the air and smoke poured in and the car rocked in time with Kelly's motion. In a sudden pause, louder than the warfare, Doc leaned over, blood dripping down his face. "Maybe you two should get out of here."

Otto peered at him. "What about you?"

"We got your back."

And it came clear. "You're part of it aren't you, Doc?"

He smiled. "We're all part of it." He turned, Colts blazing.

Otto shook his head and wondered if there was anyone on this whole blasted planet who wasn't either working for, or against, the rocket. Must have missed that briefing. "C'mon." He grabbed Ferdinand's collar and lugged him up and they both stumbled through the wreckage to the back. A slumped-over pile of chairs and ceiling exploded upward, driving both of them into the bulkhead. Otto braced for combat but it was the Hawaiian conductor, nonchalantly brushing the train off him.

He evaluated the war at the front and then looked at Otto. "This way, gentlemen," he smiled and waved a giant hand toward the back door. "Don't forget that," he pointed at the duffle as he pushed aside some debris.

They fell in as the conductor bulldozed a path to the door. Through the shattered glass, Otto saw the rest of the train Z-ing its wrecked way down the track. The firing at the front crescendoed and they all looked back to see Doc club a suit across the head with a reversed Colt while Kelly butt-stroked another and then let off a wild fusillade that barely missed Doc.

The conductor *tsk*ed. "That one's always out of control," he said and reared back and slammed into the door with his entire bulk, driving it off its hinges and down the track. He flourished a hand and grinned. "I believe this is your stop."

Otto stepped to the opening and measured the distance. Because they were canted upward, it was at least ten feet to the track. Break an ankle or get lasered? No contest and he squatted then jumped. "*Oof!*" as he landed, falling into a heap, his ankles twisting and creaking dangerously but staying in one piece.

"Heads up," he heard the Hawaiian call as he brushed himself off and turned in time to get a faceful of duffle. "*Oof!*" driven to the cinderbed, some twisted rail lancing his spleen.

"Sorry," the Hawaiian said as Otto sat up, heaving the duffle off him. The Hawaiian levered Ferdinand down to the track.

Ferdinand looked up. "You coming?"

The Hawaiian grinned. "Nah." He pulled a giant war club to

himself from the side of the entrance and hefted it. "Think I'll go help our friends upfront." He screamed something unintelligible while waving the war club over his head and was gone.

Otto, on his elbows, amazed. "Where is everybody getting these weapons?"

Ferdinand helped him up and then grabbed the duffle and they both hunched near the edge of the train. Otto peered around. Lots of smoke and flying debris up front, and lots of motion. A whole bunch of Suits moved in and out of view. A whole bunch. Won't take them long ...

A shadow eclipsed them and Otto looked up. A bat-winged ultralight swooped by, a suit at the controls. It banked to the left and out of sight, the motor silent. "What was that?" Ferdinand asked.

"Trouble," Otto quick-glanced the front again. The Suits massed there but a few detached and headed their way. "C'mon," Otto said and they sprinted to the next car, keeping as much of the train between them and the Suits as possible. On a rise in the middle of the first set of zigzagged cars, Otto saw more of the battle. Smoke carried down the whole line and there were flashes and yells and general chaos as far as he could see. The Suits were systematically going through the whole train. Suit-operated ultralights flitted here and there and everything was moving in their direction.

Not good.

Another ultralight, maybe the first one, swooped over and then jinked back. "He's spotted us," Ferdinand said. The ultralight slowed to a hover about fifty feet above drifting somewhat. The suit peered down at them, then reached inside a pocket and dropped what looked like a black tennis ball.

"Down!" Otto grabbed Ferdinand and yanked him over the rails, both tumbling down the side, entangled in the duffle. Otto looked back as the tennis ball bounced where they had just been and then expanded, forming an odd purple sphere about ten feet across with weird lightning running through it, then collapsed into itself, making a little *pffht* sound. A rush of wind smacked together where the sphere had evaporated, sonic boom slapping Otto's face, the track where they'd been standing gone. Just gone.

"What was that?" Ferdinand's eyes bugged, pressed against

the berm.

"Some kind of vacuum grenade, I'm guessing. And we sure don't want to find out where that vacuum goes." He waved at the berm. "Let's move."

They scrambled up the steep scree, Otto keeping an eye on the ultralight banking for position. Or trying to. It labored, a wing dipping toward the train and the whole craft shook as the suit made frantic movements at the controls. Looked like the wind was giving it trouble. Odd, though, Otto didn't feel any wind ...

Winds aloft. Fortuitous, perfectly timed, winds aloft. "Thank you, God," he whispered. Ferdinand, leaning against the duffle, gave him a puzzled look and Otto pointed silently at the struggling ultralight. Ferdinand nodded.

They stood, the berm giving them a panoramic view. The battle raged across the entire train, smoke and Suits and gunfire from one end to the other. The purple spheres blossomed then popped, their booms interspersing the action. Purple beams shot here and there and rifles roared.

Was that an M-16? Otto cocked his head. Yep, the unmistakable whine.

At that moment, Kelly flew out of a side window, his hands grasped around the throat of a suit he used to cushion his fall. Standing, he stomped the suit, looked up at them, gave a big thumbs-up and a grin, and ran back up the car, firing the Thompson. He reached the front and stepped right into an expanding purple sphere, which collapsed with a boom! No more Kelly.

"Mother of God," Ferdinand breathed.

Suits appeared on their side of the track and ultralights from the far ends of the train canted toward them, all focused on where they stood.

"Crap," Otto said. Standing up here in an all-white French admiral's uniform, might as well be a lighthouse. "We should go." Ferdinand eyed the massing Suits, their Nosferatu faces turned in their direction.

Otto whirled about frantically. The berm peaked where they stood and fell steeply toward the desert. Flat, brown, featureless desert, all the way to the far mountains. No cover, no place to hide, and absolutely no way to outrun the ultralights, let alone a horde of mad Suits. But what other choice?

"C'mon!" he tapped Ferdinand hard and scooped up the duffle, scrambling down the dusty berm and raising a cloud as telltale as his white uniform. They piled at the bottom and Otto fell on his back in time to watch two ultralights clear the berm. Black objects flew simultaneously from each cockpit, falling toward them.

"Move!" Otto grabbed Ferdinand and half-rolled, half-vaulted and half-dragged him and the duffle away. *Phfft phfft, boom!* *boom!* overlapped and Otto looked back to see holes where they had been standing. The ultralights swerved for another pass as two more ultralights appeared, bearing down on them.

"We're screwed," Otto said.

"Maybe not." Ferdinand was squinting toward the mountains. Otto followed his gaze. There, about a hundred yards away, a wrinkle in the desert floor. "What is that?" he asked.

Ferdinand straightened. "A ravine. A fairly long one."

"How come we couldn't see it from the berm?" Otto stopped. A ravine undetectable from the heights. They looked at each other and bolted toward it, carrying the duffle between them. An ultralight shadow fell across their path. "Break!" Otto yelled and they angled hard to the left as a *phfftboom!* sounded behind. Otto felt the rush of air dragging him back and he pushed hard, zigging again and again until he and Ferdinand reached the edge of the ravine, almost falling in because of their haste.

Otto peered down. It was deep and smooth, a sandstone rift branching off in several directions. He looked back. Several ultralights had formed up for a run at them and the whole top of the berm was black with Suits, the front edge tumbling down the side.

"Hey!" he yelled, waving his arms. The Suits froze, staring at him. Even the ultralights paused. "Watch this!" he yelled again and, grabbing Ferdinand's shoulder with one hand and the duffle with the other, stepped off the edge.

Chapter XXXV

And For Our Next Trick

They slid smoothly down, upright all the way to the cushioned, sand-filled floor. Otto looked up. A couple of ultralights buzzed past, the frantic pilots looking around but, obviously, not seeing them.

"Must think we're Houdini," Otto chuckled.

"Who?" Ferdinand was brushing sand off the duffle.

"Magician." Otto looked around. They were in a fairly open area, despite the small avalanche they'd started. Three passages stood on their right, caves with soft, bright openings like those sandstone ones in the Arizona desert. Each went in radically different directions. He turned to Ferdinand. "Okay, time to earn your keep. Which way, navigator?"

Ferdinand studied the openings and pointed at the middle one. "There," he said and gathered the duffle.

Otto almost asked, "You sure?" but held. This was the talent for the moment, so go with it. They stepped through and Otto noted the sides of the passage curved away from them and then closed rapidly at the top. The sky was still visible, but only as a narrow blue band, a deep layering blue, so beautiful, so peaceful ... Otto shook himself. Stop it!

"Wait," Ferdinand said and he stepped back, produced a hand towel, and began rubbing out their footprints. Otto watched, unsure, but then got it. The ultralights may not see them, but the walking Suits will find this spot. No need to show them which cave.

They headed through the passage, which was just wide enough to allow a side-by-side traverse, curving first to the right then the left and, at times, doubling back. A rock floor covered with spongy sand made the going rather pleasant but also left tracks. "They'll find our trail," Ferdinand said.

"Yeah." Otto glanced back, expecting a suit to turn the corner. "Don't think there's anything we can do about that. We just need to stay ahead."

A shadow fell over them and they both looked up, surprised. Against the narrow band of sky, Otto saw the silhouette of an ultralight wing. "Uh-oh," he said, punctuated by the *phfftboom!* of a vacuum grenade going off behind them. Another one went off somewhere ahead.

Ferdinand was staring up and Otto had to snap him out of sky coma. "What are they doing?" he asked, when recovered.

Otto was grim. "Carpet bombing."

"So they can see us now?"

"I don't think so. Otherwise, it'd be raining tennis balls. Their buddies in the ravine are tracking our line while these guys are forging ahead throwing grenades at random to scare us."

"They're doing a good job," Ferdinand said as they came to another junction.

"Yeah." Otto waited for him to pick a path and followed. "They're probably hoping we'll hole up."

"Should we?"

"You want them catching us?"

Ferdinand said nothing but plunged down a passage and Otto fell behind because the walls were closer here. Damn closer. Otto frowned. This passage was narrowing down to ...

Nothing.

"Great," he said, slapping the wall in frustration, "I thought you knew where you were go—"

Ferdinand held up a hand, stopping him. "Wait," he said, cocking his head and sniffing the air a bit. "There is something."

"Yeah, there's something all right." Nervously, Otto peered back, straining to hear the approaching Suits. The top of the ravine was so narrow the sky was a sliver, but a shadow flitted across it and there was another *pfhhtboom*! Louder this time. "Ferd," he said, turning, "they're getting closer so we need to double back now ..."

Ferdinand was not there. Neither was the duffle.

Otto gasped. Ravine wall and sand, that's it. "Ferd?"

An arm suddenly popped out of the wall and Otto freaked, jumping back. "Here," Ferdinand's muffled voice followed the arm, "Grab hold."

"What the hell is this?"

"It's a hidden tunnel, some kind of light at the end, maybe a cave," muffled answer. "I felt the breeze."

Light at the end of a tunnel? We have a saying about that, Ferd, involving trains. But the hand gestured frantically and Otto reached for it because there was certainly no going back. He stopped. "Wait," Otto said, "Don't move. Keep your arm out where I can see it."

The hand turned over in a gesture of "what?" but Otto frantically wiped away their footprints leading up to this spot. He jumped over the last set of prints and stomped around another wall, leaving as many tracks as he could. He hoped the approaching Suits wouldn't notice the prints were made by only one set of shoes. "Ferd!" he called when finished, "Can you hear me?"

"Barely," the muffled voice came back and the disembodied hand lifted in emphasis.

"I'm going to grab your arm real hard because I'm jumping over. The moment you feel me, pull. Got it?"

The hand gave a thumbs-up and Otto had to chuckle. Some signs were universal. Gathering himself, he leaped, trying to stay on the wall base as much as possible but slipped a little and grabbed Ferdinand's elbow as he fell over. Ferd yanked him off his feet – man, the guy was strong – cracking Otto's head – naturally – on the tunnel entrance as he tumbled inside, and landing on top of the Argentine. They both slid down an incline until rudely stopped by a big rock.

"Ouch," Otto said.

"Get off," Ferdinand replied.

Otto rolled over, rubbing his head and checking for blood but didn't find any. He sat up. "Am I bleeding?" he asked, but there was no response. Ferdinand was sitting with his back toward him, head in an angle of astonishment. Otto followed the angle.

"Good God," he breathed.

Chapter XXXVI

In The Caves Of Fairy And Doubt

They were on a short ledge overlooking a vast chamber at least a football field's length below their feet. It spread out in distances lost to view, but it wasn't the scale that took away breath. It was the fairyland.

The whole cavern glowed a very pleasant greenish-blue, like something out of a Spielberg movie. Mysterious, enchanting. Gigantic rock columns mounted from the chamber floor and out of sight, becoming pink and red and cobalt, their size and combined radiance masking the dome. Stalactites and stalagmites meshed, some blue, some red, and the walls of the cave flowed away from them for what looked like miles. A luminescent moss covered the floor, several deep-cut paths running through it, maybe water channels.

"Oh my," Ferdinand said.

"Wow," Otto agreed. "So what do you think this is?"

"The land of the Little People."

"You have those legends, too?"

Ferdinand shrugged. "Everyone does." He pulled the duffle to him and probed the ledge floor with his hands. "There's a ridge here that goes to the bottom."

"Really?" Otto scooted over and followed the line. "Yeah, it does. How 'bout that?"

"Yes." Ferdinand gave him a significant look. "How about that?"

"What? Too fortuitous for chance?"

"Of course it is." Ferdinand stood and brushed off his pants. "Every time we get into trouble, something pops up to save us."

"Well, gee, Ferd, this is Heaven, after all."

"I don't like being manipulated."

"Manipulated?" Otto arched brows at him. "Did you ever figure this is that 'close a door, open a window' thing?"

"It never worked that way on Earth. Why would it here?"

"Oh, I don't know." Otto waved an exasperated hand. "'Cause this is Heaven?"

"Are you sure?"

Otto felt like he'd been slapped. "Wait a minute. You've been here at least two hundred years longer than me, and you have doubts? Too?"

"Everyone does. Especially with these games." Ferdinand picked up the duffle. "Let's go."

Otto, still somewhat stunned, watched Ferdinand crab down the ridge. "Okay," he whispered, planted his back against the wall and shuffled sideways on a path barely wide enough to hold half his foot. It took a while but they finally reached the bottom, Otto stepped onto the moss with relief. "Soft," he said, bouncing up and down. Nice.

"Yes. Comfortable." Ferdinand shook his head. "I am surprised a bed and two maidens aren't waiting." His stance turned belligerent.

"Man, Ferd, you're starting to sound like me."

"Do I?" he whirled on Otto. "Then how about this? I am certain that, if I merely stood, then the cave will magically open and there, your wonderful ship."

Otto let out an exasperated breath, but Ferd had a point. There's always an out. Jakto had pointed him to the train; Unathi delivered him from the Suits; even Ferd pitched in with Carlton. Don't forget Claudia (like he could). As defeat loomed, there'd been escape. Otto looked up, halfway expecting the cave to do what Ferd predicted: a creaking and a rumble and the rock would part and voila! Tall, clunky, steam-wreathed, and ready to go ...

The ship.

Rocket ship ...

It hit him like a sledgehammer. Of course.

"No," Otto said. "You're wrong, dead wrong, if you'll pardon the expression. I am, too. Wrong, I mean, because obviously we're both dead. I think." He shook that off. "These escapes, these 'games' you mentioned, are part of the Opposition."

Ferdinand furrowed a brow. "How is that?"

"It's simple," Otto flicked a hand at the wondrous cave. "This fairyland, the ravine, the fortuitous rescues, all work here. It's a form of comfort in this Afterlife, which is all about comfort. But, not where we're going. Because, Ferdinand." Otto faced him. "The ship isn't what you think."

"Pardon?"

"Tell me what the ship is, your vision of it."

"Well." Ferdinand was suspicious. "I am supposing it to be a rather magnificent brig, well-made, heavy sailed, crewed by experienced and stalwart men. We will sail the Inner Sea for years until we finally come upon the Throne of God, golden on some island, having survived interesting adventures. Like Ulysses."

"Not even close."

Ferdinand narrowed. "What do you mean?"

"I'm saying that's not even close. I'm saying the ship is of a nature so alien to you, you have no reference." Otto waved a hand. "All these fortuitous little things that keep us going will end. Because we will be in *terra incognito*."

"Explain."

"You think this is simply about finding God? No, not at all. There is far more to this, Ferdinand. This is the resolution of time itself. Do you seriously think that will go unopposed? Do you seriously think it's a given? It will be a struggle, and a mortal one, let me assure you. This," he waved again, "this all ends."

Ferdinand stepped back, mimicking Otto's wave. "This never ends. It is the grace of God. It is what we count on in this realm, so how can you say grace ends?"

"Because we will no longer be in this realm."

"What are you talking about?" Ferdinand threw his hands up, then paused. "What are you doing to me, Otto?"

"Bringing you to your true destiny, Ferdinand, because it's not that kind of ship. It's a rocket."

"A what?"

"A rocket, Ferd. That will leave this planet and search the crazy stars for God's golden throne."

Ferdinand's eyes bulged. "What?"

Otto said nothing, just watched Ferdinand's moss-lit face work through the implications, shock to wonder to bafflement to ...

Anger.

"You bastard," Ferdinand said softly, "You ... you heretic!" Not so softly. Centuries had made the word lose its power, but Otto realized Ferdinand was calling him the worst thing he knew, the equivalent of "pedophile."

"Ferd," Otto put a hand on the Argentine's shoulder, which Ferdinand threw off violently. Yep, strong guy.

"You," Ferdinand pointed an accusing finger, "have made me a target. You have pulled me from my place, from my comfort, for this ... madness!"

"It's not madness, Ferd."

"It is utter insanity! In what have you immersed yourself? From whence do you get such temerity? What is this hubris!" That last shouted and it echoed through the chamber, "hubris ... hubris ... hubris!" slamming back hard and almost knocking Otto down.

Ferdinand turned his finger to point up the ridge "Those things back there are not trying to stop you. They are trying to save you!"

"No, Ferdinand! They're not!" Otto, desperate.

"Yes, they are." He paused, measuring Otto. "And they can certainly save me. From you!" He kicked the duffle viciously out of his way and began climbing the ridge.

"Wait! Don't!" Otto lunged, grabbing at Ferdinand's waist, but the little man seized his throat and hoisted him over and down. Yep, definitely strong. Otto fell heavily, the moss not cushioning enough, and lost his breath. By the time he recovered and was sitting up, Ferdinand was halfway up the ridge. There was no way Otto could catch him, and, if he did, Ferdinand would throw him back.

He stood. "Ferdinand!" Ignored, so Otto called again, "Ferdinand!"

The Platan threw a hand in disgust and kept going. Otto watched, helpless. Oh no, this can't be happening. The mission was evaporating right before his eyes. Ten more steps and Ferd was gone and Otto was lost ...

... Or was he?

Because, if Ferdinand didn't make the ship, then Otto was Crewman Number 30.

Silently, he watched Ferdinand's progress. So, it was Otto's slot all the time. Let's ignore shrinking clothes and Carlton and train-wreck silliness and focus on that. He was going on the rocket. With a smirk, Otto silently egged Ferdinand on. A few more steps, buddy boy, and Ferd was out of sight, on his way back to the welcoming embrace of the Suits, and Otto scooped up the duffle and magically, everything in it fitted and he can get rid of this stupid French admiral outfit ...

Stupid French admiral outfit.

Otto stood straight. "The uniform!" he called, "Ferdinand, the uniform!"

Ferdinand, about ready to swing over the ridge top, paused and looked back, his brows furrowed. Otto swept his hands over his get-up. "The uniform, Ferd!" Dramatic pause. "Why was it in your closet? Why?"

It took a moment, and Ferdinand was still livid, but realization softened his look. He pointed a finger at Otto. "You misled me."

"Yes."

Ferdinand chewed his lip. "Gah!" he shouted and stomped down the ridge, keeping his balance. Impressive. Otto watched Ferd's reverse progress and wondered if he should have let the guy go and then God would have no choice but to resize everything for Otto.

Wrong. God always has a Choice. And His would be to leave Otto here alone with a bag full of useless clothes, wearing a vaudeville costume and waiting for the Suits to pounce.

Roles.

Dammit.

Ferdinand reached the bottom and grabbed the duffle and stalked past Otto – who had the sense to keep out of the way – then whirled. "If." He shook a dangerous fist. "You mislead me again, I will kill you."

Otto weighed. "Deal," he said, and fell in behind.

Chapter XXXVII

The People You Meet

They walked, not speaking, whether from the tension or the wonderland, Otto wasn't sure. The glow ran the spectrums of blue and red, sometimes bright enough to hurt eyes. The moss held a steady color in all directions. Otto picked a bit of it as they moved and rubbed it between his fingers, turning them into glowsticks. He could coat himself with the moss and walk through this fairyland as a luminous blue-green giant. Might be fun.

The cave seemed to curve and Otto wondered if it was a big circle. They'd end up right back where they started, putting quite the edge on Ferdinand's already foul mood, more so if a bunch of Suits was waiting for them. Or a bunch of leprechauns. Amused by the surface dweller's befuddlement, they'd leap and chortle and "begorrah" them to death, then turn them into trees or eat their legs or something. He chuckled, earning a glare from Ferdinand, so he shut up.

The cave rose and fell and the scenery changed with it. On the upslopes, magnificent stone columns of red-to-green barred the way. Ferdinand probed them and shouldered through, dragging the duffle behind while Otto followed, staring up the long formations into the distant blur. Downslope were stalactites, giant radiant spears close enough for Otto to reach up and stroke the tips, getting more glow on his fingers.

They stepped over tinkling channels of clear water rushing through the moss. At about the tenth one, Otto stopped at the edge and peered down. A large group of tiny sparkly fish gathered and stared up at him blinking like fireflies, their gaping mouths pulsing in time with each other, a chorus of "Who are you?" or "What are you doing here?" depending on how Otto chose to interpret. He reached and they scattered, streaks of light through the water, falling stars in a cave. He splashed the water with his hand. Cold. Probably refreshing. Otto brought a palmful up to his mouth.

"I wouldn't drink that," Ferdinand warned, standing on the other side of the stream.

"Why not?"

"Cave water can make you sick."

"Here?" Slight derision.

"Here. Anywhere. We are not in the City."

"But we're still in Heaven. Afterlife. Whatever. And I don't recall running into, or hearing about, any sick people."

Ferdinand shrugged. "Nor I, nor have I caught even a cold while here. So do what you want, but you tempt fate." He turned away and paced through the moss.

Hmm. Otto sniffed the water. It had a vague chemical smell to it. Best not to tweak fate's nose and he let it drip between his fingers. Wasn't really thirsty, anyway, just curious, and that killed cats.

They were on a steeper rise than encountered so far and it was a struggle. Otto had his head down so almost ran into Ferdinand when he crested. "Why'd you stop?" Otto asked and Ferdinand, mute, pointed. "Oh," was all Otto said.

They were on top of a higher ridge than the ascent had telegraphed and below them, about a stadium's length away, the cave split off in five or six directions through as many giant holes in the wall: Gates to the Underworld. Hannibal could have marched his elephants side by side through any of them. Rills crisscrossed the floor and stalactites converged into a massive chandelier so bright the colors almost merged into one white glow, clashing with the moss. "Wow," Otto said softly.

"Yes, wow," Ferdinand studied the Gates. They all looked the same and Otto wasn't sure if Ferdinand could pick the right one. Was there even a right one?

"There." Ferdinand pointed at the third Gate to the left.

"How do you know?"

"The river."

"River?" Otto squinted and, yes, indeed, there was a rather substantial flow out of that Gate, source for the other rills. "Good eyes, Ferd."

Ferdinand glanced at him, hefted the duffle, and picked his way down the steep floor to the bottom of the chamber. Otto followed, hoping Ferd would snap out of this funk soon, at least before he saw Konstantin's patched-together rocket. At that point, he expected Ferd's head to explode.

The hike turned into a slog because the moss was thicker on the chamber floor and the river branches more numerous and it took them a while to enter the cave. The river proved more of a creek but it ran down the center of the cave, downright boiling when it reached the first of the cross channels. Otto hoped they were on the right side of the cave – the creek was too wide to jump and too fast to wade.

They pushed through. The moss turned bluer and brighter, allowing Otto to follow the curve of the cave walls up to the ceiling. No formations, all smooth, like a gigantic borer of some kind had come this way. He looked ahead nervously. Sure hope it doesn't come back.

Ferdinand kept glancing at the creek, frowning, and, after some time, scooped up a handful of water, studying it. "I thought you said it wasn't safe," Otto said.

"It is not," Ferdinand said and nodded at the water. "Look."

Otto saw flecks of blue luminescence floating in there. "What's that? The moss?"

Ferdinand held out his palm, covered with glowing pieces of mica and rock. "It is ore."

"Ore?" Otto dug at the stuff Ferd offered. Yep, rocks. Definitely not moss bits. "So what's that mean?"

"Someone is mining."

"Mining what?"

"I do not know, but they're using the river as a wash." Ferdinand closed his hand and gazed up the cave.

"I wouldn't call this a river."

"If you cannot cross it, then it is a river." Ferdinand cocked his head, listening. Otto imitated him but the creek, river, whatever, was too loud. After a moment, Ferdinand nodded. "Let us go," he said, and stepped off briskly, forcing Otto to trot.

"What's the hurry?"

"You will see."

The creek sloped upward and the way got tougher but Ferdinand kept up the pace with Otto actually enjoying it. Aerobic workout for fun, not profit, since he couldn't get any healthier here without taking on superpowers. Be nice to fly. Or lift boulders. Otto was tempted to stop and tug at a random rock or two, but Ferdinand pressed on.

After about ten minutes, the slope up-angled sharply (which explained the water's speed) and blocked their forward view. A tremendous glow waxed from the other side. Ferdinand scrambled up the almost-vertical wall, reaching the top well before Otto, and stopped on the crest, hands on hips, peering forward. "See?" he called down, satisfaction in his voice.

Otto struggled up next to him and whistled. When you're right, you're right.

A gigantic chamber opened before them, one that could easily contain two or three Carlsbad Caverns. A true river, wide as the Potomac, curved from around a bend and met the creek with enough momentum to accelerate the water up to where they stood (Weird. Shouldn't it be flowing the other way?) and over, back down the passage they'd climbed. Hundreds of conveyor belts arrayed on either side of the river, a continuous stream of ore flowing down them and into the water. The ends of the belts hooked to a honeycomb of caves all up and down the chamber walls.

People appeared at the openings on a regular beat and tilted wheelbarrows of the ore into the conveyors. From the tops of each cave, wires hung on which a series of buckets moved, all of them filled to the brim with a bright, glowing material. The aerials followed the roof of the chamber and disappeared into the top of several massive silos placed regularly beside the river, out of sight. Various other structures, barns and sheds, were scattered between the silos. A couple of water mills spun in the river. It reminded Otto of the mining scene from *Total Recall* (the Schwarzenegger one, the real one) and he rubbed his eyes to clear the image. Nope, still there.

Elevators and ladders connected the caves and people moved up and down them. Others tended equipment or buildings along the floor or inspected the conveyors and aerials while shifting the ladders. They were variously dressed, from full-blown mining coveralls to mere loincloths.

"What are they mining?" Otto asked.

"Who knows?" Ferdinand pointed at one of the aerial buckets. "It is interesting, though."

Otto agreed. "Looks like radium, but I thought it had to be refined to glow like that."

"What is radium?"

"An element that gives off tremendous heat and light. We made a helluva bomb out of it."

"What did you use it for?"

"To end a really nasty war with the Japanese."

"Japanese?" Ferdinand's eyes narrowed. "Is that what you call the people of the Japans?"

"Yeah. What'd you call them?"

"Heathens."

Otto laughed. "I don't think they'd like that."

"Whether they like it or not is immaterial. They worshiped false gods. It was holy work to bring them Christianity."

"Like the way you brought Christianity to the Indians?"

Ferdinand eyed him. "I do not like your tone."

"Whether you like it or not is immaterial, Ferd, old boy, but, you have to concede that butchering Indians, raping their women and enslaving the survivors wasn't exactly the best advertisement for the Christian Way of Life."

Ferdinand flamed. "I did not do that!"

"No doubt. You seem an honorable guy. But your compatriots did, and, I gotta tell ya, Ferd, they'd have found the Japanese weren't so easily converted."

Ferdinand stared at him then turned abruptly and headed down the hill. Otto reveled as he followed. Telling off old-time exploiters was a perk here.

The slope fell sharply and Ferd and he quickly reached the

floor. From there, both banks of the river opened, revealing a far more extensive operation straddling both sides than was apparent from the ridge top. Otto whistled. What was going on here? People hurried past them from one building to another, some of them with clipboards, some with sacks. They waved or nodded or said "hello."

"Cheerful group," Otto said.

"*Hmph*," Ferdinand grunted, still a bit sore. "Apparently, they like what they're doing."

Apparently. There was a bustle and efficiency in the air and an overall sense of being quite pleased with themselves. Guys and gals greeted each other and shook hands and a few here and there high-fived. "Must be important work," Otto said.

"Or they are getting very rich." Ferdinand was watching a happy group conferring across the river near one of the conveyor belt towers. Otto conceded that was the better explanation.

"Hi! Help you?" a perky voice called and Otto turned. A blonde woman dressed in rolled-up khaki shorts and a plaid hiking shirt knotted at the bottom – cute – very cute – waved at them from one of the silo bases. Miss America Runner-up number one. Ferdinand and he looked at each other, shrugged, and walked over. "You guys here to join a team?" she asked, a very bright, perfect smile on her perky little face.

"What teams are there?" Ferdinand asked.

"Oh!" She pulled up a clipboard and flipped a few pages. "All kinds. Excavation, refining, water management, we have openings everywhere." She looked up expectantly.

"Actually," Otto said, "we're looking for the way out."

"Out?" she was puzzled. "You mean, out of the Works?" You could hear the capital letter. "Why? Did we offend you?" She was genuinely distressed.

Otto smiled. "No. Far from it. It's actually a relief to find you all down here. We were on our way to the ..." Otto balked over "rocket," "... an old friend when we got sidetracked down here." Ferdinand frowned and Otto angled his head at him. Play along.

She caught that. "Well." There was a bit of frost in her voice. "I can't advise you on that. I suppose you could go back the way you came," and she nodded down the river.

"No, we cannot," Ferdinand said hastily.

She caught that, too, and looked worried. "Are you going to be trouble?"

Otto held up a placating hand. "Not at all. The last thing we want is a ruckus." And unwanted attention.

Unconvinced, she tapped the clipboard. "I can't help you with leaving because I don't remember how."

Otto was curious. "Really? How long have you been here?"

"Oh, gosh," she giggled, "I don't know. A little while after I got to the City, I stumbled on this place. Liked it. Stayed." The last accompanied by a whimsical shoulder shrug.

"When did you get to the City?"

"*Hmm.*" She cocked her cute little head. "It was right after Hadrada lost at Stamford Bridge, so ..." she strained at the thought.

"Wait. What?" Otto had no idea what she was talking about.

But Ferdinand apparently did and was suitably astonished. "You have been here since the Battle of Hastings?"

"Hastings? I don't know that one. My father was killed at Stamford and some of the Saxons came across me and, well." She threw out hands, clipboard and all. "Here I am!"

Otto looked at Ferdinand. "Hastings? You mean, 1066 Hastings?"

He nodded. "Yes. Stamford Bridge was the battle right before that."

Otto was impressed. He looked at the girl. "Not quite a thousand years."

"Has it been that long?" she laughed. "My, how time flies. I'm Oslava." She held out a hand. They shook and gave their names and she clasped the clipboard to herself and raised her shoulders. "Well! I think you two should take a good look around before you leave. You might change your minds. It's really important work. And besides, we are a fun bunch." She looked at them invitingly.

"I'm sure." Otto pointed at one of the buckets spinning by overhead. "What is that stuff?"

She shrugged. "Search me. Gene over there," and she pointed at a man leaning over a distant conveyor with a spanner in his hand, "calls it dilithium crystals."

"Huh?" Otto's mouth fell open. "Dilithium crystals?" He

gawked at the man. "Is that Gene Roddenberry?"

"Yeah!" She sounded surprised. "That's his name. You know him?"

"No, but I really have to talk to him." He leaned in that direction.

Ferdinand put a restraining hand on Otto's shoulder. "I do not believe we have that kind of time," he warned and gave a significant look behind them.

"But," Otto spluttered, "that's Gene Roddenberry!"

"And here." Ferdinand gestured at Oslava. "Is someone who knew Hadrada—"

"More than knew him," Oslava simpered.

"—but we have no time." Ferdinand finished with another significant look.

Oslava was suspicious. "What's with you two?"

"We ... have an appointment," Otto said, lamely.

"Right," and she gave them a sideways, knowing glance. "Look, it is none of my business, but we're pretty harmonious down here and the last thing we need is surface troubles. So." She pointed down the line of silos with her clipboard. "Why don't you go and see the boss?"

"How will we know him?" Ferdinand asked.

"Oh, you'll know him," she said, and walked away.

Ferdinand watched her go. "I would like to have talked to her about Stamford Bridge," he said, regret in his voice.

"Doubt she'd be helpful," Otto watched her go, too, admiring the walk. "She was probably putting on her makeup."

"Uhm." Ferdinand stepped off and Otto fell in beside him. A well-worn path coursed along the silos and they strolled, watching the activities. On occasion, they stopped a miner or a bureaucrat and asked for the boss and always got the same reaction, a cheerful pointing up the path. About the time Otto doubted whether a boss actually existed, they crested a small, moss-covered hill and saw a round hut off to the side, an open square doorway its only entrance. A tall black man, dressed in a long dark robe and holding a staff taller than he, stood in front.

"The boss," Ferdinand said, unnecessarily, and they made their way over. The man serenely watched their approach and, at a respectful distance, Ferdinand stopped, inclined his head, and said, "Sir, we wonder if we can trouble you for a moment."

"Certainly you may."

The man's voice was booming and silk and comfort ran up and down Otto's spine. Instant charisma.

"My name is Ferdinand Silva de Astorga, and this is my companion, Otto Boteman." Ferdinand made the appropriate gestures. "Forgive us, but we do not know the proper way to address you."

The man smiled. "Call me John."

"Johnnn ...?" Otto extended the name because he wanted the full title. This guy had to be some kind of wheel back on Earth.

John looked sagely at Otto, reading his mind. "I have been called Prester John."

Ferdinand gasped. Otto blinked. He'd heard the name before, but it was vague. Ferdinand, though, apparently held no vagueness and fell to his knees. "My lord," he breathed.

Otto blinked again, confused. John merely smiled, watching Otto, who felt a vicious tug on his pants. "Kneel, idiot!" Ferdinand hissed. "Do you not know who this is?"

"Well, I think I've heard the name," he whispered back.

"'Heard the name'?" Ferdinand, completely astonished at such ignorance. And annoyed. "You heathen! This," he gestured grandly at John, "is the greatest Christian king in history!"

Chapter XXXVIII

Legends, Myths. Whatever.

"That title more properly belongs to Constantine," John said, gesturing Ferdinand up. "I would hardly claim it."

Otto was puzzled. "Konstantin the rocket guy?"

John smiled. "No, Constantine the Great. Byzantine Emperor."

"Oh, yeah, him."

"But you *are* the greatest Christian king!" Ferdinand insisted, clutching at his chest. "You saved Africa for the Lord."

"The Lord did that," John admonished.

Otto's memory stirred and yes, he recalled stumbling across an article, probably in Wikipedia, about a mythical, medieval Christian kingdom in Africa ruled over by the wise and powerful Prester John. Could be this guy. He fitted the bill. But, emphasis on "mythical." Guy could be delusional.

Can you be delusional in Heaven?

Have you been paying attention?

"Africa, huh?" Doubt tinged Otto's voice. "Where in Africa?"

John gave him a tolerant look. "The northern reaches of the desert."

"Northern reaches ..." Doubt turned to suspicion.

"Ethiopia?"

"Yes, that was part of it."

"Really." Wait a minute… "Do you know Jakto?"

John became guarded. "Yes," he said, quietly.

"Well, isn't that a coinkidink." Suspicious to jaundiced. "Was he one of your soldiers?"

John shook his head. "He was well before my time, back in the days of my great ancestor, Saba."

"Yet, you know him." Otto narrowed. "How?"

"We just met."

"No." Otto dismissed that. "No one 'just' meets here, because I met him and now, here I am, meeting you."

"All things work together for good."

Otto threw up his hands. "Now what does that mean? I somehow end up riding around the desert with an ancient Axumite or Ethiopian soldier and now, hey, waddya know, here, in a cave, the king of Ethiopia." Otto eyed him. "Why does Ethiopia keep showing up?"

"Because of its greatness, you heathen!" Ferdinand shoved Otto aside and stood worshipfully before John. "Tell him of the magics, your Highness, the speculum, the Gates of Alexander."

John smiled indulgently. "I am afraid those are imaginings, prompted by errors of early Christian writers who said I was in India, then Asia, and who attributed to us powers we simply did not have. We were just men."

Ferdinand deflated like a kid finding out there's no Santa Klaus. "You mean, all that was untrue?"

"Fancies. As much as such wonders would have helped us, we lived by the grace of God, Who gave us victory over the Mussulman and preserved our ways." John lifted his head, a prayer on it.

"That doesn't explain why Ethiopia keeps showing up," Otto pressed.

"There are other magics," John said, simply.

Otto didn't think John was talking about rabbits out of hats. "What do you mean?"

"The miracles provided by God, such as the living symbol and proof of His Eternity, His steadfastness."

"Like, what? The Universe?" So this John guy was teleological. Or was it ontological?

John shook his head. "No, the Universe is not living."

"Dunno about that," Otto snarked. "Seems like an angry ex-wife from time to time. So who are you referring to? Christ?"

Another indulgent smile. "He is the Culmination. I am speaking of the Promise."

Nope. Not teleological, mystical. Or mythical. Choose your label. "You're losing me here, chief." Otto almost laughed at Ferdinand's aghast expression. "I thought Christ *was* the Promise."

John replied mildly, "No, He was the *One* Promised. I speak of the Promise itself. The symbol of it."

Ah. Metaphysical. Otto sighed. "You're making my head hurt. What is a symbol of a promise ... wait." Otto snapped a finger. "I get it now. Some kind of Old Testament thing, like King Solomon's mines. Indiana Jones stuff."

John furrowed a brow. "Who?"

Ferdinand furrowed two. "What?"

"Archeologist, kind of a swashbuckler." Otto paused then waved that away. "Well, not in real life. Or death. Whatever. He's a movie character. You guys know what movies are, right?"

"I've heard of them," John said.

"Okay. In his movies, he was always looking for some ancient treasure, had to fight bad guys for it. Nazis, mostly."

"What are Nazis?" Ferdinand asked.

"Really bad guys. Made your Portuguese look like choir boys."

"What kind of treasure?" John asked.

"You know, the Grail, the ... Ark. The Ark of the Covenant." A shock ran through Otto, as though someone had dropped a power cable on him. "Wait a minute. I read somewhere ... I think it was Wikipedia ... that a lot of people think the Ark is in Ethiopia ..." his voice trailed. "Oh. My. God," he breathed, staring at John. "It IS in Ethiopia."

John said nothing, merely looked away, but joy suffused his face and Otto took a step back, off balance.

"Is that true?" Ferdinand, so astonished, he could barely ask the question.

John held up a warning finger. "Please, not so loud. There are those seeking confirmation."

"Yeah, we know," Otto, rueful. "We've had a couple of run-ins."

"Not them. Their purposes are different. Others."

"Who?" Ferdinand asked.

Otto held up a hand. "How do you know who we ran into?"

John looked at him as though he was stupid.

"Okay, okay," Otto muttered, "so what do you mean by 'others'?"

"Others," and his tone brooked no further questions.

As if that ever stopped Otto before. "What do you mean 'their purposes are different'?"

"You already know." In that same "no further questions brooked" tone.

"No!" Exasperated, again. A lot of that in this here Afterlife. "No, I don't! I really don't! I have no idea why those *Matrix* refugees are trying to send me and old Ferd here into another dimension. I have no idea why they are so upset about the ship and I have absolutely no friggin' idea if this is Heaven or Hell or Purgatory and why God Himself isn't sitting in the middle of it all on a golden throne holding a scepter and dispensing universal wisdom. And just what," Otto flung a hand back toward the Works, "are you mining here?"

"Power," John said, quietly.

"Gonna have to give me a little more to go on, chief."

Ferdinand was again aghast but John only smiled. Must be used to skeptics. "It is power. Pure power, as far as I can tell, reduced to its constituents. It is the fuel of the Universe."

"Fuel of … what?" Otto fell into his best bewildered expression. "You mean, the stuff that makes the stars shine? The worlds go 'round?"

John shrugged, "Of that, I cannot say. I do know it moves the moons."

Otto flashed back to his conversation with Marc. "So they *are* artificial. How do you know that glowy stuff moves them?"

"I have seen the others take it there."

"The others. Which others, the ones you won't talk about or the ones chasing me and Ferd?" Otto slapped both sides of his head. "*Sheesh*! A *Lost* episode!"

John was puzzled. "Nothing is lost."

"Coulda fooled me," Otto muttered, "So, let me get this straight. You, the steward of the Ark and of the Magic Kingdom, Ethiopia division, crusader and vanquisher of the Mussulman – by the way, we don't say that anymore – is now in charge of mining some kind of glowy rock that one group of Nosferatus or another use to move the moons around. Is that right?"

"Nosferatus?" John was even more puzzled.

"Forget it, modern reference. Is what I said accurate?"

"Other than the odd name, yes."

"Okay, so why are you not sitting at the right hand of God or something, running some kind of Holy Division or a Corp of Angels or a few solar systems or even the City? At least the moons. I mean, you're certainly qualified. How'd you end up with this job?"

Ferdinand obviously wanted to kill Otto but John became introspective. "Well, I ..." and John paused, mused, then smiled broadly, "... really do not know!" He regarded Otto with some amazement. "I have never been asked that question."

"So you're on your death bed while your forty wives wail and fan you with ostrich feathers, then slip off and, next thing you know, here you are, running this place?"

"I only had ten wives." Said with some offense.

"Whatever."

"And I did not wake here. I came to this place later, while caravanning across the Great Empty."

"Great Empty?"

"The southern deserts, you oaf!" Ferdinand interrupted, quite incensed by Otto's attitude. "They are far from here."

"Oaf is a bit harsh, doncha think? Call me 'dubious' instead." And he eyed Prester John dubiously. "And we're already in the southern deserts. At least, under them."

Ferdinand remained incensed. "No we are not. The

southern deserts are very far away."

"But the deserts begin at the end of the train."

"Yes, but that is not the Great Empty. Those are the Hot Lands, next to the Inner Ocean and Sidelong Seas, which guide you down the Dragon's Back to where the Great Empty starts," Ferd grouched at him.

"Don't forget the Forever Woods and the Million Lakes," John added. Ferd and he exchanged appreciative glances over their shared knowledge.

"Not *Lost*." Otto raised a finger. "*The Hobbit*." They both furrowed their brows but Otto pressed. "So, John, you still haven't answered the question. How did you end up here if you were all the way out there? And why didn't you take the train?"

John flourished his staff. "These caves are extensive. I entered in the middle of the Empty and, after so much time, reached here. Trains did not exist when I arrived."

"Right, right, technology as it appears, got it. So, then, what? You showed up, they put you in charge, you've been here ever since?"

John nodded.

"So how did you meet Jakto?"

"You have a very insolent tone. Oaf," Ferdinand seethed.

Otto ignored him, raised an eyebrow at John, who regarded him coolly. "We have," he said, after a moment, "similar purposes."

"Those are?"

John was quiet for a moment, then said, "You know."

Otto closed his eyes and shook his head. "No, John, no, I've already said I don't. And I don't. And I think it would make things a lot easier if the whole lot of you would stop the silly cloak and dagger and just tell me straight out."

John chuckled dismissively. "You want me to tell you knowledge you already have. You want it explained, tidy, wrapped up. Tell me, when in all your life has that ever happened?"

"Well ..." Otto thought furiously, "Okay, point taken. So what am I supposed to do, then?"

"It isn't for any soul to tell another what he must do.

Especially here. You go in the direction you are moved, by the measure of who you are. If you and I and Jakto see the same distant city and encourage each other that way, it does not mean we will walk the same road to it."

Otto let out a long, dissatisfied breath and glared at John. "So which road do I take, then?"

John held his look briefly and then pointed at a small path barely discernible behind the hut. "That one."

Otto gauged it and, without a word, walked to where the path began. He turned. "Coming?" he asked Ferdinand.

Ferd hesitated, giving Otto a hateful look, then John a respectful one. "I wanted to ask you so much more."

"I know," and John laid a benevolent hand on Ferdinand's head. "It is all right. Those questions will be answered on your way."

"Then, your Highness, please, a blessing?"

John promptly raised the staff. "By the living God Whose Throne you seek, may your road be smooth, your travels wondrous, and your enemies confounded." He tapped Ferdinand lightly on the shoulders with the staff and raised a palm to Otto.

Otto's heart unexpectedly grew lighter. He stared at John, who turned and walked down to the Works. Ferdinand grabbed the duffle and fell in silently beside as Otto stepped off. The path already felt easier, somehow.

Chapter XXXIX

The Bridge Of Falls

"What the hey?" Otto said.

They were on top of a ridge that had taken what seemed like three days to climb. The path had been a gradual ascent from the moment they'd taken leave of Prester John, this last mile or so almost vertical. Both of them were sucking air, testament to the angle and the effort of dragging the duffle along with them. But they remained steady all the way up, testament to these Afterlife bodies. The ridge top, level and accommodating and a good place to catch breath, was also short, dropping precariously to a natural stone platform. What lay beyond caused Otto's outburst.

A stone bridge.

"It looks crossable," Ferdinand said uncertainly.

I know," Otto folded his arms. "But that's not the problem."

"What is?"

"I've seen this before."

Ferdinand blinked at him, expectant of explanation, but Otto said nothing, just stared because he didn't have one. Yet. It was a massive ramp, heavily buttressed and flanked by sheer drops into blackness, slanting at a fairly dangerous angle from the platform below to the other side where it tied in to another stone platform and the path beyond. Yep, definitely seen this before. But where?

"I thought you had never been here," Ferdinand said.

"I haven't, that's what's driving me crazy. But I know this," and he swept a hand at the bridge. "I just can't put a finger on it."

Wait.

The greenish-blue glow of the fungus cast odd shadows, throwing him. But, if it were a different kind of lighting, say fire, garish and frightful, getting brighter as something terrifying approached, then ...

Otto gasped. "No. No way."

"What is it?" Ferdinand touched his arm. Otto, struck dumb by utter disbelief, couldn't reply. Now he knew where he'd seen it before.

In a movie. *The Fellowship of the Ring*. It was the stone bridge.

"Where the Balrog attacked Gandalf!" Otto cried in pure shock.

"What?"

"It's from a movie. You said you know what a movie is."

"I did not. John did."

"Details, details. You know what I'm talking about. And that right there," Otto pointed at the bridge, "is from one I really enjoyed. Very much. Now how in the bloody hell is that possible?"

"I ... cannot say."

Otto gaped at the bridge. "There's no way. Unless this trail is constructing itself out of my head ..." he paused, startled. "Out of my head! Which means," and he whirled on Ferdinand, "I am, as I have long suspected, in a friggin' COMA!"

Ferdinand took an alarmed step back. "What?"

"Should have known, should have KNOWN!" Otto threw his hands up, infuriated. "Jesus H. Christ! Everything was heading to this point, wasn't it? You and King Canute back there," he thrust a finger over Ferdinand's shoulder, "were drawing me a map of Middle Earth, weren't you? Huh? Weren't you!" He took a menacing step toward Ferd who fell into a defensive position.

"What are you talking about?" The Platan was confused and growing angry.

Not as angry as Otto. "Oh, screw you!" Otto whirled, scrambled down the trail in more of a fall than a walk, ran through the platform and down the bridge until he stood in the middle of it. "Here I am, orcs!" he shouted to the sheer walls rising at either end, "Start shooting your arrows!" He threw his head back and arms out as "orcs!" and "arrows!" echoed back and forth across the chasm.

"Stop it!" Ferdinand rushed across the bridge and grabbed Otto's uniform coat. "You want to bring the suited ones down on us?"

Otto shook him off. "That's another thing. Those guys are right out of *The Matrix*. Or, more accurately, *Dark City*, which I thought was a BETTER MOVIE!" he shouted again. "Moviemoviemovie!" raced around them and over the side of the bridge.

"Are you insane?" Ferdinand, astounded.

"No, Ferd, I'm not." He stepped to the edge of the bridge. "I'm asleep. I'm lying in a hospital bed with tubes shoved up my nose, my wife sitting in a chair next to me wringing her hands. Could be a day, could be a week, I don't know, but that's where I am." He peered down into the forever blackness. "I am not, absolutely not, dead. I am not here, Ferd. And, you know something?" He pointed at the Platan. "Neither are you."

"Do not," Ferd whispered.

"What?" Otto leaned over, precariously, a bit of stone loosening from the bridge and falling into the darkness. "Don't wake up? I do that, you cease to exist? You don't exist, anyway, my *leetle* friend," Otto mocked with his best Al Pacino, which wasn't all that good, and glared at Ferd. "So, where did you come from? I don't have any particular interest in Argentina or Spanish conquistadors. I must have pulled you out of *The Mission*."

"I was never in a mission," Ferdinand said, "Please, Otto, step away."

"Why?" Otto made a fake move toward the edge and laughed when Ferdinand blanched. "What happens? I step off, plunge down and I WAKE UP!" Otto shouted to the ceiling, "WAKE UP! I GOTTA WAKE UP!"

UPUPUP! raced back and forth through the cavern.

"You will not wake up," Ferdinand spoke softly, "You will be forever lost."

Otto considered that. Dreams of falling were, supposedly, about loss of control. Well, suffering a major heart attack and strapped into a bed, can't lose much more control than that. But the other long-held myth of falling dreams: hit bottom, you die.

Really die.

"Ferd," Otto said, "What do you mean by 'lost forever'?"

Ferdinand gestured at the blackness. "You do not know what is down there. It could be a short fall, or it could be eternal. Either way, you will never reach your ship."

"Your ship, too, Ferd."

"No, Otto, it is not." He shook his head. "It is yours. If you fall, then I have no more reason to go there, do I?"

"Of course not, Ferd, 'cause you're not really here."

"I am actually here, Otto."

"Yeah?" Otto spun on his toes, overlapping the edge a bit, causing Ferd to start. "Then why don't you explain this?" Otto's gesture took in the bridge.

"The worlds blur."

"Excuse me?"

The Platan made an all-encompassing gesture. "What do you think, Otto?" Ferd said. "That realms of such power, like Life and Death, can be contained?"

"Huh?" Baffled, Otto almost lost his balance. "You mean Peter Jackson actually saw this bridge?"

"Who is Peter Jackson?"

"A god."

That confused Ferd even more and Otto laughed. "That's it, huh, Peter Jackson actually saw this? There he was tooling along some New Zealand highway and it appeared like a vision in the sky. Or maybe he only read about it, in *The Lord of the Rings,* and it was *Tolkien* who saw it." He paused. "Tolkien." A man of great belief. C.S. Lewis's friend, both of whom wrestled with the nature of God and His Purposes.

"Like calls to like," Ferdinand said.

"No way." Otto waved that off. "Just no way. God doesn't give visions anymore."

"Not on purpose, anyway," Ferd conceded. "But the worlds blur."

"I'm not buying it." Otto turned back to the pit. "And I'm going to show you, Ferd, old boy, that you're not real." He made ready. To hit bottom, to actually die, to relieve Sherry of her worries and fears by expiring, truly, in front of her eyes. With the insurance payouts and the will and the trust, she'd never have to worry about money again. He tensed.

"Have you never encountered the blurring of the worlds, Otto?" Ferdinand's voice behind him.

He thought. Well, maybe. Cloudy day in Alabama, walking the front yard and seeing, out of the corner of his eye, something zip into the clouds. He had whirled and scrutinized the roiling clouds but, nothing there. So, what, UFO? Angel? Bit of turbulence? Or, the time he'd been alone in the house, Sherry out shopping, and he was getting something out of the refrigerator when, *crash*! the sound of glass breaking, loud and startling, like a giant chandelier had fallen. "What the hell?" he ran into the living room, convinced someone had thrown a rock through the front window. Nothing. Searched the whole house. Nothing.

Ferdinand's arms encircled his waist and yanked him away from the edge. "Get off!" Otto fought against Ferdinand's powerful grip. "I gotta die!"

Ferdinand threw him to the ground, ending up on top. "Listen to me!" Ferdinand's harsh whisper in his ear. "You must be true to where you are!"

"Let go of me, man."

"I said listen!" Ferd held him tighter. "Let us suppose, for the sake of argument, that you are in a hospital unconscious. There is a reason for this dream, no?"

"Yeah, 'cause I'm unconscious."

"Yes, because you need the time to heal. Your body is working, repairing itself, and your mind is giving you this magnificent dream of Heaven to calm you while it does so."

"*Hmm*. Okay, so?"

"So, you must play along."

Otto pushed him off and rolled over then sat up. "What do you mean?"

"Play by the rules of your dream. Let your body work. If you violate those rules." He gestured at the edge. "Then you die."

Made sense. He was strapped and tubed and pumped full of chemicals while nurses and Sherry hovered – the bridge proved that. Were he awake, he'd be miserable as hell. At least here he was entertained. "Okay," Otto pointed at Ferd, "you're telling me, then, that I am still alive."

Ferdinand shook his head. "You are not. You have passed on and this is the Afterlife, and you are on an insane quest to find God with an impossible craft. I am here." He pointed at himself and then the bridge. "This is here. Somehow it was glimpsed and made its way into one of your movies. You will, as we move along, glimpse other familiarities because things blend. You must believe this. Otherwise, you will do something stupid."

"Stupid?" Otto looked at the edge. "What if, by jumping, I die? Really die. My wife gets the insurance and the relief. How stupid is that?"

"But you may not. You may just, simply, wake up. And there she is, having to take care of you for, how long?"

Hmm, again. His attempt to relieve her burden may increase it, instead.

"Well, I don't believe it." He gestured at the bridge. "At least, not anymore."

"Then, humor it."

"Okay," Otto stood and brushed himself off. "Okay. Humor is the watchword. I'll play along until the moment I'm convinced otherwise, then I'm going over the side."

"We'll be long gone by then."

"I'm speaking figuratively."

"Fine." Ferdinand went back for the duffle, returning with it a few minutes later and setting it down to retighten the straps.

"So what was yours?" Otto asked.

"My what?"

"Blurring of the worlds."

"Oh." He straightened. "I came into the plaza one very early morning, no one was about, and there was an angel sitting on the fountain."

"An angel? What did he look like?"

"She. All in white, shining like the sun, blonde like a Swede with blue eyes that looked like ice. Very small, even teeth."

Otto was thunderstruck. "Claudia!"

Ferdinand regarded him. "Do you mean Saint Claudia?"

"She's more than a saint and definitely an angel. What happened?"

"Well, I was a bit surprised but approached to ask if she

needed assistance, and she smiled and faded from view. Personally, I thought I had drunk too much the night before."

"No, Ferd, you didn't. You got a special revelation." One that Otto's very creative, coma-fueled brain had, no doubt, just added to the mix, but still, nice touch.

Ferdinand shrugged and finished his tying and walked down the bridge. Otto followed. When they got to the end, they both stopped and stared back. "Otto?" Ferdinand asked.

"Yep?"

"What's an orc?"

Chapter XL

Running Stars, Running Men

Finally, after what seemed like an additional three days of walking, the journey ended. But not in a good way.

After turning a corner of the continually ascending, but narrowing, trail, they'd run smack into sheer rock face. The trail ended smack at its base. Otto rendered his verdict: "This is a joke."

Ferdinand held up a hand. "Not necessarily."

"Oh, c'mon," Otto held up two hands. "We're screwed. We have to go back. And it won't be Balrogs waiting for us at the bridge but those *Dark City* idiots." Otto was going to add some unpleasant descriptions of Prester John, but held his peace.

"Not necessarily," Ferdinand repeated and slung the duffle across his back then took a step forward. He placed a hand on the rock face, exploring it ...

... and disappeared.

"Stop doing that!" Otto called and placed his hands on the same spot but found nothing.

Nothing.

All right, Ferdinand's arm should pop back out and he'd grab it and be yanked through like last time, so, wait. Otto did. Minutes passed. No arm.

"Ferd?" he called, nervous.

Silence.

"Great. Just great." Otto scrutinized the rock face, looking for some fault or odd turn, but nothing stood out. Frantically, he slapped at the rock but it remained solid, impervious, mocking.

Well, one good thing, instead of walking all the way back to the bridge and jumping off, he could just beat his head against this wall. Now *that's* an appropriate metaphor. There had to be an exit here somewhere, though, or did Ferdinand simply disintegrate? "Like an agent," he muttered, and wondered if he'd been led a merry chase. Suits were, right now, back up the trail with a newly reconstituted Ferd high-fiving while falling all over themselves laughing.

Jerks.

He sat down. Okay, the last time this happened was back at the ravine. What had Ferdinand said? "I felt the breeze." *Hmm.* A picture flashed in his mind: ten years old, standing with Dad in an open field. "How do you tell wind direction?" Dad smiling, he shrugging. Dad popped a finger in his mouth and then held it out. "The cold side is the wind." Otto copied him and found the wind and faced it and brought the kite to bear and it soared, just soared. That had been a good day.

Otto popped a finger in his mouth and held it up. Immediately, the side of it facing the rock went cold. So, a breeze. He stood and kept wetting his finger, following the subtle variations of the temperature until he bent around a previously unnoticed outcropping. The cold was strongest here and he placed his hand against the rock ...

It went through.

"Eureka!" Otto probed and found the opening, quite narrow. He squeezed forward, grateful it was smooth and not abrading the skin on his cheeks. About ten feet in, the rock narrowed sharply and Otto was sure he was trapped but made a final effort, catching his foot on some ledge and falling straight through, right on his face. "Figures," he muttered and turned over.

The stars.

"Thank you, God!" he whispered fiercely and watched them whip overhead, appearing over the edge of a cliff to his left and disappearing as they reached the edge of another cliff towering over his right, like a crowd running frantically from one display to another. Maybe that was it – all the stars in the universe gathered here to catch a glimpse of Heaven, jostling each other for a look, then went back home. You'd think someone on Earth would have noticed that.

And, of course, right overhead, the moons – stationary, so midnight or after. He eyed them. Latchemondy was probably up there right now staring down at him. Or Suits were, directing ultralights to his position where they'd drop those dimensional grenades and *pfhhtboom*! there he'd be, on the glass plain of hell. He shuddered. Time to go.

He sat up and looked around. He was in a bowl formed by a short, walled canyon, soft sand underneath him, the cave entrance obscured but he was sure he could find it again, if need be. Obviously in a desert, but whether the Hot Lands or the Great Empty ... sheesh, he was starting to talk like John and Ferd. Speaking of whom ...

Neither hide nor hair. Dude skedaddled and Otto had to wonder why. Not like him to leave the obvious spot from where Otto would emerge. Unless he had no choice.

Otto studied the area, looking for trouble. Nothing moved. All was silent, except for the passing of a slight breeze. He felt a pleasant loneliness, a sense of the desert's eternity, lands blasted by heat and wind all day but at night, still, breathing, the reduction of life to its barest elements. Nice place to lie back, just lie back for a while, watch the stars race, see if the Inside Out Man did, indeed, come back ...

Hey!

Otto shook himself hard and tore his eyes away from the stars and jerked back up to a sitting position. Ah, man! Hypnosky! Come on, that's only supposed to happen during the day, not at night! Otto resolved to keep his eyes level until he got out of whatever was weaving this spell. Had to find Ferd. Had to get to the rocket. He lurched to his feet and examined the ground and there, a trail, God-provided, or the natural lay of the land? Who knew and who cared? It was the obvious way to go.

The bowl narrowed to sheer wall mere yards down the path, allowing only one-person passage. The light dimmed as the cliffs cut off the moons and Otto put a hand on the rock as guide. It was a winding trail with a lot of switchbacks and Otto figured he'd spend a couple of days in here when he stumbled over something, falling flat on his face. Again.

"Dammit," he breathed and kicked at the obstruction, which was soft and canvas.

The duffle.

Uh-oh.

He felt around to see if Ferd was lying here, too, but no, just the bag. Now, what caused him to drop this? The need to run like hell? Otto hunched and looked up the cliff face to what little sky was exposed, but no bat wings loomed nor did Suits cling, lizard-like, to the sides. He pulled the duffle to himself and stood. Okay, little hard to get the damn thing through this narrow path and maybe Ferd had dropped it in disgust, but that seemed out of character. More likely something bad happened, like a dimensional grenade.

"Great." Otto wondered why God let that happen. Aren't You supposed to be on our side? Question for later. Hoisting the bag in front of him, he stepped fast and hard and ...

... right off a cliff.

"*Ack*!" he yelped as he tumbled Buster Keaton style down a sandy slope, the duffle following in perfect synch and knocking him off his feet every time he recovered. The sand was soft with no purchase and he hit the bottom hard, the duffle smacking his head as sand tidal-waved over him.

"*Pfhet*!" He blew sand out of his face and hurled the duffle away and sat up, instantly pinned against the wall by six or seven spears. "*Hey*!"

"Here's another one!" someone at the end of one of the spears yelled and viciously drove the point a little deeper.

"Stop it!" Otto grabbed at the spear. "That hurts!"

"Then don't move, spy!" Spear Voice said and jabbed again and Otto thought it wise to obey. He looked sideways. Ferdinand was next to him, similarly sand-covered and pinned by an additional set of spears. "Where'd you go?" Otto whispered.

"The enemy flew over," Ferd whispered back, "I had to run."

"Stop talking!" This from someone on a horse behind the spearmen. Guy sounded familiar. "What are you doing out here?"

"Running," Otto said.

"They're not running!" Spear Voice shouted. "They're spying for the Long Faces!"

"Long Faces?" Otto cocked his head. "I call them Suits."

"Shut up!" Spear Voice jabbed again. Otto could see him better now – long wild hair framing even wilder eyes, ragged beard and moustache, probably a real ...

Tartar?

Otto sat up straight and pushed the spear aside. "Knock it off," he said to Spear Boy and peered hard toward the back, at the guy on the horse. "Kenny?" he asked.

The man on the horse started and pushed forward a bit, leaning to get a better look. The moons lit him. Not Kenny.

"Sam!" Otto cried.

Sam slack-jawed. "Otto! What in all of God's creation are you doing out here?"

"Getting bushwhacked by you guys. Again." He glared at the Tartar. "Mind letting me up?" The Tartar looked at Sam, who nodded, and spears were raised, except for the ones holding Ferdinand. "Him, too," Otto said and those were raised and they helped each other to their feet, using the cliff wall as a brace as they brushed off sand. "So," Ferdinand said grimly, "you do have other friends."

Otto smiled as he handed over the duffle. "Wow, you called me your friend."

"Shut up."

Sam dismounted and gave Otto a big hug. "Good to see you, man."

"You, too." Otto rubbed at the rapidly healing wound on his chest. "Although I really wish you guys would stop poking me every time I show up."

Otto introduced Ferdinand and he and Sam shook hands and Sam then introduced the twenty or twenty-five others. The Tartar turned out to be a Galatian Celt named Kastor. "My father was king of the Tectosage!" he proclaimed.

Otto cocked his head. "I've heard that word before."

"Of course you have!" Kastor stroked the spear across his chest in some kind of salute. "We took the plains of Anatolia. Who could not have heard of such greatness?" Another spear salute.

"Oh, brother." Sam rolled his eyes, and Kastor gave him a haughty look.

"I never heard of you guys before I got here," Otto clarified and then furrowed his brow. "Now where was that ..." a light bulb went on and Otto snapped a finger. "Of course! Claudia! She said she was

Tectosage! Of Galatia!"

Kastor bowed a reverent head, "Ah, yes, Saint Claudia, of the golden hair and wondrous ales. She is a daughter to me, some generations removed."

Otto shook his head. "This place." He looked at Sam. "Where's everybody else?"

The mood turned grim. "Running," Sam said.

"What's going on?"

"Those Long Faces, Suits, whatever, attacked us about a week ago."

"Yes!" Kastor brandished his spear. "Demons, evil ones! Throwing their death eggs from on high and shooting their knife beams!" He pounded out a frenzied war dance. "I will tear out their hearts! I will take their heads! I will—"

"All right, all right!" Sam calmed him. He made a face at Otto. "Berserker."

"Why'd they attack?"

"Beats me. We were camped over with a group of Inuit—"

"Eskimos?" Right word or not, Otto was still amazed. "In the desert?"

"They were trying something different. Anyway, we were having a high old time eating blubber and doing that crazy trampoline thing when the Long Faces swarmed us."

"I lost comrades!" Kastor shouted and resumed his frenzied dance, but this time he mourned.

"Yeah," Sam sympathized. "I ain't never seen weapons like that."

"I know," Otto agreed. "Machine Gun Kelly got taken by one of those grenades."

Sam's eyebrows rose. "The gangster?"

"The very one. Met him on the train, along with Doc Holliday."

Sam chuckled. "The people you run into here."

"Speaking of that," Otto said, "I met your wife."

"Grace! Really!" Sam laughed. "You met her? Where is she?"

Otto hesitated, wondering if Grace's living arrangements would cause Sam hurt. "She's ... in the City. Has a lot of kids."

Sam slapped his knees in delight. "Good ole Grace. She was a pistol."

"She still is. She helped me out when the Suits were after me."

Sam's eyes narrowed. "The Suits were after you?"

"Uh, well ... yeah."

"And here you are," Sam said it softly. The Tartars exchanged glances, gripped spears, and stared at Otto and Ferdinand. The hostility went up a notch and Kastor took a step forward. "Why were they after you?" he asked, shoulders set to belligerence.

Welp, stepped in it again, Otto old boy, confirmed by Ferdinand's disgusted shake of the head. Fine, and he squared on Kastor. "They want to keep us away from the rocket," he announced.

"The rocket?" Sam was puzzled. "Why do they want to do that?"

"Because," Otto said, "when we get there, it's taking off."

"Oh, not this again." Sam groaned. "That thing isn't going anywhere."

"Yes, it is, Sam, with us on board." Otto flipped a thumb between Ferdinand and him. "And we're going to find God."

A collective gasp went up from the Tartars. "Blasphemy!" someone called, immediately taken up by several more.

"It's not blasphemy!" Otto spoke over them. "It's our mission!"

A roar of disapproval and the crowd pressed him back. "You stirred the Long Faces!" Kastor shook a fist. "You called them on us!"

"We didn't stir them!" Otto pushed the Celt back. "They ... came on their own!"

Sam confronted him. "Then why have the Suits surrounded the rocket?"

Startling, that. "What?"

Sam nodded. "Yes. Completely surrounded it. No one can get in or out."

Ferdinand and Otto exchanged looks. "It seems," Ferdinand concluded, "you are, indeed, onto something."

"You sure are!" Kastor pushed his face into Ferdinand's. "You're the reason we're running!" A roar of agreement this time. Kastor turned wildly to the crowd. "We've lost our tribe because of these two! If we give them up, then we'll have peace!" Another roar of agreement, followed by a lot of spear shaking.

Not good.

Otto took a prudent step back as Sam reared his horse and

forced his way in front. "This one." Sam pointed at Otto. "IS tribe!"

"But this one isn't!" Kastor sidestepped Sam and pushed his spear at Ferdinand's chest. Others ran past Sam and joined Kastor, threatening Ferdinand.

"*Hey!*" Otto jumped in front of them. "He's with me!" but they grabbed Otto and threw him to the side. A discussion broke out, led by Kastor, about staking Ferdinand and pulling off a little skin and maybe roasting him for a while before giving him to the Suits or Long Faces or what-have-you. Conclusion? The Suits will go away and then we can find Kenny and reform and have a good time again.

Otto pushed at the crowd surrounding Ferdinand but they hurled him back. Sam cried "Wait!" and tried to ride between the mob and their target but was also pushed back. Any moment, Ferdinand would be a shish kabob, courtesy of the increasingly frenzied Kastor.

"Stop!" Ferdinand shouted in a voice so penetrating it cut right through the yelling and froze the crowd. The rioters, even Kastor, were brought up short. Otto was surprised. Didn't know the little guy had it in him.

Ferdinand coolly pushed away several of the spears, glared back at the wielders, and then stepped onto a convenient boulder. He looked disdainfully over the crowd. "Are you Tartars?" he asked, the sneer evident. "Or," he said after a dramatic pause, "are you women?"

That elicited another collective gasp, and some outrage from the three or four spear-wielding girls. Otto was dumbfounded. Any moment now, Ferd is a shish kabob.

Ferdinand raised a dramatic finger, "Because! Women run from their enemies." Another pause. "Tartars don't."

The wind went out of them at once. They stared at Ferdinand and then Otto and then exchanged sheepish looks. Otto had to smile. Damn, Ferd, good job.

Kastor, after a moment, took a step and bowed before Ferdinand. "You have my spear," he said and presented it in both hands and there was a shout and a raising of spears and hearty calls of fellowship, the murderous intent of moments before forgotten. A battle cry went up, Otto joining it.

Sam reared his horse back, shouting above them all, "Drive the Suits from our land!"

"Drive them!" the Tartars responded and did that weird desert ululation Otto thought a province of Bedouins. Someone pulled out a drum and the war dance erupted, led by the crazy Kastor, of course. Otto maneuvered over to Ferdinand, who was still on the rock, watching all this with great satisfaction. "Nice work."

Ferdinand shrugged. "Sometimes you have to motivate the troops."

Otto laughed as the Tartars danced. In the midst of it, preparations to leave, spears bundled and packs assembled and horses saddled. Otto went over to Sam. "Where's Kenny?"

"Off to the south."

"Does he have everyone else with him?"

"No. Moses has one group, Jakto the other."

"You know where they are?"

"We can find them."

"Good." Otto settled and watched the preparations and felt a stir. Enemies stalk our land, and we fight. We fight. War in the Afterlife. Who'da thunk it?

Abruptly, he was pushed off balance and the Platan cap ripped from his head and tossed over Sam's horse. He turned, combat ready, the blood call working its magic.

A horse stood there, innocently gazing at him. "Flicka," Otto snorted, "I mighta known."

Sam chuckled.

Chapter XLI

The Gathering Of Armies

They rode south, guided by the double moons and a desert rat named John Myers. "Worked with Joe Walker on the Humboldt," he said, cheerfully, as Otto rode with him.

"I have no idea what that is."

"That's the fur trappin' way out of Ft. Laramie. Joe was the master." John shook an admiring head. "That man could find an alabaster trail on a white mountain in a snowstorm."

"When was this?"

"Forties," John said, nonchalant, and Otto figured he meant 1840s, Gold Rush days.

"So I'm guessing you've been all over this desert."

"Yep." John spat a wad of something. "Stayed in the City for a while but the desert's got a call to it, ya know?"

Yes, Otto did know.

"Sumpin' about it." John gazed over the flat, admiration deep in his eyes. "Ain't nothing here between you and God."

Otto stared at the old scout. "You've seen God?"

"Every day." John swept a hand over the landscape. "Everywhere."

Ah, metaphor. Or simile. Or peyote.

"Sometimes, He even talks to me."

"What?" Does peyote make you hear voices?

"Why so surprised?" John smiled. "He's talkin' to you now."

Otto considered. Yes, God was, but the words were different. "John, am I crazy?" meaning his quest.

John laughed out loud. "We all are, son!" and he spurred forward to examine two opposed outcroppings, like a door in the desert. The column stopped as he disappeared between the fingers of rock. The rest stood by, spears ready, nervous eyes to the moons, expecting a bat shape to flick across it, herald of another Suit attack.

"Sam," Otto spoke low as the ex-harem guy rode up, "what do you think happens to the people hit by the Suits' beams?"

"Dunno."

"Do they reconstitute?"

"Didn't stay around long enough to find out."

"What about the grenades?"

"You mean, where do the victims go?"

Otto nodded.

Sam let out a breath. "Otto, I wish I knew. I haven't seen anybody come back who got hit. Maybe they get transported so far away they haven't reached us yet. Or, maybe to the moons. Why you asking?"

"Because, Sam," Otto dropped to a whisper, "what we're doing could be the Afterlife version of suicide."

Sam said nothing for a moment. "Otto, you know I was in WWI, right?"

Now that was interesting. "No. And, really?"

"Yeah, I was young and stupid. Was in the 93rd, which Black Jack immediately gave to the French. Black Jack don' wan' no black back," and he grinned. Otto figured it was a troop slogan. "Anyways, I fought, got gassed, got home, got a job, married Grace, got here." He raised a finger. "But, point is, I fought. For something I believed in, even if Black Jack kept us out of the parades."

"I get that, Sam." After all, he'd fought his own wars.

"No, you don't. Anything you did, was expected. Ninety-third, we did it for pride only. Takes a special kind of thinking to fight a battle for no reward. Takes a sense of personal honor. A commitment to an ideal."

Otto paused. "Now, Sam, I *do* get it."

Sam slapped him on the shoulder. "Now, I think you do. So don't worry about the boys." He jerked a thumb back at the column.

"They're in this."

John suddenly appeared between the fingers, reared his horse, and waved an excited hat. "Found 'em!" Sam shouted and the column whooped and spurred their horses.

Moses was waiting for them on the other side. "Hey!" he cried joyfully, lifting Otto off the ground after they all dismounted. "Where'd you come from?"

"Long story, most of it ending with, 'I'm the reason you're running from the Suits.'"

Moses shrugged. "You, me, whoever. So who's in charge of the counterattack?"

"My, word travels fast." Otto chuckled and pointed at Ferdinand. "Guess he is."

Moses slapped Otto's shoulders and walked over to Ferd, the two of them immediately consulting. Moses's camp, secreted under a couple of rock overhangs, was safe from air attack and had two or three escape points. Man had an eye for the tactical, Otto concluded. Best guy to talk with Ferd, then. Better than Otto, anyways.

He found a spot near a covered fire. "Don't do anything stupid," Otto warned Flicka as he unloaded his bedroll and javelins. Flicka grinned at him but behaved herself. Otto then strolled over to the center fire, where the two groups had gathered to listen.

Moses had drawn a map in the sand and Otto leaned over to look. Good rendition of the locale around the rocket. "See," Moses pointed out various passes in the surrounding mountains. "You've got four approaches, at the compass points. The Long Faces have spread themselves pretty evenly around the fence. There's enough of them to slow down any push we make through any of the passes, giving the rest of 'em time to concentrate against us at the attack point."

"*Hmm.*" Ferdinand studied the sand map. "They're on interior lines, too. They can shift faster than we can."

"And they've got airpower," Otto added.

Everybody looked at each other and Kastor began to cry. Sam patted him gently on the back. "Stop it. We'll figure out something."

But Otto wasn't so sure. Maybe if they had corresponding weapons, something to counter the lasers and grenades and ultralights, they could pull this off, but all they had were spears and bows and maybe a couple of flintlocks. There's no way they could drive the Suits out of the desert; it's like Apaches against the cavalry – lots of fun for a while, but, ultimately, they'd end up on a reservation.

So, don't drive the Suits out of the desert.

He blinked.

The Suits had attacked Kenny because, obviously, they were hoping to find Otto and Ferdinand. Failing that, they'd gone to Plan B: keep Otto and Ferdinand out of Star City. They hadn't made a move on Star City itself, which was odd because they could save themselves all this trouble by destroying the place. Be easy; drop a few grenades, loose a couple of lasers and, *poof*! No more base. No more rocket.

But they hadn't gone after the rocket. They'd gone after Otto and Ferdinand. Because ...

... because bases, and rockets, can be rebuilt. Crewmen can't.

See how long it's taken for the requisite thirty people to show up?

So, destroying Star City and the rocket does them no good. Destroying the last crewman, though ...

... meant there was no need to take on the entire Suit army. No need at all. Just break through a portion of it, hustle Ferdinand on board and, *boom*, launch. The Suits lose.

And leave. Of their own accord.

While he mused, Flicka snatched his hat and threw it over the crowd. "Dang horse," he muttered and went after it.

Horse.

He stopped and looked back at Flicka, who was chuckling. "Sam," he called over the crowd, "anybody bring down one of those gliders yet?"

"I hit one with my sling." A Tartar, dressed more like a shepherd in a single white tunic with a matching white cloth wrapped around his head, stepped out of the crowd. A doubled-over piece of cloth circled his chest and another served as a waist sash. Looked like a school-crossing guard. Otto realized all three pieces of cloth were slings. Three slings? Impressive.

"What was the result?"

"It moved away from us like this." The little shepherd canted his hand. "Like it was damaged. The pilot was trying to regain control."

"*Hmm*." Otto pursed his lips. "As fragile a craft as they look."

Otto pointed at the headband sling. "How good are you with that?"

The shepherd grinned, whipped off the sling, and sent five pebbles crashing into the side of a distant outcropping in as many seconds, shattering it.

"Holy Moly!" Otto was astounded. "Where did you learn to do that?"

"Gymnesiai."

"In the gym?"

"No." The shepherd shook his head. "Gymnesiai. The Romans called it Balearus."

Ferdinand's eyebrows rose. "The Balearic Islands. You are a Balearic slinger." The shepherd bowed his head in assent.

Otto was even more impressed. "I heard of you guys. You're real badasses with those slings." He looked around. "How'd that word translate?"

"Best fighter," said Ferdinand.

"Tough spear," Kastor added.

"Badass," the shepherd replied and Otto had to laugh. Some things were universal.

"What's your name?" Otto asked the slinger.

"Tyrus."

Otto evaluated him. "I take it you've used that sling in combat."

"Yes!" Tyrus nodded vigorously. "I was with Hannibal at Cannae."

Ferdinand almost fell over. "You were at Cannae?"

"Yes," Tyrus's eyes shone. "A great victory. You know of it?"

"I do, indeed!" Ferdinand proclaimed. "It is world-famous. I must speak to you of it!"

Cannae? Hannibal? "Wait," Otto held up a hand. "Let's do the history lesson later. What I want to know is, how'd you end up here?"

"This desert has been part of my wanderings."

"No. I don't mean here," Otto pointed at the sand, "I mean *here*." And his arms took in the world. "You are obviously not a Christian."

Ferdinand was a bit annoyed. "I thought we had settled this point."

Otto brushed that away. "I thought so, too, and I didn't ask Kastor because he was sloshing around the Mideast and may have run into some Israelites. But there's no way this guy," Otto gestured at Tyrus, "did."

"The people of Canaan?" Tyrus queried.

"Huh? Oh yeah, I guess that's how Israelite would translate."

Tyrus snorted. "I knew many of them. Phoenicia found my islands in ancient days and there was much trade between us. I am named after their city of Tyre."

Otto said nothing. Too dumbfounded.

Ferdinand looked at him. "Don't ask anymore. If you are not convinced of the overwhelming grace of God by now—"

"All right, all right." Otto waved him off. "It's just, none of this fits the template and having him here," he nodded at Tyrus, "seems more evidence that, well ..."

"Yes?" Ferdinand encouraged.

"That I'm not in a coma." There. Said.

"You're not."

"Yeah, well, jury's still out, Ferd." Otto looked at Tyrus. "Are there other slingers here?"

"There are others scattered about this world, but none here with me."

"*Hmm*. How hard would it be for you to teach some others the sling there?"

"I could show them, but it's a matter of practice."

"Well, then." Otto clapped Tyrus on the shoulder. "Pick a couple of guys and get to it. You're now officially our anti-aircraft battery."

Tyrus grinned and grabbed a couple of Tartars and they went off to the other side of the outcropping. In moments, there was the sound of rocks shattering against cliffs.

"What exactly are you planning?" Moses asked.

"It's simple, really." Otto squatted by the sand map as the others gathered around. "We've been thinking about how to smash the Suits and drive them away, which is impossible. We're too outgunned. But, we don't have to. All we have to do is give them a reason to leave."

Moses and Ferdinand exchanged glances. "How?" Ferdinand asked.

Otto looked at the Argentine. "They're here because they don't want you and me to reach the rocket. If we reach it, they fail." He paused. "They fail, they leave."

A moment's silence to absorb this.

"And what if they don't?" Moses asked.

Otto shrugged. "Then you guys will have a lot of fun ambushing them until they round you up and put you on Fort Sill. Either way, you're screwed." Another pause. "But if I'm right, then they're screwed the moment the rocket lifts."

A buzz of conversation from the onlookers, ranging from those who thought Otto was nuts to those grasping at the slim hope provided. Slim hope won.

"Okay," Moses became the slim-hope spokesman. "So, how do we get you to the rocket?"

Otto pointed at the sand map. "We've got four avenues of attack on the base. Wherever we hit, the Suits, including the ultralights, will swarm and tear us up. So, we need to fool them, get them to commit to an area where we're not going to be, and then blast right through their thinned lines."

"And how are we going to do that?"

Otto stood and brushed off his hands. "With them." He pointed at Flicka and a couple of horse buddies horsing around the fire.

Moses, Ferdinand and the rest looked at them and then back at him. "Go on," Moses said.

"Two charges, that's what we do. We send what looks like an overwhelming force against the main gate, as huge and noisy as we can make it. That's what the Suits expect. I'm betting they only know their tactics and presume we'll do it the way they'd do it. Once they've engaged, we send a smaller, but much faster force, with Tyrus and his troop providing anti-air, against an unprotected part of the fence, cut through it and," he took in a deep breath, "hopefully, get to the rocket."

Ferdinand pursed his lips and studied the map. "It just might work."

A hubbub of excitement rose from the crowd as everyone pressed forward to look at the lines.

Otto held up a hand. "Hold on, guys, there's still a couple of major problems with this."

Kastor, who'd started an enthusiastic dance, stopped and cried, "What?"

"Well, first of all, the main charge is going to be nothing short of suicide." That quieted everyone. "You have an extremely good chance of getting smacked by a suit weapon, and we have no idea what happens to anyone who gets smacked. So you'd have to be crazy to do it."

Concerned murmurs punctuated the crowd. Kastor flicked them away. "It is war. It is what happens," and the murmurs turned to agreement.

Otto snorted. "Guys, do you understand this is, essentially, the Charge of the Light Brigade?"

Mostly puzzled looks. But then a man dressed in a red waistcoat with a flintlock pistol and a sword in a hippie tie-dyed sash which didn't go with his outfit at all, big muttonchops, big moustache, and a high forehead, stepped out. "Excuse me." The man cleared his throat. "Did you mean the charge of the British Calvary at Balaclava during the Crimean War?"

"Well, yeah, I think so."

The man clicked his heels together and bowed slightly. "Captain John Augustus Oldham, formerly of the 13th Light Dragoons, which participated magnificently in that charge."

Otto was flabbergasted. "You were there?"

Captain Oldham nodded. "Indeed. My participation landed me here, in this wondrous world." He stroked the tie-dye sash lovingly. "My troublesome horse bolted during the charge and I found myself first among the Russian guns." He smiled. "First class for one's personal legend, not so for surviving a battle. I would very much like a chance to do it again."

A cheer went up among the troop and they flocked around Oldham, clamoring to join him. Otto laughed. "Well, Captain, looks like you've got another brigade." Oldham turned and smiled, giving a thumbs-up.

"So that's one problem solved," Ferdinand said. "What's the other?"

Otto sighed, "Not enough people."

At that moment, there was a rumbling toward the south and everyone turned, reaching for weapons as a huge cavalry force burst among them, whooping and hollering and waving swords and spears. And right up front—

"Kenny!" Otto yelped.

"Hey, Otto!" Kenny leaped from his horse and embraced him.

"Heard you needed some help!"

"Yeah," Jakto materialized next to him, grinning. "We couldn't miss this."

"Wow, just ... wow," was all Otto could say, hugging both of them as an impromptu party of welcome broke out among the reunited Tartars, Kastor leading the dance, of course. Hurriedly, Otto and Ferdinand outlined the plan to them, gaining Kenny's more than enthusiastic endorsement. "Great! This is great! I'll be happy to lead the second charge!" and he puffed out his chest.

"Yeah, well." Otto high-fived him. "You'd be my first choice. 'Course, if we had a real lancer here, someone like Pashtun—"

"Good to see you again, Otto," a quiet, lilting voice spoke in his ear.

"Pashtun!" Otto hugged the Marathan. "What are you doing here?"

"Well, I could not very well stay with those persons with long faces interfering with my business, could I?"

"No, I suppose not. What about Box?"

"Even those strange beings with their strange aircraft and their closed ways need a drink or two."

"Good. So, are you up for this?"

"A chance to mount my horse and level my spear with two good arms and legs and drive into an enemy – not the British, unfortunately," and he threw a baleful glance at Oldham celebrating in the distance, "but an enemy strange and invading my lands?" He smiled viciously. "What do you think?"

Otto clapped hands in appreciation and stepped back, standing next to Ferdinand as the party took off in earnest, drinks and food breaking out among wilder dances, if that were possible. Ferdinand looked at him. "A door closes. A window opens."

Otto just laughed.

Chapter XLII

Battle

A horseman crying a high, weird yip streaked out of the rocks, lance pressed along the horse's flank. About halfway to Star City's main gate, he hauled over and dropped out of the saddle, did a somersault on the side of the horse, remounted, spun the horse around to dance it on the rear legs.

"That Vachir," Kenny, crouching behind the ridge overlooking the base, chuckled. "Always showing off."

Otto watched the spectacle. "He is going to shoot one of 'em, right?"

"Yeah, don't worry," Jakto clapped him on the shoulder. "He's a real Mongol."

"So how did he get here ... oh, never mind," and Otto settled in. A bag of popcorn would go nice with the show.

They had a good view. The rocket gleamed in the middle of the base, its misshapenness a thing of curious beauty. Steam rose as gantries were frantically pulled to it and away and workers ran hoses back and forth and up and down.

"It looks like they're getting ready to launch," Otto said to Ferdinand, on edge.

"Wouldn't you?" Jakto said and swept a hand pointedly over the scene. An army of Suits surrounded the place. Ten or twelve ultralights buzzed the perimeter as the mass of Suits roiled and moved like a stormy ocean. Within the fence, Star City residents peered anxiously from behind hastily built barricades. They brandished weapons, ranging from pitchforks to machine guns. The Suits ignored them and focused on Vachir, instead.

"I wonder why the base people don't attack the Suits with those Foxbats," Otto mused.

Ferdinand, puzzled, swung toward him. "Do you think the Suits are susceptible to bat bites?"

Otto didn't even smile. "Not that kind of bat."

"I don't think the Foxbats are armed," Kenny said. "They used 'em to test engines or something."

"Oh."

As Vachir continued his antics, the Suit mob surged, doubling up in front of the main gate while extending their flanks. Ultralights canted toward the new position. "See how they swarm?" Ferdinand pointed out.

"Yeah," Otto said, "figured they'd bunch up. They seem to hold us in contempt."

"Not so sure." Ferdinand studied the layout. "There are still plenty of Suits walking around the perimeter."

"Granted," Otto confirmed, "but they're all heading toward the gate. Do you see how they're cold-shouldering the base people?"

"Yes."

"As I thought, they're more intent on keeping us out than keeping them in."

Ferdinand grunted. "That may be helpful. Once we move, the base people can attack from the rear."

"If they will."

Ferdinand watched Vachir's performance. "I cannot believe they would never consider a feint," he said as the Mongol danced the horse while yelling obscenities along the lines of, "May your children be fathered by goats!" Otto smiled. Had to be a Mongol thing.

"Again, contempt," Otto offered. "I'm betting their only experience of us is here, where we only play at war."

"*Hey!*" Kenny sounded hurt. "We do a pretty good job."

"Yeah, but ... wait." He focused on Vachir. "He's going to shoot."

The Mongol held his ground for a second and then bolted along the suit front. Lines of purple light hissed around Vachir but he dodged and weaved through the laser blasts. "Man, he's good," Otto said.

"Why I chose him," Kenny sounded proud and Otto had to chuckle. Humans, taking credit where rarely due.

"The airships," Ferdinand said quietly and they watched, apprehensive, as the batwings converged above Vachir. The pilots were readying grenades.

"He really needs to get moving," Otto said.

Vachir must have heard him because he wheeled and zipped under the ultralights, straight for the line. The Suits thickened at his point of impact, as did the hot purple beams, when the Mongol cut sharply right, whipped up his short bow and fired an arrow straight into a random suit's chest.

The suit evaporated. There was a collective gasp.

"Did you see that?" Kenny, stupefied.

"Yeah!" Otto was equally knocked for a loop. "That didn't happen on the train."

"Perhaps it is the purity of these weapons?" Ferdinand murmured.

Otto considered. No indiscriminate gunpowder involved, just human strength and skill. *Hmm.* He glanced at Ferdinand's duffle. So much for pulling out the Contender.

Otto watched as Vachir streaked down the line, firing arrows rapidly, his targets dissolving into thin air. The raging Suits collided in their haste to follow him while the batwings spread out behind the horse, lofting grenades that exploded a second behind. Whether intended or not, Vachir was leading the entire Suit army away from the gate.

"Now would be a good time," Ferdinand said.

They scrambled down the rock, falling more than anything, arriving in a collective heap of grunts and *oofs* at the feet of the amazed horde.

"We'll get the others ready," Kenny said and he and Jakto ran off.

Otto shouted, "Captain!"

Oldham spurred his horse forward. "Suh!" he shouted back, giving Otto the English salute.

Otto grinned and returned it. "You may fire when ready, Gridley," he said as solemnly as he could. He almost laughed at Oldham's confused expression, but the captain saluted again, wheeled his horse and yelled, "Assemble!"

A wild cheer went up from the six or seven hundred horsemen

arrayed along the flat spot behind the ridge as they formed a column and began a dusty march through the small pass. Otto watched as they filed past, the leader of each cohort giving a salute in whatever manner they'd been trained. By the time the first third of the column had reached him, Otto had gotten everything from "*Eleleu!*" to "*Sieg Heil!*"

"Spartans and Nazis." Otto muttered. "Last people I expected to see here."

"You've spoken of these Nazis before," Ferdinand said. "Were they as bad as you imply?"

"Not as bad as my old boss." Otto watched approvingly as Moses rode up, dressed in Otto's Platan uniform. "How do I look?" he asked.

"Like a French admiral."

Moses laughed, "And you look like a field hand. They're going to figure this out pretty quick, though." Moses extended his coal-black arm significantly.

"Maybe," Otto agreed, "but it'll sure confuse the hell out of 'em for a few minutes."

Tabitha, dressed almost exactly like Ferdinand, pulled up beside Moses. She had a replica of Ferdinand's duffle slung to the side of the horse. "And just what am I supposed to do with this?" she asked, patting the duffle bag.

"Wave it around a lot," Otto said.

"Yeah, that'll look natural," she snorted.

"Well, you know, just make it conspicuous. And stick close to him." Otto pointed at Moses.

"Ride next to a big handsome man?" She smiled lasciviously. "You don't have to ask." Moses rolled his eyes and the two of them joined the column.

"Who's the girl?" Ferdinand asked.

"Trouble," Otto said. Ferdinand and he scooted through the last of the horsemen and ran to where the second group impatiently waited.

"Shouldn't we get moving?" Jakto said from the top of his horse.

"Yeah." Otto looked around. "Where's Pashtun?"

"Here." The Marathan broke through the ranks to present himself. Pashtun straddled a beautiful white Arabian with a long golden mane, but the horse wasn't half as resplendent as Pashtun himself. He wore a dazzling white tunic and wrap-around pants, all trimmed in gold, a high white turban on his head with a blood-red ruby in the middle. Two jewel-encrusted daggers hung from his gold brocade vest. Pashtun's beard trimmed and pointed, his eyes fierce, he gripped a long white spear with a cruel black point shaped like a leaf.

"Pashtun!" Otto goggled. "You're magnificent!"

The Marathan grinned and reared the horse, then settled down. "This is the standard uniform of a warrior displaying the honor of combat, my friend. And I thank you for the opportunity to do so again."

"Not me. Those Suits." Otto pointed through the pass. "And Pashtun, gotta tell ya, don't get into a hand-to-hand with them. They're really tough and really strong. Just go straight through."

"Yes," the Marathan replied flatly. "Straight through to the rocket, this I understand. And it would be most beneficial to the beginnings of this charge if you and your companion would take your places so this magnificent warrior," and he flourished a hand at himself, "may once again relive the glories of a fallen empire while bringing you safely to your objective."

"All right, all right." Otto waved and moved off.

"Does he always talk like that?" Ferdinand asked.

"Always," Otto said. "Now where's that blasted ... *Oof*!" Something big and hard hit him in the upper back, almost upending him as he stumbled forward two or three steps. He caught himself and whirled, ready to punch somebody, but stopped because, of course, "Flicka."

The horse grinned as the column cracked up. "You up for this?" Otto asked and Flicka nodded in excitement. Otto mounted. "No games," he warned the horse, which whinnied in agreement. "And leave the hat alone." Otto cocked the stained straw boater Moses had given him. Comfortable. Ferdinand had found a coal-black charger and stood ready. Otto raised an eyebrow at Pashtun.

The Marathan stood tall in his saddle raised the spear overhead, and shouted, "*Har*! *Har*! *Mahadev*!"

The words did not translate but their sentiment did and Otto felt a thrill course up his spine as he raised his lance in answer and shouted, "Jehovah!" He didn't know why he said that; the word came unbidden but it was a double thrill to hear Ferdinand and hundreds of others echo the same words or a variation. Pashtun looked them over with approval, wheeled his horse, and they were off.

The column broke immediately into a run, sweeping wide around the opposite end of the small pass and heading straight north for the next one. The riders settled until they rode more or less four abreast, flanked down from each other to provide protection. Dust and thunder filled the air and Otto caught himself smiling like a lunatic. Jeez, no wonder cavalrymen loved their jobs! "*Eeeehaaah!*" he yelled and echoed on every side by others as thrilled as him.

Kenny rode up, laughing. "Isn't this great?"

"Beats Viking raids," Otto agreed.

"Speaking of which," Kenny jerked a thumb back and Otto looked. Erick was about three ranks back, a giant battle-axe held before him, grim purpose in his eyes. He saw Otto and nodded curtly.

"I'll be," Otto said and Kenny grinned and pulled away.

They made their swing west and cut across the back face of the ridge. Openings in the rock allowed glimpses of the plain and they could see dust in the direction of the main gate. "What's happening?" Otto shouted to Ferdinand, who shook his head.

"I can't tell!"

Pashtun veered hard south and tore through a very narrow pass, the floor rising sharply and cutting west and then north again. Restricted to three abreast, all the pass would accommodate, they slowed as they climbed the rise. At the top, the rock suddenly opened and Pashtun's lance went straight in the air. They spread out around him in line, coming to a halt. They were on top of the pass, the land breaking to the plain below.

Otto stared. "Wow," he said.

To their front was Star City's west side, Suits running here and there, three strands of wire fronting more barricades. Off to their right, Oldham's brigade advanced on the main gate in three distinct ranks. Flags flew and trumpets sounded. Oldham was out front, or at least Otto assumed it was Oldham by the red waistcoat and martial air. The Suits had formed a half-moon around the front of the gate, extending the moon's arms across Oldham's flanks as more Suits abandoned their positions around the perimeter to join the main defense. Batwings hovered toward the back of the Suit formation, readying a massive attack.

"They don't even see us!" Kenny crowed.

"Not yet, at least," Jakto cautioned.

Oldham raised his arms and the ranks suddenly stopped. He

wheeled to face them and trumpets sounded and shouts of "*Huzzah!*" rolled across the plain.

"Huzzah?" Otto looked at Kenny, who shrugged.

"He wanted them to do it."

Oldham turned back around and drew his sword. A moment of stillness, the only sound an odd whirr as the ultralights jockeyed. Oldham waved his sword forward and the three ranks, simultaneously, stepped off.

Otto whistled, "Nice."

"Yeah," Sam agreed, "and they didn't even practice it."

Otto made out Moses in the middle of the second rank, the sharp white uniform standing out. That had to be Tabitha next to him, or at least the rider looked a bit overburdened. "God go with you," Otto breathed because it looked like the Suits had spotted Moses, too, a surge in their lines reinforcing the area his rank would hit. Oldham raised his sword and the ranks picked up speed.

"Bet we're seeing an instant replay," Kenny whispered to Otto, who could only watch.

"What does that mean?" Ferdinand asked.

Otto pointed at the charge, which was rapidly gaining speed. "This has happened before."

Oldham dropped his sword and, in a flash, the charge was at full gallop, the warrior cries of six hundred raving horsemen filling the plain. Thunder and earthquake, roar and screams and the suit front lines recoiled, as would any sane creatures watching sword-and-spear-waving cavalry bearing down on it. Heavy horse, Mongol horde, cuirassiers, Stuart and Custer and Crazy Horse, awe and terror and thrill and power in the moments before a line of cavalry reached its target.

As it did.

In seconds, Oldham's charge closed the gap and the front rank collided with the Suits like an avalanche against a stone wall, the shock of it sending both sides reeling, the sound that of mountains imploding. Otto watched, speechless, as Suits evaporated en masse at the end of lances, riders disappeared under the blossom of grenades or were cut in half by lasers.

"My God," Kenny breathed.

"Gentleman," Pashtun said, "I am thinking that now would be an excellent time for us to go." Otto looked to the front and saw how empty it was. Any remaining Suits were running toward the main fight, as were most of the rocket people manning the inner barricades. Pashtun raised his spear high then leveled it at the fence. "To the rocket!" he yelled.

"The rocket!" they all cheered and lowered their spears and they were off.

They had the advantage of the downhill and were at full speed by the time the pass leveled out, the fence rushing up to them. The last of the Suits had turned at the cheer and ran back but there weren't enough of them. Those Suits at the main gate not engaged with Oldham's charge also ran back to support, but there was no way they'd get there in time.

The ultralights were another matter.

As if by simultaneous command, all of the craft banked away from the main battle and headed toward Pashtun's charge. The bats quickly formed two attack lines, one behind the other, and gull-winged their formation to overlap the column.

"Tyrus!" Otto yelled and the slinger wheeled out, along with four other Tartars. They slammed to a halt and dropped to the ground, spreading out in line to meet the batwings. As the column roared past, Tyrus and his crew loaded their slings and fired with a rapidity Otto didn't think possible. Man they were good! Deadly missiles flew toward the approaching ultralights.

Bedlam.

The first wave of rocks crashed into the prow of the batwing attack, snapping the struts of the first three and bringing them straight down. The flanking craft turned hard and crashed into their neighbors, a process repeated along the whole gull-wing as ultralights scrambled to avoid each other and the whizzing rocks. Tyrus and his crew redoubled their efforts and batwings fell, grenades igniting when they hit the ground, swallowing the crashed craft, pilot and all.

The column cheered wildly and Tyrus, face flushed and happy, waved acknowledgment. But the first group of Suits was coming up fast and Tyrus rounded on them, redirecting his battery's efforts. Volleys of rock smashed into the vanguard breaking it up. The Suits fired back and one of Tyrus's men exploded in a purple beam. "Get out of there!" Otto yelled.

"No! We'll hold!" Tyrus yelled back and launched another salvo.

"You brave bastard," Otto said in admiration and pushed on.

Pashtun and the front lancers cut through the remaining Suits, evaporating them like soap bubbles on a summer's day. They reached the fence line and Otto presumed they would simply crash through but, no: Pashtun's Arabian sailed over, as did the rest of the column. Flicka left her feet and Otto was looking down at crappy barbed wire for a moment, then braced himself for impact— "*Ack!*" as Flicka hit the ground hard but still charging and then they were sailing again, this time over the barrier, looking down at the astonished faces of a few die hard rocketmen.

"That was amazing!" Otto smacked Flicka on the neck and the horse laughed.

"Wow! High five!" Kenny yelled and he and Otto slapped hands while Ferdinand looked at them as if they were crazy.

"You may be a bit premature," he said and pointed.

The Suits had broken off their attack on Tyrus and now paralleled the column, smashing through the fence line, rushing to intercept at a farther point. Otto saw the front gate between the buildings as the main suit force realized the trick and turned and poured through, the remainder of Oldham's force in pursuit but unable to stop them. Suits swept aside barriers and defenders and ran madly up the avenue, intent on Pashtun.

The rocket stood, tall and gleaming, steam pouring out from its side, about ten avenues away. Frenzied activity around it telegraphed the crew's intention to launch before the Suits got there, with or without Ferdinand. And it looked like without. The converging Suits would reach the intersection before they did. Otto's heart sank.

"Otto! Break!" Pashtun yelled and waved at a side street.

"Go!" Kenny urged. "We'll take the Suits. You two go!"

Otto and Ferdinand exchanged frantic glances and Otto spurred Flicka hard, cutting through an opening to their left, Ferdinand hot on his heels. Otto looked back.

"*Mahadeeeeev!*" Pashtun roared full in the stirrups, braced, leaning eagerly to war, the saints of a thousand battles in his voice. The column roared back an answering battle cry and, as Pashtun steadied his spear, they readied their own and charged, screaming Tartars and screaming horses storming the intersection.

The wedge caught the front of the Suits like a tidal wave, a thousand linebackers hitting a thousand linesmen, Pashtun in the van, and it was almost cartoonish to see Suits and horsemen flying through the air. Purple eggs exploded and beams raced across the front and arrows blotted out the sky and everything became a blur of men and horses and weapons. But the Suits stopped, thrown back.

Stunned, Otto could only watch. A nineteenth-century cavalry charge against a twenty-second-century army, and the cavalry was winning. Unbelievable. "Wish my son could see this!" he toned, but, really, no need. His son would, in his own good time, have an eternity of this and other incredible sights. A song rose in Otto's heart and the song led to the rocket.

Everyone's song led somewhere.

The battle raged. Pashtun's lance rose and fell like a scythe among the Suits, horses and beams swirling in and out of the maelstrom. The Suits couldn't go forward, Pashtun couldn't push them back.

"We should take advantage of this," Ferdinand said in his ear.

Yes, they should, and Otto spotted an opening at the next block that aimed straight at the steaming rocket and he pointed and Flicka took it.

The horse was magic, straight out fast and lean, Ferdinand's charger glued to him. They rushed a barrier, riflemen bristling behind it and lowering their barrels to fire.

"We're with you!" Otto called and they hesitated and the horses were past, racing for an inner fence and its shut gate, the riflemen there hastily threw it open as the horses flew inside.

A man stood apart from the gate, watching them.

Chapter XLIII

Launch

Otto pulled up to him. "I knew you'd be back," Konstantin grinned.

"What do we do?" Otto yelled.

Konstantin pointed toward the base of the rocket. "Head to the other side. They're loading there," he said, triumphantly, "and go with God." A pause. "Don't break my rocket." He waved them on.

Didn't have to tell them twice. Otto and Ferdinand spurred their horses as workers scurried out of the way yelling for them to hurry. Steam billowed from the rocket, clouding the street as they approached, a distinct rumble coming from the engines. Ferdinand's eyes widened with alarm and he reined his horse, but Otto grabbed the charger's halter. "It's all right!" he shouted. "It's normal!" and pulled Ferdinand along.

They skirted the base, more workers yelling "Hurry!" Around the other side, Otto saw a gantry rising to an opening about three-quarters of the way up the rocket. A line of people snaked along the gantry stairs, but there were still quite a few milling about a low building attached to the bottom. Otto made for it, yanked Flicka to a halt, and dropped hard out of the saddle.

Amelia was standing there, clipboard in hand. "'Bout time you got here," she said through gritted teeth.

"We were a little busy," Otto said, leaning over and catching his breath.

"Aren't we all?" Amelia snorted and glared at Ferdinand. "Who's this?"

"Your navigator," Otto said.

Amelia gaped at Ferdinand, then at Otto. "You've brought us someone else? Instead of you?"

And, right then, confirmation.

He was too late.

Like he didn't already know that.

"A navigator?" Marc, dressed in coveralls and carrying a duffle, stepped out of the remaining group. "A real honest-to-God navigator?"

"I am not sure you can truly call me that." Ferdinand slid off the charger. "I did map the Plata and its estuaries."

"Close enough." Marc dropped his duffle and gave Ferdinand a big hug, startling the Platan. "You owe me ten credits," he said to Amelia. Others came over, smiling and clapping Ferdinand on the back.

"All right, all right," Amelia was even more irritated. She jerked a thumb at the gantry. "Get moving. Those Suit things won't stay off forever."

"You call them Suits, too?" Otto asked.

"Yeah, heard it somewhere," she said absently and returned to her clipboard. The others grabbed their bags, including Ferdinand's, and headed up the stairs. Otto stood quietly beside Flicka, who knew a bad moment when she saw it, so behaved. Ferdinand was engaged in deep conversation with Marc, both lost in azimuth and plot and course. The line was moving steadily and Ferdinand was the last on it.

The last.

Otto looked at Amelia. "When did you start loading?"

"About thirty minutes ago."

"How'd you know to do that?"

Her glance was hard. "When the Suits showed up, we knew we were in trouble and had to get away. But we also knew it meant the last crewman was coming. We thought it was you, but Ferdinand is an excellent choice." Her look softened. "You did a good thing."

"Thanks." Otto tried not to sound bitter. "So, was it some guy named Bernard who replaced me?"

Her eyebrows rose. "Yes. Bernard of Cluny. How did you know that?"

"Heard it somewhere."

There was a pause and Amelia's frown deepened. Something crashed back toward the battle. "We have to go," she said.

Otto's throat tightened. "Will there be another ship?"

She shrugged. "Ask Konstantin." She pulled at her duffle and placed the clipboard inside.

"That'll take a while." Otto was surprised by the tears in his voice.

She glanced at him. "What else do you have to do?" And she stepped up the platform.

Otto moved back and put an arm around Flicka's neck, watching as Amelia made her way up. The rest of the line was still going, but they'd all be inside in a few moments. He couldn't see Ferdinand anymore. The Platan, no doubt, didn't give him another thought: new adventures tended to erase old ones. Flicka gently nudged him and Otto appreciated the supporting gesture. "Thanks, old friend," he said. "Figure you and I will be sticking together for a while." Flicka perked up at that but Otto didn't feel it.

He looked back toward the battle. Lots of dust and motion over there and he should go put in his two cents. He wouldn't mind tangling with some Suits right now, hand-to-hand or otherwise, holding them off until the rocket was gone, which, given the increased rumbling, should be any moment. Then what? Stay with Kenny for a few months, maybe find out what happened to Doc and Machine Gun and be a third hand in their perpetual poker game, sign on with Columbus and explore the endless seas? At least he wouldn't be bored.

Or fulfilled.

He looked at the rocket. His quest, his purpose, the resolution of his entire life, was right there. In just a few minutes, it would be out of reach, until another ship was built and launched ...

Fat chance of that.

Even if the Suits left enough of Star City intact to begin again, Otto doubted he could ever round up another crew. There weren't enough like-minded people here, people willing to leave the comforts of condo and ale hall to board another slapped-together rust bucket. How long had it taken to assemble this particular group of misfits? Face it. Ninety-nine percent of the human race weren't interested. Culling the non-lotus would be a Herculean task.

What else do you have to do?

Amelia's words rang in his ears and he saw the sense of it. Not one rocket but a fleet of them, a launch every hundred years or so, the time it would take for the next generation and its one percent of seekers to get here. Battling Suits and then getting away and following the trail of the first rocket, which never came back because it was either successful, the crew standing in awe before the Throne itself, or lost, and it was his job to find out what happened and make the next leg until he, too, was successful or lost, and then others behind him came looking. It could be as eternal and futile as Kenny's raids but just as endearing and satisfying and always with the hope of success.

Hope.

"Where are You?" Otto whispered to the sky. But the sky did not whisper back, nor did it mesmerize. God, apparently, knew a hard moment, too.

Otto stared up at the now quiet sky. Hope was a gift; Hope was corollary to Grace. We can hope You will stir a Finger and make a tiny ripple, a Sign of Your Satisfaction, that You are Well Pleased with the effort expended. Spur the Hope, Lord ...

Nothing.

Otto shook his head. What did you expect? God had been out of the miracle business for quite a few millennia. Doubt He'll pick this moment to resume. "Let's go make ourselves useful," Otto said to Flicka and mounted and the horse rose a bit, eager to be off.

"What are you doing?"

That voice. An angel singing in his ear. He turned.

Claudia.

She stood on the platform, the wind sweeping her yellow hair and the light of the Mesmer sky full in her ocean blue eyes.

Otto's heart stopped. "I ..."

She waved him frantically to her. "Come on."

"What?"

"Now!" and she stamped a foot so prettily.

Otto looked at Flicka, who rolled her head and threw it toward Claudia in such a "get your butt moving!" gesture that Otto almost laughed. "Really?" he asked, and Flicka actually looked exasperated, then twisted about, grabbed Otto's hat and pitched it toward the gantry.

Good enough.

Otto sprang from the saddle and grabbed Claudia's outstretched hand because she had already turned toward the gantry and the two of them were racing up it, hat be damned, the whole way clear and the door, a bigger door than he imagined, was still open, held by Marc who grinned, ear to ear, urging them on. Otto looked off and saw the battle still raging, nearer now, the Suits flanking Pashtun's position and pouring around the sides toward the rocket and one or two of them looked up and saw Otto and, whoa, the malevolence ... "Let's get out of here!" he urged Claudia.

As Marc slammed the door and threw a gigantic wheel to seal it, Otto took in the chamber. Big. Real big. A series of couches laid end to end and side to side with the crew strapped or strapping themselves in, corridors leading away. He was stunned. "How did you guys do this?"

Claudia placed her hands beautifully around his neck and smiled. "Ask Konstantin. When we get back." Her smile was dazzling and pure and Otto could not help it ...

He kissed her.

A round of applause from the nearby couches, as Otto's world soared and sung and spun and stopped and this was, this was, all of existence, right now.

"Hate to break this up," Marc's voice broke it up. "But we've only got seconds."

Otto tore away and stared, breathless, into Claudia's shimmering eyes. "No. We've got forever."

"What's THIS?" Amelia appeared at the end of the couches, astonished.

Claudia slid out of Otto's arms but left a hand in Otto's and stood defiant. "He's going. He deserves it."

Amelia shook her head, orders to pop the hatch and throw Otto out definitely on her lips but she stopped and did not say it. "All right," she pointed the clipboard at Claudia, "but you're going to take care of him. Share your food, your place, everything."

Claudia smiled. "No problem."

Amelia threw her hands in the air. "What are you waiting for? Get strapped in!" and Amelia turned and pelted for the far side of the room and a ladder going up. Claudia pulled Otto through the rows, heading for an empty couch. They ran past Gus and Karl, who gave thumbs-up and smiled, and Claudia said "Hurry!" and pointed at an empty couch and Otto saw it was too small. "There's no way."

"There's always a way," she said and pushed him to lie sideways and she threw herself next to him and draped a webbing of belts over them both and pulled them tight and settled into him, a perfect fit, just perfect. Otto saw Marc leaping into his own couch a couple of rows away, an astonished Ferdinand a row beyond that, staring at Claudia. Of course. The angel of the fountain.

The ever-present rumble rose suddenly to a roar and the room shook like a car careening off the side of a mountain. Otto gasped and Claudia burrowed deep into him and squeezed tight. A dizzying motion and a twelve thousand pound weight fell on Otto's head, crushing him into the seat and he couldn't even gasp or breathe and his vision disappeared and he knew, knew, that the coma he'd been in since this whole thing began was either coming to an end and he would wake screaming in the hospital bed he was halfway certain was his real abode …

Or he was on his way to find God.

The room canted and dipped, the roller coaster ride the worst ever, Otto going from completely weightlessness to five or six tons; he felt like throwing up but how could he do that to Claudia, who clung to him and shook and occasionally sobbed and he was responsible for her, responsible now.

Then it stopped.

Then it was quiet.

Amelia's voice, awestruck, came over a crackly loudspeaker, "We're away."

A moment of stunned silence, then wild, raucous cheering and good-natured insults raced around the room, some of them directed at Otto, and he laughed and fumbled for the webbing, but Claudia stopped him. "Not yet, not until Amelia says so."

Okay. He gazed into her crinkled, amused eyes. "We're going to find God," he whispered.

"I know," she whispered back. They kissed again.

All of existence. Here. Right now

.

Cast of Characters

The People of the City

1. Otto Boteman. Recently Arrived.

2. Frank Vaughn. Greeter. Beaten to death by his mother in 1965, when he was ten years old.

3. Ferdinand Silva de Astorga. Purveyor of fine wines and tobaccos. Eighteenth-century explorer of the Plata.

4. Ian. Carriage driver. Engineer from Glasgow.

5. Claudia. Barkeep and brewer. Fourth-century Christian martyr. http://www.holytrinityorthodox.com/calendar/los/May/18-01.htm

6. Ralph Hamor. Drinker. Helped found Jamestown. http://en.wikipedia.org/wiki/Ralph_Hamor

7. Steward. Australian transportee, guv'nor

8. The conductor. Nineteenth-century clipper ship crewman.

9. Cyril the Greek. Train rider. Nestorian evangelist of China in the seventh century. http://www.syriacstudies.com/2013/12/14/the-nestorian-church-the-ancient-christians-church-of-mesopotamia-the-early-nestorians/

10. Theodore. Cyril's pal.

11. Doc Holliday. Gambler. Noted Western gunman.
http://en.wikipedia.org/wiki/Doc_Holliday

12. Augustus. Cardplayer. Dutch settler of New York.
http://en.wikipedia.org/wiki/New_Netherland

13. Frank. Cardplayer. WW2 vet. Interested in Frida.
http://en.wikipedia.org/wiki/Battle_of_the_Bulge

14. Frida. Twelfth-century Maltese interested in Frank.
http://en.wikipedia.org/wiki/Malta

15. Big Nose Kate. Occasional train passenger. Noted Western
figure. http://en.wikipedia.org/wiki/Big_Nose_Kate

16. Jacob Schiff. Financier. Noted philanthropist of the 1890s.
http://en.wikipedia.org/wiki/Jacob_H._Schiff

17. Carl Jung. Maybe.

18. Rousseau. Definitely.

19. Unathi. Proprietor of crystal. Nineteenth-century Zulu
warrior.

20. Grace. House mom. Sam's wife.

21. The kids. Unathi and Grace's, that is. Not the murderous little
trolls in the desert.

22. A redneck jester. Formerly of the Stonewall Brigade, died at
Second Manassas. https://www.battlefields.org/learn/civil-
war/battles/second-manassas

23. William Godwin. Librarian. English philosopher, father of
Mary Shelley. http://en.wikipedia.org/wiki/William_Godwin

24. Admiral Zeno. Good-natured smart-alec. Defender of Venice.
http://www.britannica.com/EBchecked/topic/656525/Carlo-Zeno

25. A kimono-wearing Incan. Curro Occlo, wife of Incan
emperor Manco who fought the Spanish to a standstill.
https://www.thoughtco.com/manco-incas-rebellion-1535-
2136544

26. A couple of drunk Umbrians.
https://en.wikipedia.org/wiki/Umbria

27. A tender of street lamps. William Murdoch, first to use coal gas to light his home. https://intriguing-history.com/gas-lights-lamplighters/

28. Charles Darwin. Librarian. Naturalist. http://en.wikipedia.org/wiki/Charles_Darwin

29. Ralph Waldo Emerson. Librarian. Philosopher. http://en.wikipedia.org/wiki/Ralph_Waldo_Emerson

30. Madalyn Murray O'Hair. Librarian. Troublemaker. http://en.wikipedia.org/wiki/Madalyn_Murray_O'Hair

31. Testy fifteenth-century Russian nun.

32. Georges LeMaitre. Library patron. Astronomer. http://en.wikipedia.org/wiki/Georges_Lema%C3%AEtre

33. Edmund Hoyle. Gamester. http://en.wikipedia.org/wiki/Edmund_Hoyle

34. Fred Hoyle. Another astronomer. What's with all the astronomers? http://en.wikipedia.org/wiki/Fred_Hoyle

35. The green-and-gold barista. A mariner with Dias. https://en.wikipedia.org/wiki/Bartolomeu_Dias

36. Ebenezer Cook. Carriage driver. Factor by trade. http://en.wikipedia.org/wiki/Ebenezer_Cooke_(poet)

37. Carlton, the doorman. Former hitman.

38. George "Machine Gun" Kelly. Cardsharp. Criminal. http://en.wikipedia.org/wiki/Machine_Gun_Kelly

The People of Out

1. Nellie Cashman. Hotel proprietor. One helluva woman. http://en.wikipedia.org/wiki/Nellie_Cashman

2. Charley Utter. Cartage. Friend of Wild Bill Hickock. http://en.wikipedia.org/wiki/Charlie_Utter

3. Moy Jin Mun. Stationmaster. Among other achievements, built the first Chinese railroad in the US. http://www.threetoughchinamen.com/moybrothers.html

4. Pashtun. Traveler of Out. Eighteenth-century Maratha Lancer. Not a fan of the British. http://en.wikipedia.org/wiki/Maratha_Empire

5. Cook.

6. Henry "Box" Brown. Proprietor. Had an interesting escape from slavery. http://en.wikipedia.org/wiki/Henry_Box_Brown

7. Sir Edmund Hilary. Guide. Climber of mountains. http://en.wikipedia.org/wiki/Edmund_Hillary

8. H. Rider Haggard. Mapper. Writer of early action thrillers. http://en.wikipedia.org/wiki/Henry_Rider_Haggard

9. Christopher Columbus. Famous explorer.

10. Angela. Secretary. Likes Pashtun and red licorice.

11. Konstantin Tsiolkovsky. Manager of Star City. Pioneer rocket man. http://en.wikipedia.org/wiki/Konstantin_Tsiolkovsky

12. Robert Heinlein. Needs no introduction.

13. C. S Forester. Admiral of the new British Navy. Noted author. http://en.wikipedia.org/wiki/C._S._Forester

14. Oslava. Mining administrator. Good friend of Harold Hadrada. http://en.wikipedia.org/wiki/Harald_III_of_Norway

15. Gene Roddenberry. Mining engineer. Also needs no introduction.

16. Prester John. Boss of the Works. Noted King. http://en.wikipedia.org/wiki/Prester_John

The Crew

1. Gustavo Guerricaechevarria. Fabrics. Tenth-century Basque weaver.

2. Karl Voorsen. Structural repair. Falkenberg blacksmith of the nineteenth century.

3. Amelia Earhart. Captain of the ship. Famous aviatrix.

4. Marc Aaronson. Astronomer.

https://en.wikipedia.org/wiki/Marc_Aaronson

5. Ho. Fourteenth-century Chinese scribe.

6. Hongi Hika. Noted nineteenth-century Maori warrior. Pretty good warrior here, too. https://en.wikipedia.org/wiki/Hongi_Hika

7. Akiko. Twelfth-century geisha. Soon to be a lot of trouble.

8. Sergeant Krauss. Reluctant Wehrmacht soldier.

9. Bernard of Cluny. Medieval poet.
https://en.wikipedia.org/wiki/Bernard_of_Cluny

People of the Desert Tribes

1. Kenny. Chief of the Tartars. Goths, before that. 1970s accountant from Illinois.

2. Moses. Harem guy. Slave in 1830s Louisiana.

3. Jakto. Harem guy. Soldier of Axum.

4. Sam. Harem guy. St. Louis train porter in the 1930s.

5. Flicka. The mischievous horse.

6. Erick the Viking. No, not the Monty Python one.

7. Tabitha. Seventeenth-century party girl.

8. Kastor. Part-time Tartar. Prince of the Tectosage.
http://en.wikipedia.org/wiki/Tectosage

9. John Myers. Guide. Old West scout.
http://www.history.idaho.gov/sites/default/files/uploads/reference-series/0290.pdf

10. Tyrus. Balearic slinger.
http://en.wikipedia.org/wiki/Balearic_Islands

11. Captain John Augustus Oldham. Cavalry officer. Was in the Light Brigade. http://en.wikipedia.org/wiki/13th_Light_Dragoons

12. Vachir. A real Mongol.

The Ship Looking For God ...

Chapter I

Weights and measures

"I…just don't believe any of this," Otto said.

Marc, peering through binoculars out the forward viewport, grinned. "Neither do I."

Otto tried to think of a good, single word that summed up his overwhelming, and persistent, sense of disbelief. "Stunned?" Well, yeah, when you jump from the middle of an epic cavalry charge through a horde of weird, suit-wearing angels or demons or whatever those things were into the hold of a slapdash rocket then cling for dear life to the dear and beautiful Claudia as the rocket takes off… "stunned" might be a good choice. Except, it's underwhelming. "Astonished?" Nah, same problem. "Astounded?"

Gobsmacked.

Yeah, that's it. "So…how'd this happen?"

Marc shrugged. "You put enough combustible fuel into the open end of a closed system, you can launch anything into orbit. It's science. You can rely on science."

Otto, of course, had been referring to the entire spectrum of recent events, but he'd settle for a specific. "Yeah? Then, tell me, Mr. Science Guy, why aren't we weightless?"

Another shrug. "Beats me. That's not science. At least, no science I know."

"Been A Lot Of That Lately," Otto Muttered. Indeed. Ever

since Otto had keeled over in his driveway from a massive heart attack and woken face down on a cobblestoned street smack in the middle of the most fabulous City in the universe ... or not in the universe. Next to the universe, or outside of it or, whatever the heck Mr. Latchemondy had said ... he'd run into an unending series of "no science" things, like the hypnosky, the velocity stars.

This silly, duct-taped, jury-rigged rocket.

"Surprised we didn't blow up," Otto said.

"What?"

"Nothing. What are you looking at, anyway?"

"The little moon." Marc gestured out the porthole with the binoculars. "It's weird."

Otto pressed around Marc's shoulder. "You mean, weirder than the normal weird?"

"As difficult as that is to conceive. But, it looks completely natural."

"Why is that weird?"

"Because of its motion." Marc swooped his hands like a fighter pilot describing a maneuver. "It's all wrong, so it must be artificial."

Otto craned for a better look, "Prester John said it was powered."

"Prester John? THE Prester John? You met him?"

"In the flesh ... or whatever we are now. He's running some kind of mining operation in the caves under Out." Otto pointed a thumb behind. "Ferdinand met him, too."

"I did!" Ferdinand enthusiastically called from his station at the console. "And I found him to be a most extraordinary man!"

The Argentine returned to his clipboard, scribbling through several sheets of paper. Trying to come up with some kind of map, no doubt; after all, he was the navigator.

"What were you doing under Out?" Marc asked.

"Running. So why is it weird for a powered moon to look natural?"

"No tech before its time, remember?" Marc said, "If it was made of fiberglass or something, okay, but we humans can't power a full-sized real moon like that, or, at least, not when I checked out." He raised confirming eyebrows at Otto.

"Couldn't when I died ... or fell into this coma ... either."
Marc smirked. "Still think you're dreaming, huh?"
"Don't you?"
A non-committal waggle of fingers. "Anyway," Marc said, continuing the finger waggle out the porthole, "that moon looks like a genu-wine piece of space rock, so the Suits must have better tech than us."
Otto knuckle rapped him on the head, "Hello, McFly! Combat lasers? Dimensional grenades?"
Marc laughed with a bit of puzzlement, shoved Otto back, and pushed the binocs at the glass.
"Who are these McFlys, some Irish family?"
That voice, crystal ringing in the wind ... Claudia. Otto had a sudden urge to give her another in a long series of absolutely devastating kisses. Devastating for him, anyway. He smiled, "No. Movie character."
"Ah," she nodded. "Like Pyrgopolynices."
Otto blinked. "Yeah, him."
Her brows crinkled in amusement, knowing immediately he had no clue, but she was too much of a lady to call him out. Too much of a woman. Otto succumbed to urge and reached for her.
"Knock it off, you two," Marc didn't turn. Eyes in back of head. "The rest of us are getting bored."
"You mean, 'jealous'," Otto said and swept her up, or she swept him up, couldn't really tell and there, another kiss of sheer ecstasy, sheer eternity, the two of them whirlpooling away. It was the physical equivalent of the hypnosky.
About twelve years later, they returned. "Done?" Marc asked.
"For now," Claudia said, stars in her eyes. Otto was still incapable of speech, so just grunted.
"All right!" A sharp bark behind them caused both to jump. Captain Earhart (don't call her Amelia; you'll get a fat lip) stood in front of the console, glowering at them both. "You're not here to lip wrestle. Help Marc keep an eye on the moon. We want to get past it, not through it." She turned the glower on Ferdinand.
Otto gave an exaggerated salute and an exaggerated Scotty accent, "Aye, Captain! But we're gonna need more power!"
Marc burst out laughing, no puzzlement this time, as Amelia

stared at Otto. "What?"

Otto waved it down. "Nothing. A reference that only Marc and I get," he said to her and Claudia and Ferdinand, and the rest of the pre-Trekkies here on the … bridge, yeah, that's what we'll call this room filled with instruments and steering and navigators. Mr. Sulu, ahead full.

Her glower turned murderous. "Fine. One day you two will explain what's so funny about that. As for now." She pointed a finger with murderous intent. "Eyes on that moon!"

"Ever hear of radar?" Otto snarked then realized that no, Amelia hadn't, so he raised conciliatory hands and got back on task.

"You're going to get thrown out the airlock," Marc said.

"Probably," Otto agreed. "By the way, guess who else was down there with Prester John."

"I give up."

"Gene Roddenberry."

"No kidding!"

"Yeah, and he calls the glowy stuff they're mining, 'dilithium crystals'."

"Glowy stuff, huh?" Marc, thoughtful, as he scrutinized the moon. Otto, unable to see a blasted thing around Marc's shoulders, sighed, and looked at Claudia. "I'm feeling a bit useless."

"Well, you ARE a stowaway," she dimpled and took his arm and leaned into him, but not in affection, more to brace herself as she gazed past Marc out the porthole.

Otto grinned, "And whose fault is that?"

She chuckled and Otto moved and they were closing in for another time-stopping kiss when Marc said, "Uh-oh."

"C'mon, man," Otto groused, "You're killing the mood."

"Good," Marc said, tapping the porthole, "'cause I need your undivided attention. Something's out there."

"What?" Claudia and Otto chorused and crowded the glass. "I don't see anything," Otto said.

Wordlessly, Marc handed him the binocs and pointed towards the upper right quadrant of the fast-approaching little moon, back-dropped by the much bigger primary moon that blocked the view of the Jovian world they'd just launched from containing the City and Out and whatever the heck else was down there and … wow. This must be remarkably similar to what Neil Armstrong saw as he got closer to the Sea of Tranquility. Except for the extra moon, of course. Otto would love to spend the next few years just gawking at it all, but there were other priorities. Like spotting whatever Marc had spotted. He adjusted the wheel, marveling at the instant focus. Good stuff. What do you expect from Flemish lens grinders? "I'm still not … wait." There, a bright speck, ill defined, moving against the little moon's surface. "Uh-oh."

Claudia took the binocs out of his hands and peered hard. "Yes. Uh-oh." She watched for a moment then looked at them both. "We should tell the Captain."

"Tell me what?" Amelia was suddenly at their shoulders.

Marc gestured at the port. "We've got company."

"Dammit," Amelia said under her breath and pushed her way in, taking the binocs from Claudia to locate the intruder. Sudden breath-intake and she whispered, "The Japanese."

Otto stared. "Wait." He pointed out the window. "They're Japanese?"

"Don't be ridiculous!" she snapped, still riveted.

"Well, then why …" Hit him like a water balloon. "So that's what happened."

"That's what happened what?" She was clearly becoming irritated.

"To you and Fred Noonan."

Amelia glared at him. "Excuse me?"

"There's a theory, just a theory, mind you, that you and Fred were spying on the Japanese, and they didn't take very kindly to it." Otto put on an innocent expression. "Care to comment?"

Storm clouds gathered and, after a moment, she said, "Don't ever, *ever* ask me anything like that again. Or you'll be walking home!" and she turned angrily back to the porthole.

Claudia stood bewildered as Marc and Otto exchanged knowing looks. "Bingo," Marc mouthed.

Amelia tensed. "It's stopped," she said, "Right in our way." She chewed on her lower lip, then wheeled and stalked over to the console, hovering over the pilot, a World War Two Wehrmacht sergeant named Josef. "Evasive maneuvers," Amelia ordered.

Josef regarded her. "What?"

"You heard me."

"Um … how?"

Amelia was incredulous. "I thought you knew how to fly this thing!"

"Captain," Josef said, quietly, "I drove a trolley car in Heilbronn before I was drafted. I spent the war in a stable taking care of horses. You have much more time with aircraft than I do."

"But we trained you!"

"Yes. To hold a straight line, to ease into orbits that Mr. Aronsen," he gestured at Marc, "calculates, but not to jink all over the sky."

"Is that even possible to do?" Ferdinand, sitting next to Josef, asked.

"Whether it is or isn't, we have to do *something*!" She glanced back towards the port. "I don't want to run into whatever that is."

Someone cleared a throat. All of them looked at the hole in the middle of the floor from which a ladder to the lower crew quarters peeked. A sleek head of black hair, topping a pair of glistening beady eyes, peeked at them from the top rung. "Captain," beady eyes said, "I would advise a very gentle, very gradual course of maneuver."

"Who's that?" Otto whispered to Marc.

"Taccola," Marc whispered back, "crew engineer. Was some kind of inventor, around da Vinci's time."

"Really?" Otto made a mental note to schedule some time with the little crow.

Amelia bore down. "What are you trying to tell me, Tac?"

"I am not convinced the ship could withstand the strains of hard turns. Nor that we have the fuel for it."

Otto stepped to the ladder where he could see Taccola dangling, "We didn't bring enough fuel?"

Tac blinked at him. "Not for excessive maneuvers, no. Who are you, again?"

"Otto Boteman," Otto extended a hand – not as greeting, but to haul the engineer up. "Lately of Washington, DC. Seems a little shortsighted not to bring enough fuel, doncha think?"

Tac ignored the hand as he climbed up, regarded Otto coolly, then turned to Amelia. "Captain," he emphasized the word, dismissing Otto, "the extra weight" – he rolled eyes back at Otto – "changes all calculations."

Otto started. "Wait a minute. You're saying this is my fault?"

Tac merely raised eyebrows at Amelia, who gave a long, exasperated sigh. "We figured a crew of thirty. You," she pointed at Otto, "are number thirty-one." Her point included Claudia, who flushed. After all, she was the one who'd dragged him onboard.

"Now hold on," Otto raised a defensive hand. "Tolerances are built into everything. Right, engineer?" This to Tac.

"Yes, they are," a new voice broke in and everyone turned to see Karl, a Falkenberg blacksmith from the 1800s, clear the ladder. "But within expected standards. Your additional weight is unexpected." He and Tac exchanged approving glances. Nerds.

"C'mon, Captain," Otto said. "There's nothing *that* sensitive."

"Except for weight," Amelia looked mournful. "That's downright critical in an aircraft."

"This isn't an aircraft." Otto pointed out.

"Principle still applies."

The others examined him, some with hostility, no doubt wondering how easily he'd fit through the airlock. Claudia, her flush deepening, threw a defensive hand at Otto. "If it weren't for him, we wouldn't have taken off!"

"That's true for everyone in Star City!" Amelia barked, "But we certainly didn't take all of them with us, did we?"

Claudia's mouth became a tight line. The stares between the two women were now baleful and Otto was struck. A good old fashioned cat fight, right here in orbit.

"Hate to break up this charming conversation," Marc called from the viewport, "but there's been a development."

That was enough to shift the crowd's attention. "What?" Amelia asked.

"Our little visitor is no longer in the way. It's, instead, coming alongside …" A loud clang raised a startled yell throughout as the ship shuddered and lurched.

"I think it's attached itself," Marc said.

At that moment, the ship pitched hard, as if it had run into a wall or something. All were thrown off their feet. Otto grabbed Claudia as he flew by and cushioned her as they collided with the bulkhead. "*Oof*!" he yelped.

"Exactly my sentiments," Marc said as he unpeeled his face from the port glass.

"Thank you," Claudia whispered as she helped Otto up. He was tempted to try another kiss, but this probably wasn't the best of times. Especially with a still-hostile crowd regaining its feet.

"What's going on?" Amelia demanded of Marc.

"Your guess is good as mine, Captain."

Amelia was about to provide a guess of her own when the ship rolled hard to the right, throwing them all again. Otto landed in a tangle with Marc. "Say, while we have a moment," he said, "is what Tac said true? Is this ship that delicate?"

"Very good question," Marc unfolded a leg from underneath Otto's back. "And I have absolutely no idea. I'm an astronomer, not a structural engineer."

"Yeah, but that still puts you light-years ahead of these relics." Otto gestured at Tac and Ferdinand in a pile near the console. "No pun intended."

"No pun noted."

Otto chuckled and crawled across to Claudia, who was trapped under Karl's massive arms. "Hands off my woman, Viking."

Karl looked offended. "I am Swede, not Viking."

"Six of one … you all right?" he asked Claudia as he helped her up. Who knew if the extraordinary healing powers of the City extended into near space?

She gave a little, charming curtsy. "I am, kind sir, and it is quite rude to refer to one's opposite as a possession."

"You're right. Sorry."

Her eye-twinkle signaled forgiveness. Otto, though, had never learned to leave things alone. "So, tell me then, how did Romans refer to their slaves?"

Claudia lost the twinkle and took on the same offended look as Karl, but Amelia saved his bacon by loudly bringing them back to, er, reality when she called out, "Battle stations!"

Otto almost laughed aloud. "Did you actually say that?"

Yes, she had. And the effect was immediate.

Karl and Tac zipped down the ladder as Marc and Claudia threw open hatches and took out weapons, Marc grabbing a double-barreled Savage .12 as Claudia wielded a short Roman sword. Even Amelia strapped on a Webley. The scrambling sounds from below indicated similar actions taking place. Only Otto and Ferdinand stood motionless, bewildered.

"Don't you have a weapon?" Amelia yelped at Ferdinand. No need to include Otto since he was just dead weight.

"I … don't know," Ferdinand replied as Amelia's color rose.

"Wait." Otto's upraised hand stopped the pending eruption. "He does." He turned to Ferdinand, "Get your duffle. There's a pistol in it." Otto should know; it had been his duffle first. Ferdinand slipped off.

He was back in moments, the gigantic Contender .44 in one hand and the box of ammo in the other. Otto showed him how to load it. "Beats a flintlock, hey?"

Ferdinand hefted it, admiration in his eyes. "If I had had such a thing against the Portuguese …"

"You said the same about Machine Gun Kelly's Thompson," Otto reminded him as the others took positions around the porthole and other possible hull-breach locations.

"Yes, and both are true."

Otto was about to launch a philosophical argument about anachronistic weapons and their effect on history, say a nuke during the Civil War, when Amelia called, "Ferdinand!" She gestured angrily at the ladder opening, "Take that post. Repel all boarders!"

Otto raised an eyebrow. "Did you actually say that?"

Something nudged his hand and Otto looked down. Claudia was pushing the leather scabbard from her sword at him. "Here."

He took it, the leather drooping over. "So what do I do with this?"

"Slap someone with it," and she took the opposite position from Ferdinand.

Otto held it up, the leather flapping in his face. "Great," he said, but she didn't hear him because she was focused on the ladder, fire in her eyes, grim purpose about her mouth, the sword ready. Valkyrie.

"Don't mess with Celts," Marc observed as he moved to the side of the port.

"How'd you know she's Celt?"

"Tectosage from Ancyra?" Marc shook his head, "What else could she be?" And he went into a combat stance, shotgun across his chest.

Otto figured his best use in this situation was as spoiler, so he moved to the middle, ready to scabbard-slap whoever, or whatever, broke through the hull. Everyone stood ready as moments passed. More moments passed. Then more.

Then nothing.

They all looked at each other, a bit sheepish. Amelia frowned. "Did they attach, or not?" she asked Marc.

"Believe so."

"Well, then …"

No chance to frame the coming question because the ship suddenly jolted, knocking them off their feet yet again, and accelerated.

"Dammit!" Amelia swore as they all scrambled back to a standing position. "What's going on?"

Marc was at the porthole. "Well, we're moving again."

"No kidding. What direction?"

"Right at the moon," he said, grimly.

www.ingramcontent.com/pod-product-compliance
Lightning Source LLC
Chambersburg PA
CBHW050509110726
47899CB00005B/1383